Heat of Unrest

Book 2 in the Carnal Fever Trilogy

Riley Kade

Manifold Publishing LLC

Paperback: 978-1-957572-03-1

E-book: 978-1-957572-02-4

Cover design by Ebook Launch

Internal design by J.W. Donley

Manifold Publishing LLC

315 Prospect St.

Unit 5206

Bellingham, WA 98227

Contents

Prologue

Troy Hyun didn't look both ways before crossing the street. Nor did he wave to the old woman who always sat in the little window of her family home, watching the hustle and bustle of the busy Washington, D.C. streets.

Today, his mind was on one thing, and it seemed far more immediate than where his feet might take him. The memories of thick black smoke, screams, and chaos echoed around the chamber of his crowded thoughts.

"Sorry," he mumbled, only vaguely aware that someone had clearly just bumped into him, and not the other way around.

Though really, if he were to force himself to focus on anything, it shouldn't be his physical surroundings – it should be on the interview he had in approximately twenty minutes. He had been relieved to get the callback that morning and had rapidly assured the caller that he could certainly come in for a follow-up later that day.

It wasn't that Troy was so desperate to find work, it was this work in particular that he wanted. If he could get a job as a scribe in Congress, he could be in the room all the time, hearing all the inner workings, possibly making connections. Perhaps one day he would have his own seat at the table, be able to make some kind of difference.

On this day in particular, he wanted nothing more than to live up to the precious, albeit small legacy his mother had left behind. It was her birthday, after all, and he wanted to celebrate it by getting this job, not by remembering how she'd died.

He heard screams again, somewhere in the back of his mind.

No... wait. Someone was actually screaming. It was coming from over his shoulder. He turned just in time to see a man hurl a flaming bottle into the second-story window of an apartment building.

Troy didn't hesitate. His legs were moving before he was even sure of the details of the unfolding scene. Two men, dressed head-to-toe in black, were disappearing out of sight by the time Troy reached the base of the building. The attackers had managed to light fires in several places on the lower floors, and the five-story complex had active flames pouring from most of the lower windows.

He faltered then. It wasn't that his parents hadn't taught him anything about fire pulling. They had both been fire nymphs after all. It wasn't even that he was definitely going to miss the interview he had so desperately wanted since moving to the city. The tiny bubble of excitement in him burst at that realization.

No. He hesitated for the same reason anyone in his position would. No fire nymph could handle an entire building on their own. It would take two or three for a job like this. That is, if they were all professionals and particularly skilled at pulling. He was neither of those things. In fact, he had a propensity for stimulating fires more than dousing them, exactly like most fire nymphs still in the youth of their early twenties.

A window opened to his right, one story up. It didn't yet have flames decorating its interior. What it did have was a young woman begging the stranger on the ground below to catch her baby. Troy didn't have a chance to see if the toss was successful as he pulled open the front doors and ran into the empty lobby.

There was barely even smoke given the speed at which everything had ignited, and the rich orange and red of a young blaze glowed all around him. He paused to inhale its beauty before stepping forward and reaching out a hand to the nearest tendril. Troy couldn't help but caress it tenderly, despite the violence of the situation. He'd always found it strange to have the thing that fed him be something that was so dangerous to others.

The shouting from somewhere overhead helped him focus his intentions, and he moved his outstretched hand in a gesture to invite the flame to come closer. He had to work hard to stay calm, to let the glowing tendrils come into him. The excitement of so much molten power made him want to get lost in it, to stoke the flame, as it were. He took several steadying breaths before stepping full-on into the lit hall and pulling with all the intention he could muster.

Troy couldn't be sure of the passage of time. He'd never been in the presence of such a large blaze. A minute passed. Or perhaps several. When he looked around him again, the hall was dull and dark.

Despite the blaze on the other side of the entranceway, he ran to chase the flames up the spiral stairway. If he could clear some kind of path, at least people could escape. He choked a bit on the air as he entered the tiny passage. Ducking low for oxygen, he continued the clumsy work of absorbing the alluring substance eating away at one of the walls. His clothes were now completely on fire, and he vaguely registered the fact his wallet was burning to pieces as he crawled the stairwell. He left the passage smoky and flame-free in his wake.

When he emerged on the second floor, he found a crowded hallway. Everyone had withdrawn from their rooms and was looking around frantically. That was, everyone closest to him – there was a separating barrier of flames midway down the hall. The people who had registered there might be a path for them took off past him down the stairwell while Troy stumbled forward to open up the hall.

He was beginning to feel a bit funny, almost drunk. He locked eyes with a young boy on the other side of the hall and kept his thoughts on him as he fought to keep pulling in more fresh flame. The boy seemed oddly calm in comparison to the adults around him, almost like he didn't understand what was happening, but wanted to be good in the face of so many afraid grown-ups.

Troy needed the boy to never learn what would happen if the pretty lights reached him. He doubled his efforts. His chest heaved with the effort now, and he heard himself making small punctuating cries, as if he was engaged in an act of pleasure and not desperation.

The instant there was the tiniest path past him, people began to crawl their way out. He too kept low to the ground, feeling light-headed from the lack of oxygen. A few minutes later he was alone again, kneeling in the middle of the hall and doing everything he could to stay awake and focused. A piece of wall collapsed somewhere to his left, but he didn't turn to stare. It was too much effort.

In fact, he found himself struggling to care or to remember why he was there in the first place as the sensations overwhelmed him. Fire licked across his now-naked body, and for a moment all he wanted was to return the gesture. He imagined running a hand across the edge of the flames and helping them grow bigger and stronger. He was alive like he had never been before, even as his consciousness was fading.

Troy didn't want to sleep. He didn't want to miss a moment of this. And he still needed to do something. He wasn't sure what that thing was, only that it was important and that it would probably feel good the way this felt good. He opened his eyes briefly, not realizing they'd been closed, and caught one last breathtaking sight of the burning hallway before everything went dark.

Chapter 1

Auspicious meetings

Sadie crested the false summit and paused to look back at Jimmy. He was moving as if half-asleep, but when he reached her, the look of effort on his face turned into a smile. His warm brown eyes fixed on hers as he slid a hand around her waist to pull her close. When he leaned to kiss her, however, Sadie shook her head.

"You need to keep up your strength, or we'll never get there," she said.

"Maybe I don't want to get there," he whispered.

Jimmy pulled her tighter, but kept his lips from touching hers. He was aroused again, though she couldn't fathom how he had any energy left to be hard when their skin wasn't directly touching.

"Don't you want to bathe, maybe eat a hot meal?" Sadie asked.

"No," he said as he scooped one of her auburn curls behind her ear. He had continued to wear gloves, and Sadie wasn't sure if it was out of habit or intention. After all, even if they did continue to cross the line into skin contact, it was inconvenient for every instant of direct touch to turn into a sexual encounter. And as they had had cause to learn that morning, it seemed impossible to leave off at just a kiss.

Who could blame them for this though? When they had spent all the months since her Becoming unwilling to do something as simple and wonderful as touching tongue to tongue, or hands to backs. No, not *unwilling* – Sadie had been more than willing since the moment her sexual awakening had been sparked by her transition into the succubus life.

The problem had never been that she hadn't wanted this level of intimacy with her best friend. After all, before her touch began to cause sexual pleasure, they had always been physically close. Nor had it been his lack of desire, as she could clearly read from the red light which flowed from him to her, or see in the images of scenes surrounding him which defined his sexuality.

Before a few nights ago, those scenes had told the story of his sexual history, and current dreams, thoughts, and desires. She was able to see in them his first sexual experience, a fumbling thing with his one and only girlfriend before her. And she could see all his feelings toward herself, Sadie. Jimmy had wanted her since puberty, and loved her all of their lives.

And even if she couldn't see it directly, she would still know that he truly loved her, given the way he'd been able to resist her touch. She had fought for months to keep their relationship platonic, pretending she didn't want him that way. At the time, she had been sure that if they had tried, they would immediately abandon their resolve not to touch skin-to-skin. And the second she'd touched him, the intensity of it would take over. Given how much she wanted him, she doubted she would have any control at all over herself. And then she would feed from him, and neither of them would be able to stop it.

She had been a fool not to trust him though. Jimmy was too strong for that, so much more than she could ever have imagined. People traveled from all over to be with succubi, craving the unbridled ecstasy they could bring. But Sadie hadn't wanted to turn her closest friendship into one of addictive need.

Gabriel, the succubus who had helped her through her transformation, had warned her against the dangers of sleeping with someone you loved. And when Sadie had decided to tell Jimmy the truth about her feelings for him, she'd confessed her fears, and told him she didn't want to feed from him, which meant no touching. And somehow,

Jimmy had been able to deliver. He had held firm to her wishes and found ways for them to be intimate without skin contact. Which they had done for months.

But the many sexual encounters that followed her confession of love for him, all the scenes that had come to surround him after that dam had broken, were now nearly invisible. When she looked at him now, holding her tight at the top of a mountain in the Cascades, all she could see was what had happened two days ago.

It shouldn't have happened. They'd been meant to reach the encampment after only a few days' trek through the mountains, but when they'd gotten lost and it had already been too long since she had last fed, there'd been only one resort left. And now, it was all they both saw. When she looked at his face, she couldn't help but remember the sight of it contorted in pleasurable agony. The images surrounding him were dominated by what it had felt like to finally kiss her, after wanting to for so many years.

As they stood there, content to look over each other's expressions, warm with excitement and wearing matching grins, it seemed they would never get to their destination. Sadie knew they couldn't be so selfish, though. It was, after all, fairly important they completed this simple task.

She didn't understand why the diary of a succubus from the 1920s had landed in her hands, but now that she knew its contents, it was clear that it could play a vital role in preventing the coming war between humans and feeders – the war that the Coalition of prominent feeder families had been working toward for generations, just waiting until tensions had reached a peak. Moreover, the diary was useless unless they got it to the people equipped to do something about it.

Luckily, those people were nearby now, nestled high in the Cascades of Washington State. Sadie and Jimmy had been fortunate to get to work alongside some of them back in Seattle – that was, before the city collapsed into chaos and destruction – and they were anxious to find them again in the safety of the mountains.

Sadie wiggled out of Jimmy's arms and kept walking. The autumn air was quite cool this high up, and as they rounded the next bend, the view of the valley below was spectacular. If the journey hadn't consisted of the biggest emotional rollercoaster ride of her life, Sadie would have likely shown the scenery better appreciation.

She gaped at the patches of blue water and green trees below them, then up at the snow-capped peaks above and adjusted her gloves. They should be nearly there. Sadie turned to ask Jimmy if he remembered the code words they were supposed to say when they arrived. She thought she had it, but wanted to make sure their memories matched. After all, they had been through a lot since Luciana had given them the words five days ago.

Only, as she opened her mouth to speak, something struck her from the side, knocking her to the ground. She tumbled into a patch of wildflowers just off the trail, her pack coming off her shoulders as she rolled twice and landed on her back with a man on top of her. Sadie bucked her hips, trying to get a good grip with her heel against the ground so as to launch him off her, but he was stronger and used his own feet to slide hers until her legs were straight.

She saw Jimmy out of the corner of her eye and knew reinforcements were coming. Preparing to up her own efforts as Jimmy struck, Sadie pretended to give up. Only right as she went limp, the man held out an arm in the direction of Jimmy's approach and flames came to light around the man's hand. Everyone froze.

The fire nymph tore his gaze from Jimmy's and focused it back on her. Their faces were a foot apart, and their panting sounded loud in the sudden quiet.

He didn't have much in the way of sexual history. There was a memory of an attractive blond woman, a succubus, she realized, though he'd never been with her. There were a series of vague sexual dreams about the woman. There were also more distant memories of another woman, possibly a girlfriend, but the scenes were dull and dry.

Altogether, it wasn't a lot for a grown man. When people had little in the way of a sex life, their physical features always stood out more to her. A fact which was most annoying in this particular moment, as he happened to be quite attractive. Black strands of hair framed his face in an appealing way as deep brown eyes flitted quickly over her own features.

Sadie pouted as she watched a red strand of light begin to flow from her to him, indicating attraction. She was immensely grateful that she was the only succubus around and therefore no one else could see what she saw. She was also grateful the man didn't return the feeling.

She was released from the pressure of his gaze when Jimmy drew his attention by speaking the coded question, "Is that a dove's cry I hear?"

Jimmy was several feet back with his hands raised in a pacifying gesture, the ball of fire burning menacingly between them. The fire nymph didn't give the expected response – clearly he wasn't who they were looking for.

"Only if you've got an ear to the ground," a woman said from a location over Sadie's head and out of her sight. She recognized that voice. Sadie's heart skipped a beat as the sound of Hetia's footfalls drew nearer.

"Troy," Hetia chided.

The man shook his head. Despite the fact that Hetia had spoken the correct response, Troy didn't release her or the flame.

"And the coin?" he asked.

"In my pocket," Sadie said, gesturing with her gaze to the lefthand pocket of her jeans. Troy shifted his weight and slid his hand along her hip to retrieve the coin. Her breath caught and his eyes narrowed. He probably thought her reaction was about the coin. Why was he so suspicious?

Troy lifted the coin into the light and looked it over.

"Where did you get this?" he asked.

"Luciana," Sadie said. The name didn't seem to mean anything to him.

"Troy," Hetia repeated, her voice coming from somewhere above.

"They're succubi," Troy said. "They probably seduced the code and coin out of this Luciana. They're likely working with Siphon." An image of the blond succubus sprung to his thoughts as he said the name Siphon. *Interesting,* Troy's sexual history had something to do with congressman Siphon, the most prominent succubus in the public limelight and one of the primary leaders of the Coalition.

"That's unlikely," Hetia said. "Anyone could be spies, which is why Luciana takes her time recruiting people. And the man is human. At least he was last time I saw him."

Troy's head snapped up. "You know them?"

"Yes. They were working with the United back in Seattle. Luciana must have decided she could trust them enough to send them here. Now get off her."

He still didn't budge.

It happened fast. A hand appeared on the ground to the right of Sadie's head as a thigh collided with Troy's chest. The woman flipped him to his back next to her and landed on her feet over him. The flame died.

Sadie sat up as Jimmy rushed to her. She accepted his hand, but her gaze didn't stray from the woman now in front of her. Sadie knew that Hetia had fair hair, and a slight frame which entirely contradicted her commanding nature. She also knew she was an incredibly powerful earthquake nymph. The last time Sadie had seen her she was single-handedly holding off an entire mob, after all. But that was not what caught Sadie's eye when she looked at her. The woman was so completely covered in sexual imagery, Sadie barely even noticed her penetrating grey-eyed stare.

Only, in this moment, the imagery was not dominated by many encounters with many people, though she could see Hetia had had many lovers. No, it was mostly of one thing only: Sadie. She was completely covered with the memory of the one night they'd spent together. And though it was a memorable night, Sadie didn't see the point in the woman holding so tightly to it, when the last time Sadie had tried to initiate something, the woman had rejected her.

"Hetia," Sadie breathed, smoothing out her rumpled hair and standing up straighter.

Hetia held out a hand for Troy, which he accepted with a grin.

"Impressive," he said as he dusted himself off. "I see more everyday why Amadi called you the big gun."

"No. That's not the reason," Hetia said. She gave Troy the

smallest hint of a grin to match his before relaxing her face as she turned to Sadie.

Sadie's stomach jumped into her throat as Hetia's gaze locked on hers.

"Seems you have a habit of saving me," Sadie said a bit breathlessly. Troy's smile fell instantly. He ran a hand through his hair as he looked from her to Jimmy and back to Hetia.

"And how did you meet them again?" he asked.

"The woman approached me at a bar, before they'd gotten involved in the movement," Hetia said.

Troy raised his eyebrows. "She picked you up?" he asked.

"Yes," Hetia said, unblinkingly. Sadie swallowed.

Troy put a hand on Hetia's arm to draw back her attention.

"You know I mean you no disrespect. You're skilled and smart, and a wicked Stones player, but honestly, if you spent the night with her, that's even more reason not to trust your judgment. How do we know she wasn't trying to get in through you from the beginning?"

"Because she never knew I was involved. She thought I was a bodyguard," Hetia said.

"Maybe she did know, and she's been playing you all along. Like you thought the man was human. Maybe that was just an act to prove she respects humans enough to have one as a friend."

"I'm human," Jimmy said, removing his gloves.

"It doesn't matter if you are or not," Hetia said. "Humans, nymphs, and human feeders are all welcome here."

Troy seemed to think it did matter, as his posture didn't change. Jimmy took a few slow steps forward and held out his hand.

"Jimmy," Sadie said "You shouldn't have to do that. As Hetia just said, it shouldn't matter. Unless these people are as bigoted as the opposition." She directed a glare at Troy.

"If it helps, it helps," Jimmy said.

Troy eyed his hand nervously, but after only a moment's hesitation, he accepted the offering. He held it for just a second before nodding in satisfaction and releasing it.

Jimmy offered his right hand then, this time in greeting.

"James Baker," he said.

"Troy Hyun," the man replied. His expression lightened as he accepted the handshake, but returned to skeptical as he looked back at Sadie.

"And it's Hypatia Pierce," Sadie's rescuer told Jimmy. "But you can call me Hetia."

"I remember," Jimmy said, alluding to their brief encounter last year.

Sadie stepped forward to introduce herself to the man who had attacked her. Troy looked at her gloved hand a long time, while Sadie glared daggers at him, feeling increasingly humiliated. Eventually though, he seemed to force himself to reach out. He shook it quickly as she mumbled, "Sadie Hall."

"This way," Hetia said, stepping between them and starting off down the path without looking back. Jimmy took Sadie's nearly rejected hand in his own and pulled her to follow Hetia. Forced to stop scowling at Troy, she stomped along next to her friend while her attacker pulled up the rear, and it was all she could do not to glance over her shoulder at him.

Hetia led them up around three more bends before darting off the path and down through a thicket. Sadie stepped in front of Jimmy so they could travel single-file and focused her energy on not getting whacked with branches as Hetia released them in front of her. At some point the woman disappeared completely, and Sadie braced to push through the dense growth, but before she could, light appeared in a rush.

Hetia had pulled back the brambles, and she held them at bay to let the three of them pass into an open expanse. Sadie stepped by her slowly, wishing she could pause and talk to the woman, but Hetia gave her a cool stare and then turned to watch Jimmy coming through behind Sadie, with one hand on her back.

The four of them paused to look down on the little valley nestled between surrounding mountains. A couple dozen thatched houses were spread among the web of footpaths and gardens. Some dwellings contained goats, or chickens; some puffed clouds of smoke through little chimneys.

Strangely, there weren't many people. One man was out gardening a few houses down. As Hetia led them past him, he raised a hand in greeting, looked them over, and continued his work. They passed one of the houses billowing smoke, and an elderly woman reached out the window and grabbed a few herbs off the sill.

They saw no one else.

"Where is everybody?" Sadie asked.

Hetia spoke over her shoulder as they walked.

"They're all over at the planning tent. Dee, uhh Andre, got a letter a few days ago from one of our spies. They'd been deep and sent ahead that they had some big news to share in person. He returned from the meeting last night and called an assembly this morning."

Sadie and Jimmy had both stopped walking at the name Andre. And Troy had said the name Amadi earlier. She'd been too distracted to register it.

"Andre Amadi?" Sadie asked.

"Yeah," Hetia said. Troy again looked at them suspiciously.

"Why? How could that name mean anything to you?" he asked, squaring his shoulders to face her.

Sadie and Jimmy exchanged a look. They had already agreed to give the box to these people. Having come to trust them, it seemed like the most logical step. But the ocean nymph who had died trying to get the box to its destination had told them to give it only to Andre Amadi. It seemed they had finally fallen in with the right people, and it had led them to the man they were hoping to find.

Sadie shrugged off her backpack and retrieved the beautiful wooden box. "I don't understand why, but somehow this ended up in my hands." She glanced up at Hetia and Troy to gauge their reactions. They blinked back at her.

"What is it?" Hetia asked.

Sadie looked to Jimmy. "It's something for Amadi," he said. "A woman died outside our house. She had been trying to get this to him. She was an ocean nymph."

Hetia furrowed her brow, but Sadie couldn't tell if the information meant anything to her.

"Come," Hetia said, and kept walking.

After a few minutes of silence, Jimmy brought the conversation back to something else Hetia had just mentioned. "Is that mostly what you all do here? Spy?"

"No, but it's a large part of our efforts. Though it's been a challenge to successfully infiltrate any useful networks. The person who delivered this big news is the only real success, no one even knows what they look like except Amadi."

"A good thing since we don't know that they don't have their own spies here," Troy said from the back.

"Amadi says they barely know we exist, and don't consider us much of a threat," Hetia continued. "And he's the one who would know. He's responsible for organizing the network. He's the only one of us who knows the full picture."

"And who are *they* exactly?" Sadie asked, wondering how much Hetia's knowledge overlapped with what she had learned from the diary.

"They're called the Coalition," Hetia said. "They're made up of human feeders and nymphs. Really, they're anyone hoping to enslave humans. Though Dee – Amadi that is –believes the Siphon family is driving much of the effort."

"And what is the United doing to stop them?" Sadie pried.

"Well, the Coalition has generations on us since we've only been around a couple decades, but mainly we're trying to uncover who the main drivers are and intercept their efforts at the source. However, Dee's also been building an army of recruits from all over, people ready to fight if need be. After the Coalition driven fracture of the government into human vs. feeder this past summer, it has been much easier to find such people."

These were long speeches for Hetia. Sadie hadn't known her to be so forthcoming before. The woman must be excited to see her, or at least Sadie could hope that was the reason.

After they'd made their way past a dozen houses, they veered left down a little stone path. Sadie could hear a steady trickle of water mingled with voices as Hetia led them to the edge of the gathering. There were about fifty people spread around the creek. Some sat on rocks with their feet in the water. Others sat on blankets and logs.

They were all adults. In fact, at the age of twenty, Sadie and Jimmy likely ranked among the youngest members present.

There was one man on his feet, and he spoke loudly enough to be heard comfortably over the sounds of nature, which was his only competition since there was no chatter from the assembly sitting in rapt attention.

"They're gathering forces on the coast of Massachusetts. They have a stock of imported weapons, something called machine guns that can rapidly fire multiple rounds." Several people gasped audibly at that. "We're not sure what they're waiting for, but they'll likely move soon. We still know very little about the extent of their strength or their plan of action. Though now that we have their location, we can give some anonymous warning to the human government. What we really need, though, are more people on the inside." The man's gaze paused on each person he looked at, as if he were having a one-on-one conversation with everyone there.

"It will be a dangerous game," he continued, "trying to get past Siphon's defenses, but his desperation for more fighters will act in our favor. We'll double down on training as we formulate our plan. Everyone get sleep tonight. We might have to move swiftly if the war breaks out in full. Our efforts at prevention will have to be scaled back as we prepare to counteract their attacks. It's not what anyone wanted, but here we are." The man ran a hand over his smooth head. "Let's just hope our other efforts bear fruit, since this would be a dangerous thing to settle with violence."

The crowd must have been used to reading the man's body language, because they understood he was done almost all at once. Conversation erupted as the throng dispersed. People made their way past Hetia, Troy, Jimmy, and Sadie as if they were part of the scenery, so swept up they were in their own debates. Sadie caught snippets.

"Didn't see this coming..."

"If there are only a couple hundred, Amadi might be able to..."

"How can we stand back while..."

"Should we continue trying to..."

The crowd dispersed, leaving only the speaker and the four of them. The man stared out at the creek in contemplation for a minute while Hetia kept them back. Eventually, he turned, spotted them, and closed the gap rapidly; wearing an expression of action.

"Hetia, you heard?" he asked.

"Yes," she said. "Troublesome news."

He put a hand affectionately on the side of her head. "We can talk about it tomorrow. Who are your guests?"

She gave him their full names. "They were working with Luciana in Seattle. Sadie's a human feeder." Hetia turned to Sadie and explained, "We are in need of more human feeders as spies." She gestured back at the man next to her. "And this is my – this is Andre Amadi," she said.

Amadi pushed up his glasses and reached out in greeting. He took Sadie's hand in both of his own, nodding at the sight of her gloves. She knew her mouth had been hanging open for the past several minutes, and she snapped it closed before giving him a polite head bob. Though she couldn't look away from him.

It wasn't his physical features that drew her in. In fact, she barely noticed them over the emotion in the scenes that told her the story of his sexual self. They blurred and clashed around him like a storm, and Sadie found herself panting as she took it in.

There were two things about him which grabbed her. First was the fact that he and Hetia shared a strong blue line between them, indicating they were close family. Since Hetia's skin was very fair and Amadi's a dark brown, it was unlikely they were biologically related. Was this the friend of her father's who had raised her? If only Hetia had said his name out loud back when they'd first met, it would have saved them a lot of time.

Second, and this was the thing that had Sadie struck dumb, was his sexual history. He had been with only one woman all his life. She could see intense scenes from their youth together, but also decades of love and desire. Though a few memories shone above the throng. The first time the woman had touched him Sadie could see, almost feel, his emotions as she ripped off her gloves and scooped up his face.

This man was the lifelong partner of a succubus. And he seemed perfectly healthy.

Chapter 2

The rabbit hole

Everyone was staring at them in silence, Sadie frozen with her hand still in the Amadi's. He was smiling at her knowingly – clearly he knew what she could see on him, and he nodded once in acknowledgement. Sadie came to when Jimmy shifted and the movement caught her eye. She stepped back, clearing her throat.

"It's nice to meet you, sir," she said, perhaps a bit robotically as she tried to focus her thoughts.

Sadie had so many questions. She could see the scenes and even the emotions of them, but she couldn't read his thoughts. Did he regret the dynamic at all? Was the relationship addictive, the way Gabriel's scroll had described? What was life for him outside of the scenes she could see? Where was the woman now?

Hetia cleared her throat. Sadie looked at the others and almost laughed as they all wore identical frowns of puzzlement. She didn't know what to say to explain away the moment, so she tried for a distraction.

"We've brought something you should have. It ended up in our care by accident." Sadie extracted the box once more. Amadi showed no recognition as she showed it to him, so she told the story of the ocean nymph. His expression saddened as she spoke.

He reached out to touch the smooth marble surface, flipping it over. "At least now we know what happened to her." Amadi continued to rotate the box, looking for access. "I had word she had something for me. Have you opened it?"

"Yes. It contains a diary and a strange switch or button. The book has some important information in it," Sadie said. Everyone was looking on in rapt attention now. "The diary belonged to a woman named Vivienne Siphon. Does that—"

"Vivienne Siphon?" Amadi interjected. Hetia looked at him expectantly.

"Yes, you know her?" Sadie asked.

"She was Congressman Siphon's great-great-grandmother. I don't know much else. This is welcome news though." He handed her back the box. "Will you be so kind?" he asked.

Sadie shifted uncomfortably.

"Well for safety, I resealed the box before getting here, but I can reopen it tonight..."

"Why not now?" Troy said in his ever-suspicious tone.

Jimmy flushed slightly.

"I, uh, I need to feed in order to open it," Sadie said.

"It's a succubus box. Of course." Amadi perked up. "I've heard of these, but never held one." He said more privately to Hetia, "Mae will be fascinated to get to study it." He was grinning as he looked back at Sadie. "This is a welcome gift. But I've forgot my manners. You're probably tired from your journey. Let's show you your bed and you can bring us the diary in the morning."

At the suggestion of bed, Sadie felt a spike in Jimmy's arousal and watched him shift to cover up the growing bulge in his pants. The fact that he had been almost constantly semi-hard since they'd slept together hadn't been a problem when they'd been traveling alone, but the situation now felt like trouble. At the feeling of him, she too was anxious to be alone again. Especially since they had the excuse of needing to open the box to justify her feeding off him at least once more.

They hadn't talked about what they were going to do about what had happened. Now that they'd started touching skin, would it be possible for them to stop? Should they? The mess of images that was Amadi filled her mind as she agonized over this topic for the hundredth time that day.

At least they could delay answering that question until tomorrow. Sadie wondered then if she had really chosen to shut the box just to have an excuse to unlock it again.

"That sounds wonderful," she told Amadi.

Troy stepped forward. "Amadi, can I talk to you alone? Please?"

The elder man nodded to Troy before turning to Hetia. "Cabin nine is free. I sent out Imani and Chloe just last night. They'll be gone for months." He turned back to Sadie. "We can talk more after you've settled in. It was a pleasure meeting you, Sadie. James." He looked into both their eyes before turning to Troy.

The fire nymph didn't speak right away, simply crossing his arms and staring at Sadie until Hetia had led them out of sight. Sadie glanced back before they turned the corner to see Amadi watching Troy in silent concern as he glared her down.

She did her best to shake off the unpleasant encounter as she followed Hetia back to the main pathway. They walked in silence, except for the few moments in which their guide paused to make introductions between them and a passing stranger. Everyone seemed glad to have newcomers.

Hetia pulled to a stop right in the middle of the cluster of cottages. Cabin nine was marked with a hand-painted sign stuck into the garden, and a little cobbled path led them from the main trail to the front door. The surrounding yard was filled with carrots, beets, and kale, which Sadie looked around affectionately, grateful again to be out of the city.

They followed Hetia through the door into the tiny, enclosed space. The walls and floor were stone and the temperature was practically freezing in comparison to the sun-warmed air from outside.

"The stone keeps it cool during the day, but also helps hold the heat from the fire during the night," Hetia told them. Sadie looked around as the three of them crowded into the cramped space between bed, wood-burning stove, shelving, countertop, and little table with two chairs.

"Dishes are under the stove. Beans and rice there. You can eat anything from the garden, and about once a week we have meat. Don't overuse the sink. Amadi refills the water tanks only once a month. Outhouse is out and to the right. Showers are down by the river." Hetia didn't look at either of them directly as she added, "Have a good night."

She paused at the door, however, and said over her shoulder, "It's good you joined us. That diary is a breakthrough."

And then they were alone.

Sadie smiled at Jimmy. Despite everything that had happened in the past week, she couldn't be happier. She finally felt as if she had found where she was meant to be. His reaction to her smile, however, quickly changed the flavor of the room. His sudden arousal hit her like a storm, and she had the impression he must have been doing his best to repress the emotion. Images of them together flashed to the front of his thoughts as he covered his erection with a hand.

"Sorry," he said. She watched him as he kicked off his shoes and sat on the bed. Sadie sat next to him and put a hand on his knee.

"What do you mean?" she asked.

He shook his head. "No, I don't mean sorry. I'm just confused." He took her hands. "Sadie, it's okay. If you're going to tell me that you want to at least try to go back to not touching. I understand. We did what we had to do. I know I've been a little out of control the past couple of days, but I also know that what happens next isn't clear. If we want to try and fight this thing, I'm willing to give it a shot."

It was remarkable that his expression looked so smooth and his words sounded so sincere when his body was crying out in such a loud protest. His inner thoughts were a hectic collage of desire that somehow managed to rival her own. He must have seen she was unconvinced because he added, "Whatever happens, we'll always have those memories."

Sadie raised her eyebrows, shocked again at his self-control. He was going to make this as easy on her as possible, just like he always did. He wasn't going to beg her to touch him, at least not outside of his private thoughts. She now knew he would never do that.

But Sadie didn't think she could go back. A few memories were not enough. She'd been looking forward all day to this bed. To her, their only alternative was to split up, to stay away from each other, to take separate cabins. And that wasn't a real option either.

"Let's decide tomorrow," Sadie said. "We still need to reopen the box." A shiver ran down her back as she said this, and Jimmy's notion that they try to resist seemed even more ridiculous. Scooting forward, she squeezed his hand in hers through the gloves. Both their bodies were trembling, and their breathing turned quickly into an identical shallow pant. She clenched her thighs together and closed her eyes to say, "Let's try and take it slow."

"Yeah. Okay," he breathed, his free hand tightening into a fist around the bed cover between them. She saw his desire to kiss her an instant before he moved, but his pace was measured. His palm on her jaw was the first skin contact.

They sucked in a breath as pleasure ripped through him. Her control wavered as his mouth crashed into hers. She reached for his zipper, fumbling clumsily with the buttons, and he helped her get his pants open, not breaking the kiss. Then they turned to pulling off her shirt together. It got tangled around her head and shoulders and they collapsed backward with him on top of her. He immediately reclaimed her mouth as they fought to free her.

Sadie sat up enough to pull an arm free, and her elbow hit him in the chest. Jimmy grunted. "Sorry," she said.

"It's fine," he mumbled before pressing his mouth back to hers as he slid his palm over her breast and down her torso. Sadie ran her hand over the muscle of his arm, equally interested in her own exploration. It seemed impossible that they would ever have enough of touching each other.

The contact allowed her to feel inside him, and she could suddenly sense his body like it was her own. With everyone before Jimmy, she had been able to take them slowly through the different stages of pleasure, but try as she might, she couldn't seem to hold him back from escalating toward climax.

Afraid they would make a mess of their clothes, Sadie tugged at the fabric around his hips. Jimmy tried to shift his weight to assist her, but paused suddenly. He closed his eyes and she watched the muscle of his jaw clench. "I'm close," he told her unnecessarily.

Sadie reached into his underwear and pulled him free just in time. He started to pulsate in her hand the second she touched him, and a second later, hot fluid began spurting all over her abdomen. He groaned as he thrust into her hand, his muscles flexing as he held himself above her.

She looked down at their bodies. Her pants were still entirely on, and Jimmy was almost completely dressed. Sadie nearly laughed at what a clumsy mess they were. She was supposed to be a natural at this, succubus and all. And yet, she couldn't help but harbor the fantasy of making him come again immediately, right there on top of her.

Fighting her impatient desires, she reached for her own buttons, while Jimmy stood up to remove his pants, his gaze tracing over her. The second her pants were off, he moved forward in a rush, coming to rest between her thighs with his shirt still on. His palm ran through the slickness on her stomach and he spread it up over her breast. The smell of his release filled her senses as he ran his wet thumb around her nipple.

Every little thing they did felt new and wholly shocking. She wasn't sure what might happen next, but with the future so uncertain, she intended to soak up every minute of it. Bucking her hips to flip him over, Jimmy assisted her in straddling him.

She could feel his rising pleasure again and it made her insides ache. Desperate for more contact, she lifted her hips and aligned him with her entrance. Jimmy gave a quick spasm as she closed over the sensitive head, and they both cried out as she took him deep inside her.

Jimmy began to emit the desperate moaning sounds he seemed to make right before orgasm, but Sadie wasn't ready. She wanted his shirt off first. "I want to see your body," she said, tugging at the material.

It was useless though. He began to convulse under her before they could pull it over his head. He got entirely caught there, with it covering his arms and the upper half of his face as he bucked his hips.

Too distracted to continue his task, he remained trapped as he writhed under her.

This time, Sadie found she had enough control to keep the climax going. Watching his body spasm under her, she began to touch herself in quick, tiny circles. He had become impossibly hard inside her and she rode him frantically as she held off his release by force. She found she enjoyed getting to watch him without him being able to see her, and she reveled in his pleasure, soaking up the show as she made herself climax around him.

Her own spasming passed and she reached to run her palms over the taut muscles of his chest. His entire body was rigid with the tension of climax, which continued to release in little waves inside him.

"Don't forget to breathe," she reminded him, resting her chest against his to whisper in his ear. His chest rose at her command as he resumed the normally standard function of getting oxygen.

"I like you like this," she said, holding his trapped elbows in her hands. He responded only with sounds of pleasure. Sadie regretted not being able to see his eyes then, but the privacy at least allowed him to focus on the feeling. So far in their interactions, he'd been so caught up with the desire to kiss her that his mind was always half-focused on that.

This time, he merely savored the sensation in his own body as all his sexual thoughts focused inward. Sadie kissed him as she released her restraint over his release. He groaned loudly as he bucked one final time before filling her with hot fluid.

She finally untangled him from the shirt, and they took in each other's expressions. For a long moment, they just stared, Jimmy catching his breath as she chewed her lip.

"God that feels so good," he said. "Every time. I can't believe it's real."

She bent down and kissed him, feeling like she might cry with the emotions coursing through her.

"That's nothing," she said. "And since we don't know what tomorrow might bring, I think we should make it good."

He laughed. "Yeah. We wouldn't want to underdo it."

Jimmy ran his hands up over her hips, before sliding his thumb between her legs. He rubbed her clit as he asked, "Can you go again?"

"Making you come gets me ready," she said, realizing only then the truth of that.

Neither of them seemed remotely sated by what had happened so far and Sadie wondered idly if any of this was normal. She thought it would be impossible to ever feel like she'd had enough of him. So ready was her body to feel him, in fact, that her own climax was just around the corner.

In sudden surprise, she rocked a few times before it hit her. Losing track of herself, she accidentally pulled Jimmy over the edge with her in a quick, single spasm climax.

She blinked her eyes open during the aftershocks to see Jimmy frozen in surprise.

"Sorry," she said instinctively. He had only just come, and she had meant to give it more time. Sadie blushed at her clumsiness, fighting through the embarrassment with a long steadying breath.

For a brief moment, their bodies relaxed, and she enjoyed the simple sensation of his warm skin against hers. He ran his hands up and down her arms in an affectionate, nonsexual way, and she went soft at the gesture.

"I can't imagine, Sadie, what you could be apologizing for. Am I missing something?"

Sadie shook her head. He didn't know how things could be with her when she was in control of herself. He'd only witnessed the hungry, fumbling Sadie, driven too much by instinct.

"It's nothing," she said. "I just didn't mean to do that. I want to take it slow. I really do, but—"

He pulled her down to kiss her and they both groaned as his pleasure spiked again. It pulsed with the rhythm of their tongues and he gripped her ass to pull her tighter. Again the plateau phase passed quickly and he rode the edge of climax.

"I can't hold it back," she panted against his mouth.

"Don't," he said. "I want it. Fuck, I like it so much."

She'd never seen Jimmy act like this. It was intoxicating hearing him ask her to make him feel good. After a summer of dating without touching, and him primarily focusing on her, she found herself wanting to bask in this new experience.

But as she watched a look of pleasurable agony overtake his expression, she began to worry about what they were doing. The excessive feeding allowed her thoughts to clear a bit, and memories of their life together flitted through her mind in a random order.

She thought back to the years before she'd manifested her succubus traits. Their friendship had defined her life. She just couldn't imagine a future without it. And before her transformation into succubus, things had been almost perfect between them. Apart from his unreciprocated attraction, that is.

Jimmy pushed his head back into the bed, eyes closed, as he resumed breathing again without needing a reminder this time. Without thinking consciously about it, Sadie increased the intensity of the orgasm. His chest twitched and hips bucked spastically in response.

As fate had it though, her sexual interest accompanied the onset of her new succubus skin, and being with Jimmy meant either avoiding skin contact or... this. And though this indulgence was the best thing she'd ever experienced, it also changed everything. Even as she basked in it, Sadie saw the words of Gabriel's scroll running through the back of her mind.

They were playing with fire, and it might destroy them.

Still, none of that made her want to hold back. All she wanted was more. Jimmy, who couldn't speak just then, was also begging for more with every one of his thoughts and emotions.

"Want to see how deep this thing goes?" she asked, idly curious about how long she'd already held him like this.

He was able to open his eyes and make contact, but he let his thoughts and body give the response as he pushed his hips up into her. Leaving behind her rational musings, she dropped into the moment with him.

Sadie let go completely. Jimmy's face went calm as he looked back at her with a look of pained ecstasy. A euphoria settled over her as their chests rose and fell together, the rhythm of their hips picking up gradually, perfectly in sync this time.

As she lost herself in his lustful craving, a strange feeling developed. Time seemed to slow to a near-halt as she examined the emotion of desire as if it were a physical object she could hold in her hands. It felt as if she were observing the moment from the outside.

Gradually, she followed the emotion backward and found herself dropped into a scene as vivid as if she were there. She was looking into a version of her own face. The sun was coming up behind her and a light breeze blew a strand of hair across her cheek. She was in Jimmy's memory from a few days ago.

"No regrets," she said in Jimmy's deep voice.

All his life he had wanted this moment. He was frozen in trepidation and anticipation as Sadie bent to kiss him. Jimmy took in her scent as their lips touched lightly, parting slightly to tentatively press their tongues together. He was finally kissing her. It was actually happening, and it felt far more raw and real than he could have imagined.

Though no longer did he have time to enjoy the feeling than a new sensation spread through him. It was like wildfire as the flutter of sexual excitement turned into very real pleasure. A deep groan reverberated out of him as the feeling grew.

He wanted more. Jimmy needed to be inside her. He got his wish only a few minutes later. After they'd clumsily found their way to the ground and removed their clothing, she'd guided him between her legs. He'd still been in shock at what was happening when she'd said "now," and he'd thrust in her for the first time.

They'd frozen there for just a moment, taking in what had just happened before he'd begun to move intently, hungrily. The explosion of sensation was a shock, and his senses were lost in it as he bucked against her, but in the background of his mind was something else. This was Sadie, he thought. It was her he was inside. It was her he was kissing. And there had never been anything in the world he had wanted more.

Sadie came out of the memory as if emerging from warm water. They were both still in the middle of a climax and an unknown amount of time had passed. She refocused her thoughts and released them. As they groaned quietly against each other's mouths, Sadie was racked with surprise at what had just happened.

The aftershocks took a full minute to pass, but when they did, she kissed him once and rapidly removed herself from further skin contact.

Propping herself up on her side, Sadie looked over at Jimmy. His hands were over his head, chest rising and falling rapidly as he caught his breath. Deciding to keep the memory dive to herself for now, she merely savored the sight of him trembling and satiated. It was a kind of rapture, doing that to him, and now that he knew what it was like to be with her, he craved it as much as she did. If the plan was to try to stop now, they were in for serious trouble.

"Jimmy?" she said, before she knew what she was going to say. She wanted to tell him that she couldn't imagine a world in which they weren't going to do that again. That despite all the warnings, she wanted to spend the rest of her life making love to him. That if she couldn't keep touching him, they would have to stay away from each other or she would go mad.

"I love you," she said, blinking back tears.

He scooped one of her curls behind her ear, releasing the contact quickly. Then he pulled the sheet up over him and reached to hug her into his side. As she tossed a thigh over his and settled in, Jimmy kissed the top of her head. "I love you, too," he said, and she couldn't help but note that, like her own, his tone had an undercurrent of fear.

Chapter 3

Suspicion and hope

Sadie woke up feeling incredible. The early rays of sunrise danced on the other side of her eyelids as she reconnected with consciousness in a rush. Energy filled her as the strong desire to get up and move directed her into action. She went slowly so as not to wake Jimmy, but he seemed so worn out that her precaution was likely unnecessary.

Creeping from the cabin, she went in search of the showers. Hetia had said they were down by the river, but that was a rather vague description, so she shot for the part of the river in which they'd met Amadi. Everyone was clearly still sleeping, and Sadie strolled freely through the encampment, enjoying the view of the simple cabins framed by mountain peaks on all sides.

The river was at the lowest point of the valley, carving out a little ravine. It came into view only once Sadie had descended down the path Hetia had led them on yesterday. Since she couldn't see showers in the small stretch before the river curved out of sight, she chose a direction at random and made her way along the water. As she walked, she noted a change in the weather off in the distance. Dark clouds were accumulating, visible only from certain angles in the ravine.

After a while, Sadie began to ascend out of the valley. This didn't seem right. Maybe she'd made a wrong turn? Before she could turn to retreat back the other direction, however, she spotted a tiny figure on the hill up ahead.

She wasn't exactly sure why, but the figure reminded her of Hetia. She was too far away to see the images that defined her, but her posture was vaguely familiar. Curious, she decided to get a little closer. Hetia's long blond hair, flowing out behind her, came into view first and Sadie's heart beat as she recognized it.

The woman stared out at the storm as Sadie slowly made her way out of the ravine. Cresting the local peak behind Hetia, Sadie caught a glimpse of the gathering clouds in full. They were intense. Though localized, they were thick and dropping what appeared to be heavy rain. Lightning flashed in the distance, followed by the remote sound of thunder.

Sadie tried to make her presence audibly noticeable so that she wouldn't frighten Hetia, though this was probably unnecessary since the woman seemed unshakable. She didn't turn as Sadie pulled up next to her, but Sadie could tell by the pulse in the red light connecting them that Hetia was aware of who was standing in her peripheral.

"Did you open the box?" Hetia asked in greeting.

Sadie pulled up to her side, and looked the woman up and down. She wore a form-fitting, thigh high dress with a tiny utility belt defining her waist. The look was appealing on her and Sadie had to force her gaze to her face as Hetia looked over at her.

"Yes. Last night," Sadie said. Hetia's gaze flitted up and down her briefly and a little thrill shot through her at the attention. For a second, she wished she'd done more with her hair, but then she caught an image of herself through the other woman's desire. Sadie blinked in surprise at the way Hetia saw her.

She turned her piercing gaze back to the storm, and Sadie followed the direction of her focus. Her heart skipped. In the distance, right in the heat of the commotion, was the figure of a man. He appeared to be strolling casually as the rain drenched him.

What was he doing out there? Lightning struck the ground a few feet from him and Sadie jumped. "Oh, shit. Is that one of ours?"

"Amadi," Hetia said.

Sadie's head snapped to her. "Wh— What's he doing?"

Hetia smoothed her dress and put her hands on her hips. "Storm nymphs don't usually live around here. They need to run into a storm at least once a week in order to feed. Not Amadi. He's strong," she said with pride. "He can create storms, not just influence them. It's one of the reasons the camp is up here. Easier to hide spontaneous weather from view."

Sadie nodded. "Amadi's... a storm nymph." She cast Hetia a sidelong glance before pressing on. "He was the one that raised you, after your father died?"

"Yes," Hetia said. Sadie asked the question to spark conversation, but she had clearly seen the lines of blue light which had connected the two when they were nearby. They were obviously family.

"He did this yesterday," Hetia said. Sadie didn't understand, but waited for further explanation. "He usually doesn't feed this often, unless... he's anxious. This news about the army isn't good." Hetia turned to her. "Let's hope that box of yours can turn the tables."

Sadie didn't reply to that. She was not optimistic. "At least our side has a rare storm nymph *and* a powerful earthquake nymph." She bobbed her head in Hetia's direction. "That was crazy what you did back there. In Seattle. You leveled a whole piece of the city."

Hetia blinked. "That isn't the hard part. The challenge is containing the quake to a small area."

"Really? Do you think you could have shaken all of Seattle?" Sadie asked.

Hetia lifted her chin. "Sure."

Sadie smiled at the clear pride in her skill. "Well, I didn't say it yesterday, but thanks for saving us."

"Anytime," Hetia said, her voice uncharacteristically soft. She didn't return the smile, but she did keep her gaze fixed on Sadie for once. A moment later, the ground under their feet began to tremble ever so slightly. Sadie spread her stance to stay standing as the earth danced, laughing as her hips swayed.

As she watched Sadie, giggling and trying to stay upright, Hetia gave the tiniest of grins. This little act of showing off was the most playful Sadie had ever seen her, and she found she liked this side of the woman best of all. It seemed a precious thing, the few moments in which she was at ease enough to relax around Sadie – a tiny glimpse of how she might be if her defenses ever came down entirely.

"Whew! That was refreshing," Amadi said, making both the women jump. The trembling in the earth stopped almost instantly.

Amadi was a few feet away, wiping the rain from his glasses without removing them from his face. She smiled as she realized they were taped down on either side of his head. She turned to share the grin with Hetia, but the woman looked embarrassed, and Sadie decided to return to a neutral expression as she looked over Amadi's shoulder at the blue sky. There was no trace of the storm apart from the few fluffy clouds that were still disbanding and the man's wet clothes.

"You were able to find sleep?" Amadi asked her.

"Yes. It was the most comfortable bed I'd been in for days," she said. Sadie wasn't sure that was actually true since she honestly couldn't remember anything about the sleep portion of her night, but it seemed likely and she wanted to say something polite.

"Excellent. And the box?" he asked.

"Open," she said.

"Good." He clapped his hands together. "We'll meet in about an hour. Give everyone time to get food in their bellies." He gestured them to begin walking back to camp before turning to the woman that was like a daughter. "Hetia, allow me to walk Ms. Hall back."

Hetia bobbed her head, and without a glance backward, veered off on an alternate path. Sadie watched her assured walk as Hetia disappeared from view. When she glanced at Amadi, she found him studying her.

"My Hetia's a unique one," he said, a twinkle in his eye.

Sadie laughed. "*That* is the only thing I know for sure about her."

"Well," he patted her back, "hang in there."

Sadie raised an eyebrow at him in question.

"Mae will be here today," he said in a non sequitur.

"Who?" Sadie searched her thoughts. Should she know that name?

"The woman you see on me," he said, suddenly serious.

Sadie's heart sped up. He was bringing it up. They were going to talk about it.

"Oh. Yes, I—" She shifted. "I assume you would know what I can see if you're the partner of a succubus."

"Yes," he said, and then with a sidelong glance, he added, "Hetia doesn't. Mae is very selective with who she's told."

Sadie nodded.

"And as a man who has spent a lot of his life trying to uncover political corruption, I think she is smart to be cautious. Our secrets are our best weapons."

"I understand. Jimmy is the only person I've told," Sadie said. "Hetia, she was like a daughter?"

"Hetia *is* my daughter, yes. Her father entrusted me with that role if anything happened to him."

"Then was Mae like her mother?" she asked, wondering if there was some history with succubi that could explain her behavior toward Sadie.

"No. Not at all. Mae has her own family, and she prefers not to be too involved with our work here. She visits me often, but I am Hetia's sole family."

Sadie's steps faltered. "Your... Mae, she doesn't live with you?"

"No. She did for the first year we were together. That was an intense time, and we couldn't seem to stand being apart, but our lives took us in different directions."

This was big news. It was so close to what Sadie really wanted to know. "And... you're okay with that?" she asked.

He nodded slowly, thoughtfully. "I'm too wrapped up in my work for more. My relationship with Mae has been the best part of my life, on par with Hetia, and it works well for me."

Sadie chewed her lip. That was all good to know, but she wished she could ask directly about the things she'd read in Gabriel's scroll. The idea of talking in more detail with Amadi, though, made her squirm. He was male and much older than her, and these were very sensitive topics. If Mae was coming, she would hold her questions for the succubus.

"You found the showers?" he asked.

Sadie shook off her musings. "Uhh no, actually."

Amadi pointed. "Down there," he said, pausing at a split in the path. "See you in an hour," he nodded, before pausing in his retreat. Sadie halted, expectantly, as Amadi added. "It's... *subtle*, reading Hetia, but make no mistake, my daughter is glad you're here."

Amadi left Sadie with her mouth hanging slightly open. Was the leader, for she had no other word for him, of the United, trying to set her up with his daughter? And was he right, *was* Hetia happy to see her?

Sadie basked in that thought as she made her way back down the path, and it was several minutes before her thoughts moved on from Hetia. She suddenly regretted having gotten so distracted as Amadi was leaving. That could have been the perfect chance to talk to him about the strange memory reading she'd experienced last night. *Next time.*

Increasingly anxious to talk to this Mae person, Sadie bounded down to the river with the same frenzied energy she'd woken up with. There were several freestanding showers, with privacy curtains around each one. Sadie hung her mildly cleaner outfit on some hooks and undressed, bringing her old underwear under the water for cleaning. A soap bar hung from a rope and she used it vigorously, never so happy to see fragrant bubbles in her life. A few minutes in, the water became much warmer than she would have expected given the location of the tank. Had the sun hit it?

Fully satisfied, she turned off the faucet and immediately began to shiver as the sound of another person showering reached her ears. People were beginning to wake, and she was glad to hear it – this day couldn't get going fast enough.

Her towel was too small to wrap around herself, but she dabbed her body dry within the curtain. The other shower went quiet as she was dressing. When she heard them exit before she was done, Sadie decided she could put on her gloves while she said hello.

Emerging from the rapidly dissipating steam of what had truly been a glorious shower, she rounded the corner to say good morning. The words died in her throat. Troy jumped back at her sudden appearance, adopting a flight or fight stance. Fire didn't appear from him this time, but Sadie still made the choice to leave off her gloves, pocketing them instead. He watched her do it, noting her decision with narrowed eyes.

"What are you doing up this early?" he asked.

Something about his suspicious tone immediately put her off. "Bathing. Like you." She crossed her arms. "Do you normally treat people this rudely?"

He at least had the grace to look a little ashamed at that, making her soften her tone as she pleaded her case. "I brought good news with me, you know? I've been helpful to the United in several ways already. You think you'd be happier to have me."

He tensed at her words, and she immediately regretted escalating the hostility. "Of course you'd think that. Well, here's a surprise for you. Not everyone falls at the feet of succubi. And let me tell you now, this too-good-to-be-true mystery box that you brought us just when we *really* needed hope, isn't fooling me. I know all about Siphon's network of succubus spies. You think you rule the world. And you may have everyone else here fooled. But me...?" He stepped forward, keeping himself just out of arm's reach as he looked her over meticulously. "I'm not taking my eyes off you."

Sadie balked. Not at his closing statement, but at the fact that it was accompanied with the smallest sliver of red light, flowing in *both* directions. The thread was minuscule though, and she had the instinct to reach out and snap it, as if such things were possible.

Deciding not to rouse his suspicion further, she opted for not snatching randomly at the air between them.

"Noted," she said on a huff, and in an effort to show how devoutly unafraid of him she was, she turned her back and stomped away. Truthfully, she was a bit daunted by his fervor *and* firepower, but she didn't really think he would outright attack her again. All the same, it was a struggle to feign an at-ease walk.

Sadie tried to shake off the outrage as she re-entered the camp. She wanted to make a good impression on the people she passed. Pasting back on a smile, which took a few minutes to become natural, Sadie made her way back to cabin nine.

She found it empty. Searching about for Jimmy in her thoughts, she could feel him somewhere to her left. Since they'd first slept together, she'd become increasingly good at sensing his presence, even from a distance. She assumed this was because she could remotely feel him thinking about her, and he was *always* thinking about her now.

Sadie ached for his presence as she made herself some oatmeal. She couldn't reconcile their experience the past few days with the life Amadi and Mae had. So far, it seemed Gabriel's doomsday scroll was right on point. She felt completely out of control in her desire, and Jimmy clearly wasn't faring any better.

As important as she knew this coming meeting was, a large part of her wanted to throw the box in the river and spend the rest of the day in bed with her best friend. Last night had been unreal, and she couldn't pull her thoughts away from his face now that she was back to fixating on it. Recalling some of the things he had said made her muscles clench, and she hugged her abdomen in response, feeling empty.

She wished he would hurry up and come back. Though then again, once he did, they would need to actually talk about their future. Deciding she would rather speak to this elder succubus first, Sadie hurried up and scarfed down her food so she could get the hell out of the danger zone.

Just as she was about to pull open the door, a knock came on the other side. She found Hetia waiting there, continuing to face outward as Sadie greeted her. "We're ready," she said, glancing over briefly. Sadie nodded and stepped onto the landing, but not before Hetia had begun to walk off. Sadie scurried to keep up as she tugged on her gloves, figuring it was probably appropriate to resume wearing them despite the aggression of certain fire nymphs.

They walked in silence down a little path, while Sadie began to feel nervous. She and Jimmy had kept their unwanted gift a secret this whole time, and now they were about to hand it over. It was a silly feeling, since the box's intended destination had been Amadi's hands all along.

Hetia led her to a decent-sized building made of stone. It had a grand archway which left the front of the building open to the elements. Inside was a large table made of the same material as the walls, and around it were seated Amadi, Troy, Patricia, and Luciana. Sadie let out a squeal, suppressing it slightly at the sight of Troy's raised eyebrow. Trying to ignore the opinion of the sour man, she ran past him to hug her friend.

"You made it! I was afraid I'd have to wait days, but you arrived right after we did," Sadie babbled.

Patricia hugged her cautiously, a bit stiff at the affection, but when Sadie pulled back her friend was smiling, her beautiful face high-lighted with impeccable make-up despite the long journey. She looked mildly surprised at the strength of Sadie's greeting. Didn't Patricia know how she felt about her?

"Well, I heard you got a little lost, ended up taking a couple extra days to get here. That couldn't have been good for your feeding," Patricia said in a question. Sadie blushed and Patricia arched an eyebrow at her.

Luciana nudged Sadie's side with one of her walking canes, and she redirected her greeting to the elder woman. "You can tell my granddaughter all about it later. Now where's that Jimmy?" she asked Sadie, pivoting on her one leg to look expectantly at the doorway.

She thought she saw Amadi shake his head in a slight gesture, before Luciana dropped the subject with a wave, resecuring her bright yellow garden hat in her typical fashion.

"Sorry," Sadie said to Amadi, but he was smiling at them all warmly.

"Don't be silly," he said. "We're all grateful everyone made it out of that crumbling city. And what are any of us fighting for if not the chance to squeal at the arrival of friends? Now, let's look at this diary."

Having momentarily forgotten their purpose, Sadie's expression grew somber as she tugged open her backpack and retrieved the box. She pulled out the loose lid first and placed it on the table before setting the open box next to it.

Patricia reached immediately for the button, extracting it gingerly and turning it over in her hands. Amadi gave that a cursory glance before lifting the diary as if it were the most precious of objects. He ran his hands over the cover and brought it to his nose to sniff it before holding it in one hand and letting it fall open naturally. His eyebrows rose and mouth turned down in a frown as he flipped through several pages, skimming rapidly.

Sadie cleared her throat. "If I can...?" She held out a hand. Amadi handed it to her and she flipped open to the last entry. "I don't know if any of the other stuff is useful, but I'd read this first."

He read silently while everyone watched. When he finally looked up it was to seek Sadie's eyes. "This is the most valuable information we have ever found. A major breakthrough," he said, making everyone except Hetia squirm impatiently.

Addressing the room, Amadi explained, "It seems the Siphon family has a much bigger plan than we'd ever imagined. And two other prominent human feeder families are implicated here. The Siphon, Maddox, and Griffiths families have been plotting this war for generations. There are hints here that each family is responsible for a piece of it. Only the heads of households know the entirety, but the youngest members," Amadi paused here to look at Troy, "know a portion of the plan. It seems your connection with the young Mia Siphon will prove even more useful than we'd thought."

Troy closed his eyes and bowed his head, before nodding, a resolved look settling over his features. As she took him in, Sadie noticed that there was a strong green line of friendship pulsating between Patricia and Troy. They... knew each other well. She couldn't help but pout at this development.

"The only solid information here as to the nature of the plan is itself still vague... something about planned attacks against nymphs and blaming humans," Amadi went on, peering back down at the diary. "Unfortunately, it doesn't tell us which attacks." Amadi pushed up his glasses. "It also says that it was these families that began the trend of calling nymphs nature feeders. The ultimate goal is to unite nature feeders, excuse me, nymphs, with human feeders, against humans." He sighed. "All a part of their war to enslave humans. Well," he clapped his hands, "it seems we finally know where to look. There is a very intentional plan out there, and it is in the hands or minds of these three families."

"I presume this plan includes the button in some way," Patricia said.

"Maybe the diary talks about that somewhere else," Luciana suggested.

"It doesn't," Sadie said.

Troy frowned. "Maybe it's in *code*."

Sadie was confused. Did he still think this was all a trick, that she was a fraud, or was he as excited as the rest of them to uncover the mystery? As for his suggestion that the diary was code, Sadie didn't want to respond to that since it had been exactly her thinking up until the last entry. Choosing to ignore Troy's suggestion rather than agree with him publicly, she turned her attention back to Amadi.

Luciana stepped in. "I'll be taking this," she said, removing the book from her granddaughter's hands.

Amadi nodded. "If there's anything to be found, Luciana will find it. Let's keep these revelations within this group. The fewer people who know what we now know, the better. Mr. Hyun, are you prepared to go in for this one?"

Troy nodded slowly. Sadie stared at him a minute and then raised her hand, but Amadi waved it away this time. "Just jump in here, Ms. Hall. God knows the rest of us do."

She cleared her throat. "I... am wondering if I could come. I got some practice spying in Seattle and I want to learn more."

Amadi considered, looking around at Luciana and Patricia. "I think that would be too much of a risk. You should get some practice elsewhere."

Sadie's shoulders slumped. Now that she'd handed over the diary, she worried that she wouldn't have enough to offer. She didn't want to become useless here. In Seattle, she'd barely contributed anything apart from the one time she'd played the spy, which had come with both a thrill and a sense of accomplishment like she'd never felt before.

Wanting to prove her value and see where such a pursuit might take her, Sadie turned to Luciana, the woman who had recruited her in the first place, to plead her case. "I did well my first time, though.

And we barely had any chance to prepare. I like the work, and am willing to train hard – to learn fast." She was rambling now, and her face flushed as she fell silent.

"It's true. You did well," the elder woman said, "but I agree with Amadi. This is too big."

Sadie hung her head in resignation, nodding her deference to their opinions.

"You can be included in the planning stages as we prepare to send Mr. Hyun in," Amadi said.

"What?" Troy said, then recognizing his tone, blushed under Amadi's gaze. "Sorry, I mean, are you sure that's a good idea?"

"It would be helpful to have a succubus on board, and if Sadie's willing to be involved in the most dangerous mission yet, I say we start training her immediately," Amadi said.

"Agreed," Patricia chimed in. Luciana and Hetia nodded. Troy slumped back in his seat, defeated.

"It's decided then, we'll begin—" Amadi stopped on an inhale. Sadie saw a flurry of sharp images surround the man as deep red and black light pulsed from him to the door.

A smile overtook his face as he pushed up his glasses. "Hi," he said in such a sheepish tone that if Sadie were just meeting him now, she would have thought he were a lovestruck teenager and not a powerful middle-aged man running a national underground movement. Sadie didn't need to glance at the door to know Mae had arrived.

Chapter 4

Temptations

Sadie bit down on her lip, trying not to laugh out loud at the expression on Amadi's face. He'd known she was coming. Why was he struck dumb? Sadie followed his rapt gaze to the object of affection and found her own voice hitching. The person was stunning. All drenched in love and lust. There was too much to look at to determine anything clearly, but the overall impression left Sadie awestruck.

The scenes which defined a person were often more emotion and truth than strictly visual in nature. As such, Sadie only barely recognized the person in front of her from the swirling sexual history she saw on Amadi, and in turn, could only barely see Amadi as one of the people present in her. More than anyone Sadie had ever met, this woman had lived a rich sexual life. Gabriel hadn't looked like this. Nor had the prostitute in Arlington. Why was *this* succubus so different?

"Sorry. I was trying to wait until the end to come in," Mae said. "It seems my timing could still use some practice." She winked at Luciana.

"We're done, Mae," Hetia chimed in.

Seeming to come back to himself, Amadi said, "No, wait. Patricia, can you draw up a map of everything we know about those three families, and Hetia, start training her. Uhh, Ms. Hall that is. Oh, and does everyone know Mae Evans? This is my very good friend, my partner."

Mae released her embrace on Luciana and looked at Sadie. Her expression came to the forefront of Sadie's notice as the succubus scrutinized her. Eyes so brown they were almost black looked her over in concern as Sadie stepped forward to introduce herself, shyly offering a hand.

"It's been a while since I've run into another one of my kind." She accepted the handshake. "And how young you are. I'd almost forgotten what it's like to be newly turned."

Sadie didn't think she was that new – it had been five months after all, and a lot had happened in that time, but she could only imagine how this woman saw her. "It's... nice to meet you. Amadi told me you were coming," she said, not trying to hide her eagerness.

Mae gave her an encouraging smile before turning to Troy. "And I believe you're also new." She held out a hand to the young man. Sadie smiled at his expression. He was looking from Amadi to Mae with an amusing assortment of emotions clearly on display. Finally, he ran a hand through his hair and stepped up to take the offered hand.

"Yes, ma'am," he said with a mix of respect and uncertainty, but he seemed to settle on trusting her. "It's a pleasure to meet you," he added with absolute sincerity.

Sadie had to fight back her indignation at his near immediate trust of Mae. She couldn't help casting her mind back through her own behavior to see if there was something she'd done wrong to earn Troy's dislike. She supposed that if Mae was Amadi's partner, they'd been together long enough that she could likely be trusted, while her own arrival had been sudden, and filled with the coincidence of the box. Sadie chewed her lip, even more anxious to prove herself in some way.

Hetia stepped in to greet Mae with a handshake. The formality was strange given their tight connection to the same man. Though the succubus turned the handshake into a quick one-armed hug, releasing the younger woman after a brief squeeze.

Then without further ceremony, Hetia moved to the door and

Luciana and Patricia made to follow. Sadie and Troy realized a moment later that the meeting was officially over, and fell in line with the exodus. The both of them were fixated on Mae as they left, and nearly ran into each other in the doorway.

Troy hopped a foot away, as if she had burned him, while Sadie did her best to pretend she hadn't even noticed his nearness. They drew up on either side of Hetia as Patricia and Luciana bid them goodbye and veered off in another direction together.

Sadie laughed then. "Is he always like that around her? By the way he talked so calmly about their relationship yesterday, I really didn't expect *that*."

Hetia nodded gravely. "It passes," she said. "Give them a day or two."

"How long since they've last seen each other?" Sadie asked.

Hetia tucked back some strands of her thin hair as she thought, and Sadie watched the motion of her hand. "A few months, give or take," she said.

"Well, I don't know him well yet, but that was entertaining," Sadie said, though inwardly she was concerned at the effect Mae had had. Sadie wanted evidence that their relationship was healthy and normal. Seeing Amadi so altered brought up renewed doubt.

Troy blew out a breath. "That was unnerving," he said, echoing her private thoughts. "Amadi is a powerful man. How could he let himself be so taken in like that?"

Sadie didn't want to take the bait. Luckily, as she fought to stay silent, Hetia spoke instead. "My birth father..." she began hesitantly, and Sadie's attention snapped to her in surprise over bringing up a personal topic. "He had concerns about Mae. He thought she was a distraction. He also didn't like that she didn't want to join the work." Hetia steered them down a new path as she paused in one of her typical long silences. "And it's true, she would steal Amadi's attention. But... they're happy together. And he always comes back." Hetia spoke like it was a concession to say this.

Neither Troy nor Sadie responded to this pronouncement. Did he know Hetia well enough that he too saw this sharing as a breakthrough? Or did he know her better and already had all kinds of insight about her feelings and past? Suddenly Sadie was jealous of their potential relationship, despite the fact she was only just now noticing the tiny green line of friendship which connected them.

They stopped at a wide, semi-flat rock as big as a house that was situated on the edge of the encampment. A stone nymph had clearly molded the slab to contain several seats encircling a low, table-like surface, and a spruce tree hovered nearby, providing some shade.

Hetia hopped up to take a seat. "Not the best meeting place for Luciana, but if it's just the three of us..." she said. Troy sat next to her while Sadie took the seat directly opposite. "I've been working with Troy," Hetia said. "His experience is also still limited."

Troy smiled over at Hetia. "Not *that* limited. I was in the thick of it for a year."

"He was," Hetia told her, before replying to Troy, "but that was different. This is what I need you to learn," she said to them both. "Troy can tell you his story another day, but the recap is that he was unwittingly courted by the Siphon family. Patricia approached him separately, intentionally befriending him on the side. She wasn't sure if he would stay with the feeders when he learned more about their intentions. She saw potential in him." Troy bobbed his head as she acknowledged him. "But as someone the Coalition was intentionally recruiting, she knew he would be a valuable spy if he came to work with us."

That explained a small amount of why succubi made him nervous, but his feelings toward Sadie still seemed overblown.

"Throughout that time though," Hetia directed at Troy, "you weren't aware of what was happening under the surface. Walking back in there will be a different story."

Troy nodded, but added softly, "Though I walked myself out of there. When I learned the truth, I got out safely."

"You did. But you haven't really been tested yet. This is what we need to work on. You've been focusing on your cover story, on making the *facts* consistent, but we're dealing with human feeders. You never know who might be feeding off different emotions or physical reactions. Even though many feeders can't actually *feed* off each other, they still sense the emotions – excitement, pride, jealousy. This is the biggest challenge."

Sadie had learned a lot about such things this past year. She knew that succubi still produced pleasure in each other, though they didn't feed. While siren, like her once friend Alec, could feed off succubi, despite the fact both species were human feeders.

Hetia continued, "What I'm saying is, if what you're feeling doesn't match what someone expects, that is a giveaway."

Sadie remembered her own adventure with that kind of deception. She hadn't needed to be told this fact, and she allowed herself to feel internally smug about being ahead of Troy on this. Just when she was wishing she had some way to let him know, Hetia added, "Sadie used that to her advantage well in Seattle."

Sadie smiled and Troy clenched his jaw at her self-satisfied expression. She wasn't sure what was happening with her – she'd never felt this competitive with someone. She dropped her grin, feeling a little ashamed of herself.

"Now I'm going to give you some scenarios, and I want you to practice responding to them. First Troy, but then Sadie," Hetia said. Sadie sat up straighter, immediately excited at the game.

Hetia pulled some cards from a dress pocket. "You're surrounded by Coalition members and one of them tells you with excitement that they killed two humans last night. How do you respond?"

Sadie's smile dropped into a horrified frown. "Is that likely to happen?"

Hetia looked at her. "Possibly," she said and turned to Troy.

He thought for a moment. "I would think of the day Siphon invited me to his estate for the first time. It was a moment of excitement." He ran a hand through his hair. "Despite everything, I can still feel how that felt."

"What does that have to do with killing humans?" Sadie asked.

"Nothing. It has to do with me and my experiences, and what might give me the same feeling as the person I'm talking to. The idea of killing people repulses me, so I wouldn't think about that. But that invitation into Siphon's world... it not only made me feel alive, but it gave me a sense of being a part of something – of being on the right side of history. That's the kind of thing that would match what those feeders might be feeling."

Sadie continued to frown. Troy was a bit clever, then. His expert response annoyed her, but not nearly as much as the thread of red light that flowed from her to him as she appreciated his nuance in tackling the situation.

She shrugged and turned back to Hetia. "Give us another."

The woman flipped to a new card. "A Coalition member tells you there's someone they want you to meet and introduces you to their daughter. It is clear they're trying to set you up and the daughter is quite attractive." Hetia looked pointedly at Troy and Sadie felt there was some inside information she was missing here. "How do you respond?"

Troy took a deep breath, glanced at Sadie, and then blushed. She blinked in surprise at him. He looked away to speak. "I guess if I thought the relationship was useful in some way, then... I would try to think of someone else I find attractive and pretend the person was them."

"Good," Hetia said. "Try it now."

Troy swallowed audibly and ran a hand through his dark hair. Sadie admired the way the strands fell back into his face. She took advantage of him looking away to get to really look at him. Why did he have to be so appealing? Her unwanted feelings worsened when the image that popped into Troy's mind was of her outside the showers this morning with her hair wet. He shook his head. "I can't think of anyone," he said. "But I'll work on it."

"Sadie?" Hetia said. Was it her imagination or was the woman a little nervous to ask her this one?

"That's easy, I would remember the first time I saw you," Sadie told her simply. She didn't say it in a flirtatious voice. She meant it seriously. It was the scenario with the most amount of overlap with the one being presented. There had been an immediate spark of attraction mingled with curiosity. Having known Jimmy forever, her relationship with him was entirely different. Hetia was the right choice.

Hetia's eyes widened almost imperceptibly at this declaration, but her only other reaction was in her sudden and complete stillness.

"To get myself in the moment I would think of the smell of gin," Sadie added thoughtfully, really thinking it through. She trusted this would work fine later since it was working now. Her heart sped up as the sound of the casino echoed around in her memory.

Troy was glaring daggers at her. "This is a serious exercise, not a chance to seduce Hetia."

Sadie frowned at him. "I *know* that. You don't think I'm taking this seriously? Why do you think I gave the most honest answer I could?"

Troy furrowed his brow, but the earnest tone of her voice must have put doubt in his mind, because he considered her a long time, as if genuinely debating if he was wrong.

"That's enough for today," Hetia said. Without looking at either of them she added, "You get the idea. You both have homework. Make a list of emotions and come up with a memory to go with each of them. Then practice using triggers to drop you into each one." She jumped from the rock, landing in a smooth crouch before coming upright. "Nice work... with the gin," she said, and then without looking back, left Sadie and Troy to stare at each other.

Sadie gave him an exasperated look and hopped down after Hetia before he could say another word. She didn't want to have to listen to him blame her for their tutor leaving, so she walked in a fast-paced huff, wanting to be alone.

Troy didn't follow, and as the distance from him grew, her head cleared. *Good.* She didn't need to have him taking up any more space in her mind. Sadie wasn't sure exactly what his problem was, but she could happily be left out of it.

Luckily, she didn't have to search far for a distraction. Being left alone a minute with her thoughts, it turned out, was all it took to feel Jimmy's presence. He seemed to be in their cabin, and his thoughts were not as intense on her at the moment. Maybe now was the right time to talk about their situation. At the back of her mind, she was vaguely aware that she was looking for an excuse to be alone with Jimmy and *not* to talk, but she brushed that aside before she could look too hard at it.

Though a rush of excitement hit her as she approached cabin nine, accompanied by the rich aroma of onions sauteing in oil, reminding her of home. Jimmy was bent over the stove, looking satisfied with himself. He glanced her way and two things happened in rapid succession. A surge of sudden and rather overwhelming arousal struck him, which immediately caused the same reaction in her.

He took a steadying breath and forced his attention back to the stove as Sadie stepped toward him, all trust in her own intentions gone. She saw movement on the bed and paused. Patricia was sitting in the center of the mattress with papers sprawled out around her.

"Sadie, you're back so soon," Patricia said. "I caught Jimmy up on the conversation this morning. He agreed to help me get a map of these feeder families together. Amadi gave us clearance to look through these boxes of old notes." She pushed away some of the clutter to make space. "Would you like to join us?"

Sadie looked at the profile of Jimmy, aroused and facing the stove, then back at Patricia. She was simultaneously annoyed and very grateful for the presence of an additional person.

"Sure," she said, trying to suppress the pulsing ache that had suffused her body. Sadie made herself comfortable next to Patricia and unrolled the large paper that sat between them. It showed a very incomplete web, three separate webs in fact, of the Siphon, Maddox, and Griffiths families.

"The Griffiths aren't really mentioned anywhere," Patricia said. "The notes trace through a variety of attempts to get close to Katherine Maddox, the current president of the feeder government, and Derek Siphon since they are the two most involved in politics, and therefore the most visible. It seems that diary is the first time the Griffiths have popped up on our radar." She reached behind her and pulled another box up next to them. "This one is full of newspaper clippings regarding any tensions or major violence between feeders, nymphs, or humans. Amadi's been collecting them for decades."

Patricia was really in her element with this kind of work, and Sadie smiled affectionately as she listened to her explain everything she'd learned. At some point while the two of them were absorbed over the family map, Jimmy sat down across from her. Sadie tensed at his nearness, but didn't look up until he handed them both plates of food.

Their eyes met as she took the plate and they both paused. The memory of last night was all over him. He released the plate to run a thumb over the back of her hand, mouthing the words, *Good morning*, just for her. She mouthed the words back as if they contained all the other things she wanted to say. It was a private moment, and it seemed to last an eternity, but Patricia didn't even notice. Sadie smiled sweetly at him and placed the plate in her lap. Out loud she said, "This smells amazing."

"Hmm," Patricia agreed, taking a bite. They worked as they ate, occasionally reading something out loud if it seemed relevant. Sadie was acutely aware that Jimmy had had a persistent erection since the moment she'd walked in, and so to prevent him having to stand up again, she rose to clear the plates herself. She could feel him watching her as she stacked the dishes and returned to the bed.

As they read their way through the first stack, Sadie stretched one leg out, and Jimmy rubbed her calf through her pants affectionately. She looked up at him often, occasionally to find him watching her. They were reading so slowly that Patricia's finished pile was twice the size of theirs combined.

Sadie was impressed that he was able to focus at all given the waves of emotion she could feel rolling off him. She was no better. When he stretched his arm so his thumb could caress the back of her knee, she stopped reading for several minutes.

"I think," Patricia said, making them both jump, "that's good for now. I'm helping with food prep tonight. It's the weekly barbecue. We roast a pig." She began to pack things up. "It's a social thing. It'll be a good chance for you to get to know people."

Sadie's heart began to race. Patricia was leaving them? Should she go with her? It was undeniably clear now that staying alone here with Jimmy was not going to lead to talking. Yet she hated the idea of walking away from him. She reached down below her knee to find his hand and squeezed it. They exchanged a look, his expression matched hers as she tried to ask nonverbally for his opinion. What he *wanted* was clear, but she needed to know what he *thought*.

"Leave it out," he told Patricia, releasing Sadie's hand and pulling the papers toward him. Then he directed at her, "I can keep working here if you want to go."

Sadie wished she could feel relief at his initiative, but instead she found herself annoyed that he had the strength to remove them from temptation. Secretly, she realized now, she had hoped that they would just follow their instincts, unable to resist, and put off the conversation about the future for one more day.

Sadie nodded reluctantly. "Can I help you with the food prep?" she asked Patricia. Her friend smiled, looking pleased at this development. Sadie stood to follow Patricia to the door, but paused to look back at Jimmy. She hesitated for a second before kneeling quickly over the papers in front of him and cupping his jaw in her hand. If only she could step out of her succubus skin for a minute to kiss him goodbye. Instead, she pseudo-rubbed their noses together, keeping back a centimeter while he dug his fingers into her curls.

"We can talk tonight at the barbecue," she whispered.

"Yeah," he said, clutching her face through her hair like a lifeline. His desperate grip increased her own distress and her fear of the coming conversation made her feel rash. Before she could overthink it, Sadie closed the gap.

His surprise got lost quickly in the pleasure of the moment. She tried to memorize the feeling of his mouth against hers, their tongues pressed together, as their uncertain future pounded like a force around them. Then before they could get lost, she pulled away and turned her back on him, unable to handle the heat and love she would be sure to find in his eyes.

As the door clicked shut behind her, Sadie tried to picture how they could possibly work through their current predicament. How were they even meant to be useful to the United when their thoughts were only on one thing? And how were they supposed to resist each other now that they'd had a taste?

Amadi's dumbstruck face at the sight of Mae flashed back into her mind and suddenly Sadie didn't think it was remotely funny. As she slumped out the door and away from the person she wanted to be around the most, it seemed that both options for their future were somehow more unbearable than they'd ever been before.

Chapter 5

Barbecue of indulgence

Jimmy lay back on the bed, one arm tucked under his head and the other holding himself through his jeans. They had known. Maybe not all the details, but they had known that Sadie feeding off him would change things. He regretted his inability to join the meeting about the box that morning. He'd felt useless until Patricia had shown up. And it was disappointing that his focus was so distracted that his help was minimal.

He took pride in the things he did, whatever they were. He didn't appreciate feeling like he wasn't pulling his weight, especially when the work they had come here to do was so important. It was terrifying to imagine spending the rest of his life this caught up on a single thought. Not to mention what would happen if it got worse.

It wasn't the idea of wanting Sadie that was so concerning. He could easily spend eternity wanting to be with her. The problem was that his one-track mind was so narrow. Sex. Just sex. Just wanting more all the time. Everything, from the smell of her pillow this morning to the cool breeze that tickled his back as he showered reminded him of it.

He wanted to get lost in this moment, to put all the rest of it on hold. Having spent the summer afraid of becoming like the people in

Gabriel's scroll, Jimmy was terrified that he would never feel any other emotion than all-consuming desire for the rest of his life. What was going to happen if they kept sleeping together? Would he go mad? Would he resent her? Or even worse, would she resent him?

He wondered if she was struggling as much as he was. She'd looked pained trying to leave. Jimmy thought again of her surprise kiss. The memory had him unbuttoning his pants before he'd even noticed. The thought of her warm mouth brought him back to last night and all that had happened between them.

It was all too easy to find release to the fantasies in his head, especially since those fantasies were unexaggerated memories. In the midst of what he was doing, he realized that somewhere in the distance Sadie could probably feel him. In the past, the thought that she knew when he was doing this had made him feel shy, but in this moment it only excited him. It was a small form of communication in place of words. He was thinking about her and he was feeling good.

Ten minutes later, Jimmy found his mind had cleared. A burst of renewed energy hit him unexpectedly and he became determined to make up for lost time. Making room on the bed, he began to organize the papers. He was going to sort them into the ones that should be read in further detail versus not, and then he would read all he could before dinner.

Jimmy became so focused on the task, that he jumped when a knock came on the door some time later. Blinking at his surroundings, he recalled where he was. He'd been at it for hours. He looked at the pieces he'd added to the map in satisfaction, feeling far less useless than he had that morning.

Not wanting to keep the visitor waiting, he pulled his clothes straight and went to the door. It was Sadie. She smiled shyly at him. For a second, he wondered why she was knocking, but when she stepped back it became clear she was trying to keep herself from coming in.

"Dinner's ready," she said, her eyes dropping to his pants. Shit, he was aroused again.

Jimmy cleared his throat. "Uhh, okay. Just... give me a minute." He closed the door. It was lucky that the cabin had vegetable oil or he might have hurt himself. As embarrassed as he was at the situation, he did think it was smart to do this again if he wanted to go out in public, and seeing Sadie had only made it easier to get started.

"I'll meet you out there," she said through the door. Jimmy was grateful she wouldn't be awkwardly waiting for him to finish. He also wasn't entirely sure that she would resist coming in when he was thinking so hard on her. At least they seemed to be able to behave themselves when another person was around, because he desperately needed to get out of that cabin tonight.

When he emerged some time later, it was to an entirely empty camp. Though it was easy enough to follow the smell of food and sounds of chatter down to the riverside. As he approached, Jimmy was surprised to see how many people there actually were. Had the numbers increased since their arrival just yesterday?

There were people clustered in groups, sitting on makeshift stools of rocks and fallen logs. A small pig was half-roasted, spinning over a large fire pit. Several people, including Troy, were tending the meat. Jimmy didn't see Sadie, but a large table of food drew his attention. Noticing that many people had plates in their hands already, he went to warm up his stomach.

Jimmy shook a few hands as he ladled rice and vegetables onto a plate. He'd had an unprecedented appetite these past few days, and the smell of meat was a tease. When he'd taken more than his share, he decided finding Sadie could wait a minute, and opted for leaning against a tree to enjoy the food.

"I have never had a problem with my glasses," Amadi was saying nearby.

"Dee, you always look ridiculous. Please. For me?" Hetia was addressing Amadi in a mildly whiny tone that sounded entirely foreign on her. They were angled slightly away from Jimmy, however, so he didn't try to interrupt them with a greeting.

"Ahh, so it's about how it looks now? And here I thought it was about *safety*," Amadi said with a smile.

"Honestly, it's both," she said, throwing her hands up in frustration. "You can't go on forever taping your glasses to your head. Please.

I brought extra contact fluid back with me this time. And you don't have to wear them every day. Just when you feed."

Amadi chuckled. "I'll consider it. If it really looks that silly." He placed a hand on the side of her head and drew in her gaze. "But since when do you care about such things? Am I embarrassing you in front of someone?"

Hetia shook off his hand. "Of course not. I... just can't let you go into a battle like that. The enemy wouldn't take you seriously."

Amadi smiled. "Could be a good tactic, actually," he chuckled.

Jimmy missed the rest as he moved away, glancing back affectionately at the arguing pair. The interaction made him homesick. They were a long way from their parents now and, unfortunately, the choices of the world were becoming increasingly complex. As he thought of the conversation he was about to have with Sadie, he longed for a silly argument about glasses.

Wandering into the thick of it, Jimmy felt there was something strange about the gathering. It took a minute to realize there were no children. He'd never been to an adult barbecue before. The mood seemed rather different. Several people cuddled in each other's laps, and as he passed by a group of older women, he caught the tail end of a naughty joke.

He spotted Sadie sitting on the ground hugging her knees, her back against a log. She was watching two men play a game that seemed to involve trying to snatch a piece of paper off the other one's back. They prowled around each other, and Jimmy had to dodge their fight to reach her.

He hesitated in his approach. People sat on either side of Sadie, leaving no space for him to join. Though when she spotted him, she quickly shifted away from the man she was talking to and gestured for him to squeeze in. The man looked disappointed as he scooted back just enough to make room.

Jimmy sat pressed against Sadie to leave an inch between him and the stranger. She seemed unconcerned about this as she promptly hugged an arm around his knee, their conversation continuing uninterrupted as he settled in.

"Yeah, that's true. There are more talkers than fighters in the

United, but there's still a hell of a lot of us when you pool everyone together," the man was saying. "And the numbers are swelling rapidly right now. When I told my brothers what I was about, they all wanted to join. Amadi's been calling us all home for weeks. Something is going down. We can feel it."

"Is it mostly humans?" Sadie asked.

"Mostly, yeah. A lot of the nymphs are the mobile kind. You know?" he gestured. "Air, sunset, fire. Though we all know Amadi and his daughter are the big hitters. But nymph status doesn't always mean more of a kick. I mean really, what does a sunrise nymph have on me except a desire to get up early?"

The woman on Sadie's other side chimed in. "Oh, but it is nice to have some of them around. That fire nymph could do some damage." She nodded to Troy, who was still over at the barbecue. "Plus, he keeps the showers warm."

A woman straddling the log a few feet away added, "He could keep my bed warm too if he liked." The two women exchanged a laugh. Sadie shifted.

At their giggling, the man sandwiching in Jimmy turned to say something to the woman on the log, scooting several feet over to do so. It left Jimmy space to move away from Sadie, though he found he didn't want to, and by the way she tightened her hold on his knee, it seemed she didn't either. He put an arm around her instead and they relaxed into each other. The woman on Sadie's other side moved away too and they found themselves in a little bubble of privacy, looking out at everyone.

"It's almost like being home," she said in a private voice meant for him.

He smiled. Jimmy couldn't say he agreed, but he knew what she meant. "Except for soldier boys trying to pick you up," he said.

She squeezed his knee. "And being surrounded by spies and a major underground army of resistance," Sadie added.

"I think you underestimate my family's pigs," he told her.

She laughed and rested her head on his shoulder. "Thanks for being in my life. I love you so much," she said.

He froze in his caressing of her arm. "I love you, too," he said, and even though he wasn't sure he was ready, he added, "And will regardless of where life takes us."

She sighed. "There's still a chance for us. I wanted to find out more before I told you about it, didn't want to give false hope." He shifted and she raised her head to look at him. The eye contact turned out to be too much though, and they quickly looked back out at the men wrestling in front of them. "Amadi, he has... Well, there's a succubus, Mae. She arrived this morning."

"Amadi's sleeping with a succubus?" Jimmy said, looking toward the man on the far end of the gathering.

"No. I mean yes, he's sleeping with her, but that's not the point. They're basically married. When I look at him, I see her everywhere. They've been together for decades, and she's not even always here. She has, like, this whole other family."

"Wait, what?" he said.

"They're mad for each other. You should have seen him this morning when she walked in. And..." She shuffled her feet, then lowered her voice despite the fact no one was within earshot, "Their first time together, it was kind of like us. I could see it."

Jimmy quickly tried to suppress the memory before it took hold in his thoughts. "You're saying they're able to be together and lead their own lives. How is that possible? The scroll—"

"I know," she cut in. "It doesn't make any sense. That's why I need to talk to her. I tried to ask Amadi about it, but I got nervous."

Jimmy exhaled sharply. "This is big news. I wish you'd told me."

"I know. I'm sorry. I'm not sure what I'm doing. Every time I see you it's like my mind goes on overdrive. I can't think straight. And I just want to do the right thing." She sat up straight, removing her weight from his side. "I don't want to hurt you."

"But if this is true, maybe you're not hurting me. What if it's all just fine?" he said.

"Or what if it's not? We don't really know what's going on here. Maybe Amadi and Mae have something different about them."

One of the men fighting landed on his back in front of them. He flipped the other guy over him and cartwheeled to his feet, looking at Sadie as he did so. She didn't seem to notice as she continued, "What if we're just making it so much harder to stop? Maybe every time I touch you just leads us further down the point of no return."

He watched the man still trying to catch the eye of a succubus, despite Jimmy's arm around her. "Maybe we should lay off until you've had a chance to find out more," he suggested.

Sadie shook her head. "That makes sense, but... how? We can't even be alone for a second."

He cleared his throat and forced out the words. "Then we won't be. There are other places you could sleep tonight."

She looked up to glare at him, the expression morphing to a pout, but he added decisively, "It's the only way."

She seemed to deflate, softening back into his side as she rested her head against him. "Okay. I won't come back to the cabin tonight. But I'm not sleeping with anyone else. I don't need to. After the past few days with you I'm more than well-fed." She rested her arm between his thighs, her hand gripping his knee while they let those words settle over them. "I'll ask Patricia," she said.

Jimmy was surprised at his level of relief. Over the summer she'd slept with various other people, and it hadn't been easy, but for some reason the idea suddenly grated at him. Though before a few days ago, he hadn't really known what sleeping with a succubus was like, and he found himself retroactively jealous at all the intimacy she'd had with strangers. He tried to tamp down the emotion, but it was no use. He had to accept the truth; it was hard to share – harder than before.

Hetia stepped into the space between where they were sitting and the fire pit, and the two fighters gave each other a look and silently agreed on something. Treading lightly, the men moved to intercept the slight woman. The guy in front put his hands on the ground to forcefully swing his legs under Hetia's, while the one in back launched himself at her.

Jimmy jumped at their aggression, momentarily fearing for Hetia's safety, but it seemed she was fully aware of what was coming. Before the first guy could make contact, Hetia fell to her side in a motion that would've looked like he'd tripped her if Jimmy hadn't been watching closely. The fall carried far too much momentum to be unintentional, however, and the guy who'd attempted to tackle her found her legs wrapped around him as she flipped him over her. He landed hard on the ground, Hetia standing over him.

Everyone looked at them, but turned back to their conversation almost immediately. Apparently, the spectacle was common enough.

"Tell me what you did wrong," Hetia said, holding out her hand to help the man up.

The man on the ground smiled at her, but Jimmy didn't notice his reply as he focused in on the self-assured blond woman. Sadie had told him that Hetia was the one person she'd slept with that felt like something more serious than a simple feeding.

"They're serving it," Sadie said, pushing herself up, and grabbing Jimmy's plate off the floor in front of them. He watched her check out Hetia as she passed by, continuing to stare at the woman while she waited in line by the fire. Jimmy tried to think about how he would feel if it were Hetia's bed and not Patricia's that Sadie stayed in that night.

It wasn't like the strangers, he knew that much. The faceless people Sadie fed from were like a silent threat somewhere in the distance, while Hetia was someone he knew and liked. She was intimidating, but he felt she was a good person. Somehow that mattered. How he would react if she ever gave Sadie the time of day, he wasn't sure. They'd have to deal with that when or if it came up.

Sadie returned with her plate full of meat, and they straightened their legs out to rest it on their thighs. She moaned as she bit in and his gaze shot to her – his body growing warm. "Sorry," she said, looking away.

Though before he could stop himself, he made the same sound as the meat hit his own tongue. She bit her lip as she looked at him. "Sorry," he said, and they both laughed.

By the end of the meal, they were both aroused enough that Sadie was forced to move away. He missed her presence, but was on board with her decision. They were going to get themselves into trouble. But she licked her fingers clean from several feet away, making eye contact as she did so. Jimmy sighed at her flirtation, hugging his knees, and decided two could play that game.

He imagined pulling her onto his lap right there in front of everybody and projected his desire loud and clear. By the small smile on her face, he was sure she'd got it. Her auburn curls were glowing in the light of sunset and he began picturing the way they would sway as she rode him. He groaned at the thought, thinking he would be able to watch her forever like that. Then Sadie chewed her lip, and he got a little thrill at the effect his thoughts could have on her.

Though they were lucky that a distraction came to break them out of it when a crowd moved into their side of the fire, making a circle around the open space in the middle, as several musicians began to play an upbeat tune. People began to pass around wine and a few couples got up to dance. Jimmy and Sadie both took big swigs before sending it on.

"You wanna dance?" a woman asked him. Jimmy looked up, startled. He did love to dance, but he wasn't about to stand up.

"Uh, not right now." He cleared the husky sound out of his voice and added, "Thank you."

"You?" She turned her attention on Sadie, who for all appearances also looked to be sitting alone.

Sadie glanced at Jimmy who nodded her onward. "I'd love to," she said, getting to her feet and replacing her gloves. "Just don't touch my skin." The woman smiled and pulled her onto the increasingly popular dance floor. She took the lead, spinning Sadie around with some skill.

As Jimmy watched his friend move to the music, he felt warm all over, and wished more than ever that she was coming back with him. Why did he have to have gone and convinced her otherwise?

The music shifted and Sadie switched partners, a young man jumping in eagerly. Jimmy looked around to see he wasn't the only person watching her in particular. Among them, Hetia and that moody fire nymph, Troy. They were both tracing her with their gaze, likely thinking very different things. Jimmy watched them for several minutes as they each turned down dances. Troy's face was unreadable, but Jimmy was sure he wasn't thinking anything good. After the way he had treated Sadie yesterday, he was planning on keeping an eye on the man.

Amadi entered the far end of the gathering, drawing Jimmy's

attention. He had his arm around the waist of a woman around his age. She was petite like Hetia, though not nearly as tall, with dark skin, and hair in a million braids that spun behind her as Amadi twirled her onto the dance floor. Jimmy knew this must be the succubus Sadie had mentioned. By the way the pair were looking at each other, there could be no mistake.

He watched them dance, envious of their ability to touch so intimately and yet casually in public. In fact, intimacy seemed to be in the air. Jimmy watched the couple in front of him move together, the man's hand holding the woman's ass. A minute later, the couple disappeared up the trail to the cabins. Several more people switched to dancing close before departing together.

Off to his left, Jimmy saw Patricia's grandmother, Luciana, flirting with a man half her age, and when he looked back, they too had disappeared. By the time it was fully dark, half the people had left, and he didn't think a single one of them were sleeping.

"It's Mae," Hetia said, having come to stand next to him without his notice. "The weekly barbecue isn't always like this," she said, "but Mae brings it out in people – something to do with a special succubus talent she has." She took a swig of the half-empty bottle in her hand. "And it's the coming war. Everyone knows it's happening. Amadi's been calling the chickens home to roost." Her speech was a little slurred. "So get your kicks while you can, farm boy. Who knows what tomorrow brings." And with that, Hetia wandered off alone.

A few minutes later, Jimmy watched Troy also leave by himself, despite the clear intentions of several of the remaining women. When Patricia, who'd been sitting next to Troy, moved to depart, Sadie untangled herself from her dance partner and rushed over to talk to her. Jimmy wished he could intercept her, lift her off her feet and carry her into the woods. He watched Patricia nod, and Sadie turned toward him.

She began to approach him, but stopped midtrack. His mood must have been obvious because he watched her take a slow deep breath, running her hand along her bra line, and hesitate to come closer. Instead, she smiled sadly, blew him a kiss, and backed away. An hour later, Jimmy went to find sleep in the empty cabin.

Chapter 6

Game changer

Sadie closed the door to Patricia's cabin quietly and stepped out into the cool morning air. Luciana had been meant to share Patricia's bed, but it worked out well that her grandmother had slept elsewhere last night.

The other bed was occupied by three older women, who all snored, and Sadie realized now that they'd been given a privilege when Amadi had assigned them a cabin to themselves. He must have been allowing for the fact that she was a succubus.

And here she was, wasting that privilege. She stared longingly in the direction of cabin nine, wondering if Jimmy had slept any better than she had. Given she had to wait until he had vacated the space before collecting her spare clothes, she decided to take a morning walk. If she'd ever been in need of fresh air to clear her head, it was now.

Sadie set off in the opposite direction from the river, heading uphill. As she entered a field of grass and wildflowers, she saw Luciana coming out of a large tent. Sadie was pretty sure the tent hadn't been there the day they'd arrived. Cresting the hill revealed dozens more. People trickled out of them, gathering around tiny, makeshift fire pits as she passed. She understood better how there had been so many people at the barbecue. Amadi really was pulling together an army.

Sadie made a wide loop, heading back to camp by a different path. The field flattened out in a large expanse speckled with a few small trees, and she heard the sounds of heavy breathing before she saw its source. In a well-worn patch of ground, Hetia and Troy were circling each other. Sadie stopped in her tracks, not wanting to be seen. Retreating a few steps, she leaned against a tree to watch them.

Troy was shirtless, and they were both sweaty and grinning. They took turns attacking in quick, sudden movements punctuated by long thoughtful pauses while the green light of friendship pulsed strong between them.

Sadie had never seen Hetia look so carefree. The look on her face was relaxed and childlike in its joy. Troy was well-muscled and skilled. His hair clung to the sides of his face as he moved with assurance. They weren't evenly matched, but each time Hetia pinned him, he would let flames run across his torso and she would have to retreat.

Sadie was pretty sure she could watch this all day. Though her gaze was intent on Hetia, it kept flickering to Troy as she tried to ignore the growing attraction she saw in herself. It was unfair that she was forced to recognize her own feelings. It was all well and good to see the light connecting others, but for the first time, she wished that particular part of being a succubus would leave her alone.

A twig snapped to her right and Sadie jumped as she looked around. Mae was standing a few yards away, casually sipping coffee with a hand in her pocket. She looked at Sadie over the rim of the cup, slurping up a steamy sip. She couldn't help it, under the elder woman's gaze the image of licking Troy's chest just popped into her mind. She blushed and looked away, avoiding Mae and the eye-candy spectacle in front of her.

The older woman pulled up to her side, facing the fight. "Oh, that's definitely lickable." Sadie chewed her lip, but peered back over at Troy and Hetia. "I see you had an adventurous week," Mae continued. "What's the boy's name?"

"James. Jimmy Baker. I mean James Baker, goes by Jimmy," Sadie said, fidgeting with the button of her jacket.

Mae smiled at her, but Sadie kept her gaze forward. "That looks like a nice thing you have with him. Dee said you might want to talk about it."

Sadie shifted, not sure where to begin. The woman made it sound so casual. How could she explain all that had happened between them? There was no need to explain the lust or love since Mae could probably see it all clearly, but the larger context was... complicated.

"I guess I should start at the beginning," she said, peeking over at the woman's intimidating gaze. When Mae just slurped at the hot coffee, looking patient, Sadie took a deep breath and launched into it. She talked rapidly, finding herself gesturing in animated exasperation at each of the times she'd felt hopeless over the past year.

"And then that was it, we were two days away and there was nothing left for it, and now it's like... *impossible* to even be alone together, and then here you and Amadi are, and I just don't know what it all means."

Mae slurped again. "Let's walk," she said. Sadie was glad for the suggestion. She needed to move her body. "Tell me, can you see the early days with me and Dee?"

"I could see it on him, but you're... too complicated," Sadie admitted.

Mae nodded and then threw Sadie a wicked grin. "Well I remember it perfectly. And it was as intense and wonderful as what I see on you. Though Dee wasn't the first person I fell in love with."

"What? How is it possible that you're so... well-adjusted, when I can't even handle one Jimmy? Do these lovers have any dangerous side effects?" Sadie asked, wanting to get right to the heart of it now.

Mae laughed. It was a sweet, seductive sound. "Amadi has built a major organization over the course of decades from virtually nothing. Do you really think his relationship with me has hindered him? He's the most highly functioning, driven individual I know, apart from maybe Hetia. I think he deserves a little fun."

"But the scroll..." Sadie began.

"Tell me more about this scroll. Where'd you say it came from again?" Mae asked.

"From the succubus who helped me turn, Gabriel…" Sadie was embarrassed to realize she didn't know Gabriel's last name.

"Gabriel. Gabriel," Mae said, tapping her lip. "I think I've heard of a Gabriel. He can see when a Becoming is on its way? Wanders around the country, scanning people for new succubi?"

"I guess that's what he does," Sadie said. "I didn't ask him much. There were a lot of changes going on in my life," she added, sheepishly.

"And he gave you this scroll? What kinds of things did it say?" Mae asked.

"Let's see. It talked about the light and its meaning." Wanting suddenly to confirm everything with Mae, she listed, "Red for desire, black for love, green for friendship, and blue for family." The elder succubus nodded. "It said I would learn to sort through the images better with time, make sense of what I'm looking at. It said some succubi have additional skills. A common one is being able to recognize another succubus and their hunger on sight. I ran into a prostitute who could do that. Another common one is having an overall allure that draws in strangers. But it didn't mention Gabriel's skill, or the memory reading thing."

"The what?" Mae asked.

"The dropping into people's memories while you're sleeping with them."

Mae just raised her eyebrows.

"Twice now it's happened while I was feeding. I get a really vivid image from the person's memory," she said.

"We all get that though, I can see lots of your memories right now," Mae said.

"No, this is different. I see it from the person's perspective, like I'm in their body. The first time it happened it wasn't even a sex scene, it was the woman sitting at a table waiting impatiently for dinner to be served."

"Now *that* I haven't heard of," Mae said, and for the first time she sounded a little excited.

"And the second time was two nights ago. I fell into Jimmy's memory of our first time together."

"Hmmm. In both cases you dropped into a memory of someone wanting something, but the first one was something other than sex. Tell me more."

Sadie thought about the relevant details to share. "It wasn't anything like the sexual scenes I see when I look at people. Those are comprised of a general feeling, or sense of things. This is like I see it as if I'm there. I see people's faces and all these random details that have nothing to do with sex."

Mae stopped walking, a serious expression on her face. "Does Amadi know this?" she asked.

"No. I've barely even talked about it with Jimmy. He doesn't know about the other night."

"But you're one of Dee's spies, right?" Mae asked.

"Uhhh... not exactly. I'm in training," she said.

"But this could be invaluable. We need to tell him." She changed course, walking with purpose as they headed back to camp.

Sadie held her tongue for a minute while Mae seemed lost in thought. Just when she was about to pull her back into the conversation, however, the woman said, "I've met a variety of succubi over the years. Have several friends that I write to regularly. I've never heard of any of them, or their humans, going crazy. No homicide, suicides. No jealous rages. Well... maybe a little. Sometimes." She laughed. "But never violently," she added seriously. "Most of them are pretty happy people, actually."

Sadie shook her head, trying to make sense of how that was possible. Why would the scroll have said all those things if loving relationships between succubi and humans weren't actually dangerous?

"I don't understand," she said, shaking her head in disbelief.

Mae stopped to face her.

"Sadie. What you and Jimmy are experiencing... It's called a honeymoon phase. And apart from being particularly intense with succubi, it is mundanely normal. Just enjoy it. It doesn't last forever. Thank god," she added with a giggle. "And Jimmy's... *symptoms,* are probably a product of your love, attraction, and the fact you were really hungry the first time you fed off him." She sighed.

"If I can be frank, it sounds like the reason you're so hung up on this scroll has more to do with your own fear than anything else. I mean, you're continuing to trust some words in an old parchment over your own eyes." She held out her arms as if to indicate herself as evidence. "I think you're too afraid of your instincts. Have a little faith in yourself. Jimmy too. You two need to chill."

Sadie blinked several times as if someone had slapped her. Then she laughed. She kept laughing until the rapid tightening of her abs morphed into sobbing. Her shoulders shook as all the built-up tension she'd been carrying for months released at once. And as embarrassed as she was to be crying in front of this woman, she couldn't seem to stop the flow of tears as they poured down her face. She tried to wipe them away with her hands, worried she looked terrible. This was really too much. She needed to get it together.

Mae patted her on the shoulder, looking unphased. "You're gonna be all right, girl. Trust me. You'll work it out. I promise. Now clean yourself up. We have good news to deliver." And without further ado, she turned her back on Sadie to lead the way – the conversation clearly over.

Amadi looked concerned upon seeing Sadie's face. "What happened?" he said, bouncing to his feet. They'd found him alone in his cabin, poring over maps. Open letters lay scattered over the desk and bed.

"Oh, it's nothing," Sadie said, forcing out a smile and wishing the red in her eyes would disappear quicker.

"We had a good talk," Mae said. "And Sadie has something she'd like to tell you. Something you'll like."

"Umm, yeah, I–" Sadie cleared her throat. He was the lover of a succubus. She could talk about sexual things in front of him. Squaring her shoulders, she said, "When I'm feeding off someone, I seem to be able to drop into their memories. Sometimes. Even when what's happening in the memory isn't related to sex."

Amadi immediately held a finger in front of her lips to silence her. "Not here." He looked at the open window before gesturing them to follow him. Leading them to the same rock Hetia had used to train her and Troy, they climbed up into the seats, from where they could easily see in all directions if anyone was nearby.

"Everyone in this camp has been vetted in some way, but I haven't stayed off Siphon's radar for this long by being sloppy. The more valuable the information, the fewer people should know it. Now tell me exactly how it works." Amadi turned a serious expression on her as he spoke, and Sadie felt the sudden gravity of the information she was about to share.

Sitting up straighter, she did her best to explain with the little understanding she had. When she was done, Amadi said, "We'll need to understand it better; set up some specific tests. Can you work with Sadie on this?"

Mae nodded and Amadi turned back to her gravely. "This changes everything. Thanks to that diary, we now know the Coalition's plan is in the heads of those three families, but we've been trying to get close to Siphon and Maddox for years. You said you wanted to be a spy?"

Sadie nodded vigorously.

"Well, you're in," he said.

Her heart raced as her stomach clenched with excitement. "I really think I could be good at it," she said, remembering again the pride she'd felt after her opportunity in Seattle.

"And you might be right. I asked Luciana more about you. She thinks you have potential. But if you can read non-sexual memories, well... that *is* a game changer." Sadie could see the excitement in his eyes as he pushed up his glasses. A thought passed across his expression, and he turned to Mae. "Can you see it? When you look at this memory from a few nights ago, the sexual one, can you see anything unusual?"

Mae stared at Sadie intently for a minute before shaking her head. "All normal."

"Good. Good. Other succubi won't know. Sadie, it will be easy to get you in with Congressman Siphon. He likes to collect succubi to do his dirty work. He's able to keep close tabs on political opponents that way. The challenge will be keeping him from sending you away. We need a reason for you to need to be near him." He got up to pace back and forth along the rock. Mae watched him with a grin, her eyes flitting up and down his body.

A few minutes later, Amadi clapped his hands and sat back down. "Troy is already a trusted member of the Coalition, and a popular invite to parties among the upper echelon of the political world. When he returns, you could go as his lover. It would be him you want to stay close to. If Siphon tries to send you away to spy for him, you can say you don't want to leave Troy's side."

Amadi didn't seem to notice that she'd gone utterly still at this suggestion. "Patricia says Siphon is interested in fostering Troy as his protégé," he continued. "Siphon wants him as an in with the nymph voters. Troy was making quite a name for himself after his rise to power in the feeder capitol. Siphon will want to keep him close. If we attach you to him, you can stay close as well."

Mae cleared her throat. "I think you're forgetting that the Siphons will know that's not true. Any succubi looking at them will know they're not lovers."

"Ahh... right." Amadi nodded, then glanced over at her, looking a bit shy. "Unless... *could* it be true? That is, I hear a lot of the girls talking about him."

Sadie's eyes went wide. "No. I don't want to sleep with Troy." She crossed her arms defensively but shrunk under Mae's smiling gaze.

Amadi looked back and forth between the two women. "What else do I need to know?" he asked openly.

Mae stepped in while Sadie blushed. "They're not *uninterested* in each other," she said. "Currently, her feelings are stronger than his. He obviously has a bad history with succubi, and he doesn't trust her." Mae tapped her chin. "But I bet we could change that." She directed at Sadie.

"If you're thinking we should tell Troy about succubi's second sight, I don't like it," Amadi said.

Mae laughed. "No. Definitely not. I doubt Troy would handle that information well, and quite frankly I don't trust him with it. He is not a friend of succubi. He doesn't get to know our secrets."

Relief filled Sadie. She very much did not like the idea of Troy knowing how she felt about him, or anything else personal about her and her kind.

"And it's not necessary," Mae continued. "Succubi can only see desire, sexual histories or fantasies, we can't see mistrust. If Sadie and Troy show up acting like a shyly courting pair and there exists threads of attraction between them, that will be enough. So long as the threads are strong enough." The elder succubus directed at her.

Sadie sighed. "I can take care of it," she said, determination settling over her. This was her first chance to prove herself, she wasn't going to blow it over wanting to avoid the obnoxious fire nymph. "I'll make sure that the... *attraction* is stronger and mutual before we leave camp."

Amadi nodded. "You won't have long. The war could break out any day now. We need to get this information as quickly as we can," he said. "I will meet with Troy and tell him the new plan, or the pieces of it I can share, anyway. You two and Hetia should keep working together. Let her guide you. She has years of experience in this. And Mae can help you understand your succubus powers. We have a week, tops." He stood up. "Let's get to work."

As they were about to descend, they turned to see Hetia and Troy approaching. They'd stopped out of earshot, and Hetia had an arm out in front of Troy. "Perfect," Amadi said, gesturing them forward. They came up the path, Hetia looking curious and Troy looking more suspicious than ever. He shook his head at Sadie as she passed him. Sadie, for her part, smiled warmly at him. She at least enjoyed the way her reaction seemed to surprise and annoy him.

They left the others behind and Mae nodded to her. "Go get yourself some food. I'm going to round up some willing participants so we can run some experiments." She caught Sadie's eye. "If that's alright with you?"

She nodded. Sadie found the idea of practicing her skill under Mae's supervision exciting. It wasn't at all like spending the night with someone else. It felt like a game, one she very much wanted to get good at. And Amadi putting faith in her was a powerful natural high. She didn't want to let him down.

Though a thought occurred to her. "I'm going to tell Jimmy all this," she said in a partial question, wanting approval.

"I assumed you would," Mae said. "But no one else, okay?"

Sadie nodded.

"Meet me at the river in an hour. Near last night's fire pit," Mae told her, veering to the left and leaving Sadie standing alone to process all that had just happened.

She was going to the east to seduce information out of the most dangerous families in the country, and she was going to get to spend the rest of her life with Jimmy. And she didn't care what it took, she was going to make sure to keep him close by, since now that she knew she could have him completely, she planned on moving full steam ahead into Mae's advice. From now on, she was going to trust her instincts. She had the feeling she was going to need them.

Chapter 7

Instinct

Jimmy wasn't in their cabin when Sadie retrieved her bag, and she felt immediately deflated. She changed into her pretty blue summer dress with long sleeves since she knew it was Jimmy's favorite. On impulse, she left off her gloves, shoving them away with satisfaction.

Then despite the all-consuming, anxious excitement that was pulsing through her body, she forced herself to get some food down. She would need her energy today. Slipping back on her boots, she pulled the hair tie out of her hair, letting her curls hang loose, and stepped out into the crisp, but sunny fall day.

Sadie paused just outside the door. Taking a deep breath, she ran her hands over her own body. She felt at home in herself for the first time in a while. She hadn't realized how tense she'd been, how much she'd felt like there was something wrong with her. Now, though, she was alive. And it was time to show it.

She could feel Jimmy far in the distance as she made her way to the river. He was too far for her to pick up anything in particular about his thoughts. She hoped he was thinking about her though, because she was certainly thinking about him.

Sadie found Mae sitting on a log, talking to a young man she recognized from the previous night. She'd danced with him at some point and he had been very interested in her attention. The elder succubus had probably chosen him for precisely that reason.

"Sadie," Mae said, waving one hand for her to join them. "This is Tomas." He nodded at her shyly. "He understands that we will be practicing feeding. It's good to be able to have the guidance of an older succubus when you're just starting out." Mae pulled a small box from her pocket and handed it to him. "So that our conversation doesn't disturb you, we'd like you to wear these."

Tomas took the earplugs and put them in his lap. "Okay," he said absently, still focused on Sadie as she straddled the log facing him. He swung a leg over to do the same. "Will we actually be having sex? Right here?" he asked, looking from Sadie in front of him to Mae, now sitting behind him.

"No," Mae said, taking his hand to place a condom in it. "You'll put this on to not make a mess, but Sadie is just going to touch your skin. It will feel like sex for you though, so maybe the better answer is yes, only you'll be keeping your clothes on."

"This is so weird," he said, shaking his head, but he was smiling as he looked back at Sadie.

"Ready?" Mae asked, while Sadie nodded encouragingly at him, a familiar thrill appearing in the pit of her stomach.

He looked down and then at the condom. "No, not really," he said with a nervous laugh.

At a look from Mae, Sadie said, "I'll take care of that." She ran her fingers through his as she took the package out of his hand. His eyes widened as a sudden erection appeared between them.

Sadie unzipped his pants, secured the condom, and scooted forward until their knees were touching on either side of the log. Then she leaned forward to kiss his cheek before whispering in his ear, "If you want me to stop, just take these out." She gestured to the earplugs.

Tomas nodded and worked them into his ears as Sadie picked up his hand and placed it on her leg, just under the hem of the dress. He liked this development, and began running his thumb back and forth over the soft skin of her inner thigh. Looking past the images that surrounded him, she saw he had a sweet face. His shy smile disappeared slowly under the weight of arousal, however.

She ran her hand up and down his forearm as she built up the sensation inside him. Sadie saw no reason to rush the experience. She was enjoying it and she wanted to make sure he walked away feeling good about what had happened. After a minute, the man gave out a tiny whimper and rolled his hips forward on instinct, and she bit her lip as she looked into his eyes.

"I told him this would be more intense than he was used to, and that he might dream of you for a few days," Mae said quietly from over his shoulder. "He's prepared for whatever you feel you need to do."

Sadie nodded.

"Now try to remember what was happening last time you did this. Describe it out loud," Mae instructed.

"I – I don't know. I wasn't really thinking." Sadie closed her eyes as she tried to picture the moment with Jimmy. "I guess I was totally absorbed by what was happening. I don't remember doing or thinking anything specific."

"Have you ever tried to do it intentionally?" Mae asked.

Sadie shook her head, re-opening her eyes.

"Try now. Before orgasm. See what happens," the elder succubus told her.

Sadie had no idea how to force this. It had felt like magic the two times it had happened before. She focused intensely on the desire to drop into his mind, staring hard at the man in front of her as if she could bore right into his thoughts. Nothing unusual happened, and after a while she sucked in a deep breath, not realizing she'd been holding it, and shook her head in frustration.

"It's no problem. I wasn't expecting anything," Mae assured her. "Now try to remember how you *felt* last time."

Sadie thought for a long while, keeping Tomas just on the edge of orgasm, her heart pounding in excitement along with his. He gripped her thigh softly, staring at her breasts as she moved through his body. "I... felt very aware of the person," Sadie said, her speech heavy with her own arousal. "Like their body was an extension of my own. And my mind was completely on them. I wasn't focused on anything but their pleasure."

"Were they in the middle of climax at the time?" Mae asked.

"Jimmy was. But... the woman in the bath wasn't," Sadie said, working hard to recall the moment.

Tomas bit his lip on a moan as Sadie played with increasing the sensation. Nothing out of the ordinary happened, however, and she could feel the man's thoughts focusing in on a strong desire to climax.

"Do it," Mae said. "But hold him there."

Sadie obeyed.

His lips parted on a gasp and he closed his eyes. "Relax your thoughts," Mae told her in a calming tone. "Try to fall into him. That's how you described it earlier. Fall." Sadie tried, but still nothing happened. She began picturing her own failure and her whole body tensed. If she couldn't figure this out, Amadi's whole reason for sending her would be gone.

Tomas bucked his hips, convulsing in front of her as he opened his eyes to lock back on hers. He was making fairly loud sounds of pleasure, and a group of men heading by on the trail up the hill stopped and looked down at them.

"Keep moving," Mae called. "None of your business, boys."

They laughed and scampered away.

Her mentor turned back to her and considered a moment. "Kiss him," she said. They could both feel that he wanted her to, and she hadn't tried that yet.

Sadie gently cupped the man's face between her hands and pressed her lips to his, determined to fall into a memory. Nothing. She couldn't do it! She began to panic.

"Okay. That's enough for now," Mae said.

Sadie took a long, resigned breath and released Tomas. He gripped her face to him as he shuddered in her arms. The women let him come down a minute before removing the earplugs.

He got to his feet on shaky legs and turned to them. "Was – uhh, that what you wanted?" he asked, still out of breath.

"It was," Mae said. "Thanks for your help, Tomas."

"Yeah." He turned to go, but stopped to look at Sadie. "Thanks.

For picking me." He smiled sweetly and she found herself returning the expression.

"Good luck out there," she said.

He nodded. "Let me know if I can help again," he said with a shrug, clearly trying to look nonchalant about the offer.

"We will," Mae said, and he disappeared up the trail. The two women faced each other, still straddling the log.

"What was happening that day? With the woman in the hot tub?" Mae asked.

"Oh, god, that was a crazy day. I was at this party and I'd fed off of a ton of people. More than I ever had before. I was feeling—" Sadie stopped, a thought coming to her as Mae nodded.

"Did you feed yesterday?" Mae asked.

"No," Sadie said, nodding along now. "You're right. That's one difference between then and now. I had fed excessively both times. The situations were completely different in every other way."

"Well, that's something. But I don't think it's the whole of it," Mae said. "From the little I've seen of you, I'd say you have a habit of getting in your own head when you're stressed. There was no difference in your body language when I asked you to try intentionally and when I asked you to relax. And as much as you wanted to be with Jimmy since turning, you focused mostly on your own fear."

Sadie slumped a bit, she knew the woman was right.

"So your real homework is this. Keep it fun. I know this is important, but don't forget that you like feeding as much as the next succubus. Make sure you're enjoying yourself. Make it playful. And instead of trying to push away the unwanted thoughts, focus on the wanted ones. With a little practice, it will get easier."

Sadie nodded, sitting up straighter. She did love feeding, and she hadn't had any distracting thoughts the other night with Jimmy. If anything, the opposite – she couldn't keep her mind off him. "Okay," she said with a smile, feeling a sudden warmth and... *safety* at having Mae here. It was a relief to have someone to talk to.

"But you do need to feed regularly, and then some if possible. We'll pick this up tomorrow after you've spent a night with your boy."

Sadie nodded, her heart racing at the realization that she would get to be with Jimmy soon. At the thought, she realized that she wanted to find him immediately. She looked up at Mae through hooded eyes and the woman smirked. "Go," she gestured, impatiently. "Don't just stand here pouting about it."

Sadie smiled, barely suppressing a squeal as she trotted off. Finding Jimmy wasn't a precise science. She could sense the general direction, and as she got closer, she became sure that he was in their cabin. Sadly, he wasn't overly fixated on her. A part of her wished he had been touching himself. She wanted to walk in and take over in a surprise gesture, but clearly he was focused on something else for now.

Even so, her blood pumped hot through her veins as she drew near. She couldn't wait to tell him. Every step felt like an eternity as she climbed the path in his direction. Someone called her name and she just ignored it. Nope. Not now. She wouldn't be deterred.

"Sadie!" Patricia said again, closer now.

"No," Sadie said out loud.

Her friend stepped in her path. "What are you doing?" Patricia asked.

"I'm busy," she said.

"Clearly." Patricia clicked her tongue in disapproval. "Hetia's looking for you. She says it's important. You should meet her at the stone. Meaning the big meeting stone ov—"

"Yeah I know what the stone is," Sadie said, unreasonably taking her frustration out on the messenger.

"All right," Patricia said, putting her hands up in a position of surrender.

"Sorry," Sadie said, kicking the ground as she looked around. "Ugh, fine. I'll go find Hetia." She changed course. Pausing to make peace, she said, "Thanks for telling me."

She strongly considered doubling back, ignoring the summons entirely, but decided it wouldn't kill her to wait a few more hours. If she wanted Amadi to take her seriously, she needed to prove her reliability.

The camp was flooded with even more people than she'd seen that morning as Sadie made her way to the northern edge. Troy was sitting with his back to her, bent in silent conversation with Hetia. He was gesticulating animatedly as the blond woman listened attentively. When her eyes flicked to Sadie, Troy jumped up and moved to sit next to Hetia, looking at Sadie as if she'd intentionally snuck up on him.

"You called," Sadie said.

"Yes." Hetia looked pointedly at Troy and then Sadie. "Amadi has made a decision; given us the outline of a plan. We need to take that and flesh it out. Then get to work."

Sadie nodded and sat down across from them while Troy said, "Respectfully, this is a bad plan. Why would—" He paused, ran a hand through his hair, and lowered his voice to say to Hetia, "Can we continue talking about this in private?"

"No. We don't have time for that. We need to get things out in the open. *Now*. Amadi says we have a week." Hetia crossed her arms, looking between them.

Troy took in a slow breath. "When the succubus—"

"Sadie," Hetia interjected.

He started over. "When Sadie arrived, Amadi agreed she wasn't ready for such a big responsibility. Something happened to change his mind. Sadie met with Amadi and Mae, and bam, she was in. I know Amadi is very good at what he does, but are you sure we can trust him to make the best decision here? We still don't know what she told him." He said this last line under his breath, determinedly not looking at Sadie.

"Yes. Dee always has a reason. He would never do anything to jeopardize the United," Hetia said before turning her body toward Sadie in a way that indicated the ending of her willingness to listen patiently to Troy's objections. "Now, shortly after we recruited Troy, we removed him from under the gaze of Congressman Siphon by telling him Troy needed to go home for a while to take care of his ailing grandmother. While in fact, he's been *here*, preparing himself to return."

Hetia gave Troy an apologetic look as she continued, "Though truthfully, we had doubts about sending him back in, which is why we've been hesitating." Troy made to speak, but Hetia pushed on.

"You're a good fighter, decently skilled with your fire, and you're thoughtful when it comes to thinking through people's motivations, but... espionage needs something different. You feel all your emotions all the time. And you have too much dislike of the Siphons."

Troy clenched his jaw, but his posture relaxed as he looked thoughtful. "You're not wrong," he said, surprising Sadie.

"However, you're in a strong position given your relationship with Siphon," Hetia continued. "If you can handle this, it could be incredibly valuable. Especially if you can introduce Sadie and keep Siphon from sending her away."

Troy sighed. "Okay. You're right my dislike of the Siphons is a problem. I have work to do. But I'll do it, whatever you suggest." He took Hetia's hand. "You know I trust your leadership and guidance. And if you want me to say someone is my lover and bring her to Siphon, I will throw myself full force into that task." He looked directly at Sadie then. "The problem is, that in *this* case, I doubt any of that matters since you're very likely working with Siphon already, and if we allow you to return at all it will just wreck my cover."

"You don't really think that?" Sadie said, crossing her arms.

"How could I not? You expect me to believe it was a coincidence that you met Hetia, and... fed from her, before you'd even gotten involved with the United? And then you show up with a magic diary and within two days have wiggled your way into Amadi's head? Yeah, I may be the only one thinking clearly around you right now." He faced Hetia. "Which is why I have to be the voice of reason."

"Meeting Hetia in that bar was a coincidence," Sadie said.

"And you were there doing what? Hetia says she was spying on Hector, but you were there as a friend of a major *beaded* family," Troy said, referring to the group in Seattle who had begun actively attacking humans. They must have made national news.

"They weren't beaded at the time, and I didn't really know who they were. And who's Hector?" Sadie said.

"A friend of Siphon's. Human. Proved to be a dead-end," Hetia said.

"The rich guy who you were serving as a bodyguard?" Sadie asked, remembering her strange early encounters with Hetia.

Hetia nodded. "We thought it was interesting that Siphon would be close to a human when he detests them, so I went to investigate. Turns out they just have a lot of business dealings. It seems money is even more important than racial superiority in Siphon's world."

Sadie froze, her brow furrowing. "If you're used to spying, why aren't *you* trying to get close to the Siphons?"

Hetia fell silent a minute, considering her coolly. "Reasons," she said with a sardonic glare.

Sadie nodded, retreating in her prying, while Troy returned to his previous attack. "Strange though, how you managed to get in so easily to the inner folds of that feeder family in Seattle and then immediately hop to the United. You seem to have a knack for such things."

Sadie threw up her hands, surprised that after a lifetime of being the outsider, someone was actually accusing her of fitting in *too* well. She knew Troy didn't know what he was talking about, but still, she felt the need to defend herself on this. Addressing only Hetia, she said, "Look, I don't expect you to understand. It was a confusing time. I thought they were nice people. And they were other feeders. Jimmy saw through them immediately, but I was just happy to have friends. Especially friends that might relate to what I was going through."

Troy hesitated, his expression softening as he considered this. She thought she saw a flash of empathy in his eyes, but by the time he'd opened his mouth again it was gone. "How—"

"Troy," Hetia said softly, putting a hand on his knee. "Amadi has been doing this for decades, and we've never had an information leak. The Coalition still barely even knows or cares about our existence. They only know of Luciana and Patricia and a few other faces, but they think of them as independent agitators. Whatever he does to vet people, it must work."

Troy hesitated. The hard lines of his face were overpowered by a sweetness as he looked at the woman, and he appeared increasingly desperate to believe her. He dropped his head into his hands.

"You'll come with me?" he asked, when he looked back up.

"I can't. I'll be needed elsewhere," she said. "But I promise. If Sadie betrays you, I will level the whole state of Massachusetts."

He smiled. "I bet you say that to all the boys." Though he said this in a mock flirtatious tone, Sadie could see it was just play. The two had no attraction lines between them.

Hetia bobbed her head in acknowledgement, then dropped into a serious tone as she put a hand on his knee. "But you can trust Amadi's judgment on this. And mine. Sadie will be a good partner."

Troy ran a hand through his hair causing the strands to fall back into his face in an appealing way. He did that a lot, and Sadie couldn't help but track the motion. She dropped her gaze in annoyance before remembering she was supposed to be encouraging her interest in Troy.

Luckily, she was pulled from her confusing thoughts as Hetia turned her light gray eyes on her. "Now, the cover story." Hetia's comment left them all in silent thought for several minutes.

Troy was the first to speak. "Maybe we met on the train. If we're still practically strangers, it will explain our lack of familiarity."

"Yes. I have a friend, or acquaintance anyway, named Gabriel. He helped me during my Becoming and he lives in Massachusetts. I could've been on my way to meet him. In fact, I could find him while we're there, see where he stands in all this."

"That's a strong start," Hetia told her, getting to her feet.

"Where are you going?" Troy asked, watching her hop down off the rocky slab.

"To train the soldiers. I can hear them starting in the distance. You two," she secured her hair back in a ponytail, "are going to talk through all the little details of exactly how you met. On your own." She glared at them each in turn and then walked away without another word.

Sadie stood up, suddenly anxious. She hadn't been prepared to find herself alone with Troy out of the blue like that. She chewed her lip as she stared at the fast-moving dark clouds in the distance. They matched her restless mood. When she cast a tentative look at Troy, she caught him looking her up and down. He dropped his gaze immediately to her boots, but not before a pulse of red light emanated from him. She'd forgotten that she'd gotten dressed up that morning, intending to get attention.

She gave him a small smile, trying to make peace before they continued the conversation. He blinked back at her, apparently unimpressed. She moved to take Hetia's vacated seat next to him. Letting out a small sigh, she said, "Well, perhaps on the train, you noticed I was wearing gloves and—"

"What did you say to them?" he asked.

"Wh—" Sadie felt hesitant again. Was he really going to make this even harder than it already was?

"To Amadi and Mae? What were the magic words?" he asked, leaning in. "You said or did something. You want to work together? Tell me what it was."

She felt the urge to move away. Holding her ground by force of will, she said, "I demonstrated that I would be a good asset and Luciana backed me up. Mae did some tests and agreed." She tucked her feet up under her butt, trying to appear relaxed. "Then since you have succubus friends, you decided to start up a conversation with me, see if I knew the Siphon family personally. I said I didn't, but then—"

"Hetia says it's best to stick close to true emotions," he cut in. "Let's say we got off to a bad start. You stole my seat and—"

"Actually," she took back the floor, "in real life, you attacked *me*, so we should go with something like that."

"What reason would I have to do that?" he asked.

"You tell me. You're the one who jumped me before even asking my name," she said.

He ran a hand over his jaw, looking mildly sheepish as he considered the question. "Maybe I thought you stole my ticket and confronted you. If your plan is to betray us, then none of this backstory matters. And if you are telling the truth," he sighed, "then it would hold that I had mistakenly thought you'd done me harm."

"So you're willing to consider the idea I'm not evil?" she said.

Troy looked at her for a long time before he said, "Siphon has a habit of recruiting young succubi for his network of spies. He's the most insidiously clever person I've ever known." He sighed, looking suddenly weary. "I'm... sorry, for tackling you. Amadi trusts you, and I wish I could do the same." He sat up straighter, and gave her an unblinking stare. "I don't, though. Trust you. But I do hope I'm wrong."

Sadie relaxed a bit, feeling like this was a small breakthrough. She wouldn't have ever expected him to apologize, and the action took her off-guard.

"Thank you," she said.

He huffed out a breath. "Since I'm agreeing to do this, I might as well treat you respectfully until I have evidence of your betrayal. But I promise you this, I'll be watching you closely."

Their eyes roamed each other's expressions and Sadie had to fight not to look away. Eventually, she said, "So what happened next? After you learned I hadn't taken your ticket?"

"Well, once I trusted you, I suppose we noticed there was a spark between us," he said. Her heart beat at the truth in those words. "How often do succubi feed?" Troy asked.

"Uhh... every day. Usually," she said.

He cleared his throat. "Right... Well, then you probably took me home with you that night. You had a hotel—"

"No." She couldn't let sex be a part of their backstory. "We... uhhh, had too much tension from your initial behavior toward me. We didn't jump right into things. In fact, we haven't slept together." She noticed herself avoiding his gaze as she said this and changed course. Forcing eye contact, she blinked once. She should start paying attention to what people did when they lied.

"That's ridiculous. Would that ever happen?" he asked, his question clearly genuine.

"Jimmy and I dated for months without skin contact." She swept a curl behind her ear.

His lips parted in surprise. Then in an entirely new tone he asked, "Why?"

"Because we were afraid of hurting our friendship." She licked her lips. "My powers can be intense."

He looked away as he said, "Still, we weren't friends. That reason wouldn't make sense for us. It's simplest to assume we're sleeping together."

Sadie decided that if she could make him nervous with this topic it might kill two birds with one stone. "Have you before? Slept with a succubus?" she asked, looking him over for the answer. She could see he hadn't.

Continuing to stare at her lap he said, "No. Almost. I had a moment with Congressman Siphon's daughter, but nothing happened."

"Then you don't even know what it feels like?" she said.

"No." He was satisfyingly uncomfortable with this line of questioning.

"That would be a big lie then. Definitely not worth risking." Sadie smoothed out her dress. "Unless... you want to just try it. Briefly."

She only offered this because she knew he would refuse, but as Troy's eyes snapped to hers, a rush of desire hit her in surprise, and for a moment she thought she'd been wrong. What if he said yes?

"No... I— That can't be a good idea," he mumbled. "You're right. We'll act like we just met. Also, those details of our past shouldn't matter. Who would ask about them anyway?"

"It's about being consistent in our behavior," Sadie said. "We don't know what's going to happen there." Suddenly, she felt worried about sending Troy in not knowing what succubi could see. It seemed like a dangerous risk. "But that story will work for a while," she said. "Who knows what will happen after that, but if Siphon tries to send me away to do work for him, I will cling to our budding relationship and ask to be kept close to you."

"And then what?" he asked. Sadie shrugged.

She couldn't imagine how they were actually going to pull off having her sleep with various human feeders when succubi couldn't feed from them. She thought back to her succubus guide, Gabriel, who she'd played around with in the weeks following her Becoming. They had fun, despite their inability to feed from one another. Perhaps, such things were common, and no one would think twice about her showing interest in another human feeder. Perhaps not. Either way, Sadie supposed she'd have to play that part of the plan by ear as she met people.

"We'll see," she replied.

"Yeah, we'll see," he responded in a tone that was half-threatening and half-hopeful.

Overall, this had turned into an okay conversation. The man wasn't so bad when he wasn't in full-on attack mode. She felt herself relaxing as she contemplated the coming weeks of training and working with him. "Troy," Sadie said, softly, looking over the planes of his face. "Thanks for at least trying with me. I'm glad to have this oppor—"

A horn went off in the distance at the same time that a man ran up to them. Sadie and Troy froze as they looked at the man's expression of distress and excitement.

"Come on," he gestured. "Amadi said to bring you. It's starting. They made their move. The war's begun."

Chapter 8

Point of no return

Sadie and Troy rose to their feet in the same swift motion. He gave her an unreadable look before turning to follow the man who was now nearly out of sight. She ran after him, struggling to keep up. Troy's back quickly disappeared over the hill, and Sadie was annoyed that he'd just left her, but as she crested the peak, she found him waiting, looking impatient.

"Let's move," he said, as if she weren't already running as fast as she could. Not having breath for a retort, she just plowed past him without making eye contact and sprinted through the smattering of trees in which she'd watched him and Hetia training that morning.

There was a roar of sound up ahead, and once it came into view, they found hundreds of people arriving in the clearing filled with tents. Amadi was standing on a rock in the middle, a megaphone in hand. He seemed to be waiting for the stragglers to arrive. As more and more people squeezed in, Sadie realized how many people had actually joined the camp just in the last day.

There were at least a thousand of them, all dressed practically. The ones nearest her had a fire in their eyes as they looked around at each other in grave excitement. Sadie scanned the crowd for Jimmy, but couldn't spot him anywhere. Her search was cut off by the booming sound of Amadi clearing his throat.

"This morning there was a major attack on Middlefield, Massachusetts. Half the town was killed." Sadie's hand went to her mouth. "The rumors say it was mercenaries hired by the human government, but we suspect otherwise. The feeder government announced that they will be taking swift action to defend the people. Their army has made itself known to the world. They are stationed on the southern coast of Massachusetts and are actively recruiting to overthrow the human government." Amadi paused, pushed up his glasses, and cleared his throat. "We move out first thing tomorrow. It's not what we wanted, but we're ready for it. The captains know what to do." Amadi paused to look around at them. "Good luck to us all." He lowered the speakerphone and it acted like a signal.

As a thousand people began to move with purpose all at once, Sadie lost any hope of spotting Jimmy. Deciding to meet him back at the cabin, she nodded to Troy and trotted away through the field of tents.

"You're with Casey? Take this to him. We need to redistribute the water bags," a man said, throwing a large pack to a burly man who caught it without difficulty.

Several groups had begun to dig up the hill. Sadie watched five people haul a chest out of the ground off to her left. Looking around, she noted there were dozens more such chests being freed.

Some of the soldiers paused to stare at her as she dodged her way through the camp. One of the men smiled and she recognized him from the barbecue. She regretted they were leaving. How would she practice her memory diving once they were gone?

Putting off that worry until she could satisfy her immediate need to find her friend, she tumbled away from the encampment and into the original little group of cottages. Jimmy wasn't inside, but Sadie paused to look around the cabin in awe. There were papers strewn about in dozens of piles. A stack of boxes covered half the bed. It looked like an explosion.

A knock came on the open door behind her and she jumped. Mae was standing there wearing a worried expression. "There isn't much time," she said. "Walk with me."

Sadie followed her back into the sunlight. The rain clouds around them seemed to be trying to encroach on their camp, and Sadie realized that it was probably due to Amadi's control that they were standing in a patch of sun.

"What now?" she asked, pulling up next to Mae as the woman struck a path back toward the soldiers.

"I don't know what Amadi has shared with you, but there are many of these camps spread across the country. Anyone willing to fight will converge on the feeder army." Mae spoke in a solemn tone that sounded out of place on her. "Dee called for them to meet on the other side of the country in a week. He's sending you on ahead, though. You and Troy. Hopefully, you can get some news about what's coming."

Sadie stumbled. "What? Now?"

"Sorry, but yes. There's not time to do anything else," Mae said.

"But I still don't know if I can even do the thing we were hoping I could."

"Look, Sadie. Uncovering the Coalition's plan is really on a wish list at this point. The war has started. If you can learn something useful, great. If not... well then it will be hashed out in blood like it was probably going to be anyway," Mae said with a sigh. Then seeing Sadie's face she added, "Which won't be your fault."

Sadie's legs felt weak. She thought of her parents. Would this war make it to this side of the country? She pictured an army tearing through the tiny farming towns of the Pacific Northwest. She imagined heavy boots trampling her family home. Washington State was many long miles from Massachusetts – Sadie couldn't really even comprehend how many – and yet the concept of a war felt like a looming force that could threaten anywhere.

Mae put a hand on her shoulder, drawing back her attention. "Dee has been trying to prevent this for decades," she continued. "He has a good heart, that man. Full of optimism. But I'm proud of him for preparing such an army. It's what we need right now. If you decide you don't want to do this, that you want to go home, I wouldn't judge you."

"No. I'm in," Sadie said. "All the way." She felt the truth of her words in the steady beat of her heart, which she kept from pounding out of her chest by sheer determination.

"Good," Mae said. "Because I actually believe you can do it." She smiled at Sadie.

"And you? You're coming with me?" she asked.

"No," Mae said. "I *am* going home to my family. My other family. I have three young kids waiting for me. And we're going to ride this storm out together."

"Oh," was all Sadie could think to say. She hadn't pictured Mae with kids. Succubi couldn't bear children after their Becoming, and few did beforehand. But of course there were many ways to have a family. This didn't seem like the appropriate time to ask such personal questions, however, so instead she said, "If I leave now, how will I keep practicing? If everything is so different with Jimmy, he's not good preparation for diving into the memory of strangers. The soldiers are good stepping stones to the Coalition families. I need them."

This statement was punctuated with their arrival on the edge of the field. They looked out over the mass of people. "And you'll have them. This horde can't travel all together. They'll be making their way in groups of a hundred or so, taking different paths. We're sending you with one. Dee has asked me to choose which one." She bobbed her head to a path through the middle of the tents. "Let's walk."

Mae looked between her and the surrounding soldiers, clearly examining potential connections. By the time they'd made a loop through and back around the tents, she nodded.

"I'm sending you with Cobie's troupe. She's tough; one of Amadi's top captains. She'll get you there safely, and there's several interested soldiers you can practice on."

"Sadie," Hetia said from behind her. "We need you." The woman passed by Sadie's left, but only barely slowed as she waited for her to follow.

Sadie hesitated, speaking quietly to Mae. "But, I still don't know what to do. What if I can't—"

"Trust your instincts," Mae said. "It's been the only thing holding you back." She tapped Sadie's chest with a finger. "You're afraid of yourself. Time to let that go. And make sure you stay overfed. I think I'm right on that." She paused with a hand on her heart to look Sadie up and down and added, "Your body knows best, Sadie. Don't be afraid of it." And with that parting remark, she turned her back, leaving Sadie to follow an impatient Hetia back down the hill.

She ran to catch up to the woman setting a brisk pace in front of her. "Do you know where Jimmy is?" Sadie asked in greeting.

"Haven't seen him." Hetia spoke absentmindedly, the pulsing lines of attraction which normally flowed from her when they were close together were more muted than Sadie had seen. Clearly her mind was on other things.

"Where are you going now?" Sadie asked, jogging to keep up.

"I'll join the fight," Hetia turned her head slightly as if she were going to look at Sadie, but changed her mind. "Which troupe did Mae pick for you?" she asked.

"Umm, Cobie's I think," Sadie said.

Hetia was silent a minute, and then she said, "I'll travel with you across the country. I should keep training you, and make sure you get there safely."

"Oh, I should be safe, I'm traveling with a whole—" Suddenly Sadie realized what she was saying, and dropped off awkwardly. Hetia was determinedly not looking over at her, and a minute later Sadie mumbled, "I think that's a good idea. Better safe than sorry."

They turned down the path to the large stone meeting room in which she'd given Amadi the diary. Hetia led the way through the expansive entrance to find the table populated by Amadi, Luciana, and Troy. The men appeared tense, coiled springs ready to let loose, but Luciana sported her typical garden party look, loose white dress and giant pink sun hat, which stood out against her bronze skin.

Amadi clapped his hands once at their entrance, breaking the conversation. "I should get back out there. I'll leave you to it." He kissed Luciana and Patricia on the cheek, shook Troy's hand, and then crossed to face Sadie. "Hopefully we'll meet again, Sadie Hall." He put a hand on her shoulder and leaned in. "And just know, that whatever Mae told you, I think a lot is riding on the work you and Troy will be doing." His voice became a near whisper, "I haven't given up that there's another way."

Sadie's knees felt weak as he left. What had she gotten herself into?

The moment he'd gone, Patricia said, "Now, regarding the living situation."

Sadie was still standing there shaking as Patricia began to lay out all the details of how they'd travel and where they'd stay once they arrived. Eventually Troy and Sadie finished going over their backstory. Hetia came in and out, bringing food on her final return.

And it was there, with Sadie sitting on the edge of the table, legs crossed and one foot tapping the air anxiously, Troy leaning against the stone at her side, and the other women caught in their own conversation in the corner, that Jimmy walked in.

Everyone looked up at once at the sound. Sadie's eyes were so caught up on the sight of him that it wasn't until he began to unroll a large piece of parchment that she even noticed he was carrying something.

"I finished it," he said. "Here's everything we have on the three families." Sadie's eyes dropped to the elaborate map he was unfurling. It showed three family trees and next to each name were scribbled notes of various lengths.

"This is incredible," Patricia said, coming over to help him weigh down the corners. She rubbed a hand over his back with a familiarity Sadie hadn't seen between them before. Apparently a lot had happened in the past twenty-four hours. It made her miss Jimmy despite the fact they were in the same room. She tried to catch his eye, but he seemed to be deliberately avoiding her gaze.

"I was thinking," Jimmy said, and Sadie watched his hands as he rolled up his sleeves, "That Sadie could start here. This guy, Jax, seems to be the weakest link."

Sadie stopped listening. She just wanted to be alone with him. This was the worst time to be making elaborate plans. She didn't care.

Tomorrow, she was sure, would be different, but right now she wanted only for the rest of the world to leave them in peace.

No one seemed remotely inclined to do so, however, since they continued to chat into the night. The sun had been set for hours, the stone room lit by oil lamps which Troy had ignited around them, and her eyes were starting to droop, when they finally agreed on a plan.

Jimmy was sitting on the other end of the table from her. His features were cast in the warm glow of the flames and Sadie was sleepily watching his forearms as he gestured over the map. "What do you think?" he asked her.

For a moment she didn't realize he was speaking directly to her since his gaze was fixed on the table in front of her hands.

"Uhh, yes. Yes, I think it's good." She reached for some water to clear the dryness from her throat. Everyone suddenly looked half-asleep. Her agreement was the final note.

"We're getting up in a few hours," Luciana said. "Let's be in our beds when the sun finds us."

They rose together. Patricia rolled up the map, tucked it under her arm, and they followed Hetia from the room. Jimmy went out next and Sadie pulled up the rear, leaving her unable to see him as they walked. Her gaze was fixed on the little flame in Troy's hand in front of her, which he held high to light everyone's path.

The air was cool, smelling of the rain, and Sadie felt sharply aware of her own body as she made the slow trek back to cabin nine. Goose-bumps prickled up her arm and she noticed the feeling of the smooth skin of her legs swishing past each other under her dress. Everything felt a little unreal as she took in the smell and feel of the world, and time must have slowed on her, since a lifetime appeared contained in that short walk.

Luciana and Patricia left them first. Then Hetia branched off. Troy stayed with them to their door. There was no moon that night and it would've been incredibly dark without him. Sadie was grateful for the light, but more grateful when he left.

Jimmy turned halfway to face her and said to the ground, "You're staying here?"

"Yes," she said.

He showed her his back again as he placed one hand on the door. "Wait here a minute," he said over his shoulder. She saw him reach for something just inside the door and disappear. A minute later a soft glow trickled out of the cabin. She followed it in and leaned back against the door as it closed behind her. The papers which had dominated the space earlier were mostly contained now, and Jimmy moved the boxes from the bed before leaning against the far wall.

"Do you want me to take the floor?" he asked, still not quite meeting her eye.

"No," she said, it coming out in an unexpected whisper. He was hers. Completely. There was nothing to come between them except that gap of space he was still leaving her.

"It's late. We should get to sleep," he said. "You took the wall last time. Do you want to get in first?" He looked to the bed.

She pushed herself off the door and stepped toward him. "No," she said again.

He kept his gaze averted right up until she stepped into him. His eyelids were heavy as he searched her face for the meaning of her actions.

"Mae?" he asked, his eyes going wide with hope and surprise.

"We can talk about it in the morning," she said, drawing her nose along his jaw to inhale the intoxicating scent of him before brushing her lips against the side of his neck. He slid his hands from his pockets to clutch her hips, saying her name on an exhale. "I want to make love to you, Jimmy. Without guilt or fear. I want you to take me. Take anything you want. I'm yours."

He was utterly frozen, though she could feel him processing her words as the waves of lust between them grew in leaps and bounds. Slowly, he ran a hand up her arm, caressing her bare skin. They had only an instant to enjoy the stillness of the moment before the contact set off an avalanche. He cupped her face in both hands and pulled her mouth to his as they simultaneously made a move for the bed, their feet walking in sync so as not to force space between their bodies. When Sadie's calves hit the edge, he scooped her legs up around him and tumbled forward.

The scene felt increasingly like a wrestling match as she fought to remove his shirt while he fought to keep kissing her. With the full force of his weight on her, however, it seemed she'd just have to be patient. He settled between her legs, rolling his hips in a slow grind. With her limited ability to move, she could only respond to his pace. Sadie arched her back in waves, letting him kiss her. She tried to be patient, but as much as she reveled in the feeling of his tongue against hers, she wanted the rest of him.

Eventually, he expanded his focus enough to run a hand up under her dress. He'd somehow removed his glove, and the increase in skin contact caused him to groan loudly as her control slipped. Not wanting to make a mess of her favorite dress, she tried to pull it up. "Jimmy?" she pleaded against his mouth.

He understood. As he hiked her dress up to her waist, she undid his pants, and when he relaxed his weight back down, she put him inside her.

Jimmy paused, pressing his forehead against hers as his thumb caressed her cheek. They breathed into each other's mouths on a simultaneous groan. "Will you stay here? Right here inside me? Forever?" she asked.

"Yes," he breathed, punctuating the word with his hips. And then said the word again before filling her mouth. And again before rolling his whole body into hers.

The war. The plan. The coming dawn. It all lay forgotten as Sadie followed her impulses down a well of emotion, punctuated by the very real feel of a hand on a back or the quiet panting which filled the space between them. The well was deep and daunting, but she decided to trust that it had a bottom. So with every ounce of herself that she had to give, she let it swallow her.

Chapter 9

The upper hand

Troy was glad to get up early. He couldn't sleep anyway. No matter how many times he replayed her actions, her words, her face, he just couldn't seem to make a decision. He desperately wanted to believe her, but all of this smelled of the Siphon family. It was made even more suspicious by the way everyone was treating the woman. There were things people weren't telling him, and he didn't trust it. Why did no one else see it? She was too matter-of-fact, too genuine, too appealing. Someone like that didn't end up in this world of politics and war.

He dipped his razor back into the river and dried his face. The camp behind him was waking up. It was time. All he could do for now was play along, throw himself into their mission like it was the real thing until proven otherwise. He found Hetia standing at the door of Sadie's cabin. She seemed to be hesitating to knock. When he pulled up next to her, he could see why.

Troy decided to help her out. Taking the plunge, he gave two loud knocks, and then moved away from the door as the sounds inside suddenly reached a crescendo. Hetia followed his fast retreat. They faced each other on the trail, looking equally discomforted.

"Do you want to talk about it?" Troy asked, gesturing with his head to the succubus' cabin.

Hetia sucked her teeth and straightened her back, falling silent as she looked away.

"I mean," Troy tried again, "it was less than a year ago that I suddenly found out I was courting a fascist who wanted to enslave humans. I think I have some experience in wanting someone I shouldn't."

Hetia gave him a sad smile.

When she still didn't speak, he went on, "I think you're right to protect your heart. The more you care about someone, the more power they have to hurt you with betrayal. And this is a dangerous world we're swimming in."

He put a hand on her shoulder, and a moment later she placed hers on top of it. He wanted to offer her a hug, but somehow didn't think she'd respond well to that. As he pulled back, however, she squeezed his fingers and said, "Thank you."

They exchanged a nod of understanding. "I'll go get Luciana and Patricia," he offered.

It took an hour to get them assembled in the field with their troupe. The woman leading them, Cobie, was tall and knew how to project her voice. "It's a half day's walk down the east side. Carriages are waiting to take us to the nearest train station. The drivers are friendly, but you should not share any details about where we're going in their presence," the captain told the crowd before leading the way.

Luciana, Patricia, Hetia, Sadie, Jimmy, and Troy stuck together near the back. Even so, they seemed to be perpetually holding up the soldiers behind them. Luciana was always going to be limited in speed with her walking crutches over rough terrain, but somehow Jimmy was the slowest of all of them. He looked as if he were sleepwalking, half-dead on his feet. He never complained though, as he stared with determination at the ground, putting one foot in front of the other.

Troy worried about him increasingly. The man nearly stumbled twice and they weren't always walking along the safest of paths. It left Troy wishing they were on better terms so he could offer him a shoulder to lean on. The succubus seemed concerned too, but was only in a slightly better state herself. Were they sick or had they just stayed up all night?

The instant the two reached the end of the path, and they were the last ones to do so, Luciana ushered them up into the back of one of the many large carriages. They were asleep the second their butts touched the wooden slats of the truck bed. Jimmy sat in the far corner and Sadie leaned on his shoulder, their arms around each other.

Troy's worry lightened when he caught the glint in Luciana's eye. She had on a small smirk as she looked them over. She wasn't concerned. "We'll have to make sure those two get some sleep tonight," she said in hushed tones, throwing in a wink just for him. As the carriage jostled to life, she added loud enough for the others to hear, "Mae told me it would be for the boy's health if some of the soldiers entertained the succubus a bit."

A few of the men smiled. "I volunteer," said a man in a pink shirt.

"Happy to serve in any way I can," another added.

The exchange left a sour taste in Troy's mouth, but it was all none of his business really. Something he repeated to himself as he went back over their cover story, trying to make it feel like a real memory.

They'd met on a train. He'd suspected her of stealing his ticket, but it had just been a misunderstanding. His mind drifted to being alone with the succubus in a train bathroom. He shook his head, trying to dislodge the banter of soldiers around him from his thoughts. Their conversation was confusing his intentions.

Though Troy must have eventually lost focus altogether and drifted off, because he found himself jerking awake at the sudden lack of jostling movement. People were jumping out of the back by the time he recalled where he was. Troy was soaked in sweat and could feel his arousal the instant he shifted. What had he been dreaming? Embarrassed, he frantically tried to think unsexy thoughts before he stood up. For some reason, the blurred image of curly auburn hair, dripping wet, played in the background.

He hopped discreetly over the side and paused to adjust his backpack while he let his heart rate calm. They were just outside a train station, and in the time it took them to unload, a train had arrived.

The six of them shared a car with four of the soldiers, all men who had expressed interest in the succubus. Troy took the corner furthest from the young lovers, but their presence was everywhere. They looked perfectly awake now, continuously rubbing each other's arms and playing with each other's fingers. After most of the car had drifted off to sleep themselves, he caught them exchange a significant look and disappear together.

Troy assumed they'd gone to the bathroom, and the idea reminded him of his dream somehow, but the details slipped away the instant he attempted to hold onto them. The pair returned a half hour later, looking giddy as they plopped back into their spot and broke out some food to share. Troy closed his eyes before they noticed him watching, but he didn't sleep again.

More carriages picked them up at the other end, and another ride and short walk later, they found themselves at a different United camp. It had been a particularly long day, coming out of the mountains, and everyone went right to bed. Luciana made the lovers share her tent, but Troy blessedly was invited to room with some of the soldiers from their train car.

He woke up early, to someone calling his name. "Psst, Troy? Time to work." He slowly accepted the fact that it was Hetia who was trying to rouse him, and so he couldn't refuse. Ten minutes later, he found himself in a far corner of the camp, looking into Sadie's sleepy face, and feeling like the past few days had passed in a kind of continuous dream.

"Here. Drink up," Hetia said, handing them both hot coffee.

The session went surprisingly smoothly. It seemed that they worked well together when he was playing along that everything was fine between them. Hetia drilled into them with a pressure she hadn't previously shown, however, and they all seemed acutely aware that they only had a handful of days before they'd need these skills for real. The urgency lent them focus and camaraderie, and by the time they broke apart several hours later, Troy found himself returning Sadie's smile, forgetting for a minute that she might be his enemy.

The next day went equally well, and by the fourth morning of their trip, Hetia allowed Troy to sleep in so she could work with Sadie in particular. For a minute, Troy was worried about leaving them alone together, but he could see in the determined look on Hetia's face that the decision was all business.

That, combined with his general exhaustion, allowed Troy to sleep well that night. He was alone when he came to, and the tent was warm with sunlight. The heat invited him outside, and he went in search of the showers. Finding them full, he redirected his path toward running water, which he could hear trickling nearby.

Troy heard Sadie laugh before he saw her. There were ten or so people that had decided to bathe in the river, the succubus among them. The water was slow-moving, wide and deep, easy enough to submerge in. Many of the people were in various states of dress, but the succubus appeared to be naked. Her back was to him and she was bobbing lightly in the water with the pink shirt soldier from the other day in front of her. Troy felt heat stir in him as his thoughts buzzed hectically.

"Join us," one of them waved at him. Troy looked around hesitantly before stripping down to his boxers, and diving in headfirst. The water was refreshing and seemed to cool off his mood. That is until he heard the pink shirt man groan nearby. Several of the men smiled. "Wanna go next?" one of them directed at him. "She's insatiable."

Troy swallowed. What had he walked in on? "No. Thank you," he mumbled. Troy swam away from the crowd and dunked his head to escape the sounds of pleasure and casual chatter at his back.

"Not too far! There's an undercurrent," a man called to him when he reappeared.

Troy could feel the surge of the water below him, the calm surface clearly misleading. He floated on his back to return to the succubus and her groupies, staring at the light dancing through the leaves above as water swished past his ears. The beautiful scenery served to calm his thoughts. He wasn't going to let her get to him. Or at least he wasn't going to let her see she was getting to him. He would prove to her that he at least was entirely immune to her charm.

The sound of masculine pleasure hit his ears the instant he re-emerged, only now it had intensified greatly. The man wasn't particularly loud. Rather, it was the rawness of the sounds that caught the ear. Troy couldn't help himself, he looked in their direction. They weren't even kissing. She was merely pressed against him, cheek to cheek. Troy shivered at the look on the man's face.

He had to get out of there. Only, the cold water had lost its effect on cooling his heated blood. He decided to give it a minute. Not wanting to speak to any of the men, he turned his back on the scene. Eventually, the sounds behind him stopped, and mercifully the men began departing.

"Tomorrow," Sadie said to someone in a husky voice.

"You get what you needed?" a male voice asked.

"Oh yes. Thank you," she said without a hint of seductive undertones. "But I'd still like to feed from the rest of you before we get there."

She was so direct. What a strange world this woman lived in. Troy turned around only when the voices had gone, only to find himself alone with her. She didn't seem to realize he was there. Half-turned away from him and covered to the neck by water, her eyes roamed the surface in front of her.

Troy tried to step away to exit the water out of sight, but his movement caught her attention. His heart pounded as she turned. He was afraid to see hungry eyes directed at him, but as her gaze found his, he was surprised at what he found. She looked calm and was that... thoughtful? Her eyes seemed to come into focus on him, however, and her expression changed.

"Troy. I didn't see you."

"Sorry," he replied, feeling like he'd intentionally been spying on her in the bath. "I was just leaving," he added in a tone he hoped was casual.

Not quite ready to exit the water, he made his walk to shore slowly. Sadie looked him up and down as his torso emerged, her face now sporting an unreadable expression. She turned her full attention to him, clearing her throat. "Have you had a chance with this?" she said, holding out a pale bar of soap. He looked at her wet, naked hand, uncertain what to do. "I won't touch your skin. You don't have to be afraid of that," she added softly.

Troy lifted his chin. "I'm not," he said, and then closed the gap with determination. He held out his hand below hers. She stood up, lifting her torso out of the water and dropped the bar into his finger. Troy stared determinedly at her face. "Thank you."

His instinct was to back up, but he didn't want to give her that satisfaction. Hoping she couldn't see his aroused state, he soaped down his body right there. She didn't look away from his eyes and so he matched her behavior. Two could play this game.

"Did you... sleep well?" she asked. Her tone was so conversational and contained none of the usual bite they used so frequently with each other that he was immediately suspicious.

"Very well. Thank you," he said, dipping down to rinse off. "You?"

"Oh! I slept great. Luciana was a blessing with her presence. I honestly felt terrible slowing things down the other day. So did Jimmy." She reached out her hand for the bar. He handed it to her in a trance. Were they really just having a normal conversation like this? He ran his hands over his body, trying to remove soap with cold water while he figured out how to respond.

"Well, that's good then," he said. "I'm... glad you slept well."

"Me too," she said in what sounded like genuine relief. "And I think I'm almost ready... for what we have to do," she added. Her eyes were soft and yet determined as she said this. They were pretty eyes, and as she refocused on him, he felt like she was seeing right through him.

"Are you?" the woman asked. She was looking at him intently now, and a bit of heat appeared in her gaze. It made the question feel like a mix of challenge and flirtation, especially when she let her gaze travel up and down his torso. Troy did his best not to look nervous. Matching her expression with his own, he stepped closer.

"Of course," he said. Deciding to copy her action, he looked her up and down, his gaze lingering briefly on her hard nipples. "I've been preparing for this for months. I'm ready for anything." His body agreed, and suddenly he wasn't sure if he wasn't in fact flirting with this woman in truth.

She smiled. Sweeping a strand of wet hair behind her ear, she looked down. The pointed direction of her gaze made it clear she could see his erection, and when she locked back onto his face it was with a knowing look. "I'll give you some privacy," she said with an obnoxious twinkle in her eye. "See you, Troy," she added as she turned her back to him.

He was glad she didn't look back at his expression as he watched her walk out of the water. Despite his best efforts, he had clearly lost the upper hand in that conversation. She was good. He had to give her that. This was an opportunity, he told himself as he lifted his hips out of the water to use the soap as lubricant. It was all training to see Mia again.

Not that Siphon's daughter really had any effect on him now. It had taken a few weeks after learning of the woman's true nature for the attraction to go away, and he doubted it would return upon seeing her now. He despised them too much. Still, Sadie would be good practice for navigating conversations with succubi.

He just needed to take care of himself more often. He didn't want to get caught twice with his pants down in front of Sadie. The way she had moved between seduction, casual friendship, and smug opponent had been masterful. He still wasn't sure what she was playing at, but he knew he would have to keep his head clear at all times.

Troy groaned as the spasms of pleasure hit him. Images of Sadie's naked body passed briefly through his thoughts until the moment was over, then he tamped them down with a ten-foot pole while he cleaned himself off. He strolled into camp with renewed energy for what lay ahead, having decided one thing for sure: nothing about this mission was going to be boring.

Chapter 10

Shiny, pretty things

Sadie couldn't help but be satisfied at her progress those past few days. Not only had she successfully memory dived, twice, but she'd had an unexpected chance to increase the connection with Troy. Unfortunately, her actions had come with consequences. The image of Troy walking out of the water had stayed in a relevant part of her thoughts for several days. A surprising feat given the other memories with which it had to compete.

It was incredibly unfair that all this was happening with Jimmy right as their lives had taken such a big turn. Sadie wished she could put all the rest of it on hold for a week, or maybe a lifetime. She'd have to pull herself together if she was going to be ready for what was coming next.

She washed down her breakfast with a big swill of cool water and passed the jug to Patricia, while the soldier she'd fed from last night smiled at her from across the fire. This would be their last morning together, and she would miss them. The troupe had been perfect company. Though she'd only been feeding off them in order to practice the memory diving, not because her ventures with Jimmy had left her remotely hungry. But they were all so nice and helpful.

Plus, all the extra feeding had left a permanent buzzing under her skin, a feeling of being more alive than usual, and as Mae had predicted, it made it significantly easier to do her little trick. But more than that, it had put her in a permanently good mood. She found herself attracted to just about everyone around her in one way or another. Or maybe they were just all amazing and it wasn't her mood at all.

The soldiers had entertained her in every way they could, and the muscles of her face ached from all the laughing she'd done the previous night. Cobie impressed her with her skill and command. Even Troy... she smiled up at him as he came to join them around the morning fire. Even he had his merits.

Someone put another flask in her hand and she took a grateful swig while Hetia appeared from the same direction Troy had come. Sadie waved at her. Hetia didn't sit with them often, so Sadie beamed at her when she pulled up next to her. The blond woman narrowed her eyes as she held out a hand for the flask.

"Good fight?" Sadie asked, looking from Hetia to Troy.

Hetia opened the flask and sniffed its contents, then looked confused. It was water. Did Hetia think she'd been drinking something else?

"It was alright," Troy said in answer to her question. "Uhh, are you feeling okay?"

"Yeah, I feel great actually," she said, beaming as Jimmy appeared through the little path down to the water. He smiled back at her and it just seemed the morning couldn't get any better.

They packed up in a blur, and within the hour were ready to say their goodbyes. Cobie's troupe would head to join up with the rest of the United encampment, while Sadie would continue on to Maddox, Massachusetts, the home to the Siphon family as well as the feeder government after they'd split from the joint system. Though she hadn't followed much of the news this past summer, she knew that the human government had stayed in Washington D.C., producing a solid species divide.

Sadie watched the soldiers pile into the wagons with sadness, and then rushed off into the woods to pee one last time. As she was pulling back on her pants, she heard a twig break to her right, and fell silent at Patricia's whispered voice.

"All I'm saying is, Troy really mistrusts her. Perhaps it would be best just to tell him."

There was a long pause, and then Hetia spoke in a voice so low Sadie barely recognized it as hers. "Troy will come around. He's a clever man. Best to keep secrets in their place."

Patricia made a sound of protest, but Hetia pushed on, "Dee hasn't kept us off the Coalition's radar this long by revealing secrets any time it's convenient. The more valuable the information, the fewer people should know it."

Clearly that was to be the last word because the women walked off without another sound. Sadie, curious about what they might reveal that would make Troy trust her, decided to wait until their footsteps had faded before standing up from her squatting position in the tall grass. Troy's reaction to her unusual journey into the United had left her self-conscious that others might suspect her, and she couldn't stand the thought of Patricia's or Hetia's eyes narrowed on her if they found her *accidentally* eavesdropping. Even if it truly was an accident.

Hurrying back to the others, Sadie arrived just in time to wave at Cobie, Luciana, and the soldiers as the drivers fired up the engines. She looked around frantically for Hetia, afraid that she'd missed her, but the woman pulled up next to her. Sadie turned to face her, suddenly wondering the best way to say goodbye. She couldn't help but wring her hands as she said, "I hope you won't be too reckless out there."

Hetia stepped closer, much closer. Sadie's breath caught as she paused only a few inches from her face. "Don't worry," Hetia said. "I've been training my whole life for this. It's you that needs to be careful." Sadie caught a distinct image in Hetia's mind just before she leaned in, and her heart stopped. Though Hetia paused short of what she'd imagined, she did lightly brush her lips against Sadie's, making brief skin contact.

For a second, Sadie was utterly surprised, and she froze in complete paralysis as the contact gave her access to the feel of Hetia's body. The woman's heart was pounding fast and hard in a way that contrasted entirely with her outwardly calm demeanor.

Then Hetia pulled back. "Don't let them get in your head. Only you can decide who you are," she whispered, and the subject change left Sadie even more confused as Hetia backed up. "Good luck, succubus," she added, looking her up and down without shame before turning and hopping up on the back of the wagon just as it began to lurch away.

Sadie couldn't help but feel a sinking fear that this could be the last time she ever saw the woman. Her stomach clenched with regret and worry, but the troupe quickly disappeared over the hill, and there was nothing to do except to watch them be carried away.

Sadie would just have to trust that Hetia wouldn't do anything too rash, and that they'd see each other when this was all over. Still, her mood grew heavy as she sat down next to Jimmy. It was just the four of them now, and the full weight of the responsibility she'd taken on settled over her.

Patricia was also quiet after her teary goodbye with her grand-mother, and they passed the day in mutual contemplation, with Sadie curled in Jimmy's arms, and Troy occasionally rubbing Patricia's back.

By the time the sun had set, they'd arrived at an inn on the edge of town in Maddox. The four of them rented a single, large room and slept across two beds and the floor. They had intended to get a few rooms, but the inn was booked up. "In fact," the innkeeper told them, "every inn is booked up around here. You're not the only ones on their way out of, or into, the city."

It was true. As they sat around the breakfast table in the cafeteria that morning, the chatter around them gave the first glimpse of what they'd be walking into.

"It's like Seattle all over again," Sadie said, scowling at her sausage as she tried three times to skewer it. It simply rolled over in its juices, avoiding her fork.

"I'm not so sure," Patricia said, tilting her head to listen. "Some-thing different is happening here. At the bar last night, I spoke for a while to an older gentleman. He said the demographics of the city have shifted rapidly in the past few months. Human feeders are congregating here. And when the attack came a few days ago, the humans began to leave in droves. Many of them are moving closer to the capital in D.C. which, as the home of the human government, is turning into a kind of human-only territory."

"And the nymphs?" Troy asked, pushing away his empty plate.

"Split. Some are sticking with the humans. Many are staying here. As we learned in the diary," Patricia nodded to Sadie, "the Coalition began calling nymphs nature feeders decades ago to increase their feeling of camaraderie with human feeders. However, within the nymph community, there are clearly mixed loyalties when it comes to the government split."

"The human government's push to decrease land protections certainly didn't help," Troy huffed. "And we all know that the Coalition had some kind of hand in that recent policy shift. I doubt it came from within the human government alone."

"Hmm." Patricia nodded. "I'm sure making the humans into the bad guys on that one was an intentional part of the Coalition plan. It's perfectly on brand for them." She slid something across the table to Troy. "But onto our own plans... Here's the letter you sent Siphon, along with his reply. I'm getting good at mimicking your handwriting." She smiled. "Anyway. I figured you should see it before we get there."

Sadie's gaze snapped away from Jimmy and back to the conversation. She stilled her anxiously tapping foot and sat up straighter. She was antsy over not getting to be alone with him last night, but this was no time to be thinking about that.

"Should I see the letter, too?" Sadie asked.

"Yes, probably," Patricia said, but Troy looked anxious as Sadie moved closer to read over his shoulder.

Patricia continued. "We'll be going into the east side. It's very Coalition-heavy. Jimmy here will need to keep a low profile. I still recommend against him going at all, but—" Sadie opened her mouth, and Patricia held up a hand. "*But*... I know that is not an option."

Sadie laced her fingers through Jimmy's. No one was going to separate them now that they could finally be together. "We'll be careful," Sadie assured the group.

They took a train into the heart of the east side, emerging onto a gorgeous station. Polished marble floors met marble walls in crisp corners. Everything was tidy and Sadie and Jimmy looked grotesquely underdressed against the fashionable attire of the people around them. Patricia looked her usual fancy self, in a tight skirt and stylish knit top. She'd even put on heels once they'd arrived on firm ground. Troy was wearing a tailor-made suit that he must have been lugging around all this time. It looked obnoxiously good on him.

They caught a shiny, yellow cab and Sadie did her best to act like the experience of getting into a car in a city was perfectly common for her. "That's the old courthouse there," the driver pointed out. "Now the capitol for the feeder government. You can find all the big names there if you go during the week. Congressman Siphon is always happy to shake some hands, welcome new feeders to the area." The man surveyed them in the mirror. His eyes dropped to Sadie's gloves and he gave an approving nod.

The clean look of everything vanished after about ten blocks, morphing into an array of color. Brightly lit signs shone down from every direction, and the buildings bustled with activity.

The cab let them out in front of the tallest hotel Sadie had ever seen. Her head fell back as she watched it disappear into the sky. On the left was a casino, and on the right a long line of people waited outside a theater.

They followed Patricia up the stairs. Two identically dressed men opened the double doors for them, revealing an expansive lobby. Sadie did her best not to gawk as she crossed the sparkling floor in her muddy boots.

Troy, however, looked at home as he stepped up to the counter.

"Hyun," he said.

"Yes, of course sir. Welcome back." The woman smiled. "Your rooms are all taken care of. You'll be in suites 340 and 341."

She handed him the keys along with a suggestive grin. Or perhaps it only appeared that way, since Sadie could see what the woman was feeling. He smiled back, then said, "My friends have had a long journey. Would you mind sending lunch directly to our rooms?"

"Chicken or lobster, sir?" she asked.

"Chicken for all, I think. Thank you." Troy pocketed the keys before leading the way into this strange new world.

Outside their rooms, he handed a key to room 340 over to Patricia, and gave 341 to Sadie and Jimmy, but they all entered suite 341 together. Sadie had expected the room to be as elaborate as the lobby downstairs, but it was simple and reasonably sized. She would have been impressed had she just left home, but Alec's suite in Seattle had been far more grandiose than this.

"What, no bathtub in the living room?" she said with a smirk, recalling Alec's parties.

"Bathtub in the living room?" Troy asked.

"Yeah, I stayed in a place in Seattle like that," she told him.

He smiled, then shook his head on a laugh. "It's called a hot tub."

She crossed her arms. "What?"

"A hot tub. It's for relaxing with friends, not bathing," he said, and though he seemed to be trying to suppress the grin on his face, Sadie felt as if he were openly mocking her, regardless.

She looked him up and down. Troy was standing there in his suit with his hands in his pockets. He looked far too at ease. If it had been anyone else correcting her she would have laughed along with them at her mistake, but she found nothing amusing in this interaction.

Sadie lifted her chin. "You seem pretty comfortable here, don't you? I didn't realize your background was so *extravagant*." She smoothed out her rumpled shirt. "I'm surprised you didn't use your family money to get a private cabin back at camp."

"Okay." Jimmy stepped in with a hand on her waist. "Let's not say anything we'll regret."

Sadie was all too ruffled though, and the stress had her on edge. "Are you personally paying for all this then?" she asked, suddenly curious to know more about his history here.

"Siphon opened an account for me when he took me under his wing last year. This is all at his will," Troy said, looking somber and patient despite her attacking tone. "I had your closet stocked ahead of time."

Sadie softened at that. "Oh," was all she could think to say. She looked at the ground, suddenly uncomfortable under his gaze.

"Let's take a shower," Jimmy said, rescuing her. Luckily, the sound of him saying those words in her ear was immediately distracting, and it helped her shake away her embarrassment. Patricia led Troy from the room, and Sadie forced her gaze away from Troy's back. She had other things to think about now.

In fact, it only took Jimmy kissing the back of her neck and running a hand across her stomach, skin-to-skin, to immediately forget the interaction. It ended up taking them a full hour to make it to the shower, and by the time they had emerged, Sadie was starving.

She opened the door, only just remembering a knock they had ignored earlier. The hallway was empty. Guilt at her rudeness twisted her stomach, adding to her disappointment at missing the delivery.

"Nothing?" Jimmy asked, the same contrite expression plaguing his features.

"Sorry," she said.

He shrugged. "It was worth it," he told her, breaking into a smile. Her stomach grumbled, but the look in his eyes drew her back in. They were both still naked, it would be easy to go again. Forgetting the missed meal, she stepped forward to kiss him, throwing off her towel.

A knock came from the closet. They paused to stare at it. When it came again, they both moved to cover themselves before Sadie went to open it. Discovering it locked, Jimmy retrieved their key.

Patricia was on the other end, their room visible behind her. Clearly, what had appeared to be a closet was actually a convenient adjoining door. The other woman had changed into a fine green dress, her hair slicked back in a way she hadn't seen her with since Seattle. She was holding out a tray, and as the smell wafted into their room, Sadie sighed gratefully.

"We collected it for you," her friend explained. "Come over when you're dressed."

"Thanks Patricia," Jimmy said, reaching around Sadie to take a plate.

Sadie finished eating first and went to open the actual closet. "Wow. Siphon must really be loaded to give away all this for free."

"Well, it's not exactly free. More like fancy clothes in exchange for Troy's loyalty," Jimmy said.

Sadie frowned as she looked back at the closet. It was a strange thing, to be enjoying the hospitality of the man they were there to spy on. She ran her hand through the various dresses and chose a pretty yellow one made of lacy fabric. She twirled in front of Jimmy.

"Nice," he said. "Though it looks like it would tear easily."

She laughed. "I'm not mucking out a chicken coop. It's supposed to be *delicate.*"

He sighed. "I know. I'm just nervous. If it were up to me, you'd be going in with full body armor."

"I know." She put a hand on his head. "I'll be careful. Trust me."

Ten minutes later, they knocked on the connecting door between the rooms. Troy answered, looked Sadie up and down, and said simply, "No. That won't do." Then without explanation he pushed past her. "Come on," he said over his shoulder when she didn't budge. She complied in frustration while Jimmy shared an exasperated look with her before leaving to join Patricia.

Troy opened the closet and ran his hands over various items, pulling them out halfway to get a peek. He settled on a dark green, satin dress that looked far too small for her. "This one," he said and tossed it on the bed. "With these." He reached down and extracted some heels.

"What's wrong with the yellow?" she asked.

"It's for a summer event. More of an outdoor thing. You'd stand out like a sore thumb in it. I'm taking you to a formal evening party."

She crossed her arms, making no move to accept his suggestion.

He sighed. "Just trust me on this one. Please?"

She picked up the green satin and stroked its soft surface. "Won't people wonder where I got such expensive things if I grew up on a farm?" she asked seriously.

"No. When people have money they assume everyone else does too. They'd only think about it if you looked out of place. Besides, I bought it for you, didn't I? Perhaps it's one of the reasons you're with me? So I'll buy you pretty things?" he said with a shrug.

She balked. "I'm pretty sure my character isn't so shallow."

"Actually, I think she is. It would explain a lot of her coming behavior toward the Maddox son," he said.

Sadie walked around him. "No, I think she goes for Jax because he's experienced and she knows he can keep her satisfied." Sadie went for this explanation in particular hoping to make Troy feel privately defensive about his limited experience. "Perhaps the dress was my grandmother's, and I don't care for your money or connections."

He stepped closer, seeming unruffled by her jab. "No, I think you do. Why would you have followed me here when there's barely even any chemistry between us?"

As they looked over each other's heated faces, Troy's words stood out like a bold-faced lie. He ran a hand through his hair in the gesture that looked so good on him, and his gaze flicked briefly to her lips. For a minute, Sadie thought he was actually flirting with her, but then she decided he was just trying to get to her the same way she had when she'd teased him back in the river.

Well, this was a situation she knew how to handle. "Maybe you're right. Perhaps we should be focused on trying to change our complete lack of chemistry." She unclasped the hook at the back of her neck with one hand. "It might be all more convincing if we just get that over with." She let the dress drop.

Troy backed up so fast it was almost comical, but his eyes did flit over her before turning away. "I'll see you over there," he mumbled.

Sadie felt better about the hot tub incident. It seemed the man didn't always have a retort for everything either.

Turning her back on him, she held up the dress and looked it over hesitantly. It turned out to fit her exactly, but left little to the imagination. It was knee-length and classy, but also tighter than she was used to and more low-cut. She stared at herself in the mirror and asked, "Why not just go naked?" In the end, she decided she very much liked the dress. Sadie also donned the shoes. She might as well practice walking in them now.

The connecting door to 340 was open this time and as she pushed her way in, three sets of eyes froze to stare at her. "Oh Sadie, you look amazing. Troy has great taste." Patricia smiled from her to him. "And he knows this world, so trust him in there."

Troy grinned at her, crossing his arms.

"Right, well we should get going," Sadie said. She put on a pair of elegant black gloves which came up to her elbows and reached to squeeze Jimmy's hand.

"Stay focused," Jimmy said. "Do you remember all their names?"

"Phoenix is the youngest Maddox son, the one they're grooming for politics, Jax is the eldest. Jax is the womanizing drunk who would be easiest to get close to, but Phoenix likely has more information since the family trusts him. Their daughter is a homebody, so I shouldn't expect to see her. She's also married and unlikely to be interested in either of us."

Jimmy nodded.

"See you on the other side," Troy said to Patricia before leading the way out.

Sadie caught one last glimpse of Jimmy's worried expression before the door closed, leaving her and Troy alone in the hallway.

"Have you been to this place before?" Sadie asked on their way down in the elevator.

"I have. It's a ballroom that frequently hosts fundraisers. Tonight, it will be a container for all the sins of the world, for I doubt Jax would have thrown his brother a birthday party that wasn't dripping with debauchery." He gave her a look that made her narrow her eyes.

"If you're thinking I'll fit right in, you can keep it to yourself." Sadie crossed her arms.

Troy's eyes widened a smidge. "No, I – I wasn't thinking anything like that." He chewed his lip before breaking the eye contact to stare straight ahead. "I was thinking you might be just the right person to have with me for this, and... I was really hoping you're actually on my side."

Sadie's posture softened, and she was glad he wasn't looking at her as she blushed with embarrassment at her assumption. Then Troy added, "Though you're barely trained, and know nothing about the world we're walking into, so you might actually ruin everything." She flushed deeper, this time with anger. The doors opened, and she glared at the back of Troy's head as she followed him, unable to think of any retort to his perfectly accurate description of the situation.

Again, the cab let them out only a handful of blocks away, but this time Sadie was grateful as she preferred not to have to walk too far in these wretched heels. "There's pen and paper in that purse if you learn anything you'd like to write down," Troy said as they walked toward the front entrance. "Just don't leave your bag laying around after."

"No? But I had planned on writing the words *I should really tell the United, the resistance to the Coalition, this* in big letters on a napkin and then just abandoning it at the bar," she said.

"Good plan," he whispered, plastering on a smile as they passed the doorman, and Sadie quickly copied the expression, trying to tamp down her annoyed mood.

Troy put a hand on her back as they entered the room, his palm warm through her dress, and for a second she was distracted by the gesture. Though it quickly reminded her of the role she was there to play.

She was *so* glad to be here with Troy, she told herself. Wasn't he sexy and glamorous? And she just couldn't wait to meet all these lovely people. She was just sure she'd fit right in.

Troy took two glasses of champagne off a passing tray carried by a very strangely dressed man and handed one to her.

"Don't drink too much," he told her.

"Wow. You really are full of all the good advice today," she said, increasingly annoyed at his lack of confidence in her.

"Troy Hyun?" A melodic, high-pitched voice said to their right.

"And let me do most of the talking," he whispered, directing them toward the woman.

"And Sadie Hall," Sadie said, holding out a hand to the woman with a strong line of red desire connecting her to Troy. "I don't believe we've met."

"No. I— We haven't," the woman said, accepting the handshake with a sneer.

"Where have you been, Troy?" she sang. "We've missed you these last months." Her tone was whiny and fake. Sadie instantly disliked her. Which was good practice. She looked for something appealing about her. Her make-up was impeccable. It was almost a work of art. And she had many genuine friendship lines with the other people in the room, which Sadie couldn't say for most of the guests.

What a creative and friendly person, she told herself, trying to feel it.

"Oh, he was looking after his grandmother. She was very ill," Sadie said before Troy could speak. "But it was good for me, otherwise maybe we wouldn't have met."

"Yes. Uhh, Shirley, would you excuse us?" Troy said, steering them away.

"Now, remember Troy, to keep your emotions in check. A lot of these people are feeders, and we never know what someone might be feeding off of," she said through a smile, leaning into his arm around her.

He sighed. "I'm sorry about the drinking comment. And... the ones before it."

Sadie nearly stumbled at the genuine apology.

"I've just been preparing all summer for this, and there's a lot more riding on it than we'd thought a couple months ago," he added. "We can't mess it up."

Sadie was spared having to respond when Troy pulled them to a stop. "There he is. Jax Maddox."

She followed his gaze to the man at the back of the room. He was wearing an elaborate dark purple suit decorated with gold trim, which was cut so low it showed off half his bare chest. A crowd flanked him, most of them interested women.

Troy led them in a brief pass nearby, and Sadie smiled shyly to the man.

"Troy!" Jax shouted unceremoniously.

Troy smiled and led them over to him, dropping his hand from Sadie's back.

"Who's your friend?" Jax asked.

"This is Sadie. We met on the road. I thought this town could use another succubus," Troy said with a grin.

"It could at that. The Siphons are all business sometimes, and Derek's always sending the new ones away." He mock-pouted for

Troy's benefit before turning his attention on Sadie. "Where are you staying then?" His gaze traveled unabashedly over her curves.

"The Lanburg Hotel, next to the old opera house," Troy said. "Are you familiar?"

The man smiled. "Very. The Lanburg is always well-stocked. I'm heading there after."

By the slight slur in the man's speech, Sadie didn't think he needed more liquor. Then at the images in the front of his thoughts, she realized he might not have meant that the hotel was stocked with alcohol.

She went over the notes in Jimmy's handwriting that she'd read next to Jax's name. They knew he kept several rooms at the Lanburg and had a rotating slew of women in and out of them. There were ladies that liked to travel to the theater, and Jax's parties were well-known as the post-theater entertainment. It had been easy to identify him as their starting place.

"We might see you there then," Sadie said. "Though I bet you have a much better room than us."

"Top floor," Jax said. "You'll have to come see it. Both of you," he added.

"We'd love that," Sadie smiled, looking him up and down and biting her lip, before turning to Troy.

He wasn't listening though, his gaze fixed over her shoulder. Sadie didn't turn immediately, and she was still absorbing the expression on Troy's face when he spoke in barely more than a whisper, his entire body rigid. "He's here."

The words were simple, and yet the unfiltered emotion he let slip into them made Sadie's stomach drop. She had only one guess of who had arrived.

Chapter 11

Birthday boy

"Siphon," Jax said, following Troy's gaze. "It's a surprise to see him here. He's a busy man these days."

"Would you introduce me to the congressman?" Sadie said, leaning into Troy to get his attention. "I've been dying to meet him."

This seemed to pull him out of his trance. Sadie hoped there were no excitement feeders in the room as she was pretty sure Troy's heart was pounding. Outwardly, he made a full recovery.

"Of course, babe." He swept her up and they strolled slowly in Siphon's direction. There was no need to rush, as the man was busy shaking a variety of hands. Everyone seemed to want to greet him.

"I didn't think he'd be here. It's just a silly birthday party," Troy said.

"But this is good right? A chance to meet in a smaller setting?" Sadie said, still confused at his reaction.

"I just thought I had one more day... before we'd be face-to-face," he said, a slight breathiness in his voice.

Just as Sadie began to be worried at Troy's behavior, the fear disappeared from his face and she got hit with a solid image of her naked.

For a single heartbeat she was confused, but then she understood. *Good boy. Think of that.*

"That's better," she said, looking over his expression. "What are you thinking of?" she asked with feigned innocence.

"My grandmother's delicious casseroles. I was always so excited for them. Just like I'm excited to see Siphon." He beamed at her.

They kept smiling at each other as they watched the congressman approach. Then Troy turned and his smile got even bigger. It looked so genuine. "Oh, congressman. What a sight for sore eyes you are."

The man took his hand and turned the handshake into a one-armed hug. "Call me Derek, already. Please," he boomed, putting a hand on Troy's shoulder to look him up and down.

"You know I won't," Troy said, chuckling.

The men looked similar in some ways. They were both attractive with dark hair and fair skin, though the elder man was more phenotypically European. Sadie put in some effort to notice Siphon's physical features behind the array of sexual images, but it was much easier than it had been with Mae. He looked more like Gabriel, in fact, only he had more ongoing sexual relationships than her succubus guide.

He turned to see her assessing him and he took a moment to do the same. "I see you've made a friend," Siphon said to Troy while Sadie focused hard on the memory of her companion walking out of the river.

"Yes, sir," Troy said.

Sadie wasn't sure if he was intentionally imitating the congressman's mannerisms or not, but it made them seem even more like father and son.

"Allow me to introduce Sadie Hall. She was on her way to see an old friend when our paths collided," Troy said.

She held out her hand. "I was going to see a man named Gabriel," she said. "He helped me during my Becoming. Do you know him?"

"I do at that," Siphon said, beaming down at her. "Welcome, Sadie. It's a pleasure to make your acquaintance." Sadie inwardly groaned at the knowledge that Siphon knew Gabriel's name. Though this development could only help their cause, she felt that what

Gabriel had done for her had been a sacred thing, and she didn't like any part of that memory mingling with this fake world.

Despite this uncomfortable news though, Sadie managed to keep on a friendly expression as she looked back at the congressman. His smile was light, but his eyes continued to survey her carefully. "Come. Walk with me," he said, putting an arm around Troy. "Tell me about your trip."

Siphon led them into a second room as Troy spoke, and the crowd parted around them with cordial nods. They stopped in front of an old woman with a cane just as Troy said, "And that's when I met Sadie."

"Yes. Excellent. Troy, you remember my good friend Jan, right?" Siphon gestured to the old woman.

"Yes, of course. Nice to see you again, ma'am," Troy said.

"Jan loves to meet new friends of the family," Siphon told them, before directing at Jan, "Sadie here was just about to tell us her story."

The importance of the moment was not lost on her, and Sadie gave it all she had. She was grateful now that they'd practiced this. The parts of her story that she omitted were knit together on either end seamlessly, and she let herself feel every emotion she'd had over the last year.

Siphon was nodding along in rapt attention until she finished. "What do you think? Interesting young woman, no?" He directed at Jan. The woman, who appeared to be mute, gave one slow nod.

Siphon smiled before turning to Troy. "Will you keep entertaining Jan a moment? I'd love a chance to get to know Sadie, succubus to succubus?"

Troy's smile only slipped for a second before he said, "Of course," and turned his back on them like it was nothing.

Siphon politely took her forearm and led her in the direction of the music.

"It really is a pleasure to have you here," he said. "And not to sound too much like an overbearing father, but what are your intentions with my Troy?"

Sadie took a risk on tone and said, "Oh, I confess, they're nothing good." She shook her head contritely. "A father wouldn't want to know."

He barked a laugh, his shoulders shaking as he threw his head back. "I'm sure they are not." He smiled. "Well, I should warn you. My daughter, Mia, has her eye on the boy. You might have a fight ahead of you."

"You have a daughter?" Sadie asked.

"About your age," he said.

"That's great. I would love to meet another succubus my age," she said with the full ability to put truth into her words.

He led her around the outer edges of the dance hall and the music covered the conversations around them.

"I hope you two can get along." He smiled down at her. "She doesn't share the room well, but it looks like you can hold your own. Perhaps you'll be a perfect fit," he said. Sadie bobbed her head in agreement as he pulled them to a stop and turned to face her.

"And speaking of perfect fits, I see you have a... good friend. Since you had some fun together this morning, I assume he's here with you? You should bring him. We would love to meet the man," Siphon said.

Sadie was ready for this. "He's not really a friend. I prefer not to associate with him in public," she said.

"Ahh, a human friend then," he said. "I see now why you left him out of your story."

She ducked her head in embarrassment.

"Don't worry, your secret's safe with me. Our kind knows how *complicated* our sexualities can be. It's nothing we haven't seen before. In fact, the woman with the long red hair and freckles you see on me..." He lowered his voice conspiratorially. "She's human." Returning to his normal baritone, he continued, "And we've been together for years. It is remarkable though, the power of your connection with this man. You'll have to tell us how you do that. Or better yet, show us. I could host a private party."

It was all she could do to keep her face calm. The idea of bringing Jimmy before this man to display their relationship like a spectacle made bile rise in her throat. His gaze searched her with curiosity as she frantically tried to think of what to say.

"Excuse me, congressman?" Troy said, stepping up to them. "I love this song and I was wondering if I could steal Sadie back for it?"

"Of course, my boy. I apologize for taking your date. I'll have to make up for my rudeness by inviting you both to a fundraiser tomorrow night."

"Wouldn't miss it," Troy said, shaking his hand one last time, before scooping an arm around Sadie.

Troy led her to the middle of the floor, and they had a moment of awkwardness as he pulled her close enough to dance. His suit and her gloves were enough to keep them from direct skin contact, but Sadie did a quick check of their clothing just to be sure. He cleared his throat and asked quietly, "What did he say to you? You looked nervous."

"Nothing," Sadie said.

He locked eyes with her. "I don't think we should be keeping secrets. We're partners in this."

The last thing Sadie wanted was to increase Troy's suspicion by lying, but she couldn't tell him that Siphon could see Jimmy on her. That would be revealing a major succubus secret. "He asked if I had any other lovers and I decided it was safest not to tell a direct lie. I told him about Jimmy."

"What?" Troy said. "Don't you think that's incredibly dangerous?"

"Well, glad to have your support," she said. "Look, it's none of your business. Jimmy and I had already discussed it. He's prepared for the risk. It's safest to be as honest as possible, right?"

Troy let out a breath, making a deep-throated sound that rumbled in his chest. It was quiet and directly in her ear. She was sure he hadn't intended it, but the near groan made their closeness feel a lot more intimate. Luckily, he wasn't a succubus and couldn't see her reaction.

"And what did he think of that information?" he asked.

"He wants me to bring him over for a, uhhh, private party. But that is *not* happening. Whatever we have to do, Jimmy is staying out of sight," she said.

"Agreed," Troy whispered.

He spun them in a pivot. "What do you make of Jax? Think we can get in close with him?"

"Oh, definitely," she said, "but then again, it's his brother that probably has the real information. I think we should at least scout out Phoenix before finalizing the plan."

Jax had joined the dance floor, and after Troy spun them, she got a direct view of the man. He had a blue line emanating from him to his brother, and this time Sadie followed it to a man standing alone on a balcony. Now that was definitely a strange place for the birthday boy. Sadie smiled.

"*Or,* we should stay focused on the one we have a chance with," Troy said.

Sadie disagreed. She wanted to at least meet Phoenix. "I'm going to find a bathroom," she said as the music shifted.

"Okay. I'll wait here for you," he said.

She felt a twinge of guilt for not being honest with Troy about where she was going, but it couldn't hurt to at least talk to the man. They couldn't have known Phoenix would be hiding away alone, giving her private access. Sadie avoided catching anyone's eye for too long as she made her way up the stairs, not wanting to be stopped on her mission.

There were very few people on the second level, and when she passed by a couple they stopped talking immediately, clearly there to have a private conversation. Sadie slipped out onto the balcony over-looking the dance floor and stopped with a jolt.

"Sorry," she said as the man who she assumed was Jax's brother turned to stare at her. "I just wanted to get a look at everyone from up here. Is it okay— Do you mind if I join you?"

He nodded silently and turned back to his staring.

She examined him briefly as she pulled up to his side. He'd had a girlfriend. It looked brief and Sadie didn't think they'd been together recently. She was his only sexual experience. Physically, he was smaller and more reserved than his brother, dressed simply in all black. He would definitely be the harder of the two to get close to, but Sadie was excited for the challenge.

She also was more attracted to this man, which would make the experience more interesting. A broad sexual attraction to many people seemed to come with being a succubus, but she hadn't slept with someone she wasn't feeding off of since Gabriel. She still wasn't sure exactly how she was going to feel about it.

"It's overwhelming down there. Do you come to these things often?" she asked.

"Not when I can avoid it," he said.

She laughed. "And yet you're here today. You must have a good reason."

He nodded to the man dancing between two women. "What do you think of my brother?"

"Ahh, so it's the birthday boy, is it?" Sadie leaned against the railing to face him. "Hiding in a tower?"

"Jax seemed interested in you. Don't you want to go play with him?" Phoenix said without looking at her.

"Not really. I prefer the quiet," Sadie said.

"And the man you came with, Troy?"

"We're sharing a room. I'll see him plenty later."

He turned to her then. "Let me guess... a succubus?"

She smiled, swooping a strand of hair back behind her ear.

"You can't feed off my brother then. Is that why he doesn't interest you?" he asked.

"I came with a fire nymph. You don't think I'm well-fed?" She turned her back to the room, scooting closer to him in the process.

He smiled and it lightened his whole demeanor. "I guess a young, attractive succubus wouldn't have any trouble with that."

Good, he was flirting with her. Only, he wasn't registering much sexual interest. The red light of desire was a thin strand. He was playing it up, which meant he had other motivations.

"How old are you today?" she asked.

"I'm turning twenty."

"Hmm, a big one. We should do something fun." She ran a thumb down his tie in a bold gesture, her heart pounding at her own actions even as a determination settled over her.

"Fun's not really my thing," he said, looking past her shoulder at the dance floor below. His gaze seemed locked on the corner his brother had commandeered. Sadie looked again to see more women had joined him. Jax was sucking on the neck of the woman in front of him, and their dance party was drawing the attention of the crowd.

She only had a few guesses of what would make Phoenix flirt with a woman he was only mildly attracted to and she took an instinctual plunge. She looked from Jax to Phoenix and stared at him until he looked up at her.

"Leave with me," she said, turning her back to the room again. "Take me to your place. We don't have to do anything there. Just be the man that took the succubus home. Leave your own party early. The party your brother threw for you."

He mulled that over. For the first time, she saw a spark of curiosity behind his expression. He was tempted by this offer, and that went a long way toward confirming her theory.

Surprising her, he asked, "Would you dance with me?"

She smiled and moved closer. He grabbed her hands to stop her. "No. Not here."

Taking her fingers in his, Phoenix led them out into the hall and down the stairs. He lost some of his determination when they hit the main hall and he tried to pull them into a corner on the edge of the dance floor, but she smiled and tugged him into the center, walking backwards so that she could keep her eyes locked on his.

An almost imperceptible smile crossed his lips as he complied. It was clear he liked her attention more when other people were watching. She even observed the line of attraction pulse and grow.

Sadie caught Troy's eye as Phoenix pulled her close. He was leaning against a marble pillar, staring at her impassively. Whatever was going through Troy's mind, he was doing well to keep it from his expression.

She was aware that not only did her companion in crime not trust her, but he didn't think she was capable of much. He was probably imagining she was trying to befriend Phoenix and get into his inner circle gradually, the way they had been planning with Jax, and then see what kind of pillow talk she could get out of him.

Her own plan was very different. For one, she didn't really have a plan except to listen to Mae's advice and trust her instincts. But also, she needed only one thing: to get the subject to sleep with her. Sadie looked forward to proving to Troy just how good at this she could be.

She let loose on the dance floor, laughing and moving comfortably. That part was easy. The music was good and the room beautiful. Sadie let herself relax as if she were among friends and not enemies.

When they'd drawn enough attention to be on par with Jax, she put her arms around Phoenix's neck, careful to rest them on his covered shoulders and not touch skin. "You ready to get out of here?" she said in a breathy voice.

Again, the man surprised her. He grinned mischievously and pulled her closer. Then he scooped a hand around the back of her neck. Sadie would never have guessed that he would make skin contact in public like this. She gasped in surprise, taking a moment to recover before she returned the expression and pulled him closer.

She caught snippets of the talk around them. They'd definitely made a scene now, and when Phoenix pulled her face to his and kissed her, the crowd cheered. A wave of different emotions passed through her in that moment; a thrill at her success, a hint of desire, uncertainty over being so intimate with someone she was working against.

That last emotion was a dangerous one, and she quickly refocused her full attention on enjoying the feeling of pleasure growing in him, even if she couldn't feed from it. She needed to stay concentrated on the simple emotions, lust and excitement. She thought of Jimmy for an instant, and then probably because she could feel him watching her, she thought of Troy.

Sadie pulled away and loudly addressed the room. "What do you think, is it the birthday boy's bedtime?" she asked, her heart pounding at her publicly playful gesture. Everything about that moment, from the way she was standing to the tone she'd used, was miles away from her normal behavior. Sadie felt outside herself as she watched the spectacle and yet proud of her ability to play the role. She knew she could do this. Here was her chance to prove it.

People responded with cheers and whistles. She turned back to Phoenix and he bowed to the crowd before taking her hand and heading for the door. She waved goodnight to Troy for all to see, establishing publicly that she didn't belong exclusively to the fire nymph. Despite what she'd assumed was a certain amount of shyness on the balcony earlier, Phoenix walked across the floor with the erection from her touch quite visible.

He kept surprising her when a powerful wave of lust came off him the minute they were alone in the entranceway. The kiss had unleashed something that he'd apparently been holding back. He scooped her up in another embrace, clumsy and eager.

"Excuse me, Phoenix is it?" Troy said from a few feet away. "It's a pleasure to finally meet you. Mind if I steal Sadie a moment before you take her?"

Sadie couldn't believe he was interrupting. She wanted to scream. If she hadn't been trying to school her features, her jaw would have dropped open. What did he think he was playing at?

"Uhhh. Hmmm. If you must," Phoenix said, unimpressed at the intrusion. Sadie thought he seemed to look down his nose at Troy, as if he thought the nymph addressing him at all was inappropriate. Not accepting the handshake, he said, "I'll wait outside" before disappearing.

The instant the door had closed, Sadie rounded on Troy. "What the *hell* do you think you're doing?" If she hadn't been whispering, it would've been a shout.

"What do you think *you're* doing? This isn't the plan. Were you going to just go have sex with that stranger?" Troy said.

"Uhh... yeah! Duh, Troy. What do you think we're here for?"

"We're here to make friends with Jax. See what happens. It was never in the plan that you would definitely have to sleep with any of them," he said.

She had to force herself to close her mouth. "What are you talking about? Of course it was."

"Well, okay. Uhh, maybe. As a last resort. But hopefully it wouldn't come to that. I mean, you can't just show up and – and – throw yourself at someone you hate," he said.

Sadie was frozen as she looked over his expression. Slowly, a strange thought came to her. *Troy* was genuinely concerned about her wellbeing.

Her shoulders softened and she stepped in closer to increase their privacy. "Look, Troy. This may be hard for you to get, but things are different for me. I'm attracted to a lot of people." She dropped her gaze, feeling shy about looking into his eyes as she said that in case he realized he was included in that group. "I always thought it was going to go down like this, and I'm fine with it. In fact, it's a little fun."

Troy made a face of disgust. "I don't understand you."

"I think we've established that," she said, her expression growing somber. "Which is fine. All I need is for you to trust me."

"You know I can't," he whispered, moving closer to say, "Tell me why you're going off-plan?" She could feel his breath against hers. They were both breathing as if they were running, not locked in a disagreement. He looked stern, but his gaze dropped to her lips as she spoke. Despite the seriousness of the discussion, somewhere in the background the image of pushing her against the wall and kissing her was rolling through his thoughts.

"I don't have time to sit here and convince you to trust me," she said, crossing her arms defensively, but feeling flustered. She turned to leave, but he grabbed her wrist.

"Wait, Sadie." He took a deep breath. She stopped in surprise to hear her actual name on his lips. "If you're serious about this, let's regroup, run it by the others. Don't go out there tonight with no back-up."

"Troy," she said, moving close again to whisper. "This chance might not happen again. You have to let me do this. Now."

He swallowed. Their hard expressions softened in sync as they considered each other. Troy licked his lips and she found herself leaning in like he was a magnet. His grip on her wrist loosened. Just as she was about to wriggle the rest of the way free, however, the door opened again and Phoenix popped his head in.

The man took them in and Sadie became quickly aware of how they must look. They were standing close, gazing into each other's eyes with possible desire and confusion, Troy still holding her wrist.

"Look. I don't want to be in the middle of this," Phoenix said. Then huffing out a huge sigh, he added, "You came with him. You stay with him." And before Sadie could even register regret, the man that had been set to be her first victory closed the door in her face.

Chapter 12

The competition

Sadie blinked in surprise, staring at the hard wooden door that had just been shut in her face. She rounded on Troy. "What the hell did you just do? I *had* that guy. That was the perfect chance to get something."

"How are you drilling *me* right now? You were the one going off-plan," Troy hissed, dropping his voice as someone passed by the entranceway. They looked at the small door next to them. Sadie peaked inside it to confirm it was a closet and stepped in without looking back. She fumbled for the light while Troy shut them in.

The space was small enough that they were nearly touching. Troy sat back against a tall stool to put a foot between them, but it left their knees in contact. Sadie was acutely aware of the intimacy of their position and she could see he was too. Though he remained outwardly casual as he continued. "You're the one mucking this up. I just saved us. There was no way you were going to get anything from the younger brother."

His half-seated position put them at the same height and she used that to her advantage as she stood up tall and looked boldly into his eyes.

"I don't remember anyone deciding the plan was set in stone. The way I remember it, Hetia emphasized flexibility. I saw an opportunity and I took it. And. You. Ruined it." She wasn't proud of the way she gritted her teeth on those words, but she couldn't tamp down her rage at his interference.

The noise from outside was muffled which meant the walls were thick, but he kept his voice low as he replied. "What were you really trying to do tonight? You are clearly up to something."

He was truly infuriating. How was she supposed to get anything done like this? Not wanting to have to defend herself yet again, she opted for annoying him in return. "You're right. I just thought the younger brother was the cute one. And since all I'm interested in is sex..." She sighed. "I just couldn't help myself."

"Okay." He stood back up. "If that's how you're going to play it, then we're clearly done here. Let's just get back out there so we can make sure that when Jax takes the party back to the hotel, we're invited."

Sadie chewed her lip. "I don't think that's the best idea."

He glared at her with such disdain she would have thought he truly hated her if she couldn't also see how he felt about their current proximity. Actually, she realized then, his willingness to be in such close quarters with her was a sign that a part of him was coming to trust her.

She continued. "We all agreed the younger brother would have the best information. And I see now that if anything happened between me and Jax, Phoenix would never touch me."

Troy rubbed at his eyebrows and Sadie pulled her head back to avoid his hand mistakenly grazing her face. People sometimes forgot not to touch her skin, but ever since she'd accidentally touched Jimmy months ago, she'd become hypercautious of such things.

When his face emerged from his hand, he noticed her position and froze. He swallowed before carefully returning his arm to his side. "I can't believe you're ruining this for us."

"You're mistaken, Troy. It's your stubbornness that's ruining this."

"Ha. Right. Because—" He began, but she didn't want to hear it.

"Let's make a bet. I wasn't even going to come on this assignment originally, right? Well… then since you're so clever and since you fit in so well here, why do you even need me?" He opened his mouth, but she wasn't done. "So how about you go get what you can from Jax, and I'll take Phoenix."

For an instant he looked surprised, but then he smiled. He had an intoxicating smile though and Sadie disliked the distraction in that moment.

"Now, *that* sounds interesting," he said.

"I bet I can get something out of the younger brother much faster than you can out of Jax," she said.

Troy didn't hesitate. "You're on," he said.

"Good. Now, if *I win,* I want…" she tapped her chin, "for you to apologize to me."

He laughed. Ignoring him, she asked. "What do you want if you win?" The mood shifted slightly as a pulse of desire emanated from him. The memory of the two of them bathing in the lake was also suddenly prominent as she looked at him. The suggestiveness of the question wasn't lost on either of them, and they both looked away simultaneously.

After a long silence, Troy cleared his throat and said, "I want you to promise never to feed from Hetia. At least never again."

Sadie was shocked. She hadn't seen that coming.

"What? Why?" she said.

"Because. She's a good person and I don't want to see her get hurt. Also, she's strong and we need her in this war. I don't want her swept up in your games."

Sadie thought for a minute. Clearly his request was unreasonably bigger than her own. Then again, maybe it wasn't. Not if Hetia herself wanted to stay away from Sadie indefinitely. But the memory of the way the woman had looked at her as they'd said goodbye burned hot in her thoughts. *No,* she couldn't take this bet.

Then again, Troy didn't have her unique advantage, what could he really do to get close to Jax anyway?

She looked up through her lashes to find him studying her intently. Snaking a hand up between them, she said, "Fine. I accept."

He clasped her forearm and they shook once. Troy smiled. "You're going to regret this, succubus. I don't think you know quite what I'm capable of."

All she could do was grin.

~

Sadly, Sadie's confidence plummeted over the next three days. It turned out that Phoenix was a complete recluse, and his birthday bash had been a rare venture into the world outside. He worked seven days a week. What exactly he *did* with his time was harder to uncover. Anything she was able to learn was from talking to people who didn't know him directly.

During the day, she would chat up strangers in the nearby bars, see what she could learn about the world she was now inhabiting. She got some interesting tidbits by feeding off a few. Jimmy also made some inquiries, but with far less success.

In the evening, Troy would take her to some function, a dinner at someone's house, a private party at a bar. He usually knew half the people there, or they knew him anyway. He was well known for this heroic act he'd performed last year, trying to save everyone from a burning building. It had sky-rocketed him into the public eye – at Siphon's encouragement, that was. Sadie was tired of hearing about it. It seemed so was Troy, and yet he always smiled politely at the attention. After all, it was Siphon who was sending him to most events, and it was clear Troy was meant to be building political allies, not enemies.

At night, Sadie would spend hours in Jimmy's arms. He was helping Patricia with various tasks connected to Amadi's network of spies, but when they saw each other at the end of each day, they wouldn't get around to talking much, so she barely knew what he was up to.

It was on the fourth night, while she was sitting in the corner of the bar on the ground floor of their hotel, that she finally had a small breakthrough. A lonely man with a foot fetish sat down at the bar next to her.

He didn't try to talk to her, but when she raised her hand to order a milkshake, he looked her way and she gave him an encouraging smile.

"You're that Troy Hyun's girl, right?" he asked.

"Well, not exactly." She swiveled a bit to face him. "But we're close, yes." Just then, Troy entered the far end of the room. Jax had an arm over his shoulder and they were both laughing. A gaggle of people followed them through the lobby and into the elevator. Troy glanced left and threw her wink just before they disappeared.

"Okaaaay..." Sadie continued as the man next to her gave her a worried look. "We're not *that* close." Then she had an idea. If the man knew Troy, perhaps he knew other people in the local sphere. "Actually, I have my sights set elsewhere. Phoenix Maddox?"

He grunted. "Is that a joke? What does a succubus want with the likes of him?"

She looked at her gloved hands, acknowledging his assumption with a small smile. "He seemed nice in the one conversation I had with him. Problem is, I haven't seen him since."

"Well no shit. Doesn't get out much." He looked her over, then scooted closer, gaining some confidence. He dropped his voice slightly and said conspiratorially. "But... he does have a favorite Friday night spot."

A genuine smile broke out over her face. "Can I get you another drink?"

He waved a hand. "I'm done for the night. But if you'll sit and talk with me a while, I'll tell you all about it."

That seemed like a fair exchange. She happily spent an hour entertaining the lonely man, and the information was just a welcome bonus. She returned to her room with a glimmer of hope she might still win this bet.

Unfortunately, Friday was another six days away, and Sadie was forced to watch Troy strutting around until then. He only took her to one event that next week as he was spending practically every night partying with Jax and friends. The true low point, though, came Thursday evening.

She was in the middle of a phone call with her mother. Rain was trickling outside the phone booth and she only had another minute on her quarter. Troy was passing by with his usual crowd and he ground to a halt. Waving the others onward, he came to glare at her through the glass. What now?

"Oh, honey. I'm so glad you're staying safe and that you're making friends," her mother was saying.

"Yeah. It's been great," Sadie told her, raising her hand at Troy in a question. "Well, I should go. Time's almost up, but I'll call again soon."

"Of course, sweetie. Tell Jimmy we miss him and we love you both."

"I will Mom." She gestured at Troy to go away. "I love you." She turned her back on the man glaring at her, wanting some privacy while her eyes teared up at the words.

"Bye, sugarbug," her mother said. She sounded as if she was working a little hard to be jovial, the same as Sadie.

"Bye." Sadie hung up the phone and tore out of the booth. "What the hell are you glaring at? Can't I talk to my own mother in peace now?"

He crossed his arms. "Your mother? Why isn't Jimmy down here on the call, if you're calling *home,* that is?"

"How is that any of your business?" she asked. The truth was Jimmy was sleeping off their afternoon exertions, and she hadn't had the heart to wake him, but she didn't feel like answering to Troy just then.

"Because. You're the one trying to convince me you're not a Siphon spy and yet here you are, hiding alone in the rain to sneak in a phone call."

"Well," she said, lifting her chin and striding back toward the hotel, "This was the only time Siphon was available to meet and I never miss our weekly chats."

He pulled up beside her. "I really hope I'm wrong about you, you know?" he said.

She just shot him an annoyed glare.

"But I am looking forward to winning this bet." He grinned.

Her steps faltered. "Did you get something?" she asked, unable to keep the worry and excitement from her voice.

"Not yet," he said.

"You know what I don't understand," she said, grinding to a halt.

He raised an eyebrow.

"How you can believe I'm working for the other side, and at the same time feel smug about beating me? I mean, it's either one or the other. After all, it's not a real bet if I already know the Coalition plan. It's like you're just trying to find any reason to dislike me." She couldn't keep the hurt from her voice.

He looked thoughtful for a minute. "You're right. Maybe I am being a *little* unfair."

She blinked, crossing her arms defensively as she glared at his perfectly sincere and stupid little face. They walked in silence to the elevator. After the doors had closed on them, Troy continued, "I don't dislike you, Sadie. I think you're... clever. And alluring. And—" He turned to look at her, but didn't elaborate further. The unspoken possibilities of what else he thought of her hung in the air.

She swallowed as he faced her in full and continued to speak with absolute sincerity, almost as if he was pleading with her. "I think you showed up in our lives with this too-good-to-be-true diary, and got yourself sent on this mission with hardly any training. And even so, everyone seems to think well of you. *Which*... is exactly why I can't trust you."

She hated that she could see his point of view. His portrait of her, delivered without snark, was a bitter kind of medicine, and her conviction to beat him came back ten-fold. She wanted to prove she'd been right, that going for Phoenix wasn't going off-plan, but simply following good instincts. She wanted to prove she could be useful, and that the information she would get would be real and would change things for the United, because she was truly on their side.

"Good night, Troy," she said, her shoulders slumping under the sudden heaviness of her current failure. Wanting just to be away from him, she sped out of the elevator to rush ahead to her room.

Once she was alone with her thoughts, she allowed herself to focus on the other things he'd said. She was shocked by the way he saw her. Not the bad stuff, but the... Clever? Alluring? Where did he get those things from? True... she was now many people's sexual fantasy, but anyone who wasn't immediately caught up in the fetishization of her species must see that she's a bit awkward – highly sexual yes, but not *alluring*. And as for clever... well, the jury was definitely still out on that one.

She chewed her lip as she thought over Troy's face as he looked at her, trying to see herself through his eyes. Back home she'd always been the quiet, weird girl, and it had been a rollercoaster figuring out who she was since her Becoming. In fact, after she'd left home, it had been hard to find any place she truly belonged. There had been the siren family in Seattle, but they only liked her because she'd helped their business. And now there was the United, but Sadie couldn't help but fear that many of them too only liked her because she could help the cause... or because she was a chance for a good time, but that didn't mean they thought much of *her*.

And here was Troy thinking she'd already proven herself – that she'd actually earned her place in all this.

Sadie did her best not to wake Jimmy as she snuck back into their room, but her efforts were unnecessary. She found him sitting on the ground, his back against the bed, staring off into space.

She dropped to the ground in front of him. "Hey. Are you okay?"

"Yeah," he said, taking the hand she'd place on his knee. "I couldn't sleep."

"Are you worried about the war?" she asked. They'd been avoiding talking about it.

Jimmy surprised her when he moved swiftly to take her face between his hands. He kissed her with a kind of immediacy which made her rethink her assumption about why he'd looked so distraught, but when she tried to move closer, he sat back.

She stayed where she was, sensing something else was up. "Jimmy?"

"You know I love you," he said. Sadie thought the words sounded like trouble. She went from being hungry to worried in a single heartbeat.

"Yeah." She put her hand back on his knee, but continued to give him space.

"But I... need something more than this. I need something to do," he said.

Her muscles relaxed. "Oh," she said, almost laughing with relief. "Well, if that's all that's wrong, that seems fixable." She smiled. "I mean... I can think of plenty of things for you to do right here."

He looked at her with an expression filled with a variety of emotions, but one of them she was able to pick out clearly, and it stood out like a punch in the face. Behind desire, love, and friendship, there was unhappiness. She dropped her flirtatious body language immediately and looked at her friend.

How had she been so blind? As she thought back, she realized he'd been unhappy for days. She hadn't seen him relaxed and himself at all. Though, she mostly just saw him aroused or sleeping.

But when they'd all had lunch together on Wednesday, Jimmy had been sullen. She'd brushed it off as tiredness, but she wondered now if she hadn't been lost in what she wanted to see.

Though she looked at him now, really looked at him. Of course Jimmy couldn't be confined to a hotel room, following her around just so they could stay together. He needed work, labor. He needed to use his hands, his body. Of course this wasn't going to work. She suddenly felt like the most selfish person in the world for only just now realizing it. What a terrible plan they'd made. She'd been thinking only of her own ambitions. Her own desires.

Sadie moved closer. Taking his hand, she caressed his callouses through her gloves. "I know." They looked up at each other. "What do we do?" she asked.

"I don't know, but I can't do this long-term. I'm going to talk to Patricia in the morning."

Sadie nodded. She raged with fear that something might separate them. What if they couldn't find something worthy of Jimmy here? What if he needed to leave? Would she go with him and give up on her own goals? Obviously, being apart wasn't an option. She forced a smile onto her face even though she knew he could see through it and said, "We'll figure it out."

She suddenly felt the urgency of his kiss earlier. She moved into his lap and he wrapped his arms around her. Loving Jimmy was the one thing in her life that had the power to truly terrify her. It seemed the more she felt for him, the more she had to lose. And every day, she only wanted him more.

With a renewed fervor, she pulled him close, and they didn't get to sleep until far past midnight.

~

THE FOLLOWING EVENING, she knocked on Patricia's door just before sunset. Troy answered. His hair was wet from a recent shower and he looked happy to see her. She was taken aback, but returned the smile with suspicion.

"Is she ready?" Sadie asked.

"In the bathroom now," he said, stepping aside enough to let her pass.

"I hear you have big plans tonight," he said. She detected an undertone of sarcasm and crossed her arms in a protective stance.

"I have a lead, yes," she said simply.

"Yes. A lead." He grinned. "Phoenix hangs out in a particular bar and may or may not be there tonight. Sounds promising." He finished drying his hair and threw the towel on the bed. "Well, I had a good night. Jax's party went straight through to sunrise. He invited me to a more private function tonight. He seems to think I'm a good addition to his lifestyle. Troy Hyun fits right in."

She rotated around him as he passed to grab his jacket from the little closet. "And talking about yourself in the third person," she said. "Always an appealing character trait. How could he not like you? Sadie Hall, for one, is quite impressed."

Somehow they'd ended up closer as they moved about the room, and she caught the sweet smell that was uniquely Troy. He simply shrugged at her mockery and swung on the jacket. Sadie wished she was at least as finely dressed as him, or had made more progress. As it was, she seemed to have lost the upper hand, and was now standing there wishing she had some reason to stay close by while simultaneously wanting to get the hell away from there.

Patricia rescued her. Her friend appeared in the room dressed as elegantly as ever with heels and a shawl to match. Sadie did her best to avoid heels and was a good foot shorter than Patricia without them. She was looking from Troy to Patricia, feeling like the ugly duckling when she noticed something that hit like a cool glass of water to the face.

There were small love lines passing between the two. Had those been there last time she'd seen them together? She couldn't remember, but she hadn't seen this coming. Her reaction surprised her too. After all, it was unfair to be remotely jealous. In fact, it was ridiculous.

Her shoulders felt suddenly heavy, and a desire to slump into a chair came over her. Sadie contemplated the idea that she might actually lose this bet, decided it was for the best since she wasn't worthy of Hetia anyway, and dropped her fake smile from her face.

"Ready?" she asked Patricia with a sigh.

The woman frowned at her in concern, but nodded and moved toward the door. Sadie followed without looking back. They didn't speak as they made their way a few blocks down to a small pub, but Patricia watched her out of the corner of her eye. The place was quiet and full of academics. As per her plan, Sadie led them to a booth which had its back to the one in which Phoenix liked to sit alone and read on Fridays.

"Sadie," Patricia began the instant they were seated, "I'm going to tell you the same thing I told Troy. I only condone this bet if it helps the mission. I don't know what's eating you, but if it's a problem, you need to tell me."

"No. I— I think the bet is good. We weren't working well together anyway. Competition is better. I just didn't think I might lose."

"Ahh. Is that all? Well, it's just a bet. Losing builds character. It'll be good for you," Patricia said, noticeably relaxing before taking a sip of her wine.

"I know, it's just... I don't want to lose to *Troy*, and I agreed that if I lost... I would stay away from Hetia."

Patricia coughed to clear her bad swallow. "What? Why would you bet that?"

"Because. I wasn't going to lose. And... Hetia's not interested anyway."

Patricia narrowed her eyes. "That's not what Troy says."

"What?" Sadie froze.

"Troy says Hetia's *very* interested. They bonded a lot this summer, and she let some things slip over some drinks one night. The night of the last barbecue at camp, he found out it was *you* she'd told him about. He's been anxious about it ever since."

"Really?" Sadie asked, chewing her lip on a smile.

"Really. She's completely smitten with you."

Sadie laughed.

"What?" Patricia asked.

"Nothing. It's just... no one says smitten anymore, not even my grandmother."

"Well, mine does. Also, I don't care," Patricia said before taking a small sip.

Sadie looked her friend over. That there. *That* was exactly why she liked her. Patricia really didn't care about fitting in. If only Sadie herself could be that way. No wonder Troy liked the woman.

"What else is on your mind?" Patricia asked, narrowing her eyes.

"Oh. No, it's nothing. I was just wondering at Troy's motivations. He seems to really dislike me. It doesn't seem fair."

Patricia dabbed at her mouth, looking uncharacteristically coy. "He'll come around on you. He's been through some strange things this past year. Just try not to take it too personally."

Sadie cleared her throat, feeling suddenly nervous. "And, umm, what about you and Troy? You two seem pretty... close."

Patricia dropped her gaze to her drink. "Yeah. Well, we have a bit of a history together. I was the one that was sent to recruit him to the United. That's where I was before Seattle."

"Right. Hetia had mentioned something about that." Sadie wanted to ask about her feelings toward Troy, not because she couldn't see them herself, but because she was curious how Patricia felt about them. But she chickened out and asked instead, "What ever happened to that VJ guy? The one from Seattle who was so into you?"

"Hmmph," Patricia said. "He's back south. Once he realized I was never going to sleep with him, all his interest in me disappeared overnight."

Sadie frowned and reached to take her hand. "I'm sorry."

"Yes, well. It's his loss. We were quite close for a minute there. I thought we'd be friends for life. If all he wanted was sex, then I think I'm better off without him."

"That's true. I'm sure there's someone better for you than that," Sadie said, though her conviction wavered confusingly at the thought that person might be Troy. Though, as she thought more about it, the idea of Patricia finding a connection with someone definitely made her happy. It was just hard to be disliked by Troy while also finding him attractive, and then to throw in love lines between him and her friend...

Patricia shifted to look at the booth behind them. "Now, what am I supposed to do again?"

It took Sadie a minute to realize she was referring to their mission there that night. "Just roll with me," she said, but the last word trailed off as she caught sight of Phoenix. She looked away just in time as he scanned the room. "He's here. We have to pretend like we don't notice him," Sadie said, turning her back to the rest of the room. "I need him to think he's eavesdropping."

Patricia nodded, following along smoothly, while Phoenix sat in the booth behind them without making a noise.

Sadie directed the conversation to food for a while and then when the timing no longer aligned with Phoenix's arrival, she said, "Honestly, I don't even know why I came here." She projected her voice in a clear lament. "I barely knew Troy when I followed him here, but he seemed so determined, a real serious player, but now he's fallen in with that Jax guy and I feel like I've backed the wrong horse entirely. Why do all the men here act like children?"

"Hmmm, maybe you should just go back home. Why did you want to come here anyway?" Patricia asked, also talking slightly louder than they had been before.

"I thought I would find some, I don't know, grown-ups here. A man that was going somewhere, you know?" she said, winking at

Patricia. They were both smiling slightly and Sadie only hoped it didn't come across in their voices.

"Didn't you say there was one... what was his name? You came home talking about him last week?" Patricia prodded.

"No. He's not interested. And I don't blame him. I must seem like a silly little girl to the likes of him. I blew my chances there. But it's for the best. After all, I'm not a silly girl and I don't need to waste my time with anyone who thinks otherwise."

"No," Patricia cut in. "You're the most driven person I know. We've thought it your whole life. Sadie is going somewhere, Mom used to say. You just need to find someone who can keep up with you."

"You're right. And that guy was too obsessed with his brother to be really focused on the future. If he'd actually been worth something, he would have seen me for what I am."

"True. Ahh, like your poor ex," Patricia said. Sadie smiled inside. It seemed natural that they would keep speaking. It would be suspicious if they just talked about Phoenix and then went silent, but she hadn't thought about what other topics they could touch on. Luckily, her friend was quite quick at this.

"Yes, Michael. So sad he passed so young," Sadie said. "We would have been great together."

"True, but I always thought you could do better. He seemed a bit *soft* for you. Not enough true ambition."

Sadie loved this about Patricia. She was clever, experienced, and quick to pick up what she was thinking. A few minutes passed with them bullshitting together before Phoenix snuck away. Sadie chanced a glance right and caught his new location from the corner of her vision. He'd settled across the room.

She lowered her voice to say, "I don't think that's a bad sign. I think he probably didn't want to get caught eavesdropping."

"I agree. Now what?" Patricia asked.

"Now nothing, I guess," she said. "I think we wait to see if it worked."

"Oh shit," Patricia said, her eyes wide on something across the room. Sadie began to look, but her friend pulled her back. "No, don't draw attention," she whispered. "I shouldn't have come out with you. My face is too well-known. I'm going to blow your cover."

Sadie had never heard Patricia panicked and the effect was catching. "You need to get out of here. I'll draw attention to the other entrance," Sadie said, still uncertain what had her spooked. But trusting that Patricia had a reason, she rose quickly and slunk away with as much subtlety as she could muster.

Sadie could see the newcomer from the corner of her vision and was pleased to see he was tracking her movement rather than looking at the table she'd just fled.

"Sadie?" the man said, just as she was looking around for a way to steal attention. She jumped in surprise at the familiar voice and tried to tone down her reaction as she turned to face him.

The familiar grin of Gabriel would have been a welcome sight under different circumstances. Even now, she couldn't help but be hit by the memory of primal emotion and raw desire which comprised the time in her life in which the man had been present. Which was perhaps why the smile that took over her expression felt natural as she redirected her path in his direction.

"Gabriel. What a... surprise," she laughed.

"I could say the same. You come to this coast and you don't call," he said, taking her face in his hands. He kissed her on the lips briefly and the familiar pulse of pleasure beat once through her.

"I was coming to see *you* actually, but I got distracted," she said as she watched Patricia disappear out the door over Gabriel's shoulder.

"The sensitive blonde with the soft neck or the unrequited shirtless one?" he asked.

Sadie laughed inside at him referring to Hetia as sensitive, but then again, what he could see was limited to their sexual interactions.

She was also nervous that he could see those two so clearly even when she'd had a hundred different sexual interactions that year and was currently lost in her feelings for Jimmy. Why would Hetia and Troy stand out at all?

It occurred to her then how dangerous this situation was as she snuck a glance over Gabriel's shoulder to the new corner booth containing Phoenix. Had he seen them kiss? Did he know Gabriel?

Sadie paused to look over her succubus guide. He was dressed in his usual blue jeans and leather vest, hung open. He looked like walking sex, but far too casual to be considered good company for the woman trying to catch the attention of uptight Phoenix.

Recovering as best she could, she laughed out loud at his earlier question. "The second one, actually, but it's a long story." She pulled back a step. "I'm just on my way to meet up with someone, can we catch up later? Are you staying nearby?"

"Yeah, room six at the Old Hag. Here for a few weeks," he said.

She wondered how familiar he was with this place, and more importantly, with the people in it. "Have you been in here before? I was headed for the bathroom," she said.

"There." He nodded over her shoulder with his hands in his pockets. When she looked back at him, he was looking her up and down.

"You look good. Grown up a lot," he said, and Sadie thought she heard a hint of pride. "Don't be a stranger," he added.

She smiled, looking him up and down in turn as she backed away. "I won't. I promise."

It wasn't until she'd closed the bathroom door that she let herself feel the wave of panic. What now? Why had she said she was there to meet someone? The only other person she could approach out there was Phoenix, and she was hoping to wait for him to make that move. And what if Gabriel was sitting nearby and could hear them? Everything she said would have to be made to fit both audiences. This was a disaster.

She couldn't stay locked away forever though, so deciding to feel out the situation as she went, Sadie opened the door and re-emerged into the softly lit bar. There were only a dozen people in the place, most of them sitting alone, drinking, or reading the paper in silence. Two men, however, were sitting together. Two men, who seemed accidently determined to make her night as impossibly stressful as it could be.

Chapter 13

A surprise guest

Sadie smiled at Gabriel and Phoenix as she walked toward them. They'd both looked around at her the instant she'd emerged, as if they'd been waiting for her return. Her feet carried her slowly closer as she screamed inside.

At least she was spared having to speak first.

"Ms. Hall." Phoenix nodded at her. He had on a strange expression, which she struggled to read. "Mr. Demesko says he was there at your Becoming. He was just telling me a little about the ceremony."

Mr. Demesko? Remarkable. Gabriel had never given her his last name. She knew so little about the man who had helped her turn.

Worried at what else they might have discussed, she could only play along as innocently as possible. "Yes," she said. "He was very helpful."

Her arms felt so awkward hanging at her sides. Why could she not remember where she normally put her hands? The men stared at her, looking expectant. She smiled, frozen there.

"Uhh, you were here to meet someone?" Gabriel asked.

"Oh! Yes. Well sort of. I actually came with a friend and she had to leave, but then I saw Phoenix here and, uhh, I just wanted to come over and apologize for the other night. I didn't mean to send such mixed messaging."

Phoenix blinked back at her, cocking his head as he looked her up and down. She was clearly nervous, but perhaps that played in her favor.

"No. It's me who should apologize. I was very tense that night. I shouldn't have taken it out on you," he said.

After another pregnant pause, Gabriel added, "Join us?" He looked to Phoenix for consent and the man nodded.

Sadie adjusted her dress and took the seat across from Gabriel and next to Phoenix. Luckily neither of the men were excitement feeders, or they would have been concerned at the state of her hysteria.

Desperate to get the lay of the land, Sadie asked, "So how do you two know each other?"

Phoenix responded as Gabriel waved to the bartender and signed for two more. "Gabriel does work for the family now and again. He's graciously agreed to help my aunt with a little project."

"Your aunt Maddox, the president of the new feeder government?" Sadie asked.

"Yes. Gabriel has been a trusted support to our family."

Sade registered this with a wave of nausea. Gabriel was with the Coalition. He did work for the president of the feeder government. Maybe he was even in their inner circle.

"But what about you, Sadie? What adventures have you had since we last saw each other?" Gabriel asked.

Sadie flinched inwardly, but grinned at Gabriel in a suggestive way, "Oh, I'm sure you can guess most of it."

She glanced at Phoenix, worried this tone would put him off, but she found him looking at her with some interest. Not even at the party had he really assessed her the way he was then. Perhaps her staged conversation earlier had worked?

"Congressman Siphon told me he'd invited you tomorrow night," Phoenix said.

"Yeah." She spoke hesitantly, uncertain of the intent behind the comment.

"A very driven man, the congressman. He would be a good mentor for you, I think."

Sadie beamed. "You think he'd show that much interest in me? That's very flattering, Phoenix."

"Yes. It seems I've underestimated you. You caught the eye of the congressman, and now it seems you know our friend here as well," he said.

"I would keep an eye on this one. She was a quick study in the few weeks I spent with her," Gabriel said with genuine warmth in his tone. This time Sadie beamed for real. She hadn't realized that was how Gabriel saw her.

Following this surprise, a red thread of light began to pulse from Phoenix to her, much stronger than the night they'd met. Sadie was immediately relieved. He was finally genuinely interested. She was probably about to blow her cover, lost in a web of lies she couldn't untangle, but in that brief instant she felt as if she'd succeeded.

Thanks, Gabriel. As dangerous as his presence was for her, it seemed his comment had given her a second chance with Phoenix. And despite her fear, she was mildly comforted by the presence of her mentor. As if he were somehow there to take care of her.

Sadie couldn't help but relax, despite her better judgment. She sat back as the waiter placed a glass in front of her and changed out the one in front of Gabriel. "Orange juice?" she asked, peering into their cups.

"Gabriel doesn't drink," Phoenix chimed in. "I can order you some wine if you'd like though." He looked a question at her as he made to raise a hand.

Sadie pulled the hand down with her fingers around his wrist. "I'm fine," she said, leaving her hand where it lay. "Thanks though."

She ran her thumb over the fine embroidery of the cuff and they both looked down at the point of contact. "This is beautiful. You wore something similar the other night," she said.

Phoenix nodded. "My family are all muses. We feed off creative inspiration, and thus make a point of hiring the best artists for every facet of life."

"I bet it would be interesting to walk a day in your world," she said, not having to feign sincerity.

"I could say the same of you," he said. "I had never considered how similar succubi and muses were until hearing a little of your Becoming. But I myself am familiar with being at the center of the frenzy of a particular emotion. I grew up playing that role. Like most feeders, that part of me developed in childhood. It must have been strange being practically human for so long. Mia Siphon, the congressman's daughter, was terribly jealous of me back when we were still friends. Was it the same for you?"

Sadie wanted to steer away from talking about her own past, but she figured she had to give something to get something.

"Actually, I grew up mostly around humans. It was pretty lonely," she said.

She was happy to see a hint of pity under Phoenix's expression, especially when it was followed by an increased interest in her. She knew he related to feeling like the outcast, and this was a good opportunity to bond over that.

"My parents too were human," she added. Sadie realized immediately that this was a mistake. Phoenix sat up straighter and adjusted his sleeves which broke the contact between them.

"So, you must have thought you yourself were human then," he said.

"Well," she began, feeling a little panic again, but then at an almost imperceptible head shake from Gabriel, she realized how to respond. "Actually, we knew it was in our blood and I had always felt I was different somehow. It was no surprise to me when it came."

"Hmmm," he nodded, lost in thought for a minute. "That must have been hard." Then he smiled warmly at her. "It's lucky you found us then," he said and brushed a strand of hair behind her ear. The gesture was so sudden and unexpected it took Sadie a moment to catch up, but when his bare fingers briefly made contact with her, she became sharply aware of his body, at the pulse of pleasure. Before he broke away, she could feel he'd grown hard under the table, and he bit his lip as he looked at her.

Gabriel leaned in. "Perhaps you want to show Sadie your current projects." He added to Sadie, "His condo is just across the street."

Phoenix took a slow, deep breath, not looking at her before becoming suddenly decisive. He gave a single nod and signaled for the check. It was the same fast switch she'd seen in him at the party. It seemed to come from nowhere.

It took ten minutes to go from sitting at the table discussing their childhoods to Phoenix holding open his front door for her and Gabriel. From what she could see of his sexual history, she doubted he would have been so bold if she were not a succubus. What she couldn't tell was what was primarily driving him. He was a difficult man to follow. Was it lust? Curiosity? General interest? Perhaps a little of each.

At least she could feel the waves of desire increase the instant he closed the door. It was clear what he was hoping was going to happen. As he led the way into the living room, Gabriel gave her a small grin, and an image of her sandwiched between the two of them.

It seemed to be biologically impossible for her to be shy about such things now, but somehow Gabriel made her blood boil. She was surprised at her reaction and jerked her gaze away from him to focus on her target.

Phoenix turned on the lights and Sadie's lips parted at the hectic mess of a living space. She laughed as she looked around the condo at the various projects. She wouldn't have expected the man to be so unorganized, but she had no doubt that he was definitely a creativity feeder.

"This is incredible," she smiled. A detailed planetary system hung in the middle of the living room. One table was covered in a miniature model of the city. Next to it was a model of some other city. Every surface was covered in some half-finished project.

She went over to the table and looked from the intricate models up to their creator. "I'm surprised." She grinned. "I would have pegged you as more orderly than this."

"It helps me think. Calms my mind." Then his voice took on a new edge of excitement. "This one took me two years." He indicated the miniature city.

"And where is this one?" she asked, pointing to the unknown city.

"Right here. It's the future. It's what this place could be." He gestured to a stack of papers next to it. "These are all the changes that would need to be approved."

"Well," she stroked the side of the model of the building they were currently in, "I'm certainly impressed."

It was lucky she didn't have to fake any of this. It was also fortunate that admiring his work was the thing which seemed to please him the most. Before she could come around to join him, however, Phoenix had stepped in and pressed her against the table.

"Do you really like it?" he asked, his mouth hovering a few inches from hers.

"I do," she said, lifting her chin in a clear invitation. Phoenix licked his lips as he looked over her face. Just like the other fast actions she'd witnessed from him, there was no gap in time between him deciding to kiss her and actually leaning in.

Sadie pressed into him as he lightly caressed her lips. Unlike at the party, she didn't hold back. She wanted him to feel what it could be like with her, and she hit him with a wave of pleasure the instant he made contact.

But a few seconds later he pulled back. She was surprised when he broke away and took a full step backward. She looked at the man in front of her and found it was entirely easy to forget why she was there. This wasn't the enemy. This was a creative, ambitious young man who wanted her.

She knew Gabriel could see how they were each feeling in that moment and she was grateful for her ability to feel something for this man. As the other succubus stepped into her view, however, she could see he had his own intentions.

Gabriel was picturing her naked. He didn't need to say or do anything more to make his desires clear. As she looked from his heated expression to the quite visible erection, she found herself recalling what he'd looked like naked. That time in her life had been filled with so many new emotions and sensations that it felt like recalling a dream.

The instantaneous communication must have passed in an instant from Phoenix's perspective, but to her an entire conversation was flying by.

Phoenix turned to the other man. "How well do you know this woman, Gabriel?"

"She was living a harmless life when I found her and invited her to come back east with me." He scooped her hair behind her ear. "I'd vouch for her."

A wave of guilt struck her, and for a moment she wanted to confess everything. Then she was hit with a clear image of Phoenix kissing her and Gabriel made space expectantly. But this time, the man didn't act.

Gabriel said to him. "What is creativity, but taking risks? Didn't you say that to me once? It's that moment when an idea pops into your head and you pursue it before you have time to doubt it. It's what I've always liked about your family."

"I'm just the muse," Phoenix said, stepping back. "I prefer inspiring that impulse in others."

Gabriel smiled. "I don't think I need additional inspiration, and you can't feed off me anyway." He pulled Sadie away from the table. "None of us can," he added, "but tell me, what inspires you?"

Phoenix sat on the edge of a half-empty table. "I've never seen two succubi together. I bet it's interesting."

Gabriel wrapped his arms around Sadie's waist from behind, keeping away from her skin, and whispered in her ear, "He wants to watch."

Sadie relaxed back into him and emitted a small sigh of pleasure. This hadn't been at all how she had pictured seducing Phoenix, but she liked this new trajectory much more than her all-too-tidy earlier plan.

At least they weren't talking about the past anymore. The moment in which Gabriel somehow blew her cover had been postponed, and she was on much more confident footing in this new conversation.

Sadie removed the glove on her right hand and ran it over Gabriel's grip on her waist. She liked the feel of his forearm and took a minute to explore it with her fingers as they adjusted to the skin contact.

It was a very different experience being with someone she couldn't feed from. It left her feeling hungrier than before, but it was a fair trade-off if that person was Gabriel. She got to feel what others felt when she touched them, what Jimmy felt.

Her heart pulsed and her skin heated. Gabriel let out one of his deep-throated groans that she had come to think of as the perfect sound of male pleasure. He wrapped his arms tight around her as he kissed behind her ear.

Heat traveled between her legs and her skin puckered into goosebumps. She was already anticipating what was going to happen. Only so much had changed since the last time she had been with Gabriel. This moment felt sharper, more real than the ones in her memory.

He unzipped her dress and pulled it free from her shoulders while Sadie enjoyed the concentration of Phoenix in front of her. The man was entirely focused on her now, and the unbroken attention was intoxicating.

Gabriel slid her dress over her hips and unhooked her bra. Phoenix looked her over with a heavy gaze, but made no move to undo his own clothes. Sadie became concerned that he would only want to watch. Her plan was all for nothing if she couldn't actually touch him. She tried to take the tiniest step forward, but Gabriel scooped an arm around her and pulled her back against him.

She had no resistance as he ran a finger along the edge of her panties. She'd try again later. Right now, she wanted only for the succubus to keep touching her. The hand that wasn't holding her slid along the grove of her ass, pushing off the remaining article of clothing.

Sadie made to kick off her boots, but Gabriel whispered in her ear, "Leave them."

She was so used to being in control, she felt anxious letting him do all the work. She turned to kiss him, but he bent her shoulders forward a few inches and pulled her hips up against him. He stayed pressed against the groove of her ass as they listened to him unbuckle his belt. The room was still, quiet except for the heavy breathing coming from all three of them.

When he was free, he ran the head of his cock from her wet opening to her clit and back. They were equally slick and the direct contact made them both shudder. He slid inside her easily, moving back and forth until everything was wet before gripping her hips in both hands and burying himself entirely. Gabriel accompanied the first full thrust with an intentional pulse of pleasure. Her body expanded easily to accommodate him, but the sensation nearly sent her to her knees.

When he did it again, she thought he was going to make her climax right then.

"Gabriel," she said, uncertain of if she meant it as a plea or an affirmation.

He wrapped an arm under her breasts and pulled her back upright – or as upright as he could get her with her ass arched in the air. She was grateful for the additional support, and she tried not to collapse completely into his arms as he continued to accompany each drive of his hips with a sensation so intense her whole body shook with it.

Phoenix's jaw was soft and open, like he was under a spell. He held himself through his pants, but was otherwise still.

Sadie wanted Gabriel to touch her. She was about to beg for it when he moved his hand between her legs. Her head fell back against his chest and she kept her eyes on Phoenix as she swore.

"Yes. Fuck yes," she said. Phoenix let out an audible groan at this.

She began to writhe in Gabriel's grip, and every time she arched her back into him, he pushed in to fill her. Sadie began trembling uncontrollably as her body cried out for release. She was so caught up in her own pleasure that she only half-noticed that she was enacting her own wishes on Gabriel. She realized she was about to make him climax right as he said, "Stop." It sounded like he was speaking through gritted teeth. "Don't do that," he added.

She let out a gasp that sounded vaguely likely compliance, but found it hard to obey.

He groaned and it turned into a growl. "Control," he said, a little unsteady.

"I'm trying," she gasped, but it felt like a beast that wanted out of a cage and the bars were disintegrating.

He pulled his hand away from her, but it was too late. They were both lost in it. She clenched around him as he pulsed in her. Having given up on trying to hold back he hit her with everything he had. Not wanting to be outdone she returned the favor and she came with the sound of him growling in her ear.

Their cries turned slowly to groans and then to heavy breathing. Gabriel kissed behind her ear as he ran a hand up to cup her breast. "Damn, you've gotten strong," he said. She had never heard him sound remotely shaken before, and it filled her with a strange kind of pride.

She opened her eyes to find Phoenix unzipping his pants. Through her euphoria, Sadie was vaguely aware of why she had come there. She was worried he was just going to touch himself, and since she could see he was about to pop, she imagined that would be over quickly. Gathering herself, she projected a strong image of wanting to move closer to the man.

"Don't worry," Gabriel said, biting her ear. "We're far from done."

Then before she could fret a second longer, he lifted her by the waist and stepped toward the bed without removing himself from her. Their juices flowed down her leg as he deposited her a few feet from the table on which Phoenix was perched.

Gabriel pushed her torso down with one hand and held her hips to him with the other. His right foot hooked inside hers, and she felt him slide her legs wider.

He had deposited her face directly above the hard length of the other man, and it glistened with precum. Sadie looked up into Phoenix's flushed face before pushing him to his back. "Prop your head up," she said. "I want you to watch."

Phoenix shoved a book under his head.

"Keep your hands there," she said. "I don't want you to touch me. You're just going to lay there, and I'm going to do to you what you just watched Gabriel do to me."

Phoenix let out a little hungry groan, despite the fact she hadn't yet made skin contact.

She felt Gabriel stand upright and begin to move in her. His hands on her hips were firm, and the motion was controlled enough that her body jostled only slightly with each thrust.

Sadie looked up at Phoenix as she lapped up the wet tip in front of her. He clenched his jaw on a heavy groan the instant her tongue made contact. Slowly, she took him in her mouth, letting him take in each sensation.

She matched her rhythm to Gabriel's so she could enjoy the feeling of Phoenix in her mouth right as Gabriel filled her. She hadn't thought it could be so pleasurable to do this when she wasn't feeding. As terrifying as it had been to have her succubus mentor show up, in this moment, not a cell in her body was protesting.

She must have been projecting her satisfaction, because Gabriel responded as if she'd spoken aloud. He pumped into her hard, holding her in place with one hand on her hip, and caressed her ass with the other. His touch was always so sure. He moved with the confidence of experience, and as his hand slid along her backside and down her thigh he projected to her exactly how he felt about touching her, and Sadie felt sculpted from perfection as he studied her.

"This time, I'm going to draw it out," Gabriel said. "And I don't want you to send it back to me. You have another object of desire right in front of you."

She moaned in agreement, and Phoenix inhaled sharply as she increased the pace.

"That's good. Take out your feelings right there," Gabriel continued. "And just take what I give you as it comes."

Sadie melted at the sound of those words. She felt wide open and filled up all at the same time. She stopped arching back against him and just let the other succubus drive. His thrusts became rough and deep, but remained perfectly controlled, while she worked her hand and mouth in tandem over Phoenix. Her movements slowly lost pace with the timed control of Gabriel's, but the man in her mouth didn't seem to notice.

Phoenix was now gripping the edge of the table so hard his hands had gone white. She looked from them up to his contorted expression. This was the moment. He was going to climax, and she needed to follow him down that path. Follow him to that place inside where she could access past desires.

Before she could gather her thoughts though, she realized she was on the edge of her own orgasm. She began to panic. Gabriel had said he was going to draw this out. She wouldn't be able to think. The timing was all wrong. She needed to stop it, to change the circumstances.

But it was too late. Whatever her rational mind wanted, her body was taking precedent now. Gabriel sent the first wave through her with such slow control, she marveled at it even as her mind went blank. She convulsed in several sharp motions right as Phoenix did the same.

Through the blur of sensation, she latched onto three little words. *Trust your instincts.*

Sadie gave up trying to focus. She took in the feel of Gabriel filling her and the waves of climax crashing into her and carried Phoenix along in the same pattern. No fluid yet filled her mouth as the man pulsed in an elongated climax that perfectly matched her own.

She wanted more. He wanted more. More. Sadie heard Gabriel groan at her pleasure. And then she was falling. Falling into a blur of images that had nothing to do with sex.

Phoenix had had an angry, frustrated upbringing, and Sadie sunk into it with a shock. He wanted his brother to get down off the table. Everyone was looking. It was embarrassing. He tugged at his shirt, but the older man just pulled him up with him. No! He wouldn't go.

Sadie barely caught sight of the memory before it shifted. Unlike in the times she'd done this in the past, she found herself entirely aware of what was happening. She knew she was distinct from the person whose memories she was traveling. Though someone else seemed to be steering the ship.

She was in a classroom. A girl was sitting to her right. He'd just given the girl the note. He wanted her to smile at him, to say yes. He was so afraid. He couldn't look away from her though. She swallowed and looked down. Shit, that wasn't a good sign.

Sadie writhed in the shared body, trying to move on.

As waves of scenes of desire flitted through her mind she tried to focus in, to latch on. Parents. Things to do with parents.

She was in a kitchen, looking up at the countertop next to her. He wanted a cookie. That was all. If only the tall woman would give him another one. It would be the best thing that had ever happened. Perhaps if he cried she would figure it out?

No. Move on. She was running out of time.

Not knowing any specific details about what she was looking for made this difficult, but for some reason she couldn't name, she felt she should focus on the key pieces of Phoenix's personality. He was driven. Wanted to be held out as distinct from his brother. Wanted to carry on the family reputation with honor. These were related to the memory she sought. She knew it without being able to draw out any specific information.

Stumbling half-blind, she clawed her way into a specific room. It was a room of pride. The instant she was in it she felt that this was the key moment in her life. Her, or actually his, time had finally come. He felt warm and excited. He'd never wanted anything as much as he wanted this.

His father walked into the room.

"Sorry to keep you waiting. My two o'clock went long. Come in," the man said.

Phoenix nodded to his father's secretary and followed his senior into the large office.

Sadie was impatient. She sped through the conversation as if on fast forward.

She got caught on a moment in which the old man put a hand on his shoulder. "Well, I'm certainly glad to hear it. I'm very proud of you." Phoenix stood up straighter.

Sadie felt the familiar pull which indicated the memory dive was ending.

No. Later. Keep moving. There's something here. She had to find it.

"Do you understand what I'm telling you?" the man asked. They were by the fireplace now.

"Yes. Uhh, I think so," Phoenix said.

Sadie could hear the sound of Gabriel as a slight awareness of her own body returned.

His father smiled. "No. You don't. But that's okay. This is yours now. Read it and reread it. It's your legacy." He put both hands around his son's. "I'm trusting you with this. Not your brother. *You* will carry this on."

Phoenix nodded, keeping his eyes just wide enough that they wouldn't appear moist.

"We'll talk more next week," his father said.

As they left the office he told the woman outside, "Daisy, my son will need another appointment with me next Tuesday. Same time."

No. There was something she'd missed. She needed to go back. The pull was stronger now and she was holding on by a thread, but she needed to know. What had the man given his son?

She searched backward and caught a glimpse of the father extracting papers from a safe. Phoenix put them in his school brief-case. This wasn't the memory she needed. Where were the papers now?

The sweet taste of Phoenix in her mouth hit her senses and she had to fight away the pull to the present.

Where were the papers?

Phoenix was back home. She recognized the condo. It was the same one she was in now. The one in which she was convulsing as Gabriel finished her.

She was opening the closet next to the bathroom and looking at a safe.

Sadie heard Gabriel groan loud and clear. She was aware it was the same groan he'd started as she'd began the memory dive. They were in the same position. Her mouth was sliding up Phoenix as they moaned loudly in tandem.

Five. Two. Eight. He punched the buttons on the safe.

Her body was in ecstasy, and she clenched around Gabriel as everything sped up, reality sinking in hard.

There were two more numbers. She could feel it. She needed to see it one more time. Type it again.

Five. Two. Eight.

Gabriel hit her one last time with a thrust accompanied by pleasure that filled all her senses. She pulled her mouth off Phoenix to cry out. Her body shook several times uncontrollably before she began to come down.

She became aware of Phoenix. He was still coming. She still had time.

"Ahhh... god," he cried as he tried to push his hips up into her. His feet were hanging over the table and he had no traction to move more than an inch or two, but she matched his hungry motion by sliding her mouth over him one more time.

Sadie dropped immediately into the memory, as if she'd kept one hand in it.

Phoenix pulsed and convulsed in a spastic motion in her mouth.

He was raising his hand to type the numbers.

Fluid hit the back of her throat.

Five. Two. Eight. One.

His hips thrust once more into her and collapsed.

Seven.

The number was seven.

She swallowed and stood up, panting as if she'd run a race. Phoenix watched her like she was divinity. His body was tense as a rock and the wet shaft, hard and red, stayed pointed to the sky.

Gabriel was still inside her, moving slowly now, and massaging her breasts. She became aware then of the state of her own body. She was trembling from head to toe and her muscles felt like pudding.

"My turn," Gabriel said into her ear before nibbling on her neck. An aftershock hit her and she rocked spastically back into him.

"I want to see you," she said over her shoulder, her mind repeating the five numbers even as her desire for Gabriel captured her attention.

Before she could wonder if he'd comply, he had turned her and lifted her onto the table in between Phoenix's legs. Gabriel was back inside her in a heartbeat.

She realized then that she hadn't kissed either of these men that night, and in this moment with her body feeling so good, she desperately wanted to kiss Gabriel.

Sadie wrapped her arms around his shoulders and moved in. He pulled her calves up so that her heels kissed her upper thighs and wrapped each arm around one of her bent legs. Then he lifted slightly so he could hold her up by her ass. The position made it difficult for her to sit upright, and she found herself leaning back on her elbows.

"You can watch," he said and she got the message loud and clear that he didn't want to kiss her just then. Sadie wasn't sure why. He'd never had that feeling in the past. But she liked the show enough to move on quickly from any deep thought on the matter.

Gabriel closed his eyes and let his head fall back an inch. He projected every sexual thought and feeling he'd had about her that night loud and clear as he thrust very slowly into her. They drove together, with her taking him a little higher every time he wordlessly asked for it.

Sadie didn't care that he was clothed. She wanted to watch his face and his memories. For some reason, she couldn't see any of his usual sexual history. All she saw was her. He was giving her his undivided desire.

Except for his clenched jaw, his expression remained serene right up until the end. Despite the fact the intensity of the waves that crashed through him paralleled the ones he'd sent through her earlier, he stayed in perfect control of his movements. His grip on her remained firm, but not bruising, and he moved slowly and steadily as he filled her with fluid for the second time that night.

After his final groan, Gabriel opened his eyes and they stared at each other only briefly before he pulled out in a rush. He held himself as he reached in his pocket and extracted a soft rag, cleaned them both up, and threw the towel on the floor.

Sadie looked over her shoulder to find Phoenix fast asleep.

"They never last long after," he said, following her gaze.

"No." She smiled. "I think we wore him out."

Gabriel stepped between her thighs again, but avoided skin contact. "This was a nice surprise. Seeing you here," he said, keeping his voice low. "A very," he grinned, "productive evening."

"I'd say," she said, shaking her head. "I think I learned a lot tonight." She laughed inside at the truth in those words.

He sighed and relaxed a few inches forward, looking content. She mirrored the emotion. He nudged her nose with his in a gesture of affection as he said, "Too bad you didn't come to find me, but I was on my way here anyway. It all worked out."

She gave out a little contented sigh of her own.

"What did you say changed your mind?" he asked, sounding only mildly curious.

"Oh, you know. I met a boy. He seemed interesting," she said.

He smiled. "Yeah, I know how that goes. This is the one you haven't slept with? The one half-naked in the water?"

"Yes," she said, this time with a twinge of worry.

"He wasn't so interesting then," Gabriel said, stroking her hair. "Or is he still around?"

"Yeah, he is. We're still testing out the waters. His name is Troy, he's actually good friends with Siphon. He brought me to a party, which is where I met Phoenix," Sadie said sleepily, leaning her head into Gabriel's touch.

"Troy. I've heard Siphon say that name." Gabriel kissed her nose. "Your feelings for him are strong, much more than for Phoenix. What brought you looking for this man tonight?"

Sadie froze. A slight suspicion crept over her and a chill ran down her back. She recovered quickly, sighed, and kissed Gabriel's cheek, but she hoped he couldn't hear the sudden pounding of her heart.

Was this an interrogation? Was Gabriel here to find out about her? Had someone sent him to do this?

She opened her eyes to find him watching her. Sadie tried to relax her expression. Did she see a hint of concern in his eyes? He scooped her up and kissed her then. It was so tender and firm that she didn't have to fake the sound of contentment that escaped her. Putting away her heavy thoughts, she focused only on the emotion of being here in Gabriel's arms.

"It's complicated," she said when they broke away. "Maybe I was trying to make Troy jealous. He's holding back with me and I don't understand why. Phoenix seemed like a nice guy," she shrugged, half-closing her eyes with what was now entirely feigned drowsiness. "I just want to fit in here. I hope I can do that at Troy's side, but I'm keeping my options open."

Gabriel looked her over for a long time. She pretended not to notice and he punctuated his observation with kisses to her nose and cheek, but she felt as if she were on trial, awaiting the final judgment. She yawned, and ran her hands up and down his arms, keeping her gaze soft on his chest.

Finally, he pulled away slightly. She dared to look directly into his eyes and was relieved at what she saw there. Or more at what she didn't see – the look of shrewd assessment was gone. Gabriel didn't really consider her a friend, but in that moment a line of green light appeared from him to her. "I hope you can find a home here, too." He cupped the side of her head. "Sadie Hall."

He kissed her hand and retreated backward in a seductive swagger, returning to his usual playful demeanor. "Should I walk you home, miss?" he asked, as if he was a gentleman who had just taken her for a nightly stroll.

She laughed. "No, I think I'll sleep here a bit and find my own way."

"Well then, I'll see you around." He winked before turning to the door.

Just before he dropped out of sight, he paused and turned back. He froze there for several breaths as she became increasingly worried about what he was about to say.

"My parents were also human. It's not something I like to share around in this company though. Watch yourself."

And with that, the man who had shaken up her night in every possible way retreated out the front door, leaving her trembling, elated, and a little bit terrified.

Chapter 14

A hard night's work

The instant the door was closed, Sadie glanced behind her. Phoenix's chest rose and fell, accompanied by a light snore. She hopped down. Without wasting even a second to look over her shoulder, she beelined for the hallway. The safe was next to the bathroom off the main bedroom. If he woke up and found her, it would be very strange that she had passed up the restroom in the hallway to go to his room. Her best shot was to do this quickly.

Not daring to turn on any lights, she felt her way to the end of the hall. The door creaked slightly as she pushed it open, so she did her best to squeeze through the tiny gap. She nearly swore as she tripped over something on the floor.

Sadie reached the safe by feel, and felt out the buttons with her eyes closed for concentration. She typed the numbers carefully. At the last minute she realized it might make a sound when it opened and she had a vision of herself running down the street as Phoenix chased her.

Blessedly, it popped open with only a tiny click. By feel, she sussed out the contents: the binder and a stack of what felt like cash. Sadie memorized their position before extracting the papers. This plan was risky, and would only work if she were able to return the binder before morning, or before Phoenix noticed it was gone. But the opportunity was too good to let pass.

Her heart was beating out of her chest by the time she peered around the corner of the hallway at the sleeping man on the living room table. She had been half-sure he wouldn't be there, but again, her luck held. Sadie didn't take her eyes off him as she inched sideways to the front door.

He looked so peaceful there. She felt almost sorry for him and the world he lived in. Having caught glimpses of his memories, she thought he had a sad life here. There was no one he really loved. Not even the father he so wanted to impress. Guilt hit her at being the woman who'd betrayed him. At least she could hope he would never find out.

It wasn't until she'd stepped out onto the street that Sadie began to relax. But when she did, she looked down at the papers in her hand and almost jumped with excitement. Despite everything, this night had been a thrill. She didn't think she'd ever felt more alive as she proudly walked away with her conquest.

She hadn't stepped more than ten feet, however, when someone pulled her suddenly into the shadows. She would've screamed if not for the hand over her mouth. The hand was gloved and for a moment she thought it was Gabriel, but the scent of Patricia's perfume penetrated her panic. Her eyes adjusted and her friend's face swam into view.

"You were in there forever. I was about to send in reinforcements," Patricia said.

It hadn't been that long... had it? Sadie figured there were parts in the middle there where she'd been enjoying herself a little too much to keep proper track of time. "Sorry," she told Patricia. "Have you — man, have you been out here this whole time? Wait, what reinforcements? You have *reinforcements*?" Sadie said.

"If needed, yes. Are you okay?" Patricia asked.

"Yeah. Great." Sadie smiled.

"Good. You can tell me about it inside. I saw that succubus head that way. Which means we'll be taking the long way home." Patricia took her hand and led her between some trees. Sadie had done her part. The consequences of that night were out of her hands now. She tried to calm her trembling as she let herself be led through the dark, clutching the stolen papers to her body as if they were made of gold.

~

TROY WAS ELATED. He had won the bet, and done it in only seven days. He was sure this was his best work. All of his instincts had been right at every turn. He couldn't wait to tell Sadie.

He pushed open the door to the room he shared with Patricia and was surprised to find it empty. What time was it? Surely it was past midnight, and yet the women were still out?

A small light emanated from under the door to Sadie and Jimmy's room. Troy pressed his ear against it, but couldn't hear anything. He hesitated briefly, but concern took over and he pushed open the door to see if anyone could tell him something.

Jimmy was standing at the window with his back to the room. He looked around hopefully at Troy's entrance.

"Sorry. It's just me," Troy said, closing the gap to join him.

Jimmy nodded in acknowledgement and went back to looking out the window. Troy could tell the man didn't particularly like him, but that couldn't be helped so long as the succubus sat as a point of contention between them.

"Patricia's not back either," Troy said.

"They're probably fine," Jimmy told him.

"You're not worried?" Troy crossed his arms.

"No. They're very capable. And Sadie has stayed out all night in the past. Perhaps that was what this task called for," Jimmy said.

Troy was surprised at this. How did the man stand it?

"Patricia told me you were feeling restless here. Looking for something more to do."

Jimmy shuffled his feet in reply. Troy was hoping he could get the man to open up to him a little – it might help build some trust. And really, despite the intentions of the succubus, he really believed Jimmy was an innocent in all this.

"I understand," Troy continued. "I wouldn't be able to sit by feeling idle either. And you seem like a man that likes to work."

Jimmy nodded. "I always have. My whole life I've gotten up early, worked hard all day, looking forward to seeing Sadie." Troy stayed silent, hoping he would continue if he didn't interrupt. After a while, Jimmy added, "I miss that life. I miss it so much it hurts. Like there's a hole inside me which can't be filled up with anything else. I wish I could just take her back there."

For an instant, Troy pictured the life those two had had together and felt he'd been too harsh on Sadie. She couldn't have been taken in by Siphon and his web of spies. She couldn't be trouble when this good man loved her so genuinely.

But he shook off the image. He had to stay on guard. There were still a lot of unanswered questions regarding her involvement in all this.

"Does she know?" Troy asked. "That you want to go home?"

Jimmy shrugged. "Maybe. She probably would if she stopped to think about it, but Sadie never felt as comfortable back there as I did. I think she's pretty happy doing this work."

"And what about you?" Troy asked.

Jimmy thought a long time before answering. "I want to be involved. After all," he cleared his throat, "home might not stay the way it is if the United doesn't win this war. But what am I doing to help, really? Small tasks for Patricia?" Jimmy kicked at the floorboard.

"Why don't you join Amadi's army? You could do a lot there," Troy asked, knowing the answer.

Jimmy stayed silent. After a minute, Troy put a hand on his shoulder. The man looked at him then, and though Troy didn't think they'd resolved anything, he understood it was always helpful just to get to say some things out loud and have someone else hear them.

The moment broke when the door creaked behind them. Patricia peeked in.

"You're here," Troy said, bounding over to her. "I have great news." Sadie came in behind Patricia and Troy directed his next comment at her. "I did it. I got a solid piece of information out of

Jax." Since smugness was always unappealing, he did his best to tamp it down, but he couldn't entirely suppress the small smile.

"Really?" Patricia said, wide-eyed. "Troy, that's remarkable. No one's been able to get anything out of him and three people have tried before you. Well done." She beamed at him. "A little booze and charisma goes a long way?" she asked.

Troy shrugged in acknowledgement, but he was still smiling.

"Well? What is it?" Sadie crossed her arms.

Troy extracted a piece of paper from his breast pocket. "I wrote it down in the bathroom as soon as I could get away. I think I caught all the details." He unfolded the paper and cleared his throat. "To ensure feeder dominance there are three strategies the Coalition have been using to set up this war. As we know, each of our three key families is primarily responsible for one and keeps all the details of that piece internal to that family for safekeeping. From Jax I learned that the Maddoxes are in charge of the political sphere – the government split... getting the right people into high place and all that. Jax had some friendly times with Mia Siphon," he couldn't help but flinch at saying her name, "from which he learned that the Siphons are in charge of planned attacks against humans and building an army. And because our party friend has also kicked it with Hunter, the eldest Griffiths kid, he also knew that the Griffiths are in charge of rumors and chaos. It seems this generation isn't so big on keeping the plans a secret from each other."

"Whoa. That's a lot," Jimmy said. "That gives us the big picture."

Sadie glared at Jimmy and then Troy. "How could you have possibly gotten all that? Why would he share so much with you?" she asked, crossing her arms.

Troy ran a hand through his hair. "Patience. Charm. And... I might have slipped a little something into his drink. My mother used to give it to burn victims who were in too much pain to handle it. Jax was pretty far gone. I don't think he'll even remember telling me." Troy smiled at her. "Still think Jax was a waste of time?"

Sadie pursed her lips. "No," she sighed. "Well done."

He was taken aback. Suddenly his grin felt like too much, and he did his best to drop it.

Sadie smiled though. "Now my turn," she said and held up a binder. It was quite large and Troy was surprised he hadn't noticed it before.

"What is that?" Jimmy said, coming to stand next to her.

"This," she said as if making a public announcement, "is the document Maddox senior passed on to his youngest son. Having glanced through it just now it appears to be all of the details of their plan for political domination. It's full of names and deeds and allies and enemies. It has a whole section on the human/feeder government split and the rise of Madame Maddox to the role of president of the feeder government. Something they have been working on for three decades apparently."

"What!" Troy reached for the binder and Sadie let him take it. He flipped through with his jaw hanging open. "How... He just had this in a drawer somewhere?" Troy asked.

"A safe," Sadie said.

"A safe? How did you break into a safe?" He looked at her like she had sprouted wings.

"I didn't. I got the code out of him," Sadie said. She punctuated these words with a shrug, but she looked like she was trying too hard to appear casual.

Troy narrowed his eyes. "You're telling me... that the uptight Phoenix Maddox, the man who barely drinks and doesn't trust anyone, gave you that code?"

Sadie looked suddenly very nervous. "No. I mean. I got him to show me some special collections he has and I learned where he keeps things that are important to him, and then I... broke in while he was sleeping and found the code scribbled... on the underside of his desk."

Jimmy was frowning at Sadie and Troy didn't think that was a good sign. That lie was just too bad to believe that she had pulled this off. Why was she keeping things from them? If she really was on their side, she would tell them the truth about how she got that binder.

"Great," Troy said. "Well done. This is amazing." He handed the binder to Jimmy.

Sadie looked relieved. "Well then," she said. "I'm ready for my apology."

Troy shook his head. "No way. You didn't win. My information gave us the broad idea of each family's role."

"And mine gave all the details of one family's role." She frowned.

They both looked at Patricia. The woman held her hands up.

Perfect. That was just great. More weird Sadie behavior, and now he hadn't even won the bet.

"Fine. Neither of us wins then," Troy said.

"Or you both did," Patricia said, waving her hand impatiently. "More importantly, we need to get this copied."

"I need to return the binder before he notices it's gone," Sadie agreed.

Without another word, the two women sat down on the floor. Patricia pulled a large stack of paper out of a bag and split it into four piles while Sadie popped open the binder and carefully removed the papers. Then she too split this into four stacks.

The men joined them silently, and no one spoke for many hours. There were frequent cries of surprise as they wrote, but no one dared waste time discussing what they'd learned. Troy's wrist felt broken from so much cramping by the time they'd come to an end. He sat upright, blinking at the tiny rays of predawn beginning to creep in.

Sadie carefully replaced the original papers in the binder and stood up, shaking out her leg cramp. "Do you have a purse large enough to hold this?" she asked Patricia. Patricia nodded and returned a moment later with a sizeable bag.

"Thanks," Sadie said. "I'll get donuts and try to bring them to him as if I just went out for breakfast. If he's still sleeping, I'll just return the papers and get out of there. If not, things will get messier. I'll have to stay and wait for an opportunity."

Jimmy looked concerned at this plan, but he didn't protest.

"And as for this," Patricia said, "there are people in the city who could really use this information, but only Amadi knows who they are. We'll have to get it to him to be disseminated as quickly as possible."

Jimmy and Sadie exchanged a look. They wore identical expressions of fear and sadness. After a few breaths, however, Jimmy's turned to resolve. He tightened his jaw, nodded once, and said, "I'll go."

Sadie's eyes welled up and Troy immediately wanted to get out of there. This was a private moment that they shouldn't stay to witness.

"We should get some sleep," Patricia said, beating him to it.

"Yeah," Troy agreed, leading the way back to their room. Sadie and Jimmy didn't acknowledge their departure.

Troy closed the door with relief. He felt a small wave of pity for the man next door, but right now he just wanted to be alone with Patricia to process everything that had happened. She crossed to the mirror, and for a minute Troy just watched her taking down her hair with a sleepy smile on her face.

"Now *that* was the best day I've had in a long time," she said. "Despite the fact I spent a good part of it cramped on the floor and the other part hiding in bushes."

Troy came up next to her with a toothbrush and a frown. "I know you think I'm too hard on Sadie, but you have to admit her story of how she got those papers makes no sense. I mostly went along with it because I want her to think that I believe her, but I have never been more worried that I'm right. What if the Coalition put together that document for her and all this has been about gaining our trust so she can give this to us."

They watched each other in the mirror as they prepared for bed. Patricia looked thoughtful, but it was a full ten minutes before she replied.

"I agree she's hiding something. But her cover-up was just too clumsy to be planned," Patricia said.

Troy leaned against the doorway. "Maybe she was tired."

Patricia faced him. "Amadi has vetted her. I don't think she's lying. Perhaps we just don't know everything."

He followed her out to the beds. "Can we at least send a note through a separate channel before Jimmy gets there? I want Amadi to know what we saw."

Patricia sat down on her own bed with a sigh. "Yes. He should know at least."

Troy took the seat next to her. "Do you hate that I mistrust her so much?" he asked. "I know she's your friend."

"No. I understand why. But I'm sure you're wrong," she said.

"I hope you're right." He made to stand up, but she stopped him with a hand on his knee. She looked a little nervous, and it was a strange expression on her.

Several seconds passed like that before Patricia cleared her throat. "I was wondering." She looked down at the comforter. "Do you want to stay here tonight?"

Troy was confused. She was asking if he... wanted to stay in her bed? Was – could Patricia be coming onto him? It made no sense. He swallowed, trying to suss out how he felt about that. Patricia was stunning, but they had never really had any chemistry of that kind. He thought of her as his mentor in the beginning, and now as his friend. Well, actually, if he was being honest with himself, he thought a lot more of her than that. She'd been with him through it all this year. And he realized he really did care for her.

"I mean – I'm not asking... You know I'm not interested in sex, right? Not with anyone. I just want to... sleep next to you." She was blushing now, her eyes still fixed on the comforter.

"Oh," he said. Troy slowly relaxed before scooting closer and taking her hand. "Yeah. Yeah, I'd like that."

Patricia looked up at him then, and they let out identical nervous laughs. Hesitantly, she climbed under the covers as he walked around to the other side to avoid crawling over her. Troy lay down at her side. Feeling uncertain, he lifted his left arm to make room for her to rest her head on it. After a moment's pause, she moved into the crook of his shoulder.

Patricia let out a small sigh as she relaxed her weight on his chest. Troy had never had a woman this close to him who didn't want something sexual, and he felt all the tension from the day drain away in the warmth and smell of her presence. And before he could over think what it all meant, he'd fallen asleep.

SADIE LOOKED AT THE TIME, and it immediately pulled her from her rather sexual dream. They'd slept most of the afternoon. She'd successfully returned the binder without encountering an awake Phoenix and had returned to her own room within the hour. She'd fed off Jimmy in a quick, exhausted, low-effort sort of way and they'd collapsed into slumber before they could even attempt to discuss their future.

Though the more immediate matter now was the invitation to visit the Siphon estate. They were meant to be there in a couple hours. Troy knocked on their door halfway through her getting ready.

"We overslept," he said, still in his pajamas, which consisted of loose sweats and no shirt.

"Us too," Sadie said, looking him up and down as she slid in an earring. She couldn't help but wonder if he had opened the door that way because he knew it looked good on him. "But I'm at least ahead of you. Better get moving."

She moved to picking out shoes as the door clicked shut at her back. Sadie could feel Jimmy watching her. They'd been avoiding talking, and she was afraid to look in his direction.

"I should leave tonight," he said. "No use wasting a day."

"Ahhh, these ones." She reached into the bottom of the closet. "They'll go best with the silver trim."

"It should take me a couple days to get there and a couple to get back. We won't be apart for long," he added.

"No, these ones are stupid." Sadie threw them back in as if they'd insulted her. "I'll be tripping all over the place in them. Why can't girls just wear regular shoes?"

Then, entirely out of nowhere, she burst into tears.

Jimmy was across the room in one breath. He scooped her up from behind and held her to his chest.

"I'll be back soon. It won't be long. We can make it."

Their skin was touching and it was immediately distracting. She still had little control over her succubus skills where Jimmy was involved. She stopped crying and turned around with the strong impulse to kiss him.

He retreated as she turned. Having been jolted out of crying, she wiped her face in confusion as he sat down on the edge of the bed.

"Should you?" she asked. "Wouldn't you be better off there?"

His silence was all the reply she needed as she joined him on the bed.

"Who knows when we'll be ready to be apart," Jimmy said. "It might not be any time soon. But life is pulling us in different directions right now. I don't know, Sadie. I don't know what else to do."

She couldn't believe she hadn't seen this coming. Obviously this wasn't going to work. Jimmy, her Jimmy, couldn't just sit in this hotel room all day. They stared at each other in silence for some unknown amount of time until a knock came at the door. They stood up, but neither of them moved to answer it.

Sadie closed the gap between them and kissed him.

"I'll follow you as soon as I can," she said.

"I know." He scooped a hand around her neck and ran his thumb over her lips.

"As soon as I can," she repeated. "Just stay safe, okay? Promise?"

"Promise," he said, kissing her nose and forehead and then switching to run his hand over her breast and around her waist. "Fuck, Sadie. I don't know how we're going to do this."

"It won't be long," she said, breaking the contact by force. And before his heated gaze could pull her back in, she turned away. Grabbing her purse off the side table, she went out the door and closed it behind her in a rush.

She was face-to-face with Troy, and she really didn't want to cry in front of him, but she couldn't help herself. A few more tears came out before she could tamp them down. He disappeared and came back with a tissue. Patricia came out of the bathroom. "Oh, Sadie. I'm so sorry," she said. She helped her dry her tears and fix her make-up.

"How does it look?" Sadie asked, worried her eyes were still red. Patricia frowned.

"Try smiling a few times," Troy said.

She took the advice, smiling and laughing, until Patricia gave her the thumbs up.

"How are you feeling? Are you sure you're up for this?" Patricia asked.

"Of course! She's feeling great. Thrilled to be going," Troy said in a jovial tone. Then directed seriously at Patricia. "Never ask someone how they're feeling when they're trying not to cry. That question coming from a friend is a sure way to break them."

Sadie was surprised at this insight. And grateful. She couldn't agree more. She laughed heartily in a carefree way to practice it. Troy copied her, holding out his arm. They continued to stare at each other wide-eyed while Sadie emitted increasingly half-crazed giggles.

Patricia was looking from one of them to the other like they had lost their minds. But Troy just winked at her as Sadie laced her arm through his. Then, as if they were half-drunk, they headed for the front doors with excited grins on their faces. Sadie was certain neither of them felt an ounce of the emotion they were portraying, so she only hoped no one would be paying too much attention.

They dropped the act in the car, though, and immediately fell into looking solemnly out their respective windows. Somehow, Patricia had acquired a fancy vehicle and would be acting as their chauffeur. It allowed her to hang with the other chauffeurs of the night and possibly learn something useful through the gossip. So long as she stayed out of sight. There were certain to be people on the guest list who would recognize her, after all.

Sadie was pulled out of her own reverie by the incessant fidgeting of Troy next to her. She had never seen him like this and the sight both annoyed and worried her. She cleared her throat. "I thought you were all buddy-buddy with the congressman. Aren't you excited to be back in his world?" she asked, half-mockingly, but with real curiosity.

Troy picked at a tiny hole in the seat in front of him, while Sadie watched him with increasing concern. Just when she thought he might not reply, he cleared his throat. "When Siphon first brought me here, I thought I was the luckiest man in the world. He was charismatic, dignified, and made me feel special. Apparently, he does that with a lot of people."

Patricia looked at him in the mirror. "No. Just the ones he's grooming to help run his empire," she said. "If you hadn't been a rising star on the political landscape and a popular nymph, he wouldn't have batted an eye at you."

Sadie frowned as she realized she still didn't know much of Troy's story at all. But he didn't elaborate there. He'd gone back to looking out the window as big drops of rain pelted the glass.

Troy said as if to himself, "Yeah. That really was a hell of a year."

Chapter 15

A rising star

Troy walked into the fancy fundraiser for Congressman Maddox with a true sense of wonder at the splendor of the people, the food, the clothing, the room. He couldn't believe that three days ago, he'd just been hoping for a job as a scribe for Congress, with hopes of making a difference one day. After the fire, when the great Congressman Siphon showed up at his bedside in the hospital to ask him to share his story before a congressional committee, Troy was dumbstruck. The man had come *himself.* And he thought that *Troy* had something worth saying.

There had been an important vote coming up, and Siphon thought that Troy's testimony regarding the fire might sway the undecided. Troy hadn't been surprised to learn that the apartment building full of so many nymphs had been intentionally attacked by vigilante humans. After all, such attacks were only becoming more common these days. But he was ecstatic that the bigwigs in Washington were finally going to do something about it.

His mother had died working as a firefighter, and the story of Troy's loss and the way it mirrored his own recent near-death seemed to move people, because the vote had passed. They would be forming a new government branch to deal with internal terrorism. And he'd been a part of making it happen.

Even so, as he moved through the room of the rich and powerful, he felt like any moment someone was going to come up to him and say, "You're just some dumb kid, with no connections or money. What the hell do you think you're doing here?" Of course, he would have thought anyone who did that was a pompous fool, and yet he couldn't shake the feeling of being an imposter.

"Troy Hyun?" He turned to face a young woman in a cocktail dress.

"I'm sorry," he said, "Have we met? It's been a busy few days."

"Oh, I would recognize you anywhere." She smiled. He believed her, given the party was a masquerade and half his face was covered. "But no, we haven't met in person. Though I did just buy your poster."

"Poster?"

"Yeah, have you seen it? It came out this morning. It's being sold all over the city. Mine's hanging in my bedroom," she said a little breathlessly. "You can come see it if you want?"

Whoa. What the hell? He took a tiny step backward.

"Troy Hyun?" another woman said and he turned nervously. "Patricia Costa." She held out a hand in greeting. "Are you ready for the interview?"

He faltered. Siphon hadn't mentioned an interview. She winked at him, though, and he understood he was supposed to play along. And for some reason, he did.

"Patricia." He took her hand. "Yes. Pleasure to meet you."

"If you'll come this way," she said and led him through a side room and into a cocktail bar and lounge. She claimed a spot in the most removed corner and swiveled the stool to face him.

"Are you certain you're ready for all this?" she asked, crossing her legs carefully under her tight skirt. "She seemed to be... what's the phrase? Eating you alive?" Troy looked at her intent stare and wondered if he'd just been pulled out of the frying pot and into the fire.

"Umm. I'm not really sure what is happen—" he began, but she cut him off.

"Have you seen this yet?" She held out a newspaper.

Troy took it, but didn't look down. He was studying the part of the woman's face that he could see under the golden mask that brought out the glow in her bronze skin. Up close, he realized she was younger than she seemed, mid-twenties perhaps, only a few years older than he.

"Well, have you read it? What do you think?" she asked again.

Troy looked down at the newspaper. The front page was a picture of him. He had each arm around a fireman, and they were supporting him as they walked out of a building, which was still in flames behind them. Someone had wrapped a jacket around his waist, but his torso was bare and covered in soot and sweat. His head was slightly back and his eyes partially open, looking right at the camera. He looked like a rugged model trying to be sexy with the expression on his face. Funny, he had no memory of the moment. He'd assumed he'd gone out in stretchers.

He blushed a little at the picture and risked a glance up at the woman. Patricia had a small smirk on her face and he quickly looked back down. The article was the first one in the paper. Front page news. He read quickly and silently.

Patricia tapped her nails impatiently on the counter between them while his gaze swept over the phrases "rising star" and "champion of justice." They had printed his entire speech from the congressional floor. The paper was clearly in strong support of the human/feeder split.

"Somewhere out there my mother is turning in her grave," Troy said when he'd finished. "She would never have approved of me getting this much attention. Especially not as some kind of hero. She would want to tell her own stories to the press." He laughed.

"She'd have some stories to tell?" Patricia asked.

"Yeah. I was a very disobedient child. I never did anything bad though, I just liked a challenge. Before she passed, my mom used to do controlled burns of the forest. And one time, I buried myself under some leaves nearby and tried to suck up all the flames as she made them. I heard her swearing up a storm. She really thought something was wrong with her. Until she heard me giggling. The prank worked, but I was sick for a week."

Troy paused. Why was he rambling about his childhood? He looked more closely at the woman, Patricia, and her intent expression. A sneaking suspicion crept over him. She just had that particular look on her face. The customs around asking about such things seemed to change from town to town, but Troy figured he had some right to. After all, if her presence was affecting him, shouldn't he be allowed to ask?

"You're a feeder?"

"Yes," she said, sitting up straighter. He felt the pull to talk about his life decrease.

Troy made a guess. "A hag?"

"Yes," she said.

"I thought hags preferred older people."

Patricia pursed her lips in a small smile. "We feed off life experiences given through stories. Naturally that draws us to the elderly." She recrossed her legs. "Though that is not why I'm here with you. Tell me, this image they've painted of you, is it one you're interested in? Do you want to become a political force, fighting for feeder interests?"

Troy still wasn't exactly sure what she wanted, but he knew his answer was an unequivocal yes. That sounded like exactly the life for him. He looked down at the picture again with a mix of humility and pride then made a motion which was both a nod and a shrug and added, "*This* is pretty silly, but yes, I want to help fight against what the humans are doing."

Patricia continued to observe him shrewdly. "Well then," she said, "You'll certainly need help."

He raised his eyebrows in reply.

"I've been around these waters for a while," she said. "I share your goals. I could help you learn the lay of the land."

Troy smiled. Now that was a proposal from a stranger that he could get behind. He took a swill of his drink and swiveled to face her. "And what's your story?"

He listened with interest as she told him pieces of her youth and how she'd ended up in the city. Troy found he felt unusually comfortable with the stranger. She had a calm self-assuredness that commanded respect, and he appreciated her no nonsense way of speaking.

After an hour, he was impatient to start working with her. Pushing away their empty glasses, he said, "You said you could help me navigate this place? Where would we start?"

Patricia's heels clicked sharply against the floor as she got to her feet, while Troy jumped up with a renewed sense of purpose. They left the quiet corner of the bar and went back out to the main room. She stayed close to him as she whispered tidbits about the different guests in his ear.

"The man to your left owns two newspapers in town; including the one which printed that article on you. He is also known for regular weekend rendezvous with Congressman Siphon's wife. Which, given that he is a fellow human feeder and so she can't actually feed from him, means the relationship is purely recreational," Patricia explained. "And speaking of friends of Ms. Siphon, the little woman about to pass on your right is bonded to the Atlantic Ocean, near the ports. Nothing goes through there without her notice. She was instrumental in limiting the number of ships allowed to dock per week. She is another nature feeder that Siphon has recently welcomed into his fold."

As they meandered through the main hall, smiling and nodding at strangers, Troy tried to make careful note of every precious piece of information. He interrupted only to ask, "What about Siphon?" as the man came into view.

"Old wealth. Very supportive of the Maddox family. He was instrumental in helping Katherine Maddox come to power. There's talk of the feeder congress selecting a president. If they do, she'll be at the top of the list."

Troy made a sound like he was listening, despite the fact Patricia's last line didn't catch up to his brain for several breaths. A young blond woman dressed in a short cropped black dress and black gloves had sauntered into the room. Several heads turned to watch her.

Patricia pulled them to a halt and stepped in front of him. *"That* is Siphon's daughter. A recently turned succubus. He brought her to distract, I'm sure. If you don't want to end up making a fool of yourself, I would avoid letting her chew you up and spit you out."

Troy wasn't exactly sure what Patricia meant, giving him that warning, but the image made his whole body feel ten degrees warmer. Siphon spotted him then and gestured them over. Patricia slipped a paper into his hand. "I'll let you go here. But call me," she said and slipped away before Troy could ask her where she was going.

The congressman disengaged from another conversation to give Troy his full attention. "Tell me, son," he said, clapping him on the back. "What do you think so far? Getting on well with the other guests?"

For some reason he felt like he could be honest with Siphon. "I feel a bit like Cinderella going to the ball on borrowed time. Thanks for the clothes and coach, by the way."

"Well. It certainly suits you." Siphon looked him over. "And I'm sure you will grow into it soon enough. You're going to bring fresh energy to our movement just when we need it most. So don't sell yourself short."

Troy opened his mouth to respond just as the congressman's daughter appeared at her father's side. "I – well. I'll do my best." Troy nodded to the young woman before forcing his focus back to the congressman. "I'm excited to do whatever I can. I hope I can live up to your expectations of, uhh, bringing new energy."

"He does seem rather... *invigorating.* Don't you agree, Father?" the woman said, batting her eyes in a mock innocent expression at Siphon. The congressman didn't look at his daughter or reply to her question. Troy, however, smiled in polite acknowledgement before taking a sip from his glass to clear his mind. He'd chosen a wine with a low alcohol content, a move he was particularly pleased with now that an attractive young succubus was looking him up and down as if he was just the lollipop she'd ordered.

"We can only be grateful that so many nature feeders have chosen to join the feeder cause," the congressman continued. "Though many of our brethren have been left behind in the fracturing government as we've broken away from the mainstream in order to protect our interests. The fight needs *invigorating*—" he smirked at his daughter, "young gentlemen such as yourself to help persuade the rest of your kind to our cause."

Troy flushed under both their gazes, but managed to stutter out, "I will do my best, sir."

"We should have him for dinner sometime," Mia said, and Troy couldn't help but wonder if her words were intentionally meant as an innuendo.

"Yes. Next Wednesday," Siphon said seriously. "Say seven o'clock?"

Troy nodded. "Thank you, sir," he said, regretting the breathiness in his voice.

"Excellent." Siphon gave a decisive nod, while the congressman's daughter looked him over as if she'd already decided exactly what would be on the menu.

THE BRIGHT MEMORY FADED, and the rain pelting the car windows came back into focus. He'd been a child. It was remarkable that was only a year and a half ago.

Patricia pulled up to a stop behind a line of other vehicles waiting to get into the estate, and they made eye contact in the mirror as she said, "We're almost there." Her expression was all concern. Troy wished he could tell her he was ready to walk back into that place, but it would never be completely true. He would do what he had to, and that was all.

To avoid Patricia's ongoing worry, he looked back out into the gray evening. He was glad to have her here though. She'd been looking out for him from the beginning. Even before he had any clue of it.

TROY WALKED past the little flower boxes leading to Patricia's place on the edge of town and knocked on the familiar green door. He was bristling with excitement, and he couldn't help but look around at the sunny neighborhood with extra appreciation. When Siphon had offered to take Troy back to Massachusetts with him and put him up in a hotel near his estate, he'd been grateful to learn that Patricia kept a place nearby.

Troy had grown increasingly attached to the woman and he loved coming over every few days to talk with her about his political and social pursuits. She was always a good listener and full of helpful information. He only wished she would open up about her own life more. It felt as if he did all the talking.

But as a hag, she'd assured him that she loved hearing other people's stories. Still, he wished to know more of hers as Patricia was a mystery. She knew so much of the landscape he walked and yet she seemed to live on the edge of that world. He'd respected her wishes and not shared her name with anyone. Apparently, she had a cruel ex-husband in politics and he'd been trying to hunt her down for some time. Troy was sure she'd share more when she was ready.

Today however, he was happy to talk about his own life. He'd spent the afternoon with Mia and her friends and the woman had done nothing but show interest in him. She'd asked him about his hopes and ambitions, and when he'd said he wanted to spend his life fighting for feeder justice, she'd practically hummed with excitement. And then she'd given him the sweetest smile and suggested that he would fit well at her side as she too had such ambitions.

Troy pictured himself spending his life next to such a woman. Confident and powerful, Mia was the most self-assured person he'd met since his mother. He'd watched the dismissive way her father treated her, and the way everyone saw her as a sexual object to be used, and she never let it define her.

Mia commanded the room. She did things her way, regardless of the intentions of others. Whatever she set her mind to, he had no doubt she would succeed at it. And her presence was utterly intoxicating. He couldn't seem to get enough of her. Even though it had only been a short time, he was clearly falling hard for the woman that had welcomed him with open arms into the Siphon household.

The door clicked open and Troy smiled at Patricia as he held up a pint of ice cream.

"You don't have to bribe me to let you in," she said, but she too was smiling.

"It's more compensation for listening to me babble about my day. I warn you, I'm a little on high right now."

She gestured him in and went to the kitchen, while he sat down in his usual spot on her couch. "You know I always love hearing about your day, Troy." She handed him a spoon as she sat next to him, and he smiled in acknowledgement as he accepted the utensil. "So... how was the party?"

He made to pierce the frozen top with the spoon and found it too solid to budge. Pulling a small flame up between his fingers, he melted the top layer enough to dig in. "The party? Bleh. I guess it was kind of like this ice cream. Pretty picture, appealing, tastes like cardboard."

Patricia narrowed her eyes on him. "I thought you were enjoying all this attention."

"Am I? Maybe. I mean I am a young man, prime of life and all." He rolled his eyes at her. "Something like that would definitely go to my head. A friend would keep me away from it." He smiled.

"Do you have one of those?" she asked.

"What, a friend?" He slumped low on the couch, dropping his shoulders with extra drama. "No. You?" He passed her the carton and spoon.

"No," she said, throwing him a little smile before scooping a bite into her mouth with his spoon and passing it back. The banter was the closest they'd come to talking about their own relationship, but it was clear they'd grown equally fond of each other these past weeks.

"Well. Say you did have a friend. What would you tell them was the best part of the evening?"

"Mia." Troy laughed, unable to help himself.

Patricia jerked slightly and frowned at him. "You slept with her?"

"No. I – no, I didn't mean... It's not like that. That's what I keep telling you. If she'd wanted one night with me, she would've taken it by now. But I think she really likes me. And as I was leaving I overheard her and Congressman Siphon talking. She asked him what he thought of me and her as a couple. Siphon said he would support her taking a nymph mate. In fact, it seemed like he was even encouraging it. I think something long-term is developing here."

"Troy, I know how you feel about her, but I must caution you, Mia has many interests. I don't think things are really as serious as you believe them to be." He took back the spoon with a frown. "I just don't want to see you get hurt." She put a hand over his.

Troy trusted Patricia. She had helped prepare him many times as he adjusted to a life in politics, but he couldn't see why she kept warning him off the woman who could be his future. "We'll see," he said, feeling a smidge deflated.

"Just promise me you won't put too much hope in this," she said.

Troy shrugged. It seemed a little late for that. Even as he nodded for Patricia's benefit, all he could picture was Mia's smile, the way it quirked slightly when she was about to cause trouble. The way her eyes had lit up when she'd suggested that he should really come see her room sometime soon. The thought hummed in the background of everything else she'd said.

Though, if he was being honest with himself, he was a bit afraid to actually sleep with her. Afraid it would mean she was less interested in something long-term, afraid of all her experience and power. And yet... he couldn't seem to stop thinking about it.

Troy ran a hand through his hair and let out a long sigh. Mia was a great woman, and he would have to work hard to be worthy of her. But he certainly wasn't going to let her go because of a few warnings from Patricia. He was in deep. He knew it. And he couldn't be happier.

THUNDER STRUCK JUST before the rain grew heavier – thick drops obscuring the world outside their windows. Patricia slid the car smoothly into the circular driveway and came around to open Troy's door. They exchanged a significant look, before he turned to reach for Sadie as she came around to join him.

She looped her arm through his and they ran to get under the covering before the rain could drench them. Troy faced Sadie as she adjusted his tie while he straightened the lapel of her long coat. Just when they seemed to be ready to go inside a voice came from behind him.

"Father hinted you were coming," Mia said.

Troy froze, letting the sound of it wash over him. Then, very slowly, he turned and faced her.

❧

TROY WISHED Patricia would be coming with him. Despite being taken under Siphon's wing, he still felt the woman was his only real friend in town. Still, she continued not to want to be directly involved in his growing social circle. On this night in particular though, he didn't want to be alone.

This would be the largest event Siphon had yet invited him to, and he was anxious to make a good impression. As he stepped through the large wrought-iron gates, he took one look at the thick crowd heading toward the front door and decided to avoid it.

Ducking onto a little footpath, he followed a trail through the well-manicured grounds, taking him past vibrant gardens and sizable alcoves housing fountains and stone benches. Troy caught glimpses of the mansion as he snaked his way through the trees, until he slipped discreetly into a side entrance.

He hadn't come in this way before and his usual confident stride was hesitant as he traveled around a large statue displaying a man, upright and erect, positioned to enter a bent woman from behind. The texture of her hair gripped in his tight fist seemed so lifelike, and their expressions so raw.

Troy swallowed, then laughed, before mumbling to himself, "This is definitely the home of succubi."

This display was followed by a dimly lit passageway decorated with a long line of photographs featuring naked or nearly naked people in various tantalizing positions. Troy's eyes darted quickly from one to the next, his body growing heavy with barely suppressed arousal.

His nerves around being with Mia were quickly morphing into an all-consuming desire. If she made a move tonight, he would go easily into her bed. In fact, the moment couldn't come fast enough, and he knew he would initiate if she did not.

Troy passed through various rooms, making introductions and pausing for brief small talk until he found Congressman Siphon attending guests in a smoky room. The man patted him on the back before introducing him to various feeder families from across the country.

All of them were speaking casually, but Troy was sweating bullets. The sexual display from the side entrance was nothing compared to what he'd found in the parlor. There were three naked people, two female, serving drinks. One sat on her knees next to the couch. The other held a tray out for him upon entry. Her eyes, like the others', were cast firmly on the ground.

Siphon smiled as he noticed Troy's discomfort.

"Relax, son," he said with a wink at one of the other men. "They won't bite unless you tell them to." Siphon placed an ungloved thumb into the woman's mouth. She shuddered as he slid the thumb over her lips. Troy's eyes widened as the woman's nipples puckered and abs clenched.

Troy, who had mostly just had sex with his old girlfriend in the dark, had never realized how much he'd missed out on during his own sexual encounters. The night was turning out to be very enlightening, and he wasn't sure yet what he felt about it all.

"Come." Siphon clapped him on the back. "Walk with me." Taking him out of Maddox's arms, he led Troy away from the smoky room. "My home can be a bit of a shock if you're not used to it. You should take some fresh air if you ever find it too much. I want all my guest to feel comfortable here."

Finding his voice, Troy decided to change the subject. "Are all the guests involved in politics?"

"In one way or another. The people here tonight are a part of a network of sorts. Hi Marsha." Siphon nodded to an elderly woman coming down the grand stair well.

"Are they all human feeders?" Troy inquired as they entered a spacious chamber on the second floor.

"Mostly. In fact, funny you should ask that, as I'm taking you to meet the only other nature feeders who could make it tonight."

"Everyone else is a human feeder?" Troy was surprised at that.

"Sadly, yes." Siphon paused to look at him as they entered another side room off the main hall. "But don't worry, things have been looking up since you joined us. The number of volunteers alone has skyrocketed since you began speaking in schools. People are just confused."

Troy swallowed somberly. He was hit with a rush of pride at Siphon's words, and he knew he couldn't take such responsibility lightly. "I should do more. Perhaps travel out of state. I saw the recent pamphlets cataloging human aggression. They're well made. I should be getting them out to as many nymph communities as possible."

He thought about how many people were suffering even now and wished Siphon would have him doing more than growing political clout and talking in a few schools.

"All in good time. Patience, you have a long road to travel," Siphon gave him another look, only this time it was assessing. Troy saw a question in the man's eyes and he wondered at it. Did the congressman not fully trust him? Did he not think Troy was ready for more?

The thought left him with a sour feeling that changed his mood entirely. His earlier excitement wavered as he followed the man into another stuffy room. Two men turned as Siphon pulled up next to them. The room was filled with enough chatter that Siphon had to raise his voice to his grandiose boom in order to make the introductions.

"Daniel and Manuel, this is Troy. I think you'll find you have a lot in common." The men were twins, nearly identical, except for their hairlines.

"Actually, everyone except Derek here calls us Danny and Manny."

"I'll leave you to it," Siphon said, and Troy stared at the congressman's retreating back a second before turning to shake each man's hand.

"First time here?" Manny asked.

Troy nodded. "Is it obvious?"

"You have a bit of that look in your eye, yeah." Danny smiled. "Where are you from?"

"Michigan," Troy said, trying to get a read on these new acquaintances. They both had a twitchy presence that put him on edge, but you couldn't judge people for their mannerisms.

"No, I mean where are you really from? You look Chinese." Now *that* he could judge them for.

Troy went stiff as he said, "My father's Korean. But he lives in Michigan now." He wished he hadn't answered the question at all. Damn his politeness. Troy squirmed as he looked for an excuse to extricate himself from the conversation.

"So, what's your poison?" Manny asked.

"What? Oh, I'm not drinking tonight," Troy replied, deciding he was very much not in the mood for alcohol.

"No, I mean, what do you want out of the Coalition? More protected land? Removing voting rights from humans?" Danny asked.

"Water protection? Banning human-only towns? Mandatory service?" Manny suggested.

"Mandatory service?" Troy parroted.

"Yeah. That one's ours. We think that to teach humans about symbiotic relationships, they should all have to do service to either earth or feeder," Danny said enthusiastically.

"Service how?" Troy asked.

"Well, see... If there's a river through a city, they could clean it out. Or if a feeder needs something in particular, they could attend them; help the feeder feed."

Troy wrinkled his forehead. He was all for cleaning up rivers, but humans serving other humans was another thing.

"I'd like to see more water and land protections," Troy said. "After all, we all benefit from such things."

"Of course we do. And that's just what the humans need to be taught, to respect the natural way of things," Danny said.

As the conversation progressed, Troy was increasingly convinced Siphon had been wrong about them having much of anything in common. In fact, he found the men the height of annoying. He eventually claimed to need a restroom, and removed himself from the stuffy chamber.

Slipping through a few doors, he found a small, blessedly empty balcony. Troy looked out over the manicured lawn, his thoughts flitting from the words *should have to do service to feeders* to the enthusiastic introduction from Siphon. What exactly had those men been on about? And why in the hell had Siphon left him with them?

Kicking at the base of the rail, he looked back through the glass doors to the gathering.

He should go back in and branch out. Really get to know these people. As he scanned the crowd, however, the heads of Danny and Manny popped into sight on the far end of the room. They spotted him before disappearing behind a cluster of women heading toward the other balcony.

Troy turned his back, looking for an escape route. The ground was too far down, but he could certainly make the hop to the balcony below. Swinging his legs over the guardrail, he launched himself to freedom. He landed smoothly on his feet, running a hand through his hair and adjusting his clothes as he stood up.

He would find a different path back to the party, avoiding the part of the house which contained the irritating twins. Troy slid open the glass door and entered a much smaller room than that above.

"Nicely done," said the blond woman, brushing her hair in front of a full-length mirror. The bedroom was softly lit, and Mia sat at the vanity mirror with her back to him. He'd landed on *Mia's* balcony and barged right into her bedroom. This called for a joke, but his brain scrambled to get the words together.

"You said I should come see your room sometime," he said, feeling a little sheepish.

"It looks more like you were fleeing the festivities above. Is the party that bad?" Mia asked, looking him up and down in the reflection.

"Oh. Um... no. It's great up there actually. Very... engaging," he said. Tucking his fingers in his pockets and leaning against the doorframe in an attempt to look casual. "Though not to you maybe. Growing up around such things."

"You think a gathering like this is common?" Mia asked, laying down the brush and facing him.

"Is it not?"

Mia moved to sit on the edge of the bed, dropping a handful of pins next to her.

"Not in my lifetime." Holding open a pin with her teeth, she scooped up a strand of hair between thumb and forefinger.

Troy stole the chair from the grooming station and positioned it backward so he could straddle it, facing her. "I guess I'm lucky, then, that I arrived in time to see it."

"I'd say so." Mia spread her legs slightly as she stared him down. His body stirred. Troy reminded himself why he was there. This was a very important function. If something was going to happen with Mia, it should be after the guests went home.

"What do you think it is about this particular time that's bringing so many people together?" he asked, trying to steer to a safe subject.

"That's obvious don't you think? It's all the work my father's done. Him and his friends. He has vision and he's good at picking out *talent*." Mia smiled, pinning up the last strand of hair.

"Like me?" he asked.

"Of course. After all, without nature feeders, we'd be outnumbered against the humans ten to one. No wonder he's eager to have you on board. Hopefully you can handle it," she teased.

"Bringing more nymphs to the cause? I think so. I met with several groups of young people this week, you know? Your father has been sending me around. He seems to have real faith in me." Troy said these words less to impress Mia and more to assure himself. After the way the evening had gone, he was feeling a little untethered.

"Good. I'd like to see you at his side in the fight." She smiled.

"Or maybe in a few years you can run yourself?" Troy suggested.

"Run? Oh, for congress you mean? No, politics bores me. I get enough of that from my father. Besides, once the humans have been taught their place, I think I'll find I have more interesting things to do."

Troy blinked. "Taught their place? What do you—"

"Don't patronize me just because I have a young face. It's so tiring. Don't think I don't know exactly what you all are up to. And I'm not blind. I know Mom's been helping sneak all those guns through the port."

Troy blinked. He was frozen as his mind whirled with a hectic buzzing sensation, but he recovered with the haste needed of such a significant moment. He was pretty sure Mia was not supposed to share that with him, but if he gave away his ignorance she might not share more.

"You know your parents mean to…" He trailed off, not having enough information to actually complete the sentence.

"Of course," she shrugged.

"And why do you think they would do such a thing?" Troy asked, still hoping she would enlighten him with details of the thing he was meant to be in on.

"What do you mean? Aren't humans our most prevalent food source? We sit in a natural hierarchy. As my mother says, it's ridiculous we've let them have their own government for so long already." Her face morphed to a pout, which only increased her general attractiveness.

She focused in on him then and though Troy couldn't be sure of what she saw on his face, she narrowed her eyes in sudden suspicion. "You did know about the smuggling, right? I'm sure my father would've told you that."

Acting fast, he said, "He told me about the weapons. I just didn't realize they were coming in from overseas."

"You think he could make them here? With the pittance of iron we're allowed to extract?"

"Hmm." He nodded, trying to reconcile how in the world Siphon could support gun imports if he was fighting to increase land protections. But Mia continued to look at him suspiciously and he realized that he couldn't contemplate this information now. He had to pull himself together and get out of there without causing any more doubt in her mind.

Hopping a leg over the back of the chair to stand, he said in reference to her earlier comment, "I thought fire nymphs had the most symbiotic relationship with succubi. Does that mean you sit in a natural hierarchy above me, too?" He knelt in front of her so she'd be positioned above him, but kept himself just out of arm's reach.

It worked. Mia's suspicious frown disappeared instantly. She placed the platform of her shoe against his neck, her heel digging lightly into his shoulder. "I suppose it does," she said without even a hint of a smile; the mood in the room entirely changed.

With the view he now had up her dress, he could see the woman wore no underwear. He swallowed as his rational brain went nearly blank. Lifting his chin to gaze up into her face, he made another attempt to find out more. "And what will your role be in all this?"

Mia flipped her hair over her shoulder before responding in an almost bored tone, entirely ignoring his question. "You've been parading around, acting like you know what you're doing with all these high-society women. I've been watching you closely, you know. But the truth is, you're as a babe compared to me. You think I'm an innocent young girl and you're an experienced flirt."

Troy blinked at this remarkable assessment of them, uncertain how she could have gotten to it. But all thought of analyzing their past conversations dissolved as she dug her other heel gently around his growing erection. "But a flirt is all you are. You've never had a real moment of passion. And you crave one. I'm going to make you scream, nymph. And I'm going to enjoy it."

Right. He'd successfully distracted her from their previous conversation. Which had been about something important and bad, he was pretty sure. Mia ran a hand up her thigh, hiking her dress up to her hips.

Somewhere in the back of his mind echoed Patricia's words of warning. He was playing a dangerous game now, he knew. Mia took the tip of her right glove between her teeth and pulled it off. Troy tried to remind himself of what she had just told him about her parents. He was sure he no longer wanted to be here, and would disentangle himself as soon as the fog in his brain and limbs lifted.

She removed the heel from his shoulder and worked off the straps with nimble fingers. He watched as if in a trance as she placed her bare foot down on his thigh, covered by pants, and slid it upward to scoop under his now-untucked shirt.

"Mia!" A woman's sharp voice came from behind him. Troy whipped around and, seeing Mia's mother, jumped to his feet, covering himself. "Your father has been looking for you all night. You are supposed to be entertaining. You can dally with the fire nymph later. Now get your ass out there."

Mia gave him a hungry look, before huffing out a breath and lacing back on her shoe. Troy followed close behind her as she sulked past her mother.

"Sorry, ma'am," he said, not quite meeting the elder woman's eye. "Is there a bathroom on this floor?"

"Down there, dear," she said. Troy didn't glance back at the women as he walked away. In fact, he had to fight not to speed up as he traversed the long length of the hallway. He closed the door and leaned back against it, panting as if he'd run a mile.

What the *hell* was this? How could this be real? How could he have misunderstood so completely? Siphon. Mia. They weren't who he'd thought they were. Now that he was in a safe place to process the news, it felt as if the ground was falling out from under him.

As he thought back to the frightening conversation with Danny and Manny, and then Mia's accidental confession, snippets of conversation with Patricia from over the year penetrated his thoughts. And one thing became clear. She *knew*. She'd known all along what these people were about.

His body pulsed with desire for the woman that he'd just escaped. And for a brief instant he tried to figure out if he could still fit in her world given what he'd just learned. He gripped his hair in frustration, groaning out loud.

No. He had to get out of this place. He needed to go home early without making it seem like anything was wrong. Troy splashed some cold water on his face and plastered on a smile, checking it for legitimacy in the mirror. Then he walked back into the dangerous party.

He found Siphon in the drawing room. Troy's heart pounded as he walked up to the imposing figure and tapped him on the shoulder. Siphon turned and Troy looked into the man's face, trying desperately to understand, while he suppressed all the hurt from his expression.

"Thank you for inviting me. I'm feeling a little under the weather tonight. I might head out early," Troy said, hoping this comment wasn't going to be met with suspicion.

Siphon looked up at his daughter lingering nearby. "Yes, I imagine you are. Take care, son." He patted him absently on the shoulder. Troy felt like a robot as he turned and walked out in a casual, exaggerated swagger.

He didn't knock as he threw open the front door to Patricia's place.

"Who the hell are you?" Troy said, walking into the kitchen to confront her.

"What?" she asked. "You – left early?"

"Why do you never come to these things with me? And what do you mean I should be *careful* who I open up to? And why do you want me to make friends with Maddoxes and Siphons so badly, when you want me to be careful getting too close to Mia?" Troy's hands shook as he tried not to yell.

"Because they are powerful allies to have," Patricia said.

"To have in what? In forcing humans to serve feeders, to disband their government, to become inferior to all feeders?" With anger at the lust still lingering in his body, Troy vowed to never again be taken in by glamorous things. He'd been playing the fool, and he no longer knew who to trust in this world.

"Is that what Siphon plans to do?" Patricia asked in a tone which made it hard for Troy to read if she was actually curious or just testing him.

"If it is? Do you still want him as an ally? Do *you* think all humans are naturally inferior to feeders?" he pushed.

"What do you think?" Patricia parried.

"Sounds like slavery to me," Troy bit out.

"A harsh word for it," Patricia said with an entirely passive expression.

"Is it? And smuggling in weapons to be used in this fight. What do you call that? Do you really want to be a part of their world? Because I don't!" Troy shouted in the end, backing away to lean against the door and crossing his arms protectively over his chest. Patricia walked to stand in front of him, cupping his chin in her hand, and he couldn't avoid looking at her as she drew his attention close.

"Then let me ask you another question, Troy Hyun. Would you like to work against them?"

Chapter 16

The Siphon estate

"Father hinted you were coming," a woman said from over Troy's shoulder.

Sadie's gaze shot to her, curious at the sweet-sounding voice. When Troy turned a half-second later, he was smiling warmly, looking for all the world like he too was anxious to see the person who had spoken.

The woman walking toward them under the covered walkway was full enough of sexual encounters that Sadie recognized her as a fellow succubus. She realized now how strange it was that she used to struggle to recognize her own kind. In fact, it was blatantly obvious that this woman had turned somewhat recently, like herself, as Sadie could estimate that what she saw made up about a year or two's worth of a sexual life for a succubus.

Pushing away the many scenes of orgies that seemed to characterize her, Sadie took in the sight of the woman herself. She was tall and wearing a cropped golden dress that both emphasized her legs and matched her hair. Sadie recognized her instantly from Troy's memory.

As she took in the lines of attraction between Mia and Troy, Sadie noticed that his were almost entirely absent, probably nothing like what had been last time he was here. What he was displaying outwardly as interest was not backed up by real emotion, which would certainly be trouble. He needed to tone down the show. Which he would realize in a minute, she was sure, once he was done being so randomly sloppy.

She pushed aside her concerns, though, as she watched Mia saunter toward them with such confidence that Sadie was immediately torn between admiration and desire, two emotions she stayed close to throughout the introductions.

"Mia. Pleasure to see you again." Troy nodded. "This is Sadie Hall."

"Another succubus." Mia smiled. "You certainly do get around." Then she turned her bright eyes on Sadie and whispered conspiratorially, "Careful. He has a bit of a reputation as a tease."

None of them shook hands, so Sadie nodded her head in the same fashion Troy had.

"Oh, I know. It's one of my favorite things about him," Sadie said, then added, "So far," with a little wink at Mia.

The woman appeared to like her attitude and gave her a once-over of serious consideration before saying. "Welcome to the party. You should definitely let me show you around."

Mia led them to the main entrance as the two doormen opened the path and stepped back with their heads bowed in identical postures. Sadie followed right behind and took the opportunity as Mia's back was to them to peer over at Troy with a warning expression.

He looked back at her with concern and she realized that he wouldn't know what exactly she was on about if he didn't know she could see what he was feeling. If the plan was to seduce Mia Siphon for information, clearly Troy was exactly the wrong person to be attempting it. Which was information that really would have been useful ahead of time. And it all begged the question, what exactly did the man think he was playing at?

They just frowned at each other a second, without managing to communicate anything useful, and went back to expressions of fond excitement as they swept through the entranceway. It was wide enough for three, and Mia slowed a second to pull in on Troy's other side.

"There are a hundred notable people here tonight, so don't be too disappointed if you're not the hot topic," Mia told him. "You came back just in time though. Things are finally ramping up around here." She turned into a side door and they found themselves in a wide hall with two sweeping staircases up to a terrace which overlooked the main floor. There were indeed a good number of people there. Sadie felt suddenly nervous as she looked around at their refined clothes and manner.

Even though she was dressed just like them, she felt as if they were all about to look at her and start pointing and tittering behind finely manicured hands. She recognized, however, that it was perfectly consistent with what people might expect of her walking into this world and so if anyone who knew of her was paying attention to her emotions they would at least not be suspicious.

Mia began to fill Troy in on all the local gossip, and Sadie followed their lead as they meandered through the crowd. They paused from time to time for Troy to greet someone and make introductions. People, especially men, threw glances at Mia as they passed, and the crowd tended to shape ever so slightly around them.

The young woman seemed to take that as the natural course of things, and barely looked at any of them until they passed by Jax Maddox.

"Ahh, the life of the party," the man said, beaming at Mia. Then noticing Sadie and Troy, he added, "And then there were two." For a minute Sadie thought he meant her and Mia until she noticed Jax was looking from Mia to Troy.

At first glance, it seemed the creativity feeder was dressed surprisingly normal today, but when she looked closer it was clear that the tiny flowers covering his tie were actually interwoven drawings of dicks of all shapes and sizes. Sadie had to hold her eyes wide to keep from rolling them, feeling increasingly grateful that she'd taken Phoenix rather than this man.

Jax turned his attention on her. "And the new one... Sasha right?"

"Sadie."

She held out her hand and Jax took it in his as he said, "You know, Mia and I are throwing a party next week and you would be a great addition. Mia makes a fine centerpiece. Last week she came in bows and ribbons – only bows and ribbons," he said, smiling at Troy and then Mia before turning back to Sadie. "Perhaps you'd like to join the next such affair?"

Sadie looked to Troy for how to respond and realized quickly she was on her own. He was frozen so still, with his thoughts full of Mia and Sadie wandering mostly naked around a party together, that the overly casual grin he had pasted on his face seemed unlikely to come undone in time to help her.

Mia looked pointedly from Troy to Sadie and gave her a wink. Sadie giggled, having to feign a bit of shyness, and said, "I'll think about it."

"There'll be a host of humans and nature feeders there to feed from," Mia said. "And since they each pay a pretty penny to get in, it's a huge fundraiser. If you wanted in, you'd get some of the cut." Then she smiled. "Though that's certainly not the reason I do it."

Sadie felt like she'd played that scene before, back in Seattle, and knew it wasn't particularly for her. But she could appreciate that Mia had an affinity for being the center of attention and probably thrived in such environments. If she was going to get anything out of the woman, she had to be willing to play a little. "Actually," Sadie said, "I think that sounds like fun."

Mia's attention focused on something over Sadie's shoulder. "Perfect," she said, distractedly looking from Sadie to Troy. "I'll see you *both* there." As Mia added, "Catch you later?" to Jax and began to step toward them in the direction of whatever had caught her eye, Sadie saw in Mia's thoughts the image of her kissing Troy on the cheek as she passed.

Knowing that Troy probably didn't want this, Sadie stepped rapidly between them and said, "Great. See you in a bit." And steered the two of them away from Jax and Mia without a parting excuse.

"What was that?" Troy said. "Shouldn't we be sticking close to her? She is one of our primary targets, after all." These words came out under his breath and through gritted teeth as he addressed her with a smile that would look from a distance appropriately attentive. Just a man showing off for the girl he was courting as he led her through the grandest affair she'd ever been to.

Sadie glanced casually to their left and saw Mia's target. She froze. In a strange mix, her blood seemed to heat as her skin chilled. The person who had pulled the woman away was none other than Gabriel. He was in a suit that, though it of course accentuated his beauty, also seemed entirely out of place on him.

Mia leaned in and kissed him on the cheek, and Sadie couldn't help the twinge of jealousy she felt at the warm expressions on their faces, or at the green friendship line flowing both ways. Though it was at the tiny black love line which laced the red, that Sadie truly recoiled. Gabriel, the man who had played such a sacred role in her past, was in deep with the Siphons.

Troy followed her gaze, and she quickly looked away.

"Who's that?" he asked, abandoning his first question.

"*That*, is Gabriel, uhh, Demesko. He's the succubus who guided me through my Becoming." She maneuvered them toward the stairs. "He was also present the other night when I was with Phoenix. I sort of got the impression he was there to check me out. See if my intentions in town were honorable and all that."

Troy was looking at her with a strange expression which she couldn't read.

"And now he's here," she hissed. "I'm afraid he knows too much about me to be good for us. I'm worried he's going to ask me something about Jimmy, and I'm going to fumble and blow my whole story." They pulled to a stop on the balcony and Troy turned to look at her, the image of her naked and covered with bows and ribbons returning sharply to the front of his thoughts.

Sadie sighed. It really would have been better if she and Troy had been sleeping together. She'd be less afraid of Gabriel's prying, and they wouldn't have to go around pretending there was nothing between them. After all, it's not like they had to like each other to work out some of their other... feelings. If only he wasn't keeping one foot out the door, ready to run when she proved to be a Coalition spy.

Just as she was having the thought, however, she noticed how closely he was standing. She'd put her back to the room when they'd stopped, and Troy had stayed pressed in tight as they'd unlinked arms. His gaze flicked from hers to just over her shoulder and back, his strange expression morphing slowly into a frown.

"What is it?" Sadie asked, suddenly highly aware of the warmth of his body.

Troy quickly removed the frown. Standing up straighter, he put a hand casually on her waist in a gesture appropriate for a young couple in an intimate conversation. Though she could tell by his stiff stance and quick shallow breaths that neither of them felt remotely casual about their position.

"I just don't know what to make of you. If this is all an act, it's a really good one." He was looking at her with careful deliberation, his gaze passing over every inch of her face as if considering each piece of it. "This man Gabriel was at your transformation?"

"Yes," she breathed. "And I didn't know he would be with the Coalition. He played an important role for me. He was sort of... special."

Troy frowned. "I'm sorry. That feeling of betrayal... it can be hard." Mia, grinning flirtatiously, swam to the forefront of the sexual images surrounding him.

"Why haven't you told me more about you and Mia Siphon?" Sadie couldn't keep the question in any longer despite the fact they probably shouldn't be discussing any of this while in the middle of the Siphon estate.

Troy flinched ever so slightly, and again his gaze flickered to a place just over her shoulder and back. "It's not important."

"Troy, Mia is one of our primary targets and we were just invited to party with her. A party which will also contain Gabriel and will most likely go very badly for both of us. You have a romantic history with that woman and it is clear that she also terrifies you."

Troy took a long, deep breath, his thumb twitching awkwardly in its place on her hip as his posture stiffened further. "This is what we're here to do. Whatever has to happen, it's more important than my personal issues with Mia."

He continued to look thoughtful and Sadie decided to wait before responding. This proved worth it when he continued, "I – I can't figure out if my... *hesitation* to trust you is logical." Sadie's body went as rigid as his as she waited for him to elaborate. "Seeing Mia again – coming here – it brings back memories. And I suddenly don't know..."

Troy looked back at her with such intensity that she stopped breathing as she impatiently waited for him to continue. "On the one hand, Siphon uses succubus spies for a reason. You're all—" he dropped his gaze as he decided not to finish that thought. It was a long awkward minute before he looked back into her eyes. "But on the other hand, I can't deny that my fear is wrapped up in my past with Mia."

Sadie's lips parted in surprise, and it was then that she noticed the lines of attraction running from him to her were strong and clear. And now that she could compare them to the ones that seemed to have gone stale with Mia, she knew that Troy couldn't be too sure of his theory about her. After all, he'd mostly lost interest in the woman after he'd realized they weren't on the same side. While toward Sadie his interest had wavered day-to-day, but in a pattern that had undeniably been growing stronger.

"The night I walked out of here, I was a mess," Troy continued, as Sadie watched him silently, chewing her lip. "And even in the weeks that followed, all I felt was anger and confusion. But seeing her again, and seeing *you* – you here, in this place, I realize some things."

His grip on her waist had softened into something more natural, and Sadie's posture relaxed in response. "First, Mia never lied to me. She thought I was on her side as much as I thought she was on mine. And second, you're not her. But the ways in which you're different from her – kinder, more vulnerable and loving." Troy's voice dropped to a near whisper. "And the ways in which you're similar – bold and comfortable in your skin... they make you all a little too good to be true."

Sadie swallowed at this proclamation. "Which means you're either one of the most interesting people I've ever met, or the best actor in the world. And as much as that woman downstairs scares me, it's you that terrifies me."

They were pressed right up against each other now and Sadie's lips had parted somewhere in the middle of this speech. Her legs felt numb, and she was sure her heart was pounding out of her chest, as she cleared her throat to try and respond. She was frozen, waiting for him to follow up with some critique or snarky remark, but he too seemed lost in the moment as the grip on her waist slid higher, pulling her close. Sadie lifted her chin in invitation as the idea of kissing her swam through Troy's thoughts.

"We should get back out there," he said, slowly retreating. "We have important work to do."

Before Sadie could protest and try to pull him back into the moment, Phoenix's voice came from behind them. "Sadie?" He sounded almost... shy? As she turned and took in his expression it was quite clear that their little interaction last night had drastically changed the way he felt about her. He was even pawing the ground with one foot in a caricature of a little boy nervous to talk to a girl. Which looked rather silly as the front end of the erotic memory he had playing in the background.

A man walked up next to him and gave one friendly, albeit aggressive thump to his back. "This must be her," he said to Phoenix. The man was tall and broad, which made Phoenix look almost scrawny, but the hard lines of his face gave off the same serious vibe as Phoenix had the day she'd met him. The men also had a healthy friendship line between them. It was in fact the strongest relationship attachment Sadie had yet seen for Phoenix.

"Uhhh, Hunter, this is Sadie. Sadie... Hunter," Phoenix said, standing up straighter and adjusting his tie.

"Hunter? Hunter Griffith?" Troy said, and the name registered sharply in Sadie's mind. "We've met before," Troy said, re-introducing himself.

The men had some back and forth about a particular event from last year while Phoenix shot puppy dog eyes at Sadie. As she looked the three of them over, trying to ignore the creativity feeder as well as the small hole of guilt beginning to form in her stomach, she imagined the scene from Siphon's perspective. Here they were, the future of feeder domination. The heirs of the Griffith and Maddox plans as well as the promising young leader of the movement to bring nymphs onto their side. All that was missing was—

"Mia," Hunter said. "There you are. Your father wants you downstairs, drawing room."

"Good to see you, too," she said, stepping into their circle. "It's been months. How's the camp?" And there they were. Their three primary targets.

Hunter nodded in acknowledgement of his brusqueness. "Sorry. I haven't been in polite company in a while. Used to barking or responding to orders. Your father kindly requests your presence."

"I think he can wait," Mia said and unexpectedly took Sadie's hand. "Me and the new succubus *must* get to know each other in the language we speak best." She pulled Sadie forward as Hunter and Phoenix looked at them wistfully. Hunter wanted to follow Mia as much as Phoenix wanted to follow her, but Mia just kissed Hunter on the lips and said, "Not this time. I'm hungry." Then she directed at Troy, "You, however, are coming."

And with that, Mia pulled the two of them to a side room on the third floor. As they walked, she asked Sadie, "So when did you turn?"

"The start of last summer," she said.

"Wow, you're brand new then. I'm only a little over a year, but I still feel ravenous all the time. Have you ever been so hungry that your whole body aches and you feel this constant gnawing craving that seems almost impossible to satisfy?"

Sadie laughed. "Actually, yes."

"It can be a drag sometimes when you have other things to do, like come to this party, but lucky for us I've prepared a little back-room fun. All nymphs." She winked over her shoulder. "What did you think of Hunter and Phoenix? I, uhhh, heard you and tight pants spent the night together."

Mia probably hadn't heard that so much as she could see it on Sadie, but couldn't say so in front of Troy.

"Yeah. He's sweet," Sadie said in not too much of a stretch.

"Yes, he's totally boring," Mia agreed in a twist on Sadie's word choice. "Hunter is much more fun, but he doesn't seem to get that just because I walk around like a bitch in heat doesn't mean *he* has anything for me. I throw him a bone now and again, but you have to keep these boys in check."

Mia was talking as if Troy wasn't there, but Sadie was highly conscious of his presence. She chanced a look at him only to find an unreadable expression over a tiny wave of lust directed at both of them. She felt a little sorry for him for that and began frantically searching for a way to get Troy out of there, but Mia commanded such authority it seemed impossible to just make some weak excuse.

"They're good ones though," Mia continued. "I trust them both completely and they're hella reliable."

That was great for when the three of them inherited the world, Sadie thought, fighting down the emotion of bitterness suddenly bubbling up from the chest she'd locked it in before agreeing to do any of this.

Mia paused outside the door and really looked at her a minute. Then she said. "I've only got to hang-out with a few succubi my age since I turned, but my parents typically send them away to work for them so fast we can barely say two words to each other. So I'm going to take what I can get while I still can." Then she pushed open the door and firelight cast a warm, flickering glow over her skin.

The room was dimly lit by wall sconces and a roaring fire. It contained several couches around a little coffee table and a thick rug between the seating area and fireplace. On the couches sat seven people, all men, sipping cocktails and discussing – well, Sadie didn't know, because they fell immediately silent the instant Mia stepped through the door.

Sadie was hit with a powerful wave of very real lust. It wasn't the kind of stuff that came off men in the streets, it was more like the feeling you got right before you went pee when you knew for sure you were going to be able to because you were already in the bathroom.

Mia, who clearly felt it too, smiled mischievously over at Sadie, and she knew then that whatever was going to happen next was going to be trouble as the rational part of her brain turned to white noise, and the primal animal inside of her reared its head in excitement.

Chapter 17

A succubus greeting

Sadie quickly discovered that the animal inside her wasn't a dangerous one. It was a contented little pussycat that just wanted to rub against the furniture and playfully devour its food. And this emotion was encouraged drastically by the realization that she finally had a real playmate. Another succubus her age. Gabriel wasn't the same – he was older, more experienced, and male.

Mia, the hungry young woman at her side, was relatable in a way that instantly made Sadie feel normal. She didn't realize how much she'd been missing this. She'd felt increasingly comfortable in her own skin since her Becoming, but she'd never really got to see herself reflected in someone around her.

Despite her concern over Troy's presence in this situation, she knew now that she wasn't going to even try to get them out of this. He would just have to look out for himself, Sadie decided as she realized this was exactly where she wanted to be. And she was in luck that it aligned perfectly with their goal of getting in good with Mia.

Sadie stepped hesitantly into the room. Mia had let go of her hand a few minutes ago, but she herself was still locked together with Troy. Untangling herself from her date, Sadie put down her purse by the door and followed Mia's lead. She wasn't sure if she should introduce herself. What kind of protocol did a situation like this call for exactly?

"Sadie, this is Tucker Stone." Mia gestured to the only man standing up. He was leaning against the fireplace and he was built like his name, a large slab of stone muscle. "And his crew. They're all earth nymphs. They live in the Appalachians just west of here and they're intent on helping Father. This is their first time in town, though. And I see no harm in a little under-the-table hospitality."

Sadie nodded to Tucker, who returned with a simple expressionless bob of his head. Some of the other men smiled tentatively at her though.

One of the younger ones, much closer to her age said, "I've never met a succubus before." He had a nice jawline and gave off a generally energetic vibe. It was particularly easy to notice his appealing face since he had no sexual history to speak of, except for an old childhood crush. Sadie wasn't sure if he was up for this, and she looked dubiously at Mia who, with a flick of her eyes, seemed to say *he's all yours* before turning her attention back on Tucker.

Out of the corner of her eye she saw Troy head to the bar and pour himself a drink as she sat down next to the man that had just spoken. Up close, she realized he was probably in his mid-twenties and well-built like the rest of them.

"I'm Sadie. How did you meet Tucker?" she asked, searching for any topic of conversation.

The man grinned. "Tucker recruited me into his crew right out of high school. He saw the writing on the wall and started putting us together."

"They're the best fighters I've ever seen," Mia said over her shoulder. "You should see them training," she added with a grin. Sadie returned the expression then glanced over at Troy, who was leaning back against the minibar. They exchanged significant expressions at this news.

Sadie turned back quickly to Mia before anyone could notice. And then, without any more preamble, Mia began to unzip the back of her dress as Tucker scooped her mouth up to meet his. Strangely, Sadie found herself wishing she could just watch them. It would be interesting to see what the other woman did. Somehow, though, she didn't think that was going to be easy, as the man next to her pulled her attention back by asking, "Do you want me to take these off?" He was pointing to her heels.

She bit down a little laugh since even though he didn't know it, she desperately wanted out of those shoes. "Yes, thank you," she told him. He began to fumble with the buckles, gasping a little when his fingers made contact with her skin. She smiled around at some of the other men. Two of them were looking at Mia, but the other three nodded back to her. Two with confidence and the third with a nervous swallow of his drink.

The lines between the men indicated a strong alliance of friendship, but as far as she could see, they'd never done anything quite like this together.

When the man next to her had removed her shoes, Sadie gestured him to the clasp at the back of her neck. He unclipped it and let the dress fall loose to her waistline. Since the dress had been cut so low in the back to warrant built-in breast cups, this left her instantly nude from the waist up.

The mood shifted, and it suddenly didn't seem necessary to carry on with more polite conversation. And as long as they all seemed comfortable skipping such things, she certainly was too. She leaned over and kissed the youngest man, who jerked his eyes up just in time to focus on her face.

Out of the corner of her eye, Sadie watched Mia pull Tucker over to the coffee table and push him onto his back. Or at least she suggested with a light push that that's where he should be, and he complied. She was entirely nude now except for the heels, and Sadie watched as she kneeled on the rug to unbuckle Tucker's pants. He just put his hands behind his head and watched her coolly, but behind the facade were frantic waves of excitement. As much as he wanted to be the calm leader, internally the man was clearly shaken.

Sadie went to undo the buckle of the guy next to her, but found it too much of a challenge in their current position. It was no problem, however, since the instant he realized what she was doing, he seemed to extract himself from all his clothing in one fell swoop. Sadie missed his undressing though, as she was watching Mia free the beefy dick of Tucker Stone. The woman looked up at her just as she wrapped her mouth around the tip of it.

Tucker tried to suppress the sound that tore out of him, but it only made it come out as a whimper. She felt like she could see Mia smiling at her, though it only filled her eyes, since her mouth was fully occupied.

Sadie mentally shook herself and looked back at her own entertainment. He was stroking himself as he watched her, and she chewed her lip as she looked him over. Removing her gloves, she slid her hand around the base of the shaft to increase the sensation. "Keep going," she whispered in his ear before turning back to focus on Mia.

She felt the man's hand hitting hers as he moved it, but otherwise barely paid him any attention as she watched Tucker clenching every muscle in his body. She'd never had the chance to see this from the outside, and the sight was pretty exciting when she could focus on it with a half-calm mind. Mia, however, was clearly lost in it as she slowly worked the man until he was bucking uncontrollably under her.

"Fuck," he said so loudly that it accentuated the general silence in the room. Sadie seemed to awake from a dream as she turned to look to her right. Troy was standing behind her couch, watching the scene with no less lust than any of the other men. He had a drink in hand and a very prominent erection.

They locked eyes and Sadie was hit for the first time since walking in by a very real desire herself. Troy looked beautiful in the firelight, and she could see in his thoughts that he felt the same about her.

As she looked over his sexuality with more care than she'd previously done, she realized just how far outside his comfort zone this was. He didn't actually take sex casually. Perhaps ever. He hadn't recently, which meant whatever had gone down at Jax's party last night hadn't involved any kind of escapades.

In fact, he'd only slept with one person, and Sadie guessed it had been at least a few years ago. *Yeah...* an orgy was definitely far outside his world. But it didn't seem to matter, as Troy's heated gaze stayed fixed on her face, it seemed he only had eyes for her.

Sadie chewed her lip, feeling frustrated at the whole situation with Troy. It was entirely unfair. People should be able to act on how they felt for each other, but human relationships, it seemed, were too complicated for that. And since he didn't fully trust her and she didn't like him mistrusting her, they had to just go around at each other's throats instead of getting out all that frustration in what she was sure would be a much more productive manner.

Then a wicked idea occurred to her. Maybe this was their chance to do something the current circumstances of their relationship didn't seem to allow. After all, this was all in the name of their mission.

Keeping her eyes locked on Troy who was still leaning against the minibar behind the couch, she slid into a straddle position over the man next to her. He was about to climax and so she took over matters. Pulling his hand away, she pulled aside the thin string of her thong and lifted her hips to slide him into her.

This position put Sadie facing backward on the couch and directly in front of Troy, who swallowed noticeably and did nothing at all to hide his desire. Though the man under her was lost in excitement over what was happening and was expressing it loudly, it felt like she and Troy were alone together. He stepped forward until he was only a few feet from the back of the couch, just out of arm's reach.

Sadie rolled her hips over the man in a slow undulation, and Troy licked his lips. Wanted her own stimulation, she slid her hand along her inner thigh and under the dress pooled around her waist, letting her head fall back a little as she began to touch herself.

A wet spot began to glisten over the mound in Troy's nice dress pants and she vaguely realized they might care about that later, but just then all she could do was stare at it hungrily. He followed her gaze and swallowed again. He wrapped a hand over himself as he took a sip of his cocktail, then looked back at her with an expression too complex to read.

Was he thinking what she was thinking? That this could be an excuse for them to interact in this way? Though that would be a bit of a stretch since they were both here to get closer to Mia. But he didn't look over when the other succubus moaned loudly from somewhere behind her.

He stayed focused on Sadie, as if he too felt they were alone. In the back of her thoughts she let the man inside her climax, not wanting to make this experience too intense for him, and stopped moving as he pulsed inside her. She waited for his grip on her hips to soften before sliding him further under her and starting again. She wanted his head lower on the back of the couch so it didn't obstruct her view of Troy.

The unnamed man didn't seem to mind, as he was now face-to-face with her breasts and was happy to entertain himself. Troy took a step forward. It was the most hesitant, awkward step she'd ever seen him take, and it looked entirely out of place on him.

Her own body was getting close, and the scent of Troy was a powerful catalyst. He always smelled so good, though she was real-izing only now how much she'd come to love it. She began to writhe a little faster against her hand, suddenly chasing her own climax. She nearly jumped at his presence when the man under her asked, "Why am I still hard?"

Sadie unbit her lip long enough to pant, "Because I'm not done with you yet."

Troy's eyes flared slightly at these words and she saw his hand grip tighter over himself. She wanted him to move it. Or to undo his zipper and let her do it, but he just stood there, still as a rock, his gaze fixed on hers.

She closed her eyes as she let her sounds of pleasure mingle with the ones still coming from behind her. Sadie had learned enough at this point to know she would only climax once under these circum-stances, and didn't want to waste it right now if there was the chance of being with Troy.

Gathering up all her willpower, she made herself stop.

Sadie opened her eyes to find Troy had leaned in slightly. His mouth was parted and his brown eyes were lit up with the pleasure of watching her. She put her hand on the back of the couch, gripping it for stability as she rocked forward over the man. She loved the feeling of someone inside her when she was this close to climax, and she let herself enjoy the sensation as she looked up at Troy.

He put his hand next to hers, a few inches away. The problem with being a succubus was touching someone's skin was equivalent to sleeping with them. Which was particularly inconvenient since all she wanted to do was test the waters by taking his hand. However, such a gesture would be crossing a hard and fast line, and so she knew Troy was going to have to be the one to make that call.

If they could somehow talk about it all like grown-ups this would be easier, but instead Sadie could only move her hand slightly closer, as if she were simply getting a better grip. She placed her pinky a hair away from his thumb.

Troy went to take a sip of his drink, but it was now empty. He bit his lip as he looked back at her, and they did their best to have a silent conversation with just their glares. The conversation wasn't particularly fluid though as it just consisted of both of them asking *what do you want?* while silently waiting for the other one to answer first.

Troy's thumb twitched next to her, but then he suddenly stood up straight and shoved his hand in his pocket. Sadie, not wanting to appear like she'd been hoping he would take it, slid her own hand around the back of the man's neck and began to play absently with the hair at the nape.

At which point Troy put his glass down on the nearby side table and put that hand on the back of the couch. This left her in the frustrating position of having to decide what exactly he was playing at. Which didn't take much of a guess, since it was clear in his thoughts that he was in fact desperately hoping that she was going to make the move to reach out first.

Didn't he realize that she was the succubus here? And he was the man that was only in the room because of a mission and not because he wanted to be involved in this? Even if she couldn't see his desires, it wasn't exactly appropriate for her to make any kind of a move on him under these circumstances. Also, given his stubbornness to make her go first, she didn't particularly even want to try.

To double down, she gripped the couch in both hands and began to move in quick undulations as she used the hard backing for stability. She glared up at Troy in what she wanted to be a dare, but was probably ruined by the underlying hint of longing.

He didn't seem to be aware of exactly what was happening in their exchange, and so put his hand back in his pocket. Or maybe he was just doing it to spite her, as he was still clearly picturing himself in place of the man she was straddling.

Sadie wanted to annoy him in return, but couldn't seem to come up with anything. In the end, she just finished the man off under her while she glared daggers at Troy. He must have seen something else in her expression because he just watched raptly with his jaw clenched and an increasingly large stain of precum spread over his thin dress pants.

Mia gave out some directions and Sadie looked over her shoulder to get a visual on the scene. She was on her back now with Tucker's face between her legs. She had both hands on the ankles of two of the men on the couch over her head. And a fourth man was sitting on the table next to her, playing with her stomach and breasts. All four men were enjoying the physical contact, and Mia was soaking up the feeding like a sponge.

The remaining two men moved closer to Sadie. One pulled up on her right and the other came to stand next to Troy, who immediately moved away in response. The newcomers looked at her hopefully. Sadie stopped touching herself to reach for each of them, copying Mia in pulling in as much desire as she could while doling out pleasure freely.

The effect was a bit intoxicating, and she found her frustration at Troy finding an outlet as she got lost in the three men around her. She looked back over her shoulder at Mia who was trying to direct Tucker while not letting go of any of the men. Sadie could see that as much as Mia was enjoying the game, she was nowhere close to her own climax and she wanted Tucker to press harder and in a very specific way that he wasn't getting.

Seeing Mia's frustration made her more aware of the fact that she too wanted something she wasn't getting. The tension between her legs was so palpable that it wouldn't take much. She tried to rock her pelvis against the man under her without letting go of the other two.

It wasn't enough. Sadie felt Mia's mind lock onto her then and she turned and made eye contact with the woman. At that moment one of the men on the couch groaned loudly as Mia suddenly finished him without preamble.

Sadie saw Mia's intent before she moved and mentally consented by sending back the same image. Then she turned back to look for Troy as Mia reached out her now-available hand and clasped Sadie's ankle.

Troy was leaning against the back wall now, watching her with both hands in his pockets in some kind of stubborn refusal to touch himself. Sadie stared at him hungrily in the shadows as the contact with Mia spread pleasurable heat through her. She sent the same feeling back, trying to match the intensity as closely as possible. Her clit began to pulse, and she felt the familiar flush cover her chest and neck. Sadie stopped paying attention to anything but her own pleasure and Troy's gaze from the back of the room.

Sadie noticed that Mia's touch wasn't as strong as Gabriel's or her own, but it still felt damn good when her release finally came. She convulsed in tiny spasms as she bit down on the sudden impulse to say Troy's name out loud. She could feel his attention on her though, and she thought she made out the tiniest groan from his corner right as she finished.

Sadie blinked open her eyes to assess the situation and realized that Mia was still hungrily waiting for the same behind her. She was caressing Sadie's ankle as she enjoyed the sight of the naked man sitting next to her.

Sadie sent the same feeling back, only twice as strong. She had the impulse to show off a little for the other succubus while also being caught up in wanting to give her what she was asking for so strongly.

"Oh, god. Yes. Just like that," Mia said. Sadie heard Tucker moan from between her legs, but understood who she was really talking to.

In her inattentiveness, Sadie accidentally made the man under her come and he followed it by reaching for her face and kissing her. "That was amazing," he said.

Sadie felt guilty that she'd forgotten he was there. Remembering this was his first time she asked, "What's your name?"

He laughed. "Oh, right. It's Michael."

"Nice to meet you, Michael," she said sweetly and kissed him briefly.

Then she gave her full attention to Mia.

Sadie closed her eyes and watched the world through Mia's as she felt her hungrily crash into her own climax. She arched her chest and back off the table as she squeezed her thighs around Tucker. Sadie drew it out enough to show Mia what she could do, but didn't try to memory dive when the contact between them was so minimal. In fact, she found the whole thing rather challenging when the only place they were touching was from the two fingers Mia now had on her lower calf.

When it was over, Sadie quickly finished the other men and moved to sit in between Michael and the new guy just as Mia released her and relaxed back on the table. It took Tucker a moment to notice she had stopped writhing, but when he looked up and saw the blond woman looking quiet and sated, he crawled up her body, clearly moving to enter her.

Mia sat up. "No. I'm done," she said. She kissed Tucker and made him climax in a quick release. He expelled a large amount of fluid all over Mia's stomach, gasping as she let go of him. He looked down at himself in some surprise. "Huh. That was... interesting," he said.

"Welcome to the Siphon estate," Mia told him as she rose from the table. The other guy whose ankle she'd been fondling was still hard, and he looked at her a little wistfully, but it was clear it was over.

"Come on," she said to Sadie. "We can use my private shower. The one for the rest of you is in there," Mia told the men, pointing at a door over Troy's shoulder, and both women paused to take him in. Mia looked from Troy to Sadie and laughed. "Let's go. You can ride that boy some other time. I want to get back to the party."

And with that, Mia scooped up their clothes and walked directly into the hallway wearing nothing but her heels.

Chapter 18

The best-laid plans

Sadie grabbed her own shoes, looked at Troy with a shrug that said *I guess I'm going this way now* and scrambled after Mia.

They walked naked down the empty corridor and then past another hall that contained several finely dressed guests, who either squawked or leered at their entrance. Mia ignored them all entirely as she said to Sadie, "You're really strong. Like even more than Gabriel, you know? That was definitely awesome. You have to come to our party next week."

Sadie bobbed her head in apology to an older woman who looked at them in outrage, but Mia caught her eye as she continued. "I want to see you and Gabriel face off. That scene last night looks fun, but—" She paused to push open a door to what turned out to be her bedroom. "Think of how much better it would be if it were Troy instead of Phoenix."

The image traveled rapid-fire through Sadie's thoughts and Mia paused to look at her and smirk. "That's what I thought," she said before crossing the room and disappearing through another door. Sadie had two seconds to take in the elaborate bedroom, complete with vanity stand and bed canopy, before she caught up to her on the edge of an equally grandiose bathroom. Mia dropped their clothes onto a little table and kicked off her shoes. "Were you always that strong or have you been practicing?" she asked as she flipped on the shower and tested the temperature of the water.

"Umm. I think it was always that way. I didn't really have much comparison except Gabriel, and he left me a few weeks after I turned. He was—"

"Yeah," Mia cut in. "Gabriel was there at my Becoming too. He's good. You got lucky he found you."

"I guess I did," Sadie said, following Mia under the water. It was big enough for two, but the woman didn't seem at all concerned about them accidentally touching skin. She casually passed Sadie a bar of soap and made nothing of it when the spark of pleasure passed between them. While Sadie tried to navigate this new social situation, Mia continued to chatter with the casualness of any ordinary day with a new, potential friend.

"And the guy with the pretty brown eyes? The one that's obsessed with you or something. What's the deal there?" For a second Sadie thought she meant Troy, before she realized that didn't exactly make sense. "What's going on in those scenes? They look a little crazy in your memory. Is he some super powerful fire nymph or something? Why are you mad for him?"

Mia began to clean between her legs as Sadie soaped up her breasts. They were both carefully keeping their styled hair from direct contact with the water.

"No, that's just someone I really clicked with. I've known him a long time is all." Sadie was afraid to hold Mia's gaze as she said this and fumbled the soap so she could reach to pick it up instead. It was no use though, because she stood up to find the woman with her eyes narrowed and both hands on her hips. Clearly her evasion had just made her more suspicious. Great. Some spy work. Though she'd always known Jimmy was her weakest spot.

"He's human, isn't he? You grew up with some human boy who is now obsessed with you?"

Sadie didn't like this description and it was completely inaccurate, but she just held her breath, waiting to see how Mia would react to this news. Mia smiled and gave her shoulder a shove. "It's okay. Wow, you really haven't spent a lot of time around your kind, huh? I can't imagine what it must've been like growing up outside of a succubus family. Well, just so you know, that kind of thing happens all the time. Both of my parents have humans that they feed from in an ongoing way. Mom even has one that she keeps in the servants' quarters so he can be close by. Of course, the unspoken rule is that no one talks about it. Especially not in front of the other families." Mia stepped out of the water to let Sadie rinse off properly.

"Succubi are a little more used to these things," she continued. "After all, people are always full of contradictions, and we're used to seeing the contrast between people's bedrooms and their public masks. But the Maddoxes and Griffiths certainly wouldn't understand, so we keep any mention of *significant* relationships with humans... to ourselves." Mia gave her a pointed look for emphasis.

Sadie nodded in agreement. "Thanks for telling me. I've always felt a little guilty about that guy. We obviously have a good sexual connection, but it can be a drag having him around all the time. I'm happy to keep him out of sight though, since it's where I prefer him anyway."

This she delivered perfectly, making up for her stumble earlier. Mia nodded once and moved on in the conversation.

"And oh my god, speaking of fire nymphs, I've been wanting to get my hands on Troy ever since he disappeared last year. He's obviously moved on in his interest, but I think we could have some serious fun taking him down together."

Sadie's heart pounded at the idea all while a sick image of two lions tearing apart a gazelle popped into her head. Whatever she had to do next to get into Mia's memory, she was going to make completely sure that nothing of the sort ever happened. "Yeah," Sadie said, smiling mischievously. "That man really doesn't know what he's missing. And it might just take two of us to show him."

Mia beamed and pecked her on the lips. "I knew we were going to get along!"

Sadie smiled back with a sudden feeling of sadness. She turned her back on Mia to shut off the water right as she was struck by the horrible realization that she had some tiny, but very real desire to have a life here in Mia's world, with her as the best friend. She got the mental image of the two of them running all over town, breaking hearts together. For a brief instant, it sounded all too appealing.

By the time she'd turned to take the towel out of Mia's hand, Sadie had moved onto a general feeling of disgust at the woman's privileged life at the expense of others, guilt for wanting to be a part of it, guilt at being a part of the organization about to go to war with the beautiful succubus now smiling at her with genuine warmth, and pity that Mia could grow up believing herself so much better than humans.

Sadie made sure to let these emotions play out on a face that was bent over drying her feet and somehow managed to pull herself together before she straightened.

As they exited the bedroom, Sadie excused herself to go find her date, and Mia took that in stride, saying she should probably go respond to her father's call.

Sadie made her way back down the hall toward the room where she'd left Troy, immensely grateful there were people around, because it helped hold all her emotions at bay, but the second she turned down the second hallway she was hit again with a strong wave of guilt. Shit. Why did she feel this way?

Realizing she was going to need a minute, she darted into an unoccupied side room. She closed the door behind her and stood there in the dark taking deep, potentially calming breaths.

It was in that moment that Hetia's parting words came back to her, even though she hadn't thought of them once since: *Don't let them get in your head. Only you can decide who you are.*

Sadie didn't like this. Not at all. How was she supposed to be this close to people she was here to betray? And what the hell was Gabriel doing here? It seemed so unfair that he had to be involved. She didn't like having to be suspicious of him last night. And why did Mia have to make her feel so welcome and at home?

The door clicked open and she jumped a foot backward, nearly losing her balance in her heels. "It's me," Troy said, stepping into the darkness. "I saw you come in here." Sadie just panted with a hand over her heart as he asked, "Why are we in the dark?"

She reached out for the wall and ran her hand around until she found the switch. "I just needed a minute," she said, before flicking it on.

The first thing she saw was a memory from Troy in the bathroom just now, touching himself as he thought about what he'd just witnessed. The second thing was the room they were in. It seemed to be a rather large storage closet for sex toys.

Behind Troy was an elaborate rope contraption, and hanging directly between them were several whips that made it hard to look at each other with both eyes at once. She leaned against the wall to see him better and he did the same. Unfortunately, this positioned an insanely large dildo, which happened to be stuck to the wall, directly between their foreheads.

She batted at it impatiently, which caused it to jiggle back and forth as she tried to initiate a serious conversation about their situation. "Troy... I'm... not sure I can do this," she said, just wanting to talk about it a little so he would calm her down.

"Do... what?" he asked, and the mental image of her kissing him popped into his thoughts as a possibility.

"Spy on these people," she confessed, scattering his mental fantasy.

"What?" he said, and his expression went from surprise to worry in the span of a couple heartbeats. "What do you mean?" he asked. "We have two more people to go. And if you really are so good that you could get that code out of what's-his-face, it's not like it will take all that long."

She pushed aside his disbelief in her story about last night and went on. "Look. Before I got here, our targets were just faceless assholes who were the clear enemy. I don't think I really thought through what it would be like to come here and actually do all these intimate things with them."

He had a look like he was really digesting her words for a minute and then he nodded. "Sadie. They are the clear enemy. Siphon," and here he dropped his voice even lower than they'd been speaking, "is amassing an army that's already attacked several places and is about to clash with Amadi, and Hetia, and all our friends. Remember them?"

She gave him a grumpy look, her gaze briefly acknowledging the dildo before flicking back to him. "Of course. It's just…"

"Look, I know exactly how you feel." His tone was suddenly so gentle and understanding that it was nearly unrecognizable. "Trust me. I've been there. And I know that what you are doing is a lot more personal than my tactic, but we can't let ourselves be seduced by the allure of it all." He reached out like he was going to touch her arm, but realized she hadn't replaced her long gloves yet and instead leaned his fist against the wall next to his head. "That's the most important task we have here. Not losing ourselves in it."

Her shoulders slumped and after a minute she nodded.

"It's a glamorous world," he said, looking at the wall in the general direction of the room they'd all just been in together. "And I know it seems like you would fit in well here, but those men will be way less appealing when they're coming at us armed."

Sadie sighed. "I know. And it's not like I feel *much* for them, but they're still human beings. And I don't want to hurt anyone. When you think about it, harm is the exact opposite of my biological purpose. It's easy to find reasons to care about someone, even the enemy. It's much harder to find reasons to hate them."

Troy's whole demeanor shifted and he looked at her as if seeing her for the first time. His gaze was soft and full of empathy, and there was a kind of pained longing in it. He leaned toward her ever so slightly and bumped his forward against the dildo. With a look of that's-the-last-straw, he ducked under it so it would be behind him. This put him so close to her that she couldn't actually see his hand move and so was surprised when it landed on her waist.

Sadie swallowed as Troy opened his mouth to speak. Whatever he wanted to say to her though was clearly frozen on his tongue, because he stayed silent as his gaze roamed her face. He was radiating desire behind the uncertain expression, and she desperately wished that there was anything she could do to make him trust her once and for all.

Though it seemed that despite his ongoing reservations and his warning to not get caught up in things, the events of the hour had gotten to him, because he pulled himself against her and gave her a look that made clear he wanted to kiss her. "Sadie," he whispered in a tone that was half plea and half question. When she made no motion to discourage him and instead parted her lips hopefully, Troy leaned in.

They froze immediately at a rather unwanted sound passing by their door. Siphon's deep voice rang clear, and their hearts found a new reason to pound. "It's becoming a problem," Siphon said. "We could really use the help of a female. Sorry, I know you are quite talented, but it seems our spy is not interested in men. We need to send someone else in."

He appeared to have stopped a few feet down the hall, and it was almost too far to be able to catch the next voice. *Almost.*

"And Mia?" Gabriel asked. Sadie's anxiety spiked at hearing her once mentor converse with her enemy.

Siphon's response to the suggestion of using his daughter must have been delivered entirely in a look, but after a few seconds the congressman asked, "And what about your other girl?"

Gabriel cleared his throat. "Yes. I've vetted her. I'm sure she's with us. If she had something to confess, it would have come out of her last night. As you'll remember, I have a sort of... an affinity for this kind of thing. After I've slept with someone, I can usually tell if they're lying to me." He paused and then added decisively. "That one is unequivocally on our side. She's a good girl. And strong."

As Sadie realized with horror that they were talking about her she looked at Troy wide-eyed. He hadn't budged from his close position, not daring to make a noise, but he was glaring daggers at her.

"Good work. Now do me a favor, go keep my daughter from getting into too much trouble tonight. If you can keep her away from Jax as he becomes more intoxicated, I'll double your pay," Siphon said. They heard two pairs of footsteps pass by them as the men made their way out to the better lit parts of the house.

Troy's hand stayed on her waist as he panted out, "So that's it then. All this time." His quiet anger was frightening, and Sadie's heart pounded louder. "You should get an award. You got past Amadi, Patricia. Everyone. And here you were about to snag me too."

His muscles were contracting in violent spasms all over his body, and she knew there was nothing she could say to undo the damage that had just been done. She'd lost him completely with Gabriel's words, and her body screamed with regret that they hadn't got to kiss at least once.

Sadie realized he was thinking the same thing as the image ran strongly in his thoughts. Her body was tense with arousal and her own righteous anger and frustration, which was quickly growing to rival his. She couldn't be sure which of them moved first, or the rightness of either of them making a move under the circumstance, but they seemed in unthinking agreement as Troy pressed her up against the wall in the same instant she put her hand against the back of his bare neck and pulled him into her.

Troy's tongue entered her mouth with a moan as his hips rolled against her. They kissed like they were in an argument, trying to one-up each other in commitment. She tried to pull herself closer into him, inhaling the sweet smell of his skin while pressing her tongue against his. He tried to push her into the wall as firmly as possible and take control of the kiss with his own rhythm, which didn't entirely match hers.

This was nothing like any of the casual interactions she'd had that week. The ability to feel Troy through the skin contact was shockingly exciting. She traced through his body in her mind, the pounding of his heart, his tightly strung muscles, his abs relaxing and contracting as he moved in tiny undulations against her.

With frantic longing, her thoughts focused on the hard length of him pressed against her abdomen. Given her current lack of self-control she immediately began responding to the rhythm of his kiss, which had now thoroughly dominated her own, with pulses of pleasure.

He responded with gasps and groans that sounded so good on him she wanted to make him climax right there. She suddenly couldn't think of any good reason why she shouldn't, and she pulled Troy tighter to her and began to rapidly increase the intensity like it was a task of vital importance.

Then several horrible things happened all at once. The sweet smell of Troy disappeared, the warmth of his mouth on hers stopped, and the skin contact which gave her access to his pleasure vanished. She opened her eyes in shock at the sudden losses to find him kneeling on the ground on the other side of the closet, looking up at her.

"Shit, succubus. Why does that have to be so good? I didn't..." His chest was heaving and his jaw was clenched so tight she was surprised he could speak. "I hadn't imagined..."

She made to take a step forward, but stopped when he growled at her. "Stay back." He said the words with so little conviction they somehow turned into a plea to do the opposite.

At first she was upset that she was clearly hurting him, despite not really doing anything wrong. Except that she probably shouldn't have encouraged any of that. Though why she had to be the strong one when she was also in the midst of being accused of being a traitor, she couldn't say.

Gradually, her pity turned to outrage and she stood up straighter as she looked down at him. Her anger at him increased when she realized that despite all of that, she wanted more than anything to forget it all and resume kissing him. And he felt exactly the same way.

This all meant that neither of them wanted to do the right thing just then, and so she decided to grumpily take on the responsibility. Sadie smoothed her dress back down over her knees. "You can think what you want of me, Troy. But I'm not going to let you turn me into your source of suffering."

She walked out without another look at him, trying to compose herself as she walked toward the well-lit hall in front of her. Her whole body was trembling and she knew the other succubi would be able to see the interaction the second she ran into them. She did a quick mental check that it aligned okay with their story. It seemed to be fine. Perhaps she'd stopped their encounter so as not to get their fine clothes dirty or something. She doubted Siphon would ask about it, but it seemed worthwhile having all her answers ready, since she seemed to be terrible at coming up with them on the spot.

As she made her way back downstairs, she began to feel increasing panic that she couldn't quite identify. It was only as she was walking through the main hall, smiling at the people around her like a robot, that she realized the feeling was the one she used to get all the time back home. It was the sense that everyone around her secretly thought she was abnormal.

Until her transformation into succubus, she hadn't actually heard that many slights against her spoken out loud, but it didn't take many to leave her imagination full of all the ones that were also likely being said behind her back. Ironically, she did hear plenty after her transformation, which also happened to align with her beginning to feel somewhat comfortable in her own skin.

Unfortunately, except for when she was alone with Jimmy, she had never found anywhere that she felt at home, exactly as she was. Until joining the United. And until standing in the shower with Mia Siphon smiling warmly at her.

Her emotions were a confused mess. She couldn't seem to focus her various thoughts and worries as they swirled around her: Troy's betrayed expression behind his pulsating lust, Amadi telling her he believed in her, the armies amassing nearby. Again, Mia's face flashed into her mind and Sadie put a hand over her heart as she tried to push away the welcoming encounter with the other succubus.

All she knew was that the United was the one place she might actually fit, and if she somehow messed up this mission or if Troy did successfully convince everyone that she was sent by Siphon, she would be back to square one. Only it would hurt worse given she'd had a glimpse of what could've been.

She couldn't fathom why Gabriel had said what he had to Siphon. How had she passed his test? It really was the worst luck that Troy overheard it, as she didn't have any explanation to counter Gabriel's assertion. *But* she couldn't let this one obstacle wreck everything.

"You look a little lost," someone said to her right. Sadie took in the man grinning at her. "Anything I can help with?" he asked, holding out a drink to her. Since he already had one in his other hand, he must have spotted her and brought this one over with a mind to intercept her.

Sadie smiled at Hunter Griffith in a way that sat entirely on the surface. She knew she should match her emotions to what she was projecting outwardly since you never knew who was watching in a room full of feeders, but she just couldn't manage it.

As she accepted the drink, she couldn't help but feel as if she were the bad guy; the viper in the nest, here to bring down this beautiful world because she truly didn't belong anywhere, especially not here.

"I hear you've been making your way around. You seem to be fitting in well here. Or so my friends tell me," Hunter said, making her feel even worse.

"Everyone has been really welcoming," Sadie said, just barely keeping the sadness from reaching her voice. "And I love getting to know new people," she added, sinking deeper into the role with a strange kind of self-loathing she hadn't had when seducing Phoenix.

Hunter ducked his head on a smile. "Good to know. Unfortunately, we don't get much time off. I'm a captain in the Coalition army, and Siphon's sending us back out tonight."

"Shame," she sighed. Then she stared at him with a look that made perfectly clear she was available if he wanted it.

"But, uhh, that's not for a few hours," he said, taking a large sip of his drink and setting it down still half-full.

"Do you know where the upstairs bathroom is?" she asked.

"Yeah. I know this house very well," he grinned.

"No one's given me a tour yet. Would you mind?" she asked, setting her own drink down untouched.

Then, without the slightest desire to sleep with this man, and feeling entirely drained from what had already occurred that night, she followed him into another room and up a staircase. As they were rounding the upper corner, however, someone ground her unwanted mission to a halt.

"Sadie Hall. There you are, dear," Siphon said.

The congressman paused the instant they were face-to-face, and Sadie became suddenly self-conscious of the recent shenanigans she'd just engaged in with his daughter. She was right in assuming that was what he was taking in when Siphon turned to Hunter and said, "Will you please let my daughter know that her presence is still wanted."

Since Mia had said earlier that she was leaving to go respond to her father's call, Sadie wondered idly where she had really gone off to. But she didn't have much time to give to such thoughts as Siphon was now inviting her to follow him. Sadie nodded in acquiescence and a little relief as she left Hunter behind.

Siphon led her down the hallway, and Sadie wondered how much of his daughter's life he could see. It would be uncomfortable living with a family of succubi. As if he'd read her mind, Siphon said, "We learn to block out most of it. But when I see my daughter on you, I know something occurred, which is enough."

Sadie nodded shyly. "Sorry. I didn't mean to – she's a bit... forceful," she said, then added in a rush, "But very welcoming. I like her."

"Glad to hear it," he said, looking at her with approval as he held open a door.

They stepped into a small drawing room. It was the third such room she'd glimpsed so far, and Sadie marveled at how big the place was even as she stopped dead at the sight of Troy pacing back and forth in front of the mantle. He froze the instant they'd entered and leaned against it, trying to look as casual as possible. Troy had somehow gotten his hand on a fresh pair of trousers and looked entirely put together, as if nothing but polite conversation had occurred that evening.

"Sir," he said with a bob of his head. "Gabriel said you wanted to see me?"

Though Sadie was sure he must have been on edge at this development, he looked outwardly calm and mildly interested.

"Yes. Some unfortunate news has been brought to my attention," Siphon said, gesturing for them to take the couch. The congressman turned his back to them as he poured a drink. Sadie felt Troy glance at her as they sat down a foot apart, but she continued to stare determinedly straight ahead.

Siphon took the large armchair across from them, swirling the ice in his glass as he looked at it. "Even as a succubus, I think I can say there are few pleasures in life as sweet as fine brandy," he said before passing the glass to her.

She took a small sip and nodded in polite appreciation while doing her best to not make a face of disgust. Troy didn't hide his look when it was his turn and passed the glass back to Siphon with a laugh. "I think I'll leave this one for you."

"You know. Regardless of your vices, these things never come for free. We have to protect the precious parts of life." Siphon sipped again in slow appreciation. "And there's always someone lurking in the shadows trying to take it all from you."

Sadie had the shocking realization then that the mighty congressman was mildly too intoxicated. He had the slightest slur to his speech and wobble in his movements. His eyes were sharp though when he focused them back on her.

"The humans are amassing an army. They intend to attack any day now." He paused for dramatic effect and they both made appropriate sounds of surprise and outrage. "Luckily, I have been preparing for just such an event. I have my own little troops gathered nearby, and they are ready to counter any aggression our enemies throw at us." Sadie's face must have registered some real fear, because Siphon looked at her in concern. "Don't you worry, dear. Justice will prevail in the end. But not without a fight."

Siphon sighed. "It's hard work keeping a sizable number of troops from being infiltrated by spies. And it has become clear that someone on the inside has been passing rather detailed information about our movements. Someone at the top."

Siphon looked at her squarely. "I'm going to be frank here because I believe you are a smart and capable young woman, and Gabriel has attested to that fact. Many of the captains are men who would be rather susceptible to your charms. You are a bit of a godsend to this problem in fact. My own daughter... is a bit obvious about these things. Plus her looks tend to intimidate or build instant mistrust. You, however... have a quality. A sweet, girl-next-door energy. And though perhaps that is just your natural way, it also makes you special here. You could be a game-changing force if you were willing to do service to the cause – help root out this rat."

He leaned back in satisfaction. "A sweet-faced succubus. Your arrival is an omen that we're on the right side of history."

Sadie smiled shyly and swept her one loose strand of hair behind her ear. "That's... quite a flattering assessment," she said, not having to feign her reaction.

She couldn't be sure, but she thought she felt a wave of heat coming from Troy, as if his body temperature had just increased a few degrees. She didn't dare look at him, but her awareness of his arm a few inches from her was suddenly sharp in her thoughts.

"Only question now is. Are you up for it?" Siphon asked.

Sadie had come here with Troy to get in close with this world. He had been her main excuse for rejecting this offer, which Amadi had been certain Siphon would make upon meeting her. The idea was to stay close to the main targets. Only, Hunter Griffith was one of those targets, and she'd just learned that he was with Siphon's army.

It didn't seem that unreasonable for her to say yes. And, given everything that had just happened to her, she desperately wanted to get the hell out of there. Not to mention the fact that they had been invited to go to this party with Mia, Jax, and Gabriel, and she was sure the whole thing would be a disaster. She wasn't sure how she had managed to get past Gabriel's test, but she wasn't going to let herself end up back in such a dangerous situation.

"Sure, I'll go," she said.

Troy cleared his throat, sitting up straighter. "Uhh... don't you want to stay with me, dear?" he asked, as if choking on the words. Sadie was glad Siphon was drunk, because Troy didn't look particularly convincing in his role just then.

"That's why you're both here. I know this is a request for the two of you." Siphon faced Troy. "Would you let me borrow Sadie a while? A week or two, perhaps? I would send you along, but you have more important work to do here. You can join the fight when you're done recruiting nature feeders to the cause. Which, given the effectiveness of your charisma, might be never."

Sadie looked over at Troy. Her gaze slid from his passive expression to the tense muscles of his neck and forearms. He'd rolled up his sleeves and was holding his hands a few inches apart. He looked, very subtly, as if he were braced for an attack. It occurred to her then that Troy wasn't trying very hard to play along, because he had fully assumed the belief that she was on Siphon's side, which would mean the man knew all about the United and Troy's role in it.

He must have thought this was some kind of test, or simply a load more false information to take back. Troy smiled then – it looked like his usual one, only this time, he didn't change his ready stance in the slightest.

"It would be my honor, *sir*," Troy said, and Sadie wondered if the congressman had the awareness just then to pick up on the drop of irony Troy had clearly deliberately placed on the honorific title. Siphon seemed content, however, as he gave a decisive nod.

"Good. Now please, go enjoy the party." Siphon gestured to Troy. "Sadie can come say goodbye when we're done here."

But Sadie didn't see Troy again that night. Which, she would later think was for the best, since as he looked back at her from the doorway, his expression of betrayal sat coldly over the underlying lust that surrounded the memory of their kiss, and Sadie didn't think she could stand to see that combination a moment longer, especially when she caught sight of the thick red cord of light connecting them. It pulsed strong and thick, and despite her hurt feelings, it was flowing both ways.

Chapter 19

Isolation in a crowd

Sadie and the Coalition troupe left at dawn the next morning. The departure point contained about fifty people, twenty horses, and eleven motorcycles. Tucker Stone and his posse of earth nymphs were standing together in one corner. One of them, she assumed Michael, waved at her from afar.

Hunter arranged the ride situation to accommodate the additional ten people they'd picked up on this visit, and Sadie was loaded onto one of the bikes behind him, where she spent the rest of the morning pressed intimately against his back. The feeling was uncomfortable, and it somehow made her miss Jimmy with a sharp pain, despite having seen him just yesterday.

Her fear over when they'd be together again was too overwhelming to look at directly, and she determinedly kept it suppressed into a tight ball in the pit of her stomach. She was a bystander to her changing fate now, and as the motorcycle jostled her over roads and fields, she did her best to surrender to it.

The sun came up right before they crested the final hill into camp, and her mouth fell open. The fifty of them were just a tiny drop in the bucket of people present. There were tents for a mile at least. They couldn't see the end of them from where they were dismounting, and for the first time since joining up with the United, Sadie really understood what it meant that war was coming.

Hunter, branching off from the others, took her to the captain's quarters, a roped-off encampment on the opposite side of the field from which they'd entered. It sat on the edge of the forest and Hunter gestured to the trees as he helped her dismount. "The enemy camp is on the other side of these woods," he said, then clearly mistaking her expression added, "But don't worry. We'll keep you safe. Siphon asked us to show you a good time, and I always keep my word."

Sadie did her best to return his warm smile. Recalling Jimmy's map of the three Coalition families, she reminded herself that Hunter Griffith was an excitement feeder, and she would have to work hard to ensure her outward demeanor matched her inner feelings of enthusiasm. Not to mention that most of the captains were likely to be human feeders, and since she was there to entertain them as much as they were her, every one of them would be watching her closely.

Hunter introduced her to the twenty or so men and two women who were in the midst of having breakfast. Gesturing grandly, he said, "Sadie's a succubus, and she's going to spend some time with us until the fight breaks out. I'll take her back to Siphon when the excitement is over."

Sadie looked around at the faces of the those in charge of leading the Coalition war and had to quickly fight back a feeling of disgust. Luckily, no one seemed to notice, and Hunter's words were followed by a wave of interest from many of them.

Siphon had asked her to look for anyone sneaking off or behaving suspiciously. He'd also given her detailed instructions on questions to ask after she'd slept with someone, things only meant to catch them in a lie. Of course, she would be doing none of that. *Her* goal was to get closer to Hunter.

Nodding politely around at the uniformed crowd, Sadie accepted some bread and cheese before sitting down with her side pressed against Hunter's. He smiled at that and began telling her all about the coming battle with an enthusiasm she did her best to match.

"But how do you know their forces aren't bigger than yours?" she asked in a tone of concern. The emotion in her was luckily real, since she was very much worried over the idea that exactly the opposite was true.

"Oh, we've seen them. Our scouts indicate they're about two-thirds our size," a man who'd been trying to catch her attention said.

"Yes, but the unknown is in the number of nature feeders. And the type," a woman said. "If they have a ton of fire and earthquake feeders, we might take a big hit."

"But... we must also have such nymphs on our side?" Sadie said, immediately regretting having said nymph instead of nature feeder. She was worried it might be a sign she was an outsider to the movement, and she wanted to put them at ease.

But no one seemed to care, and Hunter even said, "Yes. We have several fire nymphs. Though I'm not so concerned over this question. After all, we have something they don't." He looked at Sadie as if waiting for her to ask.

She just gestured him on with a smile. Hunter licked his fingers clean. "Be right back," he told her with a wink.

Sadie didn't have to feign her excitement when he returned with a large black gun that looked nothing like her father's back home. "Come," he said. "I'll show you something you haven't seen."

Her heart pounded as Hunter led her into the trees, which were glowing brilliantly with the rising sun. A minute later they were alone, the sounds from the camp muffled. He smiled over at her as he loaded the weapon and Sadie did her best to smile encouragingly.

"Should I cover my ears?" she asked.

"Nah. It's the quietest gun you'll ever hear. It has a suppressor that tamps down the loudest part." Hunter took aim at the largest tree across from them.

Sadie knew what was coming and yet, she couldn't quite manage to suppress her surprise as the gun began to rapid-fire round after round in a non-stop flow. If the tree trunk had been a group of soldiers, this weapon would have mowed them down in a couple heartbeats. She did cover her ears at the end, because despite what Hunter said, the sound was still terrifying.

Hunter leaned the weapon against a tree and faced her. "What do you think?" he asked.

She knew he'd be able to tell her near-hysteria, and so decided it was best to roll with it. "That's incredible," she breathed, putting a hand over her heart. "I've never seen anything like it."

She wanted to find out how many of these they had, but couldn't ask too directly. "Will you get to use one in this coming fight?" she inquired instead.

"Me? No. The captains are all prominent feeders and are lives are too valuable to be on the front lines. We do the strategizing. Without us, these men wouldn't know where to go or who to shoot. No. The battle will be led by the lieutenants and directed by Tucker Stone."

"Tucker? I met him. I hope you have enough to arm his whole troop. I got a little intimate with them last night," Sadie said, ducking her head in feigned shyness.

Hunter chuckled. "I heard, actually. Yeah, we've got enough for Stone's people and more. Don't worry. With fifty of these guns, we'll be able to more than hold our own. After all, these people are untrained, and mostly unarmed. Tucker Stone and his merry men will be just fine." He stepped closer, and his smile faded. "We all will," he added with an intent look.

As Hunter moved within arm's reach, the distinct image of him kissing her flashed into his thoughts. Sadie tried to steady her nerves as he placed a hand on the side of her head and stroked her ear through her hair.

"You are so beautiful," he whispered. The sounds of the recent gunshots rang in her ear, and she did her best to swallow her anxiety. She could see the heavy black death machine in her peripheral and she had to fight back the urge to look at it directly as Hunter stepped into her space.

This was good. She was here for exactly this. She should kiss Hunter. He closed the last inch of space between them until his body was flush with hers. The image of her friends being mowed down by rapid-fire bullets popped into her thoughts unbidden. She flinched, and gave her head a tiny shake, blinking in confusion.

Hunter froze with his lips nearly against hers. He stood back upright, and she tensed as he withdrew a foot. "Sorry, was that too forward?" he asked.

"No, I just – It's been a long morning. I think I need a nap. That 3 a.m. wake-up is catching up with me." She tucked her hair behind her ear as she dropped her gaze, not wanting to meet his eyes a moment longer.

"Of course. I didn't mean to overwhelm you. You can rest in my quarters," he said, gesturing her toward the camp.

Sadie tried to calm her emotions by focusing on the birds and trees as Hunter led her to his tent, but the second she was alone, a sense of panic hit her. What was she doing here? She was surrounded by the enemy, and she had to carry out her objective entirely alone, having lost her one ally. The hurt face of Troy popped into her thoughts for the hundredth time that day.

If Jimmy knew how afraid she was right now, he would lose his shit.

But could she return to Amadi after what Troy overheard in that closet? She was terrified of the others rejecting her as Troy had. She needed to prove her worth first; show that she could bring them something undeniably useful.

She pictured Troy and Patricia arriving at the other camp right around then and sharing what had happened. Amadi might look at the binder she'd stolen with suspicion. Sadie couldn't help but picture Luciana and Patricia poring over the thing, looking for evidence the information was a set-up.

No. They wouldn't be so fast to accept one overheard comment. Amadi at least knew how she could have gotten the code to that safe. He would believe her story. He would assume there was a perfectly good explanation to Gabriel's vouching for her. Sadie paced back and forth as she talked herself both out and back into a state of panic.

At the sounds of footfalls, she threw herself on the cot facing the wall. She heard someone, likely Hunter, enter and place something nearby. It was probably the tea he'd said he'd bring. She feigned the breathing of slumber, and a moment later he was gone.

Sadie was relieved. She wasn't ready to deal with him. Hunter didn't turn her off in any personal way, but having seen this camp put the realization that these people meant harm into sharp relief. With that thought, Sadie was hit with further worry over her reaction to his attempted kiss earlier.

What if... she couldn't actually go through with this?

Sadie fretted over this question right up until she emerged from the nap several hours later to find the captain's quarters nearly empty. She ate lunch with a couple of the guys and then told them she wanted to take a tour. At least Gabriel's comment had done some good. Siphon had clearly sent her here with his full support, because the men seemed unconcerned at her wandering off unaccompanied. They didn't even glance her way when she ducked under the rope and went straight toward the center of the camp.

Sadie did her best to analyze her surroundings as she walked. When she'd first turned succubus, it had been hard to make sense of all the new information she saw when looking at people. She realized now, however, that somewhere in the past month she had begun to be able to tell whether or not she could feed from someone. It was a subtle thing, just a small humming under her skin when she looked at a person.

She walked for what must have been hours, taking in the people around her. In the end, Sadie decided there were roughly four human feeders for every nymph. Since she could feed off of both nymphs and humans, there was always a chance that some of that count could have included the latter, but she highly doubted it.

This meant two things: the Coalition had managed to recruit a good number of nymphs to their cause, *and yet,* they still had a long way to go. She could see now why Siphon had put so much interest in Troy's leadership. Sadie couldn't recall her human species class very well, but she knew the country had far more nymphs than human feeders, maybe ten times as many. If so, the Coalition hadn't actually won all that many hearts and minds.

"Hey, are you hungry?" a man nearby asked when she stopped to stretch.

Sadie smiled and accepted the offering of warm bread. "Thanks."

"No problem." The young man smiled, looking pleased with himself.

"I just joined up and my nerves kept me from eating breakfast," she said.

"You joined today?" he asked.

She nodded.

"Hell of a time. Hope you're ready for a fight."

She raised her eyebrows in a question as she chewed.

"Not with another town of human vermin, no," he continued. "There's a resistance force, an organized one, nearby. We're going to wipe them out later this week. It'll be something big to be a part of, but I'd get ready if I were you. It'll be any day now."

Holding up the bread in thanks, she nodded again to the man and kept walking.

For the first time, Sadie considered the idea that she was going to get caught in the fight. Why would Siphon send her to draw out a spy this close to a battle? Unless... he wasn't remotely concerned that Amadi's forces would put a dent in the Coalition's. And as Hunter had explained, none of the captains would actually be risking their own necks, anyway. She could only hope that their confidence was far overblown.

It was time to put away those heavy thoughts, though. As she wandered through the crowd of feeders back to the captain's quarters, Sadie actively practiced replacing her feeling of cold fear with raw excitement. She couldn't allow herself her true emotions here, it was too big of a risk, but the sun was shining and the field of people was bustling with energy. Sadie would need to tamp down her rational brain and immerse herself in this experience if she was going to genuinely fit in.

By the time she came around the nearest tent and spotted Hunter bent over some maps, she felt ready to re-engage. He smiled up at her and she focused in on all the things which could be appealing about him. Hunter was a man of energy and enthusiasm, which seemed to affect the other captains around him.

He stroked his finely cut beard as he chuckled at a story the man across from him was telling. Sadie repressed the words of the horrible story best she could and instead focused on Hunter's strong hands and daring smile.

Which were the two things she was still fixed on hours later as they cleaned up after dinner. She kept a hum over her brain to fight away the war chatter, tuning in only when someone said something personal.

"Can I pour you a drink?" Hunter asked.

"Sure," Sadie said, smiling up at him from her spot on the grass.

"We don't have much, I'm afraid. Do you prefer watered-down beer or bad whiskey?"

She laughed, then opened her mouth to ask for beer. "Whiskey, please," she said, changing her mind at the last minute. It might not hurt to get herself a little tipsy.

The men cheered as she smoothly downed the shot, fighting back her look of repulsion. Sadie shivered, then laughed and handed the glass back to Hunter. "Another?" he asked.

"One more," she said, winking at the captain sitting near her.

Hunter sat down between her and the other man, holding out two shots. "Cheers," he said, and they downed them looking into each other's eyes. She was going to sleep with this man and steal his memories. It was going to be fun, because he was attractive and entertaining. She had had fun that night with Phoenix, and this was no different.

Sadie let her pinky, which was still bare from when she'd taken off her gloves to eat, graze Hunter's as she passed back the glass. His breath hitched as a light wave of heat pulsed briefly through his body. For that fleeting moment, she could feel his heart beating and a clear awareness of his body captivated her thoughts. Her animal brain took over and she thought, *yes, I can do this*.

Hunter stayed by her side, watching her intently for the rest of the night as the men told stories and asked her flirtatious questions. Sadie rolled with it, playfully, and by her fourth shot, she'd practically forgotten where she was, convincing herself this was a true party with friends.

"Where are you staying tonight?" asked one of the captains whose name she'd already forgotten.

Sadie didn't hesitate to look shyly over at Hunter. He sipped his beer to cover the smile as the other men cheered. She got to her feet, glad to find herself fairly steady, and held out a hand to him. "Bedtime?" she asked.

Hunter took the hand as he rose, and the men clapped at the erection that bulged strong. "Okay, enough," he said, throwing a towel at one of them as he led Sadie back to his tent. The sounds of the other captains dimmed as they entered Hunter's dark quarters on the edge of the roped-off section that indicated their station.

She waited in the dark as Hunter bustled around lighting a couple lamps. "Ahh. That's better," he said, looking up at her from the bedside oil lamp. Sadie stepped toward him, but tripped over her feet, stumbling a bit.

"Whoa, steady there," Hunter said, catching her. "That was a lot of whiskey. I don't know how much you usually drink, but maybe I can get you some water?"

Sadie nodded as the tent spun around her. Hunter brought her a tall glass and sat her on the cot as she drank it. "Better?" he asked, stroking her hair from her face.

"I think so." She put aside the cup and moved closer. Hunter's gaze grew immediately heated and she was hit with a strong pulse of lust. He pulled her close with an arm around her waist and his eyes dropped to her lips a moment before he leaned in.

Their mouths met, and for a brief instant Sadie was repulsed by the intimacy of the kiss, but then the room swam again and she sunk into the feel of the warm body responding to her. Hunter pulled back to look at her, cupping her face between his hands now. "Wow, that's really good," he whispered. "Even better than Mia."

"Hmm," Sadie nodded, not wanting to think about the other succubus just then. She leaned forward to pull them back into the moment, but Hunter stopped her. He was still holding her head, only now he was looking back and forth between her eyes.

"Wha—?" she mumbled.

"I – I think you're pretty drunk," he said, sounding regretful.

"Yeah, a little." Sadie shrugged and put her hand around his bare wrist.

He closed his eyes on a groan, but then shook his head, looking back at her. Reaching with his other hand, he gently removed her grip.

"No, I – I think you're *too* drunk." His shoulders slumped as he scooted a couple inches away. "Too drunk to do this tonight."

"No, I'm not. I mean, maybe. But that's just in this moment, you know? But in like a minute – I'm sure it'll all be fine. Just fine," she said, vaguely aware of the slur in her speech.

"Yeah, you're gone. I shouldn't have refilled those shots. I wasn't thinking. Here." He gestured her to stand, giving her a hand when she struggled. Then he pulled back the covers and bent to remove her shoes.

"I'll sleep above the sheet," he said, refilling her water glass and putting it nearby. "We'll leave a lamp on in case you're sick in the night," he added, tucking her in before walking around to the other side of the cot.

The room spun behind her closed eyes and she tried to muster the strength to protest, but it just felt so good to be lying down. "M'okay," she mumbled in the end.

Sadie felt the weight of the man as he made himself comfortable several feet away. A minute later, she heard him unzip his pants and the cot began to rock in quick, tiny jerks. She was asleep before he'd finished.

THE SOUND of many voices pulled Sadie from her dream of Jimmy. For a brief moment, she fought to stay asleep and continue it. Her body ached with the heat of the moment and the vision of Jimmy's brown eyes grew fuzzier as she was pulled to consciousness.

Despite the fact it had only been two days since she last saw him, she could already feel the presence of a Jimmy-shaped hole, and it seemed to stem from much more than her growing hunger. She realized that they had never actually been apart this long, except perhaps when they were very small children. And in this particular moment, it felt as if he were on another planet.

The light of day hit her, and it came in the company of a pounding headache.

"Morning," Hunter said, his smiling, concerned face swimming into view. "You slept through the night. That's good."

Sadie pushed herself up. "Hmmm," she groaned, putting her forehead in her hand. "Sorry about last night."

"Don't worry about it. We had some laughs. Just promise me you'll take care of yourself today." Hunter placed a rich-smelling sandwich in her hand.

"Hmmm," she agreed without looking up.

"I'll leave you to it," he told her, and a moment later she heard his retreating steps and the swish of the tent flap.

Oh, thank goodness. She couldn't handle his kind smile while she was feeling so terrible. God, what had she been thinking? Sadie knew, of course, that she'd been trying to ease her own fears through over drinking, but now that she was sitting here nauseous in the bed of her enemy, who was being very kind to her, she wished she'd just kept her head straight.

She'd fucked up. But she was going to fix this. Forcing down the food and water, Sadie decided she would go in search of the Tucker Stone men. She hadn't fed yesterday, and she wanted to take Mae's advice and memory dive only when she was brimming over. She would stock up and get herself together for another attempt with Hunter, whose caretaking had helped to soften her ill-ease toward him.

An hour later, she was fed and watered and following Hunter's directions to Tucker's part of camp. It was even harder to control her emotions as her head continued to pound, and she stared around at the soldiers with a growing sense of panic. There were so many of them, and they looked so... excited, while she felt entirely on the outside of the shouts and smiles all around her. The sense of anticipation in the air was due to the coming fight, and she couldn't seem to suppress that knowledge.

"Sadie!" Michael said, the second she came into view. He was sitting on a log, eating alone, and his big smile made her heart ache.

"Where are the others?" she asked, looking around at the empty space.

"Training. I got a concussion this morning, and Tucker's making me take a recovery day," he said, sounding completely distraught.

"Oh. Well... That works out for us, though. I was hoping to find someone to feed from. I'm staying with a bunch of human feeders."

He grinned. "That does put a different color on the morning, yeah."

Sadie took her time getting all she could out of him, feeling only slightly guilty for exhausting the man while he was injured. As they were getting redressed, she found herself in search of something to say. "Are you excited for the coming fight?" she asked, immediately regretting bringing up the topic.

His answer surprised her, though. "Not really. I love the guys... and training has been a blast, but—" He shrugged. "I don't know, what if one of us dies? These dudes are like my brothers." Sadie sat next to him as she laced up her boots. "And I'm not sure how I'm going to feel about actually shooting at people."

She knew how she felt about it. It sounded insane. "Yeah, that would be pretty hard," she nodded sympathetically as she laced up her boot.

"I mean, don't get me wrong. I know these people deserve it. They tore up a whole town, after all. Someone's got to stop them." Michael clenched his jaw, looking suddenly older. "I just don't think it's going to be so easy wiping out thousands of people. I mean, we all still have families out there somewhere. The people I'll kill, they have parents."

Sadie felt a cold chill creep up her back. Why did he have to be so relatable? "Yeah, I know, Michael." She sighed, knowing he would soon be shooting at her friends and even so, not wanting him to get hurt either.

But the smiling face of Hunter this morning flashed into the forefront of her mind, and she recalled that despite how nice the captain looked on the outside, the real blame for all this should be laid at his feet. His, and the other feeder leaders. "That's why we have to remember that this is an ugly business. The other side started this war. We're just responding to it," she said, pleading with her own conscious.

They exchanged a sad smile. "Take care of yourself," she said in parting. Then she recalled it was her friends he'd soon be fighting and added, "And I don't think it would make you a bad soldier if you just shot at their kneecaps."

Sadie left there with renewed determination and the emotion didn't fade as she entered the second evening with the captains. She drank nothing but water that night, and by jumping in to dominate the conversation with tales of her sexual escapades, Sadie both captured attention and prevented herself from having to hear any more terrible stories from the men. By the time Hunter suggested they go to bed, she had a much steadier hand over her emotional state.

Hunter again led her into his quarters and fumbled around lighting the lamp. But the instant he turned to face her, Sadie put a hand on the back of his neck and sent a strong pulse of pleasure through it. He gasped, looking momentarily surprised, but he calmed under her gaze, and for an instant they were just two people about to kiss.

Sadie drew him toward the bed with the kiss and pivoted to push him to his back. He was very compliant in her maneuvering, and it increased her sense of control over the situation. She left most of her clothing on as she straddled him, not particularly wanting to be completely naked with this man.

He lifted his shoulder as she wrestled off his shirt, and for a moment it got stuck over his shoulders and eyes. The image of Jimmy caught like that hit her hard. She froze, her heart pounding. Hunter pulled himself free and threw aside the shirt. "What is it?" he asked. His concern, she realized, was likely not due to the fact that she'd paused but more because he could read her sudden increase in excitement.

"Nothing," she breathed, running her palms up his muscled chest. "I just really like your body."

The sound of rapid-fire bullets echoed through her thoughts, and the image of Jimmy on his back covered in blood swam into view. She shook her head, trying to clear away the unwanted disturbance. *No.* She had been doing fine. Everything had been working out. She just needed to get it back.

Increasing the pleasure coursing through him, Sadie bent to

continue their kiss. For the briefest moment, she was caught up in the warmth and feel of another body, but she couldn't hold onto it. She sat up on a gasp, as if searching for air.

"Sadie?" he asked, looking concerned now. "What is it?"

Shit. Shit. Shit.

"Sorry." She pressed her thumb and forefinger into her forehead. "I think I'm still recovering from last night."

Sadie hated that she'd apologized. She didn't like this man, she certainly didn't owe him anything, and she couldn't turn away from the fact he was a captain in an army that was about to attack her friends.

Hunter propped himself up on his elbows and looked her over with scrutiny. "Sadie, you know you don't have to do this, right? It seems like you're trying too hard, and I don't know why. No one said you have to sleep with me." Sadie looked up in time to see a small wave of doubt pass over his features. "Did they?" he asked, propping himself up to scrutinize her.

Sadie panicked at his look of suspicion. "God no! It's nothing like that," she said with so much sincerity that she almost even convinced herself. "It's just—" She recalled Hetia's advice to stick to true emotions when possible. "I think I'm falling in love with Troy. I didn't realize I would have a problem trying to sleep with someone else, but – it seems I do."

That was good. Hunter's scrutiny disappeared entirely, and his body relaxed under hers. He plopped to his back and she disentangled herself from his lap.

"I see," he sighed.

"I'm sorry," Sadie said, and then to her horror, she began to cry. Hunter paused only briefly, before moving to comfort her. Pulling the blanket up between their skin, he put an arm against her back. This only increased her confused emotions. She didn't want this man to be kind to her anymore. She didn't want to touch him or think about him a moment longer. And it wasn't even him to whom she was apologizing. She was sorry to herself.

This was a far cry from the situation she'd been in a few days ago. This was an utter disaster. She shouldn't have come here. There was no way she was going to be able to get something out of Hunter, and she was now in a very dangerous place. And worst of all, she had failed completely. She couldn't do the one thing that might save her position in the United, and even more importantly, might help stop the war.

She sobbed harder, and Hunter said, "Look, it's really not that big a deal. You think I want to sleep with you when you clearly don't want to? No... it's good we stopped. Really. It's nothing to cry over."

Sadie began to calm. She followed the soothing sound of his voice back to earth, gaining enough control to push down the remaining emotion. She nodded, drying her eyes. "You're right. I'm being totally silly. This week has just been a lot," she said through ragged breaths.

At least there was no way on earth this man would think she was a spy. After all, it seemed impossible that a spy could be this bad at her job.

"Captain?" a young man called from the door.

Sadie jumped at the sound of another person so near, her nerves were clearly stretched thin.

Hunter crossed the tent and took something from the man. She watched him open the parchment and read rapidly, then he disappeared without looking back at her. Creeping to the flap, she peered out in search of where he'd gone.

He returned a minute later, appearing in her sight without warning. Sadie jumped back as he entered. "What's going on?" she asked.

"We're attacking at dawn," he said.

She couldn't help her surprised expression. "Now?"

"Don't worry. You can just go to bed. We'll likely only need a third of the troops." He put his hands on her arms in a comforting gesture. "You'll be perfectly safe here. And in the morning, I'll send you back to your old life."

She didn't know what to say. "Oh – okay." To show she was going to follow his directions, she moved to sit on the bed. Hunter looked satisfied, gave her a quick nod of his head in parting, then grabbed his hat and left.

A third of the troops. They were awfully confident they had the upper hand here. Suddenly, her little worries about getting information didn't seem as important. Jimmy was in that camp. Hetia, and possibly Patricia and Troy, too. The faces of Amadi, Cobie, and the other soldiers rolled through her mind one after the other.

She had failed here. Hunter's kind smiles and comforting words were driving her insane, and she didn't think she could stand another night under the gaze of the Coalition. But, if she could get out of here, maybe she could offer an early warning to Amadi. If not, then she would at least be with Jimmy when this all went down, instead of utterly alone in the bed of Hunter Griffith.

Sadie made the impulsive decision with such conviction that she knew there would be no turning back. She was leaving. Now. She was going to cross the forest and find the United camp.

Chapter 20

Playing with fire

Having made the decision to leave, Sadie felt a sudden urgency, as if any moment someone was going to grab her from behind. Moving with quiet haste, she pulled on her warmest layers and fished around for some kind of light source she could take with her, finding a single tiny flashlight, which she tucked between her breasts.

The sound of movement and chatter had grown louder around her, and she wondered how in the hell she was going to make a break for it when everyone would be staying up tonight. But as she peered out through the flap into the dark, she could see a clear shot between the tents. Before she could overthink it, she darted out into the night.

A minute later she was covered by the trees, quiet except for the occasional bird call. Despite the fear and uncertainty of wandering dangerously through the woods separating two war camps, Sadie felt a sense of peace she hadn't had since crossing the country.

She was back in the forest. It wasn't her forest; the trees were strange and the sounds unusual, but it had that familiar stillness to it she just couldn't find anywhere else. The near full moon provided plenty of light, and she opted for not drawing attention to herself by using the flashlight, especially given that she found little challenge in navigating the terrain.

Everything was going to be fine, she told herself on repeat as she set a sustainable pace in what she hoped was the right direction. She would probably run into the other camp within a few hours, long before sunrise, she coached, despite not having any actual information.

This was a narrative that died sharply when an hour later she saw lights off to her right. Lights, which quickly turned out to belong to the edge of the Coalition camp. Damn. She'd managed to loop back around. A shiver ran down her back as she set off again, this time making great effort to keep the moon in the same place above her.

Unfortunately, the trees only grew thicker and there were long moments in which she couldn't find any points of reference at all. After the third time she'd tripped over something unseen, she gave in and pulled out the flashlight.

Hours passed. It was hard to tell how many. And the creeping fear morphed into a very present threat. *This* was a disaster. Though it was just as she'd begun contemplating climbing a tree and waiting for dawn, that she was hit by a glimmer of hope. The wind blew lightly past her and she caught the barest hint of fire smoke.

Could it be the United camp? Was she finally near? Suddenly worried at sneaking up on a war camp, she began to move even more quietly, taking care not to snap any twigs with her steps. Hopefully, she could get close enough to be recognized before someone tagged her as a threat from a distance.

But even though the scent of smoke increased drastically, she'd found no signs of life as another hour passed. The only change was a distant rumble, which became noticeable when Sadie stopped to listen hopefully for voices. The noise was hard to identify. It didn't sound remotely human, more like a light roar of a... fire.

Squinting into the dark behind her, she thought she could make out the coming dawn, unless – her stomach clenched – unless the *forest* was on *fire*. If so, then maybe she wasn't smelling campfires from the United camp at all. She decided it was time to pick up the pace. This was no time to conserve energy.

Breaking into a jog, she tried to set a pace she could maintain. But as the minutes passed, the evidence that there was in fact a fire at her back became more and more apparent, despite the fact the light was indeed mingling with the rising sun.

Dawn was here. And the attack was starting with fire nymphs.

Sadie lost her sense of reasoning and sped up into a full-on sprint, not caring how long she could keep it up. The forest remained empty of human life, and the image of her dying alone flashed unbidden into her mind.

She jumped at a crashing sound from behind her and a moment later a herd of deer ran past, not bothering to glance her way. The sight of other animals fleeing flipped a primal switch in her head. She didn't know where she was or in how great of danger, but she bolted through the woods with everything she had.

The roar of flames stopped increasing and soon a new sound replaced it, distinctly human this time. The fire was coming more from her left, while behind her on the right was the clamor of many feet. As they neared, she thought she heard the quiet rumble of motors, and the galloping sound of horses. They were gaining on her.

A single gunshot went off in the distance, and Sadie tripped over a branch. A moment later, the sound of fighting erupted in full. People shouted as more shots fired and somewhere in the dark woods ahead, thunder roared. Thunder. Yes, thunder was good, her brain registered after a minute.

"Amadi!" she called, in the direction of the storm. "Jimmy!"

Sadie hesitated on which direction she should continue, and decided to veer more left as she picked back up the pace. The fire smoke grew thicker, but the gunshots became fainter. She could only hope that the actual fire lagged far behind its cloud of smoke.

"Jimmy!" she called again, too out of breath to get much volume behind the cry.

From the corner of her eye, she caught sudden movement. Several figures were running full force to her left, heading in the direction of the fire. Most of their skin was bare, in the style of nymph firefighters, and Sadie thought the figure in front looked distinctly like Troy. She nearly called his name, but hesitated, uncertain of the wisdom of such a thing.

But then the figure turned and there was no doubt. Troy was here. Really here. She wasn't alone anymore. Though her relief was quickly overtaken by uncertainty as he spotted her. He called out something to the others and veered off in her direction. Troy was shirtless and wearing the flame-retardant pants of a firefighter. He looked angry, and yet, she couldn't help but be grateful to see him.

"What are you doing here?" he called as he closed the distance.

"Trying to—" She choked on the words, too out of breath to shout again with smoke in her lungs.

Troy reached her and she tried again. "I was trying to warn you about the attack, but I got lost in the dark."

She felt like she was about to cry as she waited to see how he was going to respond to her. Troy looked her up and down, then quickly glanced around them.

"You have to get out of here. Head that way." He pointed behind him. "And tie your shirt up over your mouth and nose." He hesitated, looking in the direction the other nymphs had run. "I have to go. Please, get yourself away from here."

"Troy—" she said, stepping closer. She wanted to say something to repair what had happened between them, say she'd been a fool to go off-plan. She wanted to berate him for mistrusting her and beg him not to leave her there, even if Gabriel's comment had damned her. But in the end, there were no right words.

Troy cupped her shoulders in both hands, giving her his full attention. "Sadie, I don't know what you're up to, but you can't stay here." Then retreating in his familiarity, he added, "No one deserves to get caught in a fire." Giving her a tiny shove, he said, "Hurry. You have to head that way."

He looked distracted again as he glanced in the direction of the smoke. Sadie took a tentative step away from him, before deciding there was nothing to do but follow his advice. Troy glanced back to her, before looking again in the direction of the roaring sound. Still, he didn't budge until she began to leave. As she retreated, Sadie caught a last glimpse of his worried expression before he darted away.

She didn't like being left alone again. The momentary reprieve almost made her fear worsen as it rushed back in. All the same, it did give her a glimmer of hope. Troy was nearby, dealing with the fire. He'd given her a direction to head.

She ran with more confidence as she awkwardly pulled off her jacket and threw it aside without a second thought. Then she pulled off her shirt and did as Troy had said. She was boiling hot from the running, and the feel of cool air on her skin was a relief, but there was so much smoke in her lungs already that the barrier didn't feel like much help.

Her whole body burned as she pushed onward, looking for more signs of the approaching United army. She was grateful for the dawn, which clearly showed off that she was not in a Coalition uniform. Perhaps whoever saw her next would be as directive as Troy in helping her get to safety.

Just as she was starting to feel marginally in control of her emotions, a dozen Coalition soldiers appeared through the trees on her right. Even though they were a fair distance, she could make out that half of them carried rifles. Some had bows-and-arrows; a few swords or long knives.

Sadie froze, momentarily captivated by the sight as more appeared, spread out in a creeping line for as far as she could see through the trees. Just as she turned to continue running, a twig snapped behind her. The man hesitated, equally surprised by the sight of her. He wore the uniform of the Coalition and was armed with only a knife. He was also young, perhaps younger than her.

Frightened and unarmed, she put out her hands in a pacifying gesture, but didn't know what to say. Before they had figured out what to make of each other, however, two other men appeared, sprinting through the trees. Sadie bolted.

When no shots followed, she assumed the men at least didn't carry guns. All she had to do was outrun them. Unfortunately, that didn't seem possible as footsteps crashed increasingly close behind her. Sadie pivoted and threw the flashlight at the nearest guy's head. It missed as he ducked, but she saw that he was the only one who had pursued her, which gave her some hope.

Though this guy was nothing like the young man who had frozen at the sight of her – he was out for blood. But he had only a small knife, and she knew that all she had to do was make skin contact, and she could suck the life out of him in an instant. She'd done it before, twice now, and felt confident her instincts wouldn't fail her now.

Sadie waited until he was right behind her before pretending to trip. She rolled to her back as she fell and took him in. She didn't have time to think. He stumbled over her and she reached for his ankle. It wasn't much, but the contact would have to be enough. She pulled at his life force the way she had done to Alec earlier that summer.

It didn't knock him out, but he writhed, kicking out in surprise. Not wanting to give him room to push her away, she crawled up his body and reached for his neck. As he rolled to free the arm holding the knife, she made contact and pulled again, her forehead pressed tight to his as their lips grazed. This time, he jerked once, and then went slack under her.

Sadie jumped up immediately, panting and stared down at him in shock.

"It's okay. You're okay," she told herself.

Before she could take in the enormity of the danger she'd gotten entangled in, she bolted full steam ahead toward the storm clouds. There were voices all around her now, occasionally broken by intimate sounds of fighting, and she couldn't help but look frantically left and right in between her attempts to not trip over the underbrush.

It was as Sadie was glancing to her left that she caught the flash of a Coalition uniform just behind her. She spun, jumping back in surprise as a large man pulled back to swing a sword, as if to chop her down like a tree. Sadie put her hands out on instinct as if they could ward off the blow.

Then before she could even register fear and regret, something kicked out her feet and she found herself looking up from her back at the man about to stumble over her. Mercifully, a figure collided with his chest, sending him backward. He seemed to fall in slow motion as Hetia wrapped her thighs around his head and twisted. Sadie jumped at the horrible cracking sound of his neck breaking.

She scrambled backward on her hands and feet as she watched

Hetia take out the two other soldiers nearby. Gunshots went off in the distance and Sadie looked around frantically for any other signs of danger. They seemed momentarily safe by the time Hetia had returned to hold out a hand for her.

Sadie reached to accept, forgetting she wasn't wearing gloves. They seemed to realize this at the same time and hesitated. In that brief moment of pause in the chaos, the adrenaline twisting Sadie's stomach was replaced by a wave of conscious fear. She had almost just died, multiple times. The hypothetical war was a sharp and present thing, and she was caught right in the middle of it. Caught, because she had failed to do her part and decided to flee instead.

Her previous narrative that she'd been trying to warn the Amadi camp seemed distant and silly now. Silly. Because she was just a silly girl in a big world, and she'd failed.

"Failed." Sadie shook her head. Hetia crouched in front of her with her typical unreadable expression. "I'm sorry," Sadie croaked, her throat sore from the fire smoke. She pulled off the shirt tied around her face and used it to dab up a few tears as they broke free. Sadie glanced up and found Hetia looking nervous now. Clearly uncertain what to do with a crying woman, she squatted, gently took the shirt from her, and helped clean up Sadie's face.

"It's not over yet," Hetia said, then at Sadie's expression, added, "But you're safe for now."

Sadie was embarrassed at breaking down in front of this woman, probably more so than she would be with just about anybody else, but she couldn't help the full-body shudders that seemed to be ruling her evolving physical reaction to the stress. Somewhere deep down, she knew she was safe now that Hetia was here. It was the only explanation for why she was losing it now, when she should get up and press on.

Hetia's shoulders softened a touch as she watched her, and after a moment, she moved closer. Placing a hand on the side of Sadie's head, she caressed her through her hair. "I got you. You'll be okay. I promise," Hetia told her in a soothing voice Sadie had never heard her use in any other circumstance.

Sadie nodded, beginning to relax.

Hetia's hand moved along her hair again, only this time, her thumb lightly grazed Sadie's ear. The awareness of another body shot to the forefront of Sadie's thoughts. For a brief instant she could feel the steady pulse of Hetia's heart, and it made her nervous dry sobs cease immediately. Before more than a slight wave of pleasurable heat could penetrate, Hetia had pulled back, as if having received an electric shock.

The mood altered as they each waited for the other one to respond to the mistaken touch. Sadie looked over the woman crouched so near and couldn't help but bite her lip. Her calm strength made Sadie feel safe, while her sudden pulse of desire brought an entirely different emotion.

"Why are you always rescuing me?" Sadie asked, the question coming out with a nervous giggle.

"Why are you always in trouble?" Hetia replied, the hint of a smile breaking through.

Sadie sat upright, and as the distance between them decreased, the other woman made no move to pull back. Hetia's only reaction was a slight increase in breathing, which Sadie could see in the movement at the hollow of her throat. Moving slowly, she ran a finger along the hem of Hetia's shirt, just above her breasts. When she still didn't pull back, Sadie moved her thumb onto the skin of her neck, coming to rest in the groove of her collarbone.

Like a dam breaking, Sadie was hit with a flood of images and feelings of the one night they'd spent together. It hadn't escaped her notice that Hetia's desire for her had been lessening over time, but it only now occurred to her that the woman might have been intentionally suppressing the feelings.

A clear image of them kissing shot to the front of Hetia's mind, and the thought was filled with intention. If they talked about it or thought too hard, Sadie was sure they would stop, so before either of them could question it, Sadie scooped her hand behind Hetia's head and pulled her mouth to hers.

Something about believing she'd been about to die made the kiss feel especially real. For a moment, all the fear and guilt disappeared and the sounds of the battle closing in from behind faded into the background as Hetia parted her lips to meet her tongue for tongue.

They let out simultaneous sounds of pleasure, which were dwarfed by a fresh bout of thunder at Sadie's back. And when they could clearly make out voices coming closer, neither of them stopped what they were doing.

Hetia clutched at her waist, pulling her tighter as her other hand held her face. Sadie was still shaking from the night of running, so she let the woman support her as she focused only on the feeling of Hetia's mouth on hers.

Hetia kissed Sadie with such intention that all the rest of the world seemed to fade. They quickly found a rhythm together, Sadie's whole body rocking gently with the pace of her tongue. But while Hetia appeared steady and collected, Sadie consumed her with a wildness that bordered on frantic.

Memories of their first encounter rushed to the surface in force. The way they'd talked for hours. The way Hetia had opened up and told her fond stories of her childhood. She had left out most of the larger facts at the time that Sadie now knew, and yet, it had been a glimpse into the fierce and yet playful woman she seemed to be. She had a sweetness to her that was so guarded, it felt like a precious thing whenever Sadie caught a glimpse. And despite Hetia's rejection after that night, Sadie couldn't help but want more with a desperation that was only surfacing again now that Hetia was giving her a clear yes.

They shifted at the same time to move closer, and Hetia dug her fingers into Sadie's hair. What were they doing? They needed to get up. Sadie should keep running and let Hetia get back to the fight. She pushed away that thought though and inhaled Hetia's breath. Taking comfort in this moment seemed far more immediate than dealing with their impossibly dangerous surroundings.

Hetia let out the tiniest sound of pleasure, and the bout of thunder that followed seemed to perfectly match Sadie's reaction to it. Her heart was pounding. This was nothing like the night they'd met as strangers. She'd had months to think about Hetia, letting her feelings develop, letting her get to know the woman, even if only a little.

Hetia pulled back, blinking as if in surprise. Sadie watched her extract a small knife from her miniature utility belt as an awareness of her surroundings rushed back to fill her senses. The smoke was thicker now and the sounds of fighting, fire, and thunder were all much closer than they'd been a minute ago.

Sadie frowned down at the knife, watching Hetia's steady panting. The other woman's eyes dropped back to her mouth and she thought Hetia might resume the kiss, but instead she turned and threw the blade at a man to their left that Sadie hadn't noticed until he was falling to his knees a few yards away. Hetia might have seemed distracted, but unlike Sadie, she clearly hadn't lost track of the rest of the world.

More Coalition soldiers appeared and Hetia rose for the hand-to-hand combat that she was so good at. Most of her raw fear having dissipated, Sadie watched her in awe. There was so much she didn't know... or understand about this strange woman.

How had she come to be such a skilled fighter? Why was she so afraid of starting something with Sadie when they clearly had mad chemistry? At least in the brief moments in which Hetia had let her in.

Sadie coughed on the thickening air. Dusting off her shirt, she fastened it tightly over her nose and mouth before crawling to hide against the nearest large tree. She settled into its roots just in time for an arrow to go shooting past her, traveling from the direction of the United camp. Reinforcements were coming.

In the distance beyond Hetia, Sadie could see the flames approaching now. They were backlit by the sunrise, which masked their power, but judging by the crackling roar accompanied by the large creaking of crumbling trees, this fire was a force to be reckoned with. Hopefully, Troy was alright out there, but Sadie didn't think she had any more space in her heart to worry.

She moved to glance around the trunk in the direction of the storm clouds, but jumped back as several United soldiers ran past to join the fight. Hetia let them take over as she turned back to run toward Sadie. Over her shoulder, Sadie watched two men on motorcycles appear with the flames lighting up the sky behind them. It was a terrifying sight, even before they pulled out guns and began rapidly firing in their direction.

Sadie screamed and covered her ears, while Hetia darted behind a tree just in front of her. She gestured at Sadie to move, which she did without question. Crawling to stay low, Sadie crept to the other side of the trunk until she was facing the storm. Hetia appeared at her side a moment later.

"You have to get out of here," Hetia said over the roar of surrounding noise. She glanced to Sadie's left, assessing something. "You'll head that way." She pointed at the path directly in between the coming storm and fire. There wasn't any fighting that way, but it was obvious why. The fire was fast approaching on that side – clearly it was meant to box in and concentrate the fight. That would give anyone with an automatic weapon an advantage, she supposed.

"But," Sadie panted, "the fire---"

"Amadi is close behind, he'll put it out. But if you can stay near to the flames, you won't be caught in the fighting. It's the best course," Hetia said, pulling her to her feet. For a moment, they hesitated within a foot of each other, and the space between them seemed to shrink further when one or both of them leaned in.

Another round of gunfire went off, and Sadie jumped. Hetia stood up straight, peering quickly around the trunk. She squatted to put her hand to the ground, and the sound of the shooting shifted a moment before the motor engines roared and then died.

"Go now," Hetia said up at her. Sadie hesitated, afraid of leaving Hetia behind despite her competence. "Now," she hissed.

Sadie took off running, not daring to look left as she emerged from the safety of the covering. The sounds at her back blurred together as she quickly put distance between herself and the fight.

Hetia had been right – Sadie saw no one as she ran. After some five or ten minutes, she dropped back into a walk, unable to push onward with every muscle in her body on fire. Not even after eighteen hours of farming in peak season had she ever been this exhausted. It was as if she could just drop any minute and never get up.

It wasn't long until she had switched to a slow trudge. Any minute now, she'd be safe. All she had to do was keep putting one foot in front of the other. She began to fixate on the idea of water above everything else. Images of streams and lakes flashed through her thoughts with such vividness she could almost hear them.

She paused as another herd of deer sprinted past in front of her. Good idea, deer. This smoke was the worst. She should follow them.

Lazily, Sadie turned to watch them running headfirst toward the storm. It didn't look like it had gotten much closer. She should adjust course. Looking left to assess the fire, Sadie paused in confusion. Even in a few breaths of staring, it seemed to change before her eyes. There were long tendrils barreling right for her at an unnatural pace. She couldn't make sense of it. It was as if—

On either edge of the bright and deadly substance, two humanoid figures ran, covered in flames, while the fire around them moved as if taking orders. She understood. The nymphs were moving the fire toward the storm. Toward her.

Adrenaline had a fine way of sharpening the senses. Like the deer, Sadie ran straight for the storm, the roar of crumbling trees at her back. As she neared the dark clouds, she could once again hear sounds of fighting. Gunshots mingled with the thunder, punctuated by screaming and shouting.

A tendril of fire passed on her left. She watched it in horror as she ran, losing the race with every step. It caught a tree up ahead and a loose branch crashed to earth in front of her, bright and heavy. She pivoted as the crackling sounds surrounded her, coughing on the smoke-filled air.

Just out of her peripheral vision, a tree began to fall. It came into view with a large crash and Sadie screamed, coming to an abrupt halt. It was tall, and in the distance she could see its base was in flames. Shit. Fuck.

She would have to go over it before the whole thing caught fire. Scrambling over the maze of branches, she fought to reach the trunk. It wasn't thick, and she should be able to mount it without too much difficulty. The flames were moving fast, however, and she soon realized that she wasn't going to beat them. Deciding she shouldn't get caught in the tree's branches when the rest of it went up, she moved backward to look for another path.

Positioning herself in a small patch of tree-free space, Sadie spun in a circle to analyze the trajectories of the tendrils. There were still some paths through, but she was afraid to choose the wrong one. Another tree crashed behind her and she screamed again, fighting down her panic.

As Sadie took in the newest burning trunk, a voice called out from behind it. "Where are you?" The sound of him mingled with the crackling, but Sadie thought she recognized it.

"Troy?" she called, but her voice was torn from the smoke and it was hard to project. All the same, a figure jumped the burning log, appearing in the distance in front of her. For a moment it just looked like moving flames, but as it stepped forward, a man emerged. Light tendrils clung to him as he moved toward her, but as they broke free from the tree behind, he absorbed them. His golden torso was covered with soot and sweat, and his eyes were ablaze in a way she'd never seen, but it was clearly Troy.

"Sadie? What are you doing?" he asked as he neared.

"Picking daisies," she said, breaking into a cough.

He moved within arm's reach and looked her over, then glanced around them.

"Fuck. Okay. This way," he said. Sadie followed him with hesitation as he moved straight for a wall of flame, but a moment later, another fire nymph ran by and a path cleared. Deciding it was best to follow blindly, she kept her eyes on Troy's feet as she kept close behind.

The surrounding heat lessened a little and she was hit with a wave of relief. She was almost to safety. It was almost over. The fire nymphs were taking care of it, and soon she would be okay.

Troy stopped and she nearly ran into him. Looking up, he was spinning in place. Sadie did the same, only to find they were completely surrounded. She looked back at Troy as her heart stopped in fear. He was smiling.

"What—" she choked out, taking in his carefree expression with confusion.

"It's beautiful, isn't it?" he said, looking around.

Her head swam with the smoke and exhaustion as she tried to

process the situation, and for one long, horrible moment she thought Troy had lost his mind. Then before she could drum up a fresh bout of fear, she found herself on her knees, her vision blurring. Troy knelt in front of her, his smile disappearing as he looked at her face. "Hang on. It's almost over," he said, his voice coming as if from a long distance.

No. *Not like this*, she tried to protest as she willed herself to focus, to stand back up. Troy reached to support her as she swayed on her knees. "Sadie? Can you hear me?" he asked, and she realized she'd closed her eyes. A perfect picture of Jimmy appeared in her mind, and a pain of regret and anger re-awakened her.

"Keep – moving," she said, refocusing on Troy.

"In a minute. We need to get your shirt back on so someone can carry you." He began to untie the fastening at the back of her head. Confused, Sadie opened her mouth to protest, but before she could get anything out, she was hit from above by a downpour of the coolest, most welcome rain she'd ever felt.

Her shock was so great, it took a moment to recognize the sensation, but it registered right as a loud roar of thunder sounded directly overhead. Someone ran past them as Troy held out her shirt, displaying the hole for her head. She blinked, unable to believe they were out of the fire.

"Sadie?" Troy sputtered, water pouring down his face. "I need you to help me here."

She held out her arms, but they felt like lead. Troy wrestled the shirt onto her and an awareness of him sprouted to life as his hands couldn't entirely avoid her skin. The sensation gave her a momentary flare of excitement, of life. She focused only on the pounding of his heart as he pulled her shirt down in a rush.

And then he released her, cutting off the contact. Her head swam. And within one breath and the next, she'd lost consciousness.

Chapter 21

A dangerous confession

Someone was running a hand over her head. She felt the gentle tug on her hair as his thumb caressed her temple and knew it was Jimmy. The light was dull when she blinked her eyes open. They were in a large tent. Jimmy was sitting next to her cot, looking down at her.

"It's so quiet," she said. It wasn't the most important thing to say in that moment, but her mind was foggy. Sadie was glad to hear her voice was returning, but Jimmy helped her sit up and get some water down all the same.

She slumped back into the bed, as the memory of the fire returned in sharp flashes. She thought back over all that had happened since Jimmy left only a few days ago. It echoed around her in a confusing mess.

"It was loud. The fire." Her chest tightened. "I was so alone," she said, beginning to cry. "So alone. And I thought I'd never see you again."

"Hey," he said gently, pulling back the covers and climbing in next to her. "You're here now. That's all in the past. I've got you." Jimmy held her for a long while as the tears flowed.

Eventually, her body began to relax and he kissed her temple. The contact made both their hearts race, his pounding almost in unison with her own.

Jimmy kissed her cheek through the tears and she could feel the pent-up longing in his body. It seemed like a lifetime since she'd last been next to him. Her own hunger throbbed in her and she pulled him to rest between her legs. He must have removed her wet clothes, because she was entirely naked under the warm covers.

"I'm sorry. I'm sorry I didn't leave with you," she said, fumbling at the button of his pants.

He kissed her as he held his hips up enough to give her access. When she couldn't get the zipper down, she let him take over freeing himself while she spread her own wetness around her entrance. He held back until she had lined him up before he pushed his hips flush with hers, groaning as he did so. Jimmy paused there with his eyes closed and she was momentarily distracted from her sadness as she soaked up the sensation.

He remained frozen as he opened his eyes and looked at her with that expression of love and awe he sometimes wore. "You couldn't," he said. "We had different things we needed to do." He kissed her again and added, "It's no one's fault."

Her tears were almost dry by the time he slid a hand between their bodies to touch her as he began to thrust his hips in a slow rhythm. Jimmy kept himself inside her as much as possible. He wanted to feel her wrapped around him, and he radiated this desire like a beacon even as they continued to talk in hushed tones.

"But do we? I wasn't even sure what I was doing there at the end. The feeling that I might almost belong in that place, with all those feeders and succubi, but then not. Not at all. I didn't think I could feel so lonely."

She felt Jimmy's muscles tightening with the growing tension. Without consciously thinking about it, she sent an orgasmic wave through him, her instinctual response to his excitement. He sucked in air through gritted teeth and sped up his rocking motion. "You've had that feeling before. Back home. In fact, you've felt that way all our lives," he said.

If he hadn't been thrusting inside her in heated anticipation, she might have responded with the words *nuh-huh,* but instead she fought down her gut reaction and thought about it. She supposed he was right. The feeling of seemingly belonging to a place while being on the outskirts was all too familiar to her.

"I don't know why this keeps happening to me," she said. Then before her own body could get carried away, she forced herself to relax. "I'm getting close," she said.

"Hmm," Jimmy moaned and sped up.

"No. Don't. I want you to come first. I don't—" She exhaled on a groan. "I don't like being distracted by my own climax. I'll miss yours."

Jimmy seemed to have learned that it didn't matter at what speed he moved if she was controlling the sensation. He kept the same rhythm, but clenched the pillow next to her head in his free hand as she began the pulses of pleasure that preceded release. He pressed his forehead against hers and gasped against her mouth as he came.

Though she knew it wasn't true, Sadie felt that one little sound should be enough to sustain her hunger for days. Jimmy kept moving, spastically at first as she became slick with his juices, but then intentionally as he regained focus on her.

"I missed this," he said. "And I missed you."

His fingers were slick over her now, and she felt the first little spasm of her own orgasm as he replied, "But maybe that's part of the problem. We've always been each other's whole worlds." She couldn't process what he was saying because she was busy convulsing against him with her eyes shut, but the words caught up eventually.

"What?" she panted, the second the spasms had passed.

He slowly ceased his thrusting as her body softened. Jimmy relaxed on top of her, propping his head up on one elbow, but Sadie felt tense from his comment.

"Maybe we relied too much on each other. Should've gotten out more," he said.

"What? No. You were all I had. All I've ever had. Which is my point. It was terrifying being almost welcome in Siphon's world. It was like I finally belonged somewhere, and it was someplace terrible. That's why I had to get out of there. I decided to get away by going to the Coalition camp. The Griffiths son was there, so I thought I could work on him. But then I was even more isolated. Troy had completely stopped trusting me because of something we overheard, so I'd gone alone. It felt like nowhere was safe."

He looked at her with concern. "I know. I heard you were at the camp. I couldn't believe it. I was terrified. What were you doing there, Sadie?"

"I told you. I went to find the Griffith boy," she said.

"You got the Siphon memories?" he asked, his eyes wide.

A sliver of guilt she couldn't quite place pierced her. "No. I made contact with the Siphon daughter and she... was very welcoming, but it—" It sounded a little stupid. "It didn't feel safe there. I couldn't stay."

"It didn't feel safer than a war zone?" he asked.

She swallowed. "Troy and Mia had a weird history, and I didn't want to expose him to the party she invited us to. And then Gabriel was there, and he can apparently tell when lovers are lying, though maybe not with me, I'm not sure what happened there." She was rambling and needed to give a bigger reason for leaving, but when she dug right down to it all she could say was. "They made me feel welcome, but... they're the enemy. I just couldn't take it."

He searched her face for a long time. She was really hoping he was going to explain what exactly was going on with her, but in the end he just asked, "Why wasn't Troy with you again? With all the preparations, I didn't get to speak to him."

Sadie shifted, trying to think of how best to explain. "Well... First, he's holding onto some prejudice against succubi from being burned by the Siphons last year."

Jimmy screwed up his face and then shook his head. "Troy hasn't treated you well from the beginning, but he's very devoted to the cause. He wouldn't risk it over a mistrust of succubi."

She shook her head. "No. It's not just that. He doesn't see how I could have gotten the information I did from Phoenix Maddox. He doesn't know what I can do. *And,* I was somehow able to fool Gabriel, who vouched for me in a place Troy could overhear."

Jimmy was silent a long time, but eventually he nodded along as if to some inner thought. "Troy doesn't want to just take Amadi's word for it on you. That... doesn't seem all that unreasonable. And it seems he has plenty of good reasons to be suspicious."

Sadie squirmed, and Jimmy moved off of her, putting a sheet between them to break the skin contact. He cuddled back close again though, and Sadie pouted at him as she contemplated his words. He brushed her hair out of her face as he waited patiently for her to speak.

Eventually, she couldn't help but reach two conclusions. Firstly, she'd been wrong. Now that Jimmy was taking Troy's side... *now* she'd never felt more alone. And secondly, Jimmy was completely right. Which really, really sucked.

JIMMY LEFT AN HOUR LATER. He'd agreed to help prep the medic tent. Sadie was supposed to go back to sleep, but she found her brain wouldn't turn off, despite her lingering exhaustion. It was as she was sitting propped up in bed, sipping on a large glass of warm water, that Troy appeared. He stepped through the flap, looked around, and then turned to her with his arms crossed.

"What's wrong?" Sadie asked, immediately worried someone had sent him with a message.

"The fight is coming to an end. The Coalition is pulling back," he said.

"Oh. That's great news," she said, relaxing back.

Troy narrowed his eyes. "It's just me. There's no need for the performance."

Sadie cringed, remembering he thought she was a Coalition spy. "Look, Troy—"

"I don't need to hear it," he cut in.

Sadie smoothed out the blanket, annoyed that he was going to make this harder than it already was. They glared at each other a long while, but eventually she tried to speak again.

"Thanks for saving me," she said.

He shifted, spreading his feet in a firm stance. He looked powerful standing like that, and again Sadie lamented her ongoing attraction to the man that had made her job so difficult these past few weeks.

"Of course," Troy said, his clenched jaw softening a bit.

When he continued to stand there, Sadie raised an eyebrow. "Was there something else you wanted to tell me?"

"No. I didn't come here to deliver the news. I came to keep an eye on you in case no one else does."

Sadie glared at him a moment and then sighed and sunk back into the warm blanket. She was so tired. The unknown faces of everyone who had died that morning passed like ghosts through her thoughts. She wondered if Michael and the rest of the earth nymphs had survived the day. And if they had, would they survive the next one?

After what she'd been through in the last twelve hours, it was now no longer possible to keep the idea of war in some hidden part of her brain. It was real. And many more people would be lost before it was over. Not to mention the fact that the Coalition might win. What would such a thing mean for her home, her parents?

"We did this all wrong," she said, almost as if to herself. Jimmy's words from earlier came back to her as she contemplated how differently things could have gone if she and Troy had been working together since the beginning. She had just been so defensive at his mistrust, she couldn't contemplate letting him in a little.

The sound of rapid gunfire rang in her memory, and suddenly her troubles with Troy seemed inconsequential. Sadie pushed back the blanket, wrapped the sheet around her naked body, and pushed herself upright. As she sat like that on the edge of the bed in front of him, she caught the image of herself through his eyes. He must have thought she looked beautiful wrapped in a sheet with her hair a mess as the image burned bright in his thoughts.

Sadie laughed once. What a pair they were.

"Troy? Can I ask you something?" She knew what she had to do. She'd actually been stewing on Jimmy's words for hours and there seemed only one path forward. A potentially dangerous one. After all, it seemed foolish to entrust a man who thinks she's the enemy with her most prized secrets. But then again... someone had to trust first. Maybe it should be her.

He narrowed his eyes at her question. "I suppose."

"What happened to the short woman with red hair?"

He shook his head, "What are you on about?"

"The woman you first slept with. It looks like you were together for a while. Was she a girlfriend?"

This time he blinked, looking uncertain for the first time since adopting his watchdog stance. "Is this a threat? Is Amber in trouble? Because I haven't seen her in years. Whatever you've done—"

"No." Sadie held up her hands. "I didn't even know her name." She swooped her hair behind her ear and decided to be more careful with what she said next. "I do know that the first time you slept with her, you were so nervous that you couldn't come, so you focused all your attention on her, and ended up having a really good time. You still think about it fondly, even if the later experiences weren't as great."

Troy's mouth was slightly open now, but he was still perched as if for a fight. "And I know that last night you dreamed that I appeared in your tent and begged you to make love to me. You woke up before the end, but finished the fantasy while awake. You came into your hand as you pictured me on top of you. My breasts don't really look as round as you have them in your head, you know? You must not have got a good look before, because there's more gravity here and here."

Sadie cupped the underside of her chest. She was trying to lighten the mood since he was looking increasingly alarmed, but the gesture caused a spike of arousal. Her description of the dream made the memory come back in force as well, and he swallowed as the crotch of his pants twitched. Troy decided not to acknowledge his semi-erection as he said, "You can read minds."

"No." Sadie shook her head frantically. "Not at all. But succubi can see the nature of people's relationships when we look at them. It's a long-held secret. It's what makes us good spies. We can tell who is family, friends, or lovers. We can see a person's sexual history, their sexual desires, dreams, and actions. It helps us find lovers."

His breathing was low and frantic now. She watched his abs clench and unclench.

"Some succubi have additional abilities. Like me. When I'm

feeding off someone... I can drop into their memories." She paused to watch his reaction and then added, "*That's* how I got the code from Phoenix."

Troy stepped back as if slapped, his gaze traveling back and forth over the air between them as if trying to solve a puzzle.

"You're – you're telling the truth. You have to be. How could you know—" He looked up at her, and blushed before looking away. Troy ran a hand over his jaw as he stared at the tent flap. Sadie had been so focused on the importance of telling her secret that she hadn't processed how uncomfortable this situation might be. She'd just told him that she can see exactly how he felt about her, feelings which he hadn't been particularly proud of, given their dynamic.

"I like you, too, you know?" she said, the words coming out before she could stop them. It did only seem fair to level the playing field. "I mean, I'm into you. I don't know that I *like* you," she added, but then Troy looked at her and it was her turn to look away.

The tent flap opened then, and Patricia and Hetia entered as one. Patricia looked between them, but Hetia only had eyes for her.

"What's going on?" Patricia asked, turning from Troy's flushed face to hers. Sadie was glad he wasn't still visibly aroused. It seemed better for their relationship if this moment didn't get any more awkward.

When Troy didn't answer, Sadie cleared her throat and jumped in, "Troy and I were just talking out our differences. We think we're ready to go back in." Sadie looked at him as she added, "As a team this time."

Troy blinked in surprise and Sadie held her breath, waiting to see if he would contradict her. After what felt like a lifetime, but was probably only a few seconds, he nodded. Looking back in control again, he turned to the newcomers as he said, "We're invited to a party with Mia Siphon. Since congressman Siphon doesn't know I've left yet, I could still return with none the wiser."

Hetia contemplated that for a minute and then nodded.

"Are you sure about this?" Patricia asked.

Troy looked at Sadie as he said, "I'm sure."

"When is it?" Hetia asked.

"Tomorrow night," Troy and Sadie said as one.

"And what is Sadie's reason for going back. Didn't Siphon send her to the camp to do some work for him?" Patricia asked.

There was a pause before Sadie spoke, a little hesitation in her voice this time. "I was already planning on going back and just telling Siphon I was a terrible spy, but now we have to explain why I just disappeared during the battle."

"The battle's not over," Troy said.

"Still, I'm sure Hunter Griffith has noticed my absence by now."

Troy ran a hand through his hair and looked at Hetia.

"Let's go," Hetia said to Troy. "We need to cover her tracks."

"What will you do?" Sadie asked, suddenly worried.

"Troy's going to burn down the captain's quarters," Hetia said, securing her jacket. "And I'm going to cover him. Then you can tell Siphon you fled in terror and decided staying with the soldiers was no longer for you."

"We'll have to make sure Hunter doesn't make it out of there," Troy added gravely.

"But—" Sadie stepped forward.

"We'll be back within the hour," Hetia said, sounding entirely unconcerned, and before Sadie could mount a protest for their safety, they had both slipped from the tent.

It looked like the plan was made. She was headed back in.

Chapter 22

Cooperation

Troy knocked on the hotel door, despite the fact he also had a key. They'd arrived an hour ago to get cleaned up, and he'd taken first shower before leaving to find a payphone. He knocked again, clearly hesitant to just enter.

Doing up the back of her dress, Sadie checked her reflection before opening the door. Troy was wearing that same uncertain look he'd had on all day. His feelings toward her had been evolving rapidly since she'd told him the truth, and now that he trusted her, she'd watched her own feelings toward him changing in response. The red lines of desire which connected them were now pulsating, growing stronger by the minute.

Troy didn't enter immediately, and so she held the door open wider. He was finely dressed in a dark suit, and she made an effort to not look him up and down as they took each other in. He seemed to be doing the same.

"How did it go?" she asked, stepping aside as he passed.

"I got through to the Siphon butler, left a message explaining that you were with me and that I was considering taking you to a party to help take your mind off what happened. We'll probably get an invite to come see him tomorrow, but we can cross that bridge when we get there." Troy moved to the window and stared out at the darkening sky.

Sadie went back to the vanity mirror and began pinning up her hair with the fifty bobby pins she'd already dumped on the counter. Jimmy and Patricia had stayed behind to help out at the camp, and she and Troy had been alone together for hours. And yet, they hadn't had a real conversation yet. Speaking only when necessary, they'd been interacting mostly through silence and nervous glances.

"I'm sorry," Troy said to the window as she was putting in the last pin.

"Wha – what?" she asked, looking in his direction. The sun had set and they could see each other in the reflection of the glass.

"I'm sorry... for the way I treated you. Right from the beginning, I thought you were trouble. I was wrong."

Sadie chewed her lip. "You had your reasons," she said. Though a wave of tension released from her body that she hadn't realized she'd still been carrying, and she added, "But thanks for saying it."

Troy faced her, perching back against the windowsill. "We should probably talk about some things before we go back in there."

Sadie sat on the edge of the bed to put on her heels. "Yeah," she agreed, looking up from her bent position and waiting for him to take the lead on whatever was on his mind.

He ran a hand through his hair and looked away before saying, "They can see. Siphon and Mia and other succubi. They know we haven't slept together."

"Yeah," Sadie said, sitting upright.

"Is that a problem?" Troy asked. "Is it unusual that we're supposedly a couple and yet things on that front haven't escalated? I mean, you and Mia the other night... it seems succubi usually waste no time." When she didn't respond immediately, he added, "I just want to know how to respond if Mia asks me about it."

"No. I don't think it's a problem," Sadie said, her voice coming out breathier than she'd meant it to. "Succubi need to feed every day, but someone they have a romantic interest in is... different. Think about the way Mia was with you last year. I don't think you were off to think she was interested even though nothing had happened. Also, think of me and Jimmy. It was scary for us to cross that line."

Troy swallowed, and looked back out the window. "So what's the plan?"

Sadie stood up and smoothed out her dress, glad to be moving on. "I'll take the lead, since I'll be the one getting the memory from Mia. You should just kind of – look for trouble and help me navigate it."

Sadie pulled up next to him and he faced her with a frown. "That's not a plan."

"Well, it's the best we've got. How can we know ahead of time what's going to happen in there? We're going to have to roll with it," she said, the defensive tone she was used to using with Troy returning.

"We can't know everything, but we can do better than that," he said, crossing his arms.

"Okay." She mimicked his gesture. "How? Enlighten me."

"Well – uhh," he glanced away, looking nervous again. "Are you – I mean... I have no idea how any of this works."

Sadie waited for him to go on before she tried to decipher that sentence. Eventually, he cast her a tentative glance and continued, "You're going to need to... *interact* with Mia, but you two can't actually feed off each other, so—"

"I don't know exactly how that part is going to go, but I couldn't feed off Phoenix either and everything worked out fine. That's why I'll have to figure it out once we see the situation." Sadie said this with some confidence as she was increasingly comfortable with her own improvisation.

"Is Mia into you?" he asked, unable to meet her gaze again.

"Not like that. And Mia is more into men in general, so it would be a stretch for me to try and seduce her in any way."

"Then... how?" Troy shifted, clearly nervous at this topic.

Sadie held up her hands as if to say, *I have no answer*.

Troy blew out a breath. "This is crazy. We can't go in there like this."

"What, you thought we'd map out a script or something? There are too many variables," Sadie said, a bit more brusquely than she'd meant to. His reaction was increasing her nerves, and she didn't like it.

"No, I just—" He sighed, matching her tone. "Will I, uhh, be *involved* – directly – with the memory extraction part?"

"No," Sadie said without hesitation. "I'll make sure of it," she added, completely resolute on that front.

He faced her fully and she did the same. "Okay. Then I guess we're going in blind," he said. "But I don't like it. I just don't see how we can know this won't be a disaster."

Sadie smiled. "Because, this time we'll be working together."

FIFTEEN MINUTES LATER, they were taking the large elevator up to Jax's top-floor suite. The deep bass of the music reverberated through her bones as the elevator door opened and deposited them directly into the entrance room.

They stepped into the expansive space and Sadie couldn't help but gawk. The suite must've taken up most of the top floor. Several heads turned to take them in as they entered, and it helped to focus her into playing her part. She took Troy's arm and they smiled at each other in what seemed to be their official method of getting into character.

The lights were low, and the walls mostly made of glass which drew the eye to the city below. Sadie gaped at the view before turning her attention to the people. Everyone was dressed formally, like them, and there were plenty familiar faces. They passed a few gambling tables and nodded at Jax, while Troy raised a hand to some people sitting around on couches.

Before they'd gotten too far into the party a woman came up to them. "Troy Hyun, right?" she said over the music.

Troy nodded.

"Then you get one of these." She took his hand and tied a blue string around it, before turning to Sadie. "And you? What's your species?"

"Oh. Human feeder," Sadie said. The woman took her hand, noticed the gloves and smiled knowingly up at her through thick lashes.

"And you get this. It's a young crowd tonight. And not everyone can tell, you know." She said and tied a red string around Sadie's wrist.

She wore a blue string around her own. The woman was a big fan of Mia's, but Sadie could only see one time that her desires had been satisfied.

"Do you know Mia Siphon?" Sadie asked her. "We're here as her guests. Has she arrived?"

"Yes, uhh—" The woman blushed at the mention of Mia. "This way."

She led them through a door and up a staircase to the roof. A large pool dominated the space, and the view to the city was unhindered by any protective walls running along the edge. Sadie had never seen such a thing. Two fire nymphs were keeping the place warm, with flames dancing along their own naked bodies. People swam, some naked, some in swimwear. Mia was on the far end, lounging on a reclined chair. Ironically, she was fully clothed in an elegant white dress.

They walked along the outer edge of the pool to reach her, and Sadie's heart skipped a beat as she looked over the edge of the building to the long fall to the ground below. Just as she had the thought, a man tripped the woman who was their guide and she went tumbling toward the edge.

With nothing to hold onto, she was on a clear trajectory to go right over, and only the man who had put his foot out was close enough to grab her. For a brief second, Sadie thought he was going to let her fall, but at the last minute, he reached out and grabbed her hand. She was suspended with most of her body hanging over the edge and her eyes wide with fear. The man pulled her in. "Whoops," he said with a grin.

The woman abandoned her mission to take them to Mia and instead wandered back inside, looking distinctly like she was about to throw up, while the man turned his gaze on them, his eyes dropping to Troy's wrist. Needless to say, they gave the excitement feeder as wide a birth as they could without falling into the pool.

Mia was surrounded by a small crowd and talking to a young man who was really hoping to go down on her, but when she saw them, she waved him away with one hand. The man vacated the recliner next to her and slumped off, while the young succubus smiled up at her and Troy.

Mia's legs were stretched out in front of her, and a woman knelt at her feet. She was giving Mia a foot massage with her bare hands, and her face was flushed with pleasure. Sadie glanced at the woman as they sat down. She wore no bracelet. Did that mean she was human or just not an official guest? Sadie figured both.

Troy and Sadie sat side by side, facing Mia on the long chair next to hers, and the crowd around them fell silent as Mia said, "Hot off the battlefield. Looks like my father couldn't get rid of my new friend so easily this time."

"You were in the fight?" a man standing at Mia's head asked.

"Yes. Sort of. I saw a little of it," Sadie said. She looked around at the faces with a small smile that dared someone to ask more.

"Well?" a woman said impatiently, but she too was smiling.

Troy looked at Sadie. "Why don't I take this one?" he said before rising to his feet. She wasn't sure what he was up to until every eye followed him as he moved to stand in the open space between them and the pool. If his goal was to draw them away so Sadie could have some time with Mia, he would have to do better than that.

But as they all watched him silently undo the buttons at his wrists, she had to admit he wasn't bad at holding people's attention. Troy didn't speak as he removed his shirt, folded it neatly and handed it to one of the women. Sadie looked him over and couldn't help but grin at his style of building anticipation.

"I'll tell you a tale. Told from the eyes of a young succubus trying to entertain herself with some lonely generals," he grinned and people chuckled, "and ending up caught on the edge of a battle." His voice grew deeper and bolder as he continued, "I sing of a dark and stormy morning." Troy grinned dramatically before snapping both fingers, producing two tiny flames. "As two large armies lay in wait, covered by the lingering darkness just before the dawn."

The flames grew along his arms and he began to shape them with his hands. Sadie was mesmerized as they took on the vague impressions of armies and trees separated across the expanse of his torso. No shapes were distinct, they appeared held together like rough clay carvings, but it was clear enough that anyone watching would agree what they were.

Sadie watched in awe. She'd never seen anything like this. The fire nymphs at her Becoming had likely been more skilled than Troy, but she'd never seen fire used to tell a story. As he continued, she became even more impressed at his ability to weave an interesting, mostly false, tale from her perspective on the spot.

She was lost in it enough to have nearly forgotten why they were there until he concluded the dramatic telling by declaring, "But then the fire was tragically quenched by the storm." He fell backward into the pool with his arms outstretched and covered in flames.

Everyone applauded and several people jumped in after him. When the remaining five onlookers turned to get further details out of her directly, Sadie replied, "And that was about it." She shrugged, looking apologetic, but it worked to quickly lose their interest. Troy in the pool became the life of the party, and Sadie found herself alone with Mia and the masseuse.

Mia glanced at the woman and she stopped the massaging and retreated.

"So... what exactly is going on with you and Troy? And when do I get to meet the other boy?" Mia asked.

The change of subject was fast, but Sadie caught up quickly. Clearly Mia didn't care much about war stories. She could relate. "Well... I'm pretty private about the other guy, and I'm taking things slow with Troy," she said, kicking her feet out to lay back in imitation of Mia. "I want to wait until things are really tense between us. As you can see, I'm into that kind of thing."

Mia looked at her for a really long time. "I can't really suss out all that. It's too much to look at."

Sadie remembered feeling the same way while trying to make sense of Mae's history. Though her sexual past with Jimmy was much more limited in time. Perhaps Mia hadn't been developing that skill as quickly as Sadie was.

"But I meant, what happened the past few days," Mia said. "Why are thing so different between you if you didn't fuck?"

"What?" Sadie said, genuinely confused this time.

As she spoke, Mia held up a hand and gestured to the corner. There were a few men chatting in the distance, and Sadie hadn't noticed until just then that they were keeping a constant eye in their direction. At Mia's command, they came to stand in front of them.

"I mean. A few days ago you didn't have anything but early lust between you, and now you're suddenly friends. And he's way more into you. What did you do?"

Mia's gaze travelled back and forth over the men she'd summoned, settling for a minute on one of the ones she'd been with several times before. But then she grinned and pointed to the guy on the end. He was a little older, probably in his thirties, and had no sexual history with the woman. The man went hard the second she looked at him and Mia smiled appreciatively at the bulge in his pants.

"Uhhh...it's been an intense week," Sadie said. "I think we just bonded over everything that's been going on." The other men slumped away and the chosen one came to stand at Mia's feet.

"Well, I'd be careful," Mia cut in. "He used to look at me like that until he went home to look after his dead aunt or whatever. He definitely has a one-track mind. I'd jump on that before it's gone. In fact," Mia lifted herself into a more upright position, "I was thinking you could show me how you do that special thing you do."

Sadie's heart skipped two beats. What did that mean? Could Mia see the memory diving? "Um... what's that?"

"You know, this really intense thing you and that guy have going. I want to see you do that to Troy. Wouldn't that be a fun first time together?" Mia tucked her feet up under her. "And then I could copy it with this guy."

Sadie was at a loss for a few seconds, but then her brain kicked into overdrive. First off, she wasn't in love with anyone else, so even with Troy she wasn't sure she could mimic the way things were with Jimmy. Plus she couldn't tell Mia that she was in love with a human and therefore couldn't explain why things were so different with him. Second, there was no way in hell she was going to feed off Troy with Mia watching. Even if the idea would be exciting in a different reality, in this one, Troy would hate that. And therefore, so would she.

Sadie laughed. "I'm pretty sure that was just from a lot of practice with a single person. I doubt I could—" But then an idea occurred to her. A way in. "Though... it's not a bad idea. We could try it."

She was going to make sure Troy was unavailable for this game, but the guise of skill sharing might be the perfect way to get closer to Mia. Steering the conversation along those lines, she decided to ask her own question.

"It's been a lonely year since the change," Sadie said. "I've been wondering, after a party like this when you feed off a lot of people, do you get this kind of buzzed feeling?"

Mia played with her own clavicles. "Of course. That's part of the fun."

"But then," Sadie pushed herself up, genuinely wanting to talk about this, "a few days later, you feel kind of... flat. And worn out?"

"Ha. Yeah. I used to fix that by just having someone in bed with me every morning. If you feed right away it takes the edge off."

The man shifted at their feet. They looked at him. "Should I..."

Mia handed him a condom, which she fished from some invisible pocket. "Why don't you put this on."

"I thought—" the man began.

"It's so you don't make a mess on my dress while you're eating me out," she said. Mia turned back to her. "Or you can just set a hard limit. If there's no one around worth taking home, I'll just cap myself at three."

Sadie nodded, genuinely appreciating the advice. After all, Mia really did have a lot more experience with group feedings. Though after she was done with this spy work, Sadie doubted she would seek out anything like this again. It was fun the first few times, but she didn't seem to enjoy it as much as Mia. "And how many is this tonight?"

"This is number two." Mia pulled her dress up and got comfortable. "And probably the last. No one's really catching my eye."

An image popped clearly into Mia's mind. Troy standing at her feet with Sadie kneeling in front of him, her mouth around his cock. The woman smiled at her as Sadie blushed. "Or maybe I just have other things on my mind," Mia said with a wink.

This wasn't good. If Mia was fixated on watching her and Troy, how was Sadie supposed to get closer to her? She sent back the image with a slight modification. She replaced Troy with the man currently writhing with his head between Mia's legs and she put herself straddling Mia's thighs.

Mia sent the image back. She kept the two of them in contact, but put Troy back as the leading man. Sadie smiled and returned the exact same image, appearing to agree. Then she bit her lip. It wasn't hard to be excited about the idea, and so she didn't have to fake the emotion. Though Mia needed to think it was a solid yes from her or she would be suspicious when Sadie told her Troy couldn't be found.

Which it looked like she wasn't going to get the chance to do, as Troy had just emerged from the pool in his underwear and was headed their way. Sadie could see him out of the corner of her eye over Mia's shoulder, but she didn't dare look directly at him. Instead, she looked at Mia's dress. "What's the fabric? It looks so smooth," she said. As Mia directed her gaze at her stomach, Sadie shot a quick look in Troy's direction and shook her head once.

He stopped dead. For a moment she was worried he was going to argue, but then she remembered they were a team now. He backed up and, gathering up his dry shirt, made for the stairs.

"—so that's how they get it so soft," Mia was saying as she caught her eye.

"Oh, sorry," Sadie said, when Mia spotted her looking around. "I was just searching for Troy. Did he get out of the pool?" She pushed herself up and feigned looking around. Mia frowned as it became apparent he was missing.

"I'll go get him," Sadie said. Mia relaxed into the lounge, spreading her thighs further as she made herself comfortable, and watched Sadie rise with an excited smile. She turned her back on the woman, fighting down guilt at all the deception. In a different world, this might have been a fun night with the other succubus. Sadly, she was not here to enjoy herself, and her actual task was of utmost importance.

Sadie traced Troy's path down the stairs and scanned the room. He was talking to the bartender, but had his eyes on the doorway and was already looking her way when she spotted him. He excused himself and disappeared down a hallway. She followed and found him in line for the bathroom. Somehow he had acquired a fresh pair of pants, which were draped over one arm.

There was only one person in line in front of them, but it meant they couldn't speak openly. Partially to make conversation, Sadie asked "Where did you learn to do that?" She looked at the ceiling to indicate, *that thing you just did upstairs.*

"My drama teacher in high school was a muse, a uhh, creativity feeder like the Maddoxes," Troy said. "It was my favorite class."

"Theater kid? Huh, I guess I can see that. You are quite the performer." He seemed thrown by her complimenting him. For a second, he searched her face to see if there was some double meaning in her words. There wasn't.

"What about you?" he asked, as someone exited the bathroom and the woman at the front of the line replaced them.

"Me? I guess I liked math. Figuring stuff out." Her words died suddenly as Troy stepped into her the instant the bathroom door closed, leaving them alone in the hallway.

"Congressman Siphon is coming. I just heard that he wants to talk to Jax about something. Are we ready with our story?"

"Yeah. I think so. It might be better if he didn't see us just yet, though. I think I'm close to getting something. It's just..." Sadie blushed.

"What is it?" Troy said, his concern adding to hers.

She bit her lip. "Mia's really fixated on you. I mean... on us."

The door opened and they waited until the woman was out of sight before replacing her, entering in a hurry. "What does that mean?" Troy asked once the bathroom door was locked.

Sadie sighed. "Mia's not really into anyone here tonight. She keeps picturing one thing and won't let it go."

"And that is?" Troy pressed.

This was no time to be vague, but still she hesitated. "She wants to watch me go down on you."

Troy swallowed, immediately looking away. And even though his breathing quickened and he sent out a strong pulse of desire, Sadie couldn't help but notice that he also took the tiniest step back.

"And will that work?" he asked, his voice suddenly husky.

"Yeah. She likes the idea of her and I being in contact while she watches. She'd be focused on you, but I could still... do what I needed to do. It's the perfect plan. Except for the fact we need to remove you from it. I'm thinking that if I tell her you couldn't be found – maybe she'd move on in her interest."

Troy nodded. The image she'd just painted still sharp in his mind, but the lust coming off him was a wavering thing.

"And if she doesn't?" he said.

Someone knocked on the door. "Just a minute," Sadie called.

They faced each other and Sadie chewed her lip. Troy's eyes dropped to her mouth and he swallowed. Then like an unstoppable wave, the image of her mouth wrapped around him became sharp and real. He took in a steadying breath, not breaking eye contact.

"Troy," Sadie said, "you wouldn't be comfortable with that. We already agreed—"

"But this is too important to fuck up. What if it's the only way? I can close my eyes, pretend that Mia's not even there. That it's just—" He caught her eye and this time he did drop his gaze.

Sadie had to fight back her own reaction to the idea. It was so tempting. But then she remembered his initial response. She couldn't see the entirety of his emotions, only the part where he *was* interested in her. But the fact that Mia was nowhere in his mental image made it clear he wouldn't be happy with her watching. Plus, she could see that he wasn't a sexual exhibitionist. He was private and intimate in his sexuality, and this would be a stretch even if they weren't in the house of their enemy.

"No." Sadie shook her head. "Not like this." As much as she wanted to be with Troy, she wouldn't combine business with pleasure. They had to get away from the thought. Somehow they were standing closer than they'd been a minute ago, and their breathing was an identical shallow pant. One of them would need to break the spell.

"You need to leave," Sadie said, leaning back against the wall.

"What?" He stood up straighter, also increasing the distance.

"I know what I need to do now, and it's not something you can help with. You should leave the party, drawing away some of the Mia groupies if possible."

He ran a hand through his hair. "I don't like the idea of leaving you here alone."

Sadie looked down at the fresh pair of pants still draped over one arm. He followed her gaze, glancing at them as if he'd forgotten they were there. In silent agreement, she turned her back and he got dressed. When she heard the zipper go up, she faced him. He tossed the wet underwear into a corner and shook out his damp hair. The pants clung low on his hips, and her gaze followed the lines of his abs downward. A primal part of her wanted desperately to drop to her knees right there and free him from that zipper.

"Leave Troy," she said. "Please. Just listen to me on this."

"And what if you're wrong about Mia picking someone else?" he asked.

"Then we'll take that chance. It's not worth forcing you to do something you don't want to do."

"And what about you?" he asked, concern written all over his face. "You don't want to do this either. Do you?"

"That's... complicated. It's not the same for me. Sex... it's different for succubi than for humans. And Mia doesn't want to sleep with me either. I'm just going to get her to let me in," Sadie said.

When he still didn't budge, she added, "I'll find a way. But you... *have* to go. Now." She said, feeling increasing panic at how long she'd already been gone.

He hesitated a moment longer. His eyes dropped to her lips and the distance between them seemed to contract again, though Sadie wasn't sure if either of them had actually moved. The image of him grabbing her face and kissing her appeared sharply in the forefront of his thoughts.

"We can't touch. She'll know I found you," Sadie whispered, half-wishing he would do it anyway.

But he just said, "I'll be close by. And I'll burn this place to the ground if I have to." Then he pulled open the bathroom door and hurried away. And with that, she was sure she'd made the right decision in trusting him. Because he now finally trusted her.

Chapter 23

Demons from the past

Now that Troy was safe, Sadie headed back upstairs with confidence. Mia didn't frighten her. In fact, if it weren't for her terrible position in the world, Sadie would very much like the woman. She leaned into that thought as she returned to the upper level.

Mia. Legs for days. Long blond hair. Hair like Hetia's. Sadie had to distract her emotions from the image of the tension that had just happened with Troy. If she was pining over that almost-kiss, Mia would see it.

Instead, she focused all her attention on the powerful daughter of her enemy, letting herself feel that lingering desire to be the woman's friend. As she spotted her, Sadie noticed the slight strand of green light that connected them, indicating that there was the beginnings of friendship. Had that been there before she'd gone downstairs and she just hadn't noticed?

Mia was in the pool with a different man than the one she'd chosen earlier. Most people were keeping their distance now, shooting envious glares at the man she was kissing, while Sadie returned to the chairs they'd occupied and dropped her dress next to Mia's.

She wasn't wearing much underneath, but she removed the rest, following the other succubi's lead. Sadie ignored the stares now directed her way as she walked with determination into the pool. She stepped behind the man and into Mia's vision, who immediately broke off the kiss. The man switched to sucking on her neck.

"Where's Troy?" Mia asked.

"Couldn't find him," Sadie said. It was a dangerous lie. One that anyone who'd seen them walk in or out of the bathroom together could refute, one that Mia would see through if she looked closely, but Sadie was too close to her goal to care.

"You said you wanted me to show you how I do that thing?" Sadie said.

Mia smiled. "With this guy?"

She shook her head. "Not with a stranger. It needs to be someone I know better." Sadie braced herself before adding, "But *you* could try it with this guy, and I could help."

If Mia wasn't into this idea, she wasn't sure what else to do. She couldn't keep casually suggesting things that put them in contact without raising suspicion. After all, Sadie wasn't particularly attracted to Mia, she'd have to have some other motivation for wanting to be so close to her.

But Sadie had been right. Now that Troy was gone, Mia was open to other suggestions. She nodded, and Sadie moved forward to place a hand on the man's back. "Put yourself inside her," she whispered in his ear.

It was all down to this. She had to make this happen. There could be no hesitation now.

"Water's terrible lube, but you won't need to move much," Mia said. Sadie was in luck that this was someone the woman was genuinely attracted to. She'd been with him before, in fact.

They worked together easily to get Mia's hips wrapped around the man, and when he was in place, Sadie stepped behind Mia and wrapped an arm around her waist. The edge of the pool was cool at her back, and it contrasted with the pleasurable heat that hit her at the contact with the other succubus.

The water lapped lightly around them as the man began to move in slow, small thrusts, and Sadie fell into the comforting feeling of desire, letting it focus her thoughts and relax her nerves. Then he leaned in to resume kissing the blond woman, and Sadie caught a shot of his face.

She nearly yelped. She knew this man. He... was one of Alec's cousins. *Alec*, the human feeder in Seattle who had briefly been her friend before trying to kill her for being a human lover. *His cousin* was a foot from her, only temporarily distracted by his situation.

Sadie quickly hid her face behind Mia's head. This was it. She had to get in and get away while he was still recovering. Worst come to worst, she could partially life-suck him so it looked like he'd had a stroke or something and then sneak away in the commotion.

But Mia would be confused if she took things too fast. Trying to calm her heart as it was attempting to beat out of her chest, Sadie did her best to refocus. She ran her hand up over Mia's breast and began playing with her nipple. Sadie felt her clench around the man inside her. Since he was a human feeder, Mia wasn't doing this to feed. Sadie could feel the woman's attraction to him.

Perhaps that was why Mia didn't seem to mind this new plan. In fact, she barely even thought of Sadie as she got lost in the feeling of it all. Mia and the man spoke dirty little phrases to each other as he slowly picked up the rhythm.

Sadie returned to gripping the woman's waist and let the sensation build. The other succubus didn't have her endurance, however, and before long the man was close to coming. Afraid that would distract Mia out of the moment, Sadie cupped the back of the man's head and fought for control.

He sucked in sharp air and cried out at the sudden contact with two succubi, but Sadie was able to keep him from climaxing.

"Yes. Keep touching me," Alec's cousin said. He moved his head around Mia's with the thought of kissing her, but Sadie just used the opportunity to hold his head there. She put her cheek on the other side of Mia's face and did her best to distract the man with enough pleasure to buckle his knees.

He managed to remain standing, but his thrusts lost all rhythm. Mia was getting closer now. It was almost time. Sadie began to relax her thoughts. At the ready.

Mia gasped in a high-pitched cry that sounded so different from her usual one. Sadie had never heard her so outside of a position of control. The sound was nice – erotic and sweet. Just as Sadie was having the thought, she realized she was about to climax herself. It had snuck up on her at the sound of the other woman's pleasure.

But she couldn't lose control. She had to hold Mia where she was. It took everything she had to let her own climax wash over her without pulling Mia along. Several gasps broke out of her and she closed her eyes, but she kept her mind on the goal. *Mia. Mia. Mia. I'm not done yet. Stay focused.* She heaved as the aftershocks replaced the high-intensity spasms.

Sadie opened her eyes. Most everyone there was watching, except for the other people who were engaged in similar activity. There was one of them that stood out in particular, however. Standing beyond the other side of the pool was a woman she recognized instantly.

In high heels and a short cut dress, was Alec's sister, Irene. She was looking right at Sadie, daggers shooting out of her eyes. And that was it. The game was up.

Irene sashayed down the stairs and she doubted she would be returning with presents. Sadie should run. She knew she should run, but she was so close to getting what they needed.

"Hold on," she whispered in Mia's ear. She rushed both her and the man to the end and pushed them into a climax at the same time. The man stopped moving as he gripped the edge of the pool.

"Fuck," Mia gasped, her head falling back on Sadie's shoulder.

Sadie tried to ignore it all. She doubled-down her focus and relaxed into Mia's past.

She'd memory dived enough times now that it could have started to feel routine. But immediately, this time felt different. She had never been so focused before. The fear driving her was even pushed to the background as she searched with unbridled determination for a memory she had no way to recognize.

Whole months of Mia's life swam past her and she discarded them at a glance. Months of her wanting to become a succubus, months of her wanting to develop breasts, months of her wanting to be allowed to go play with Phoenix on her own because she was a big kid now.

Sadie searched through all the time since her becoming with a fine comb. Surely Mia would want to know what her father was up to. There must have been a conversation somewhere like the one Phoenix's father had had with him. Though perhaps Mia wasn't as desperate to be a part of her parent's grown-up world as Phoenix had been. No. It had to be there somewhere. Mia was in her twenties. Her parents must have shared their secrets with her at this point.

Sadie focused on one thought only, of Mia wanting to be a part of her father's world. She pushed that to the front of her mind and narrowed in on it. There were several pulls in different directions at this, but the strongest one seemed to take her back in time. She found herself dropped into an emotionally charged memory in which she was very small, a young child of perhaps five, based on her height.

She was in her dad's office, and once again, he wasn't paying any attention to her.

"I need access to the inner city, Mr. Pierce. I know you have keys," her father was saying to a tall man. He was scary looking in his big suit. She grabbed her father's leg.

"Mia, Daddy's trying to work here. Why don't you find your mother." He pulled her off his body. She began to cry immediately. He always wanted her to leave. Why could she never stay! She sat down to pout.

"Can't you talk to the mayor? If you're looking for a private tour, I'm sure—" the tall man said, but her father cut him off.

"Mia, hush. No, this is a private affair. I need to get in without notice, before the repairs happen. Me and several of my men. You would be compensated enormously for your discretion and help in this matter."

Mia sobbed louder, wanting more attention. He wouldn't ignore her this time. She would be heard. She looked up to see her father looking at the other child in the room. Why was he looking at her and not Mia!

"You're about to have a teenager on your hands. You could retire early, a rich man. I'm offering you the chance to give your little girl that kind of life," her father said.

Mia wailed, but her father was so focused on the man now that he didn't flinch, at least not until the man nodded. "I accept," the tall man said.

Her father smiled. "You're a smart man." He looked down at Mia for the first time. "Now if you'll excuse me a minute. I need to take care of my daughter, and then we can talk details."

Her father scooped her up over his shoulder and began to carry her out of the room. She looked back at the tall man and the older girl. Why did she get to stay and Mia was getting cast out again! The girl, who was about twice her age, was playing quietly in the corner. She looked up at Mia, bouncing over her father's shoulder.

Sadie jolted, becoming aware of her own presence in someone else's memory. She was looking at the ten-year old face of someone she knew well. Little Hetia was looking up at her over her toys.

As Mia was brusquely handed off to a maid passing by in the hallway, Sadie came out of her memory. She fought to stay and keep looking, but the jolt of shock combined with the passage of too much time, forced her back to the present.

She surfaced to face the pool, grown Mia, Alec's cousin, and, most significantly, the scowling faces of Congressman Siphon, Irene, and Jax. Fear shot through her and she released Mia immediately, stepping free of her with guilt written all over her face.

A crowd had followed the congressman up the stairs and they were all looking down at her with loathing. Mia disappeared out of the pool in a flash, and in her peripheral Sadie saw someone hand her the white dress. Her father didn't look in his daughter's direction. He had eyes only for Sadie.

And the only piece of information she had managed to gather before getting caught was that Hetia's father had once helped Siphon do something nefarious and Hetia had been in the room.

It had all been for nothing. And now she was in some deep shit.

Chapter 24

Bound

Sadie scrambled up the stairs and out of the water, barely taking her eyes off Siphon. She jumped when she bumped into someone waiting for her. It was Gabriel. He was holding out her dress. The music of the party had been turned off and she got dressed in utter silence. Everyone was staring. When she was done, Gabriel reached for her. He pulled her to him with a firm grip on the back of her neck. She had only a second to register what was happening before she lost consciousness.

HER HEAD WAS POUNDING. Where was she? Had a truck hit her? Her limbs were weak and sore, and it was all dark. Or actually, maybe her eyes were closed. She lifted her lids as much as possible, and a blur of bright color entered her vision.

"I don't know how she managed it. To fool me that is," Gabriel was saying. "Perhaps she has some hidden talents none of us knew about. I would have thought she'd discuss them with me at her Becoming. I'm sorry, sir. I've let you down."

"I'm not disappointed in you, son. She fooled all of us. Perhaps her talents developed late. You did all you could to vet her." Siphon appeared in her vision as he spoke. "It's too bad things turned out this way. If we had only gotten to her first, she could have been a powerful asset. But alas, she can still be useful to the cause."

"Sir?" prodded a woman Sadie didn't recognize.

As her vision sharpened, she could see there were some dozen people in the room. Some wore the uniforms of the Coalition generals. Troy was standing next to Gabriel, looking still as a rock. He hadn't run then.

Phoenix was behind him. The lust-tinged puppy dog eyes he'd had last time she'd seen him were entirely gone. He looked stern and disgusted. Sadie became aware of the ropes at her wrists and ankles as she took in the rest of her surroundings. She was tied to a chair in what appeared to be a wine cellar.

"We need to recruit, and fast," Siphon said. "I'm going to put the word out. Whoever, be him general, soldier, or... fire nymph that can bring in the most new recruits in three days' time can have a night with the succubus."

This was met with pregnant silence. Broken when one of the generals said, "With all due respect, no one wants to force themselves on a bound woman. This doesn't seem like much of an offer. Also, can't uhh, succubi kill? I didn't think it was possible to—"

"It's not like that. Yes, we can kill. But what people don't know is that if you get us hungry enough, we won't want to. I'm going to leave her locked up for three days. She'll want anyone we bring her at that point. A night with a hungry succubus. That is the reward. Put out the word."

Three days? Sadie struggled against her bindings. At least they weren't going to kill her. But three days of not feeding? She knew exactly what she would be like by then, and Siphon was right, she wasn't remotely concerned about being used for recruitment. She was terrified of having no one to feed from.

The generals disappeared, and Troy made to follow them.

"Troy. Stay a minute," the congressman said. He came back and stood in front of Siphon. The older man put his hand on Troy's shoulder. "You've done well this month. I'm proud of you. And I believe you when you said you didn't sleep with her. But tell me, are you attracted to her?"

Sadie was immensely grateful she'd told Troy the truth. He knew not to lie here. He shrugged, looking guilty. "Yes. I admit I am."

"Well, then make me proud again. And don't worry. There are better women out there. You'll heal in time."

Troy nodded solemnly. He didn't glance her way as he made for the door, but he caught her eye just before it closed, and his expression was grave and full of fear. Then the heavy door clicked shut with a sound that reverberated around the chamber, and Sadie found herself alone with Gabriel and Siphon.

"What did you do to me?" she tried to say, but the words came out like a croak. Gabriel brought her some water and helped her drink it.

"I sucked some life out of you. Not enough to kill, obviously," he said.

"Gabriel's quite good at that actually. I was rather impressed," Siphon said, coming to stand next to her succubus guide; the man that had been there at the most important moment in her life. It seemed now he would be at another important moment, watching her slowly starve.

"Tell me, have you ever gone without feeding for a few days?" Siphon asked.

"You can see that I have. Twice," Sadie spat, the water having soothed enough to allow her to speak.

He smiled. "Yes. I see that." He squatted in front of her. "Well, this will be different. You see... As of right now, you're already dry. Gabriel made sure of that. Any feeding you did in the past couple days has been wiped away. You'll be begging for someone by nightfall. After three days, I doubt you'll care about anything else." He stood up. "I'll be back to ask you my questions then. And if you're very, very good, I might take mercy on you."

The men left, casting her dispassionate looks as they passed through the doorway. And then she was alone.

Hours passed. Her weak state turned to sharp hunger for food and water. Were they not going to give her anything? Her muscles ached from their trapped positions and her heart pounded in a ceaseless state of panic. The chair was fixed to the ground with heavy blocks and she quickly abandoned her attempts to shift it. Eventually, she began to cry.

The door opened right as tears fell from her chin to her chest. They dripped between her cleavage, prominently displayed in her elegant black dress.

"Oh, dear. You look a mess," a middle-aged woman in an apron said as she bustled into the room. She placed a tray on a stool nearby and came to wipe Sadie's face clean with a thick handkerchief. "Don't cry now. You have only yourself to blame, after all."

This made Sadie cry harder. Her shoulders shook with tiny, suppressed sobs.

"Here. Stop that. Stop it. Aren't you hungry?" the woman said, attacking her face again with the now damp rag.

The smell of the food penetrated her cleared nose and her stomach grumbled. Slowly, Sadie stopped crying.

"That's better. You want some eggs?" she asked.

Sadie nodded.

The woman pulled off the cover of a large plate of bacon and eggs. The scent pulled at her attention, and she accepted spoonfuls of the warm meal with gratitude, gulping down the water with equal enthusiasm.

When it was gone, she sized up the woman who'd fed her. "Are you human?"

"Don't see how that's your business," she said.

"Please, if you are. You have to help me. These people—"

The woman pulled out a large stick and pushed a button. It lit up. "I'm going to untie you now so you can use the restroom. Now if you try anything funny, this'll knock you right on your ass, understand?"

The woman vaguely looked like her mother. Or maybe it was just something in how she carried herself. Either way, Sadie was shocked by the threat coming from such a source. How could she hurt her? Didn't she want to look after Sadie? Make sure she minded her manners and showered at regular intervals? The world felt newly terrifying, and the threat coming from this woman, more than anything, sent chills down her spine.

Sadie cooperated fully as the woman took her to the bathroom just outside the hall. She didn't recognize this part of the house, but it was in the same style as the Siphon estate, confirming her suspicions about where she was being kept. She looked around frantically for anything that might help her. Maybe there was some small piece of information that would get her out of this, if only she took note of it in time.

The woman watched her pee and wash her hands, while Sadie stared at the heavy soap holder, wondering if she could smash it over the woman's head before she could zap her with that stick. But the maid was hefty and in the prime of life. Sadie didn't think she could take her even if they were on equal footing. With the brief reprieve from her bindings passing her by, she began to panic over her lack of action. But what could she do? This was not a situation for which she was remotely prepared.

A few minutes later, the woman re-secured her to the chair and left. Several hours passed before she returned to repeat the ritual. At night, she chained her to a post in one corner. The small sleeping pad and blanket would have been plenty comfortable enough for her to sleep if she'd been remotely able to do such a thing. By the next morning, she was starving in full, and not for food. Siphon had been right, it came on fast after Gabriel's depletion.

It was during lunch the next day, while she was tied to the chair, that someone other than the maid finally came to see her. Mia Siphon sauntered into the room, looking as dazzling as ever. On her hip was a toddler, peering around in curiosity.

"Take him, Ninny," Mia said, handing the boy to the maid, who put down the spoon she'd loaded up for Sadie and obeyed. "Leave us," Mia added, not taking her eyes off Sadie.

Without another word, the maid and babe disappeared.

Without preamble Mia said, "Father says you're a spy. That all this has been fake. Is it true?"

The lack of sleep combined with the stress and hunger had left Sadie slightly delirious. She couldn't help but feel as if this were all a dream through which she was floating like an outside observer. "Mia, I'm so hungry. Please. They're going to starve me and then use me. I can't take it. You... please. You have to help me."

The succubus grimaced down at her. "You look terrible," was all she said.

"I feel terrible."

"It's—" Mia crossed her arms and pouted. "You deserve this. You lied to us." There was the slightest hint of doubt in her words and Sadie clung to it with hope.

"Was that your son?" Sadie asked.

"Yes. I wanted you to meet him. Or at least I had when I thought we were going to be friends." She sighed. "I'm tired of this. I hate not knowing who you can trust around here. Every time I think—" She cleared her throat. "Just tell me *why*. I want to know."

This was a dangerous moment. Sadie didn't want to blow a chance at support, but she also wanted to ask Mia the same question. "Your father is trying to start a war. People I love will get hurt. I didn't come here to make trouble. I'm trying to do what I think is right. What about you?"

"My family has a vision. A world where feeders rule, keep the peace, keep everything in its rightful place. Don't you see how that makes sense? How everyone would be happier once things settle down?"

Sadie shook her head. "Mia. Lots of people are going to get killed. And for what? So feeders can treat humans like cattle?"

Mia pursed her lips and glowered at the bowl of cold porridge on the stool. After a minute, she took the seat the maid had vacated. "Here," she said, and lifted the spoon to Sadie's mouth. She froze in surprise that the woman was doing anything at all for her. "Well? Aren't you hungry?" Mia pushed.

Sadie resumed eating while they glared at each other. "Maybe it's not too late for you," Mia said. "I could talk to my father. He believes in people. Maybe over time you could prove yourself."

Sadie gulped down a soggy bite. "Mia, there's a whole world out there of good people just trying to live their lives. If you knew them, you wouldn't want to see them get hurt. Please—"

The woman stood up suddenly. "Like the people that attacked that town. The ones Father is fighting against?" She cast a look of sadness down at her. Sadie hadn't seen her wear any expression remotely similar before. It touched her, despite herself.

"Mia, please. It's not like that. Your father, he—" Sadie hesitated. How could she explain?

"You can keep your lies to yourself." Mia crossed her arms.

Despite the woman's glare, her devout belief in her family's morale superiority actually gave Sadie hope that if she could only show her the truth, Mia might help her. She recalled her struggle to locate the memory of her parents passing on the legacy of their family secrets. It was possible, that Mia had been fed a very limited amount of information. Perhaps the Siphons didn't fully trust their only child with the truth of all they'd done.

"Mia, let me tell you the full story, from the beginning. If you knew what I knew—"

"You know that's not going to happen," Mia said. They exchanged glares for what felt like a long while. "I guess that's all we have to say to each other." She stepped back.

Sadie slumped in her bindings. "I guess so."

"Ugh," Mia said, throwing her hands up in frustration and stomping away. Sadie thought that was the end, but a few breaths later, she'd returned carrying a wet rag. Mia hiked up her dress to kneel in front of her and aggressively began cleaning Sadie's face.

"There." She stood back up. They exchanged another long stare before Mia added, "I'm not coming back. So if you have nothing else to say to me, then…"

"I'm sorry," Sadie said. She meant it too, though not in the way Mia probably took it.

"Fine." Mia tossed the rag in the empty bowl, scowled down at her one last time, and then sauntered back out the way she came.

Sadie lost track of time as she began to drop in and out of sleep. Her dreams rotated through various sexual memories, and every time she came to, she found herself increasingly ravenous for contact.

Someone shook her awake again, and she gasped out loud as if pulled from cold water.

"I'm not hungry," she mumbled, trying to return to the dream. Her skin was warm and everything on her ached.

"I'm not the maid," a young man said. Sadie opened her eyes to find she was back on the mat in the corner. When had she been moved? It must be the middle of the night since the only light was the small lamp burning on low in one corner. "A friend sent me," he said.

Sadie propped herself up and looked at him. He was around her age and she saw immediately what he was there for. "I – I don't know what I'm supposed to... do exactly," he said.

She reached for him, but her hands were gloved. In fact, at some point someone had changed her into clothing that covered her from head to foot.

"Do you have a condom?" Sadie panted.

"Yes. Uhh... several." He pulled a pack out of his pocket.

"Get one ready. And then kiss me," she whispered, before lying back down. She watched him open the package with growing impatience. His hands were shaking, and he dropped it several times. The anticipation of having someone so near made her want to scream every second she had to wait.

He lay down next to her and put a hand awkwardly on her waist, before leaning in and finding her lips. An uncomfortable game followed in which they tried to maintain contact while he shuffled around putting on the condom. Once settled, he rested the sheathed shaft on her stomach and cupped her face with his hands.

Sadie was impressed at his ability to stay quiet. He gasped into her mouth and never completely stopped shaking, but he didn't utter any sound out loud. The condom was quite full by the time they were done, and he surprised her again by pulling out a small sack to deposit it in as well as a wet rag to clean himself. Someone had prepared him well, for she could see he had no experience with this.

"Do you work here?" Sadie asked as he rezipped his pants.

"I help tend the gardens," he told her, still breathing heavily.

"Can you get me out of this?"

"Umm. I was told to just come here and do this and then leave the estate. Find another job."

"Who told you?" she asked, sitting up as best she could.

"I don't know. He was hidden. He paid me to help cover the cost of leaving and to stay silent. Not that I would talk, anyway." He got to his feet. "I – I am sorry about your situation. I wish you well. And... I'll never forget this."

He crept across the room and slipped away. She wasn't disappointed he didn't try to do more. It would be a big risk to take for a stranger. And it seemed like someone out there at least knew where she was. Had Amadi approached the young man? It must have been him.

Sadie began to have hope. If one of the Siphons came back to see her tomorrow, they would see the sexual encounter on her and know what the man had done. In which case they'd probably starve her for three more days. But if they didn't visit, then she had a chance. She could play along with being hungry. If she appeared weak, everyone would underestimate her. If the right moment came, she would have to act fast. Siphon would be back to question her eventually.

Sadie didn't fall back asleep. When the door clicked open hours later, she jumped and had to immediately feign the deep breathing of heavy slumber. She heard the buzz of the maid's taze-stick a second before she shoved her shoulder.

"Hmm," she moaned in protest.

"Time to get moving. We need to clean you up," the woman said.

"Can't. Not hungry." Sadie made sure to slur each word.

"Oh yes you are. And tomorrow's your big day. Gotta get you cleaned up." The woman pulled hard on her arm, forcing her upright. She had to sell this right though, so she flopped back down. Sadie heard the buzzing sound of the taser decrease and realized with horror that the maid was about to use it. She pictured Jimmy's face. She had to get back to him.

But it turned out that the fear of the small shock dominated over the experience of it. She yelped and sat up.

There were two other women standing behind the maid, and the three of them dragged her to the bathroom, where they spent the morning bathing and grooming her. Sadie didn't have to fake her weakness much. Despite feeding off a stranger in the night, she was still shockingly depleted, though her mind was blessedly sharp again.

When her hair and face were presentable, they wrapped her in a robe and took her to a new room. It was beautiful, mostly empty except for two fireplaces at either end. In the center was a man standing next to a strange contraption.

The maid removed Sadie's robe and displayed her in front of him. Though he looked at her with desire, she didn't see any clear images that would mean this was the person who had won her.

When the women stepped back, she made to collapse to her knees, but the man stepped forward and caught her with gloved hands.

"No matter. You won't need to hold yourself up," he said.

The man led her forward and proceeded to string her up to the wooden thing in the center of the room using dozens of tiny ropes. They were a deep red color and very soft. Sadie watched in fascination as he worked on her for hours. It was difficult to not let her curiosity outshine her hungry succubus act, but she made sure to keep looking longingly at the man. She repeated any of the things she could remember having said to Jimmy last time she was hungry. If anyone suspected her performance, they didn't show it.

When the man stood back to admire his work, real lust shot out of him for the first time. He smiled. "You look radiant," he said, making a gesture to the women in the corner. The maid disappeared at his signal and the man took a thin robe and draped it around her, tying it loosely just under her breasts.

The maid returned with five people in tow. Two men and one woman in captain's uniforms. One man of soldier rank. And Troy.

"These are your top contenders," the man who'd tied her up said. "Fancy any of them?" Sadie looked over the five people hungrily, and there was truth in her expression. But it wasn't until her eyes landed on Troy that she remembered exactly how starved she was. He wore a well-fitted suit, rolled up casually at the sleeves, and the sight of him made her whole body throb.

He ran a hand through his hair before putting it in his pocket, and she traced the movement with her gaze. Though he was attempting to look casual she could see in his forearms that his muscles were taught.

"Well, of course you do. That's the whole point," the man contin-ued, winking at Troy.

"You have all done well recruiting." He reached out and pulled open the robe he had just tied. Somehow it fell all the way to the floor at his gesture. "And you have twenty-four hours left to take the top spot."

Sadie's muscles clenched at the wave of desire that hit her from everyone present. Even the three women that had groomed her that morning were sizing her up. The ropes managed to cover a lot while not covering anything. They laced under her breasts and accentuated her abdomen and hips. Her arms were in a triangle over her head with her wrists wrapped together.

Troy was staring at a spot just over her head, but his eyes kept flitting to hers. Images popped into his mind and then disappeared as if he was doing his best to suppress the thoughts. In fact, he was the only one of the men who wasn't at least partially hard. The rest of them raked their eyes over her hungrily and Sadie returned the expression. She realized only the soldier and Troy could actually feed her though, as the captains were all human feeders.

As if she'd read her thoughts, one of the captains asked, "What assurances do I have that she won't kill me? I can't feed her after all."

"That is the last thing on her mind. Trust me," the man said. "Besides. If she killed you, we would do the same to her. While if she plays nicely, we'll give her something good to eat." The man ran a gloved finger between her breasts and Sadie didn't have to fake the small sound of desire that escaped her.

Troy's eyes caught hers, and he swallowed noticeably, before his gaze flitted quickly up and down her naked form. He grew hard like the rest of the men, and Sadie immediately hated that all these other people were here. Suddenly, she didn't care about her goal of getting out of there safely. All she wanted now was for Troy to win.

But even that was a day away.

The man in the night had done something for her, but what she really wanted was the man standing ten feet from her. The one she'd begun to share friendship lines with. The one with the hint of fear behind his gaze. The one trying to save her.

"Will she be tied up like that? It doesn't seem like very good access," one of the other captains said.

"Ahh. That's what this is for. You pull this rope here and it will lift and spread her knees." Sadie closed her eyes against the images running through Troy's thoughts at that. She had to be patient. He would come for her. Tomorrow. Patience. She just had to trust him. Sadie took a deep breath and looked at each of the other contenders, trying to distract herself.

"Well, let's get back to work then," the one female captain said. Their brains were filled with lust as they hurried from the room, each and every one of them appearing determined as all hell.

Troy shot her one final look as they left and she found there was so much she wanted to say to him. He too seemed to be trying to communicate too much. She got none of it except for what she could clearly see, desire, longing, and a strong pulse of the green light of friendship. She was sure that the full picture of his thoughts and emotions was as a mess as her own.

"I'll wait here," she said as if to all of them.

The next morning, they went through the same ritual, only this time Sadie barely had to fake her feverish state. She had dreamed repeatedly of Troy. With her hands tied to the anchor all night, she spent most of her waking time rubbing her thighs together, wanting pressure between them.

As the craftsman began to restring her, she became hyperaware that he was in fact not a human feeder. Whether he was a nymph or human she couldn't tell. It didn't matter so long as he could feed her. She watched his hands and eyes intently. He had a small goatee and nimble fingers. She hadn't paid him much mind yesterday, but now that she was far hungrier, he shot to the forefront of her attention.

This time as he worked, he kept shooting glances at her. He wore a small smirk and a semi-erection nearly the entire time. "Tucker Stone is a lucky man," he said as he finished.

"What?" The elder maid said. "He – he wasn't even in the room yesterday."

"Yes, well... Everyone was surprised. The competition has been heated; the talk of the whole army. You have served the cause well." The man smiled at her again and this time, Sadie felt a little sick at the whole situation. "But after the humans attacked the foothills, Mr.

Stone was able to recruit large groups of the mountain nymphs. They're hard people. Not afraid of a fight. He more than doubled the numbers of the next contender."

"Well, then I guess you're lucky too. Tucker Stone is quite the man," the maid directed at her as she came nearer to observe the final product. Sadie couldn't believe her bad luck. If she hadn't been so far gone with lust she would have cried.

"When will he be here?" Sadie asked, her voice a sultry, breathy thing that she barely recognized.

"Around five. Three hours from now. Siphon wanted to talk to you beforehand, but it seems he was detained with some emergency. We're supposed to leave you like this until Tucker arrives."

The man pulled something from his pocket and secured it around her hips. It was a small object shaped like a semi-flat stone. He placed it so it rested against her clit and fastened it with ties around her upper thighs and waist. Then he pulled out another device, pushed a button, and set it on the ground next to her.

"It's succubus designed. Very special," he said.

Sadie looked at it all curiously. Nothing happened.

"It was a pleasure meeting you," said the man who had tied her up. Before Sadie could mount any protest, guards ushered everyone from the room and she found herself alone.

For several minutes it was quiet except for her spastic breathing. Then the stone between her legs began to vibrate. Sadie gasped in shock. It was fast and the sensation shot through her with surprising speed.

It was just what she'd wanted all night. Torn between wanting to feed and wanting to be touched, the ache and hunger mingled like sugar and honey. The vibration slowed over time, however, and as she approached the release of the tension between her legs it turned back off.

Sadie blinked down at her body in surprise. Did it die? She was right on the edge. If it turned back on for just a few more seconds...

She writhed against the ropes, trying to push against it, but it was no use. There was no way to create pressure from her position. After a while she gave up and let her head lull against her chest. If she could fall back asleep, she could at least dream of the things she craved.

There was nothing to do, but relax in her ropes. Her body was too tense to lose consciousness though, and she couldn't imagine actually sleeping. She focused on her breathing, trying to calm herself. Her thighs eventually went soft and she began to come down from the after-effects of the vibrator's work. And then it turned back on.

Sadie was so grateful that she didn't see what was coming. It repeated the process exactly as before. The vibration slowed over time and died just before she could climax. How did it know? The words of the man as he departed came back to her. The toy was succubus made, and clearly designed for one purpose.

This time Sadie couldn't get herself to relax. The idea that the stone might turn back on any minute hung heavy in her thoughts. Her erotic fantasies of Troy which had plagued her all night returned in force as she pulled against the many ropes that restricted her movement.

It waited longer the third time. She had just begun to suspect it had all been a coincidence when it came back on. This time she tried not to play along. If she could resist the growing tension between her legs, perhaps it would leave her alone. Her efforts only served to drag out the moment before it shut down. This time she cried out in frustration.

"Fuck. Please. If you're out there. Somebody help me. Please." She writhed again in vain. Nothing seemed to get her out of what was happening. The time ticked away at a glacial speed. After a while she lost all ability to tell how long had passed. It did seem that the duration for which the stone lay still increased each turn and the amount of time it took to bring her to the edge shrunk.

After a long, tortuous period she found herself panting and writhing for long periods of stillness, only to get a few seconds of vibration. She was right on the edge. Permanently. She needed someone to touch her. And she desperately needed to feed.

Where was Tucker Stone? Had the first hour passed? Had he been delayed? The vibrator turned back on and Sadie threw her head back and cried out.

"Shit. God. Fuck." She balked, writhing with everything she had. It shut off almost immediately and she bucked spastically against the ties. Sadie was sucking in air through her teeth in quick, rapid breaths as she slowly brought down her chin and opened her eyes. She froze in shock.

Troy was standing in front of her.

Chapter 25

Released

Troy's lips were parted and his face flushed. He snapped his mouth shut and stood up straighter the instant their eyes met.

"Wha— How did you get in here?" Sadie whispered. It didn't seem like the most relevant question, but her brain wasn't exactly firing on all four cylinders.

"Drugged the guards," he said, flipping open a pocket knife. "Sorry I couldn't get in sooner." He approached her and began scouting out a place to cut the ropes. "Amadi's first plan was to have me recruit a bunch of our own people to insert them into the Coalition army. Which we did. But we couldn't get enough volunteers to beat out Tucker. We thought since I still have Siphon's trust enough to be allowed to walk through his front doors, the back-up plan was for me to break you out." He stepped closer and began messing with the ropes at her wrists. Up close she could see he was shaking, she'd never seen him so nervous.

"You're blowing your cover then?" Sadie asked in a quiet voice that barely filled the space between them.

"Yes."

"But all the recruits. They won't be accepted now." She inhaled his scent as she watched him work. "And having you on the inside—"

"The whole plan has changed. I'll explain later. Right now—"

"Ow!" Sadie said as the knife nicked her wrist.

"Damnit. The ropes are too close to your skin. I can't seem to get under them." He pocketed the knife.

"You could untie them," she said.

He looked back up at her wrists. "How? There's no knot here."

"Maybe it doesn't start there. Do you see a beginning anywhere?" she asked. He looked at her neck and arms, his gaze determinedly avoiding her eyes. When he found nothing, he hesitated a moment before tracing the ropes that ran over the rest of her body.

His hands were gloved, but when his fingers ran along the ropes under her breasts she sucked in air audibly. Troy paused, swallowed, and then continued south apparently attempting to pretend nothing had happened. But as he traced the ropes around her thighs a whimper escaped her.

He froze again and this time his pants moved as he began to grow hard. Sadie thought her body would explode with desire at the sight of it, especially when it was followed by a wave of lust. She was just about to broach the topic of him stopping this nonsense and kissing her when he said, "You look like a pig."

"What? Did you just call me a pig?" she squealed in a way that probably wasn't a counter argument.

"Yes. They've trussed you up like a pig, all bound and decorated like that. Why any man would want to—" He faltered.

His misdirection was pointless though. He knew she could see how he was feeling. Not that she needed to see inside his thoughts and emotions. Troy cleared his throat as it became even more visibly apparent exactly how much he liked what he was looking at.

And it was in that moment that the stone turned back on. Sadie had entirely forgotten about it. She cried out again, every muscle in her body going taut as she struggled in vain against the ropes. It lasted only a few seconds.

"Fuck!" she said as it died. "Can you turn that goddamn thing off?"

"Wha— What is it?" Troy asked, staring openly at her crotch now.

Sadie didn't really want Troy to know exactly what it did so she spat out. "What does it look like?"

"It just vibrates for a few seconds?" He continued his search of the ropes as he added "Why?" He would have sold the question as casual if she didn't have eyes or ears.

"In the beginning it went for longer."

"In the beginning? How long have you been here?"

"Tsst. I don't know, Troy. An hour. It vibrates for some amount of time and then turns off when I'm about to come, okay?"

His gaze shot to her hard as rock nipples and then the flush in her face and neck before dropping back to the stone. "Oh," was all he said, but a sheen of precum appeared over the mound in his pants.

"The button is on the floor," Sadie breathed. Troy bent down and clicked it. When he stood back up, her gaze rested heavy on his crotch. He caught her staring and they made eye-contact.

"Troy." Sadie practically panted his name. "I have barely fed. I've been here for an hour with that stone. Even if you do get me untied, you'd practically have to carry me out of here. I need—" She took a deep breath. "I want you to do what Tucker Stone was meant to do."

Troy froze. "Now? Here?"

"Now," Sadie said, unconsciously undulating in her bindings.

Troy stared at her for what felt like a lifetime. It was obvious he wanted to as much as she did. His thoughts were such a frantic mess of images and desires, she could barely track them. But she'd learned that people were complicated. His answer came when all his thoughts sharpened into the single image of him kissing her.

He closed his eyes briefly and took in a long, measured breath. When he reopened them, he looked, all too slowly, from her lips to her bound wrists as Sadie grew increasingly impatient. His face was flushed but determined as he said, "You're asking me to... have sex with you."

"Yes." The word came out through gritted teeth. She was feeling especially exposed in her need and didn't like having to wait for him to comply.

After what felt like a lifetime he asked in a whisper, "What do I do?"

Her body jerked in her bindings as she realized she would soon get to feed. "You want the sex talk? Haven't you ever fucked a girl before?" she said, far more crassly than she'd meant to. Her vulnerable position mixed with her desire had her more on edge in her relationship with Troy than perhaps she'd ever been. She was literally in his hands and she needed something desperately that only he could give. It made her want to lash out.

"Yes." He glared at her. "I— But not like this." His tone sharpened to match hers. Her question was also entirely rhetorical since she knew his experience. He wasn't one for jumping into bed. Though... his feelings for her were far beyond something casual. He wanted to do this as much as she did. And yet, what she was asking was still a large step away from what he was used to. Even if he'd had a hundred girlfriends, nothing would be good preparation for being with a succubus when she was not only hungry, but as aroused as it was humanly possible to be.

"Well, unless you want to get them dirty, I would take off some clothing before touching me," she said, more gently this time. Sadie strongly suspected that the instant they made skin contact, things would escalate quickly.

Troy stepped back and undid his belt buckle. His shirt was rolled up at the sleeves and his forearms flexed as he moved. Her gaze passed back and forth between his arms and the attention-stealing mound in his pants. Sadie bit down on her lip, trying to distract herself away from audibly groaning with longing as he pulled himself free. She took in the sight of him and, with some embarrassment, began to pant.

Troy paused there a second and it became apparent that he was enjoying her checking him out. He stayed back where she could see him as he pulled off the gloves he'd worn for her benefit. His expression was perfectly innocent, but she could see what he was thinking and feel what he was feeling. He was elated by her unsuppressed interest.

"You know we don't have a lot of time here, Troy. Right? Are you intentionally going as slowly as possible?"

"Actually, the guards are the only people in this wing of the house today and they'll be out for hours. We have about seventy minutes before Tucker is supposed to arrive." He stepped forward then, holding the erection to his abdomen so it didn't touch her skin. "You're just impatient," he said in awe, as if he couldn't believe the state of her.

"Or maybe we're in a very dangerous situation and you're being an idiot." God why had she said that! All she wanted was for him to touch her and he might hurry up and do it if she could just *not* goad him. But didn't he realize how desperate she was? This was not the time for games.

"Then tell me what you want," he said, his voice deep and heavy with arousal.

She tried to groan in annoyance, but it came out more like a plea. He was so close it was all she could do not to beg him to kiss her immediately. Sadie did her best to steady her voice before saying, "Pull that." She gestured with her eyes to the rope hanging from the pulley next to her.

Troy frowned at the thing as he began to tug. Apparently, he'd forgotten the explanation from yesterday. Her legs moved and he stepped back in surprise, flushing as her lower half shifted until her knees were on either side of her ribs. He looked right between her legs, and her clit throbbed against the stone.

Sadie stared into his dark brown eyes and commanded, "Now put yourself inside me." Her voice was definitely pleading now. She could only hope he didn't recognize it as such behind the order. He swallowed, then blessedly, moved closer. Stepping up to her, their faces a few inches apart, his gaze rested on her lips.

"Don't you want me to warm you up or something?" She raised an eyebrow. "Right, I just mean..." He ran a hand over himself, his eyes flicking back to her lips. "Do you want me to kiss you?" Troy appeared to be playing the same game she was and trying to play it cool, but the husky undertone in his question was an audible betrayal.

She stopped herself on the verge of saying yes. She looked at his lips in turn, desperate to feel them against her. She wanted his tongue in her mouth. Yet somehow, the sentimentality of it felt too in contrast to their treatment of each other. All their competitive, antagonistic exchanges of the past shone sharp in her thoughts, adding to her current vulnerability. She did want him to kiss her, of course, but she didn't want to be the one to ask for it.

"It's not necessary," she replied, "but if you want to get more warmed up, you can play with my body." It was intentionally cold and his face hardened.

"Glad to know we're sticking to necessities," he said. But as he looked down at the rest of her, it became clear that he did want to touch her. He blinked and looked back into her eyes.

She thought he was going to begin caressing her breasts as he was imagining, but with a determined expression, he closed the inch of space between them and slid just inside her entrance. She was so shocked at his sudden decision that she gasped out a high-pitched cry. They watched each other's faces, unspeaking, as he pushed his hips flush with hers in one deep motion.

Troy pulled back and thrust again. He paused there, buried in her, as they took in each other's expressions. Sadie was trembling all over and she bit back a whimper of elation at the contact. He groaned at the sound and then began to move in her, slowly, tentatively. It was only then that he began to explore her body, finding nipples and hips and collarbone. Running his palm down her stomach, he slid his thumb under the stone and over her clit.

"What about this?" he panted. "Is this necessary?"

She wanted to cut him off with a quick *no*, but the word resisted her. Someone was finally touching her. And this time it wasn't going to stop when she got close. Her hips bucked against him involuntarily and he clenched his jaw against the smile threatening to overtake his face. His own pleasure as he moved inside her, however, vied for dominance over his self-satisfaction and his expression grew serious; his gaze heated.

He massaged her in tiny circles that matched the rhythm of his hips, and the sensation coursed through her in a searing wave. She bit her lip, but a loud exclamation still escaped her. It echoed around the room and Sadie sincerely hoped he'd been right about no one being around.

"Does this feel good? Do you like it?" he whispered in her ear and the husky sound of his voice was filled with his own desire. But as he pulled back to look at her, she saw he was still biting back a grin. He was just a little too satisfied that he was giving her what she wanted most. For a second, she considered actually headbutting him, but in the next moment she lost all ability to generate coherent thoughts.

The first spasm hit and heat flooded her entire body. Her head fell back and eyes clamped shut as she strained hard against the ropes. Troy switched to thrusting into her hard and fast, even as he kept his touch on her clit light and slow. It was exactly the combination to send her immediately over the edge while drawing out the moment.

She clenched around his rough pumping as her body convulsed repeatedly. All of her motions were involuntary as she twitched and shook and strained against the bindings around her knees and wrists. He set the pace, and all she could do was take it. And take it she did. Gratefully. She cried out his name several times with a longing she was sure she would regret later.

When she finally began to come back down, she blinked her eyes open and found his. The smirk was gone. His face was all deep lust now and she had personally never been hungrier for it. And even more than that. He had got to watch her climax, to enjoy her suffering and pleading in a situation in which he had all the control. She decided it was time for payback.

He had slowed his movement for a second after she climaxed, but he picked back up the pace. Troy was on the edge and he began chasing it, believing he was about to come. But Sadie took over.

"Are you close?" she asked rhetorically. He growled in response, speeding up. His face was near enough that she was able to kiss his clenched his jaw. She felt every muscle in him tighten as he pushed against the edge of the orgasm. Sadie let one wave of climax pierce through him, before continuing to hold him at the point of highest tension.

"I'm right there," he panted.

"I know," she said in her sweetest voice. "Aren't you going to come for me?"

"Yes. Yes, you feel so good. I'm right there," he repeated as if willing himself over the edge.

She waited as he said her name several times, thrown in between various divine swearing, and then she said, "You know that I can control your orgasm, right?"

His gaze shot to hers.

"I mean. You pursued a succubus for several months, surely you know we can control the pleasure of someone we're touching." Troy's eyes went wide and his lips parted. She waited for her words to sink in fully before saying, "So tell me, do you like this?" She sent another wave through him, much stronger this time. He bucked sharply into her as a deep rumbling moan escaped his throat. "How about this?" she teased and did it again.

Troy didn't answer, but eventually he opened his eyes to look her over. He ran a hand over her calf and breast and then sped up his thrusts. She rewarded his speed by not sending any more orgasmic waves his way. He went back to being on the edge, frantically trying to chase his own release.

"Try slowing down," she said, grinning at him. His lust was intoxicating. It fed her hunger like the finest of meals.

He didn't obey at first, continuing to pound into her. His body pushed the stone against her clit and she felt her own body re-igniting. Just as she became uncertain that she actually wanted him to slow, he abruptly stopped moving. He looked at her, panting and clenching his jaw.

"Are you telling the truth?" he asked.

She smiled. "Haven't you learned? I rarely lie to you."

He moved deep in her once and she responded with a pulse of pleasure. He groaned and pulled back. She sent a stronger wave to match the next deep thrust. "Do you understand the game?" she asked, soaking up his tense face.

"I understand," he said as he buried himself in her again with a satisfied moan. She wouldn't let him speed up. Only if he maintained control would she reward him. Troy's whole body was tight as he asked for more with each deep, slow thrust.

But after a minute of gradually building toward climax, he again began to chase it. The instant he pumped twice in fast succession, she took him back to the pre-orgasmic state. She was proud of her control under the circumstances. She couldn't have done this a few months ago.

He sucked in a sharp breath and pressed his forehead to hers. "God, I'm so close." Troy slowed back down and she rewarded him with the tiniest taste of what he wanted. He groaned again in that deep, back of the throat way.

"I can make it feel so good. Better than you can imagine," Sadie panted, her own breathing ragged with desire.

"Do it," he gasped, gripping both her knees in each arm and trailing his lips down her neck.

"I will. All you have to do is say please," she said. And now she was the one who wore the self-satisfied smirk. Sadie had never talked like this to anybody, and she was shocked at her own boldness. Or perhaps she would have been if she hadn't been so far gone in the moment. But right now, she reveled in the idea of making Troy beg.

He could have pulled out of her and finished himself. She couldn't have stopped that. But it wouldn't have been the same as what she was offering. And his thoughts were fixated solely on her. The image of her arms bound above her head and her knees pulled up remained in the front of his mind as he desperately pumped into her. But try as he might, he had to concede that she was in fact in control of his climax, if nothing else.

He nipped at her neck with his teeth and nuzzled his face against her ear. Then, very quietly, he said. "Yes. I like it," he breathed against her neck. "Finish it."

"Magic word?" she said.

And then, to her utter satisfaction, he leaned in and whispered in a voice barely audible even at this close distance, "Please."

Sadie wasn't smiling now. The sound of his plea was nearly enough to make her come. She wanted to feel him pounding against her again. "Okay," she panted. "Go as fast as you want. I'll match you." This was just what he'd wanted. He resumed pounding into her, even rougher than before, and she matched each thrust with an increasingly powerful climactic wave.

She entirely released her restraint over his pleasure, letting the full force of it overtake him, and in her highly aroused and hungry state, that was a thing to be reckoned with. He bucked inside her in fast, spastic motions. "Oh my god, Sadie. Yes. That's—" His words dissolved into incoherent sounds as she gave him all she had.

She strained against the chains as the rich sensations of his body filling her, and his hands holding her, sent her to the edge, but it was the sight of him that sent her over. Her own climax passed within a few heartbeats, and she felt a small victory for getting to orgasm without him smugly observing her.

Sadie was glad to move beyond her own release as she wanted nothing more now than to soak up the sight of Troy. He had one arm over their heads, holding one of her wrists and the other in a bruising grip on her ass. His eyes were closed and jaw clenched with his head tilted slightly back. She drew out the moment, making each pleasurable pulse as intense as possible. A voice in her head chided her that she should probably stop now, but another, much more respectable voice in Sadie's opinion, reminded her he was a fire nymph and could probably take anything she threw at him.

She rode it out until all her hunger was satisfied, bathing in the moment in a state of absolute ecstasy until she let him finish. Troy gave one last cry, and stilled, buried deep inside her, his chest heaving as if he'd just sprinted for miles.

After a minute, he relaxed his forehead against hers with their noses touching.

"Did you like that?" she whispered, attempting to mimic his earlier tone. The obnoxious man didn't reply. She wanted to hear him say yes. She wished she could force the word out of him. Instead, he rubbed his nose against hers as his breathing slowly quieted. His lips brushed her cheek. Sadie opened her eyes to find that his were closed. He looked so serene.

His mouth slid to brush hers, which parted in response. Sadie wasn't sure who moved first, but they began hesitantly to massage tongues and lips; their breath mingling. He sighed in satisfaction, the quiet rumble reverberating from his chest to hers.

Sadie's mind went soft. She wanted her hands free so she could hug him to her, run her fingers through his hair, and caress his face. She wanted to deepen the kiss and then keep kissing him all afternoon.

But the enormity of their circumstances moved back to the forefront of her thoughts. What were they doing? They had to get the hell out of there. Troy immediately noticed her disengagement from the embrace, and he pulled back a few inches, opening his eyes.

Neither of them were grinning now. He ran his thumb over her cheek as his gaze darted between her eyes. "I'm sorry. I was being an idiot before. I wasn't thinking straight." His body shook in an aftershock. "It's not every day you have a hungry succubus beg you to fuck her."

"I didn't beg," she cut in immediately.

"Of course not." He smiled, but then his face fell. "But you did… because you were hungry. Very hungry. Sadie, did I do the wrong thing? Was I taking advantage?"

She shook her head. "No. That isn't possible. I needed to feed and you helped. As you should have." Then at the look on his face, she added, "I *wanted* you to."

Troy was still inside her, and he pulsed as she continued to look at him. He bent to kiss her again and this time there was no hesitation from either of them. His mouth was warm and firm on hers, and after a minute he began to gently thrust his hips in time with the prodding of his tongue. Troy didn't break the kiss once as he moved in a slow, deep rhythm.

They were both trembling by the time he was on the edge again. Sadie could feel her own climax coming and slowed his down so they could come together. Troy's chest heaved against her as she panted into his mouth, and unlike the first time, their sounds of pleasure were quiet and intimate.

Troy ran his hands along the insides of her spread thighs before traveling up to cup her breasts. She could feel his desire like a living thing, hot and raw. He savored her body as if it were the only thing in the world. Which it might as well have been for all either of them remembered their dangerous circumstances.

It shouldn't have been enough, but the gentle pressure of the stone pressing into her eventually sent her over the edge. "Troy," she cried against his lips at the same time that he let out a deep groan. He pinched her tender nipples as he came, his mind locked on the sound of her cries.

It took several minutes for them to come down from the high, but when they did, Sadie felt like herself again. Her hunger was gone and her thoughts clear and sharp.

Troy pulled out of her slowly and stepped back. He was covered in sweat, and unlike earlier, his eyes roamed unabashedly over her body as he did up his pants. They didn't speak as he put back on his gloves and moved to untie the stone at her waist. He pocketed it, along with the button on the floor, giving her a sheepish shrug as he did so.

Before he could go back to working on untying her, she had an idea, the first good idea she'd had since her hunger had consumed her thoughts.

"Burn it," she said.

He blinked.

"We don't have time for you to figure out how to untie me. But you could try to burn it."

Troy continued to look at her in drowsy contentment for a few long seconds before his brain too seemed to kick back in. His gaze snapped up to her wrists. His finger caressed the wooden shaft that held up her hands, assessing. Then he reached for the tightly coiled metal wire that pulled up her knees. The rope was secured around two small loops at the end of the coils.

Troy cleared his throat. "I might be able to melt the metal here, that will be the easy part. But—"

"We'll start there then," Sadie said, feeling increasingly vulnerable about her position.

He gripped one of the coils in a fist and after a minute it began to glow. Sadie jumped as he snapped a chunk of it free. One leg fell to the floor. He repeated the process until she was standing on her own two feet again, and then re-examined her wrists. He snapped his fingers and the glow of a small flame illuminated his look of concentration.

After a few seconds, it went out. He tried again and managed to hold it slightly longer, but he appeared to be trying much harder than usual.

"You're weak," Sadie said, feeling guilty over how carried away she'd gotten.

Troy just tightened his jaw in concentration and a few breaths later Sadie felt sharp heat emanating from a place just above her hands. She sucked in breath as it became painful.

"Troy?" she said, uncertain if she was going to be able to handle this. He reached up with his other hand and the feeling lessened. She assumed he was cupping the flame to shield her.

"How's that?" he whispered tenderly.

"Better," she said and found her voice mirrored his. Her body trembled slightly and she was momentarily consumed with a feeling of fragility. She wished they could pause time and curl up in each other's arms for a while.

Her wrists snapped free, and Troy gasped triumphantly before looking down into her face. She needed to get away from that look, they were in danger here.

"Let's move," she said before reaching for the thin robe that lay at the foot of the post. Sadie was conscious of Troy still watching her. He didn't seem to want to look away, but she avoided his gaze as she covered herself as best she could in the light fabric before facing the door. "Which way?"

Troy stepped in front and led her down several hallways and up one floor. He didn't pause to explain why they were going up, and she didn't ask. It seemed the looming threat of their situation had finally reached both their senses as they practically ran through the maze of the mansion.

"Stop," Sadie said abruptly and far too loud, but she had just spotted something worth pausing over. Sprinting through the open door, she confirmed her suspicion. This was the office from Mia's memory. The one in which Siphon had met with Hetia's father.

She began searching the desk.

"What are we looking for?"

"I don't know," she said, her voice coming out frantic. "But this is his work office. There must be something worth finding in here." Her sense of failure hadn't fully left her body, and she was still desperate to find anything useful to take back. She was grateful when Troy moved to explore the cabinet, pitching in.

Voices in the hallway made them freeze. "Not sure how long they've been down. I ran the second I saw it." It was the maid who had tended her.

"It's okay. You did the right thing. We've got it from here," a man said. They were nearby, moving rapidly. Sadie turned in time to watch them pass just outside the open door. The man wore a gun at his side, and she thanked their good luck that neither of them glanced left.

"Get the staff upstairs," the man said as his voice faded in the distance. "And don't worry. There's security at every exit. They're not going anywhere."

"We have to move," Troy said. Sadie ignored him. This could be her last opportunity. She couldn't walk away with just one pitiful memory from Mia. She shuffled around pens and stationary and felt around in the back of each drawer. Nothing. She ran to the cabinet to take over Troy's abandoned search. The bottom drawer had a lock.

"Can you burn it?" she asked.

"Sadie, we don't have time for this."

"Please!"

He ran a hand through his hair, glancing back at the open door, then knelt next to her and gripped the lock in one fist. It took much longer than the coil, and Sadie began to regret forcing the issue. Her ears strained to hear footsteps, but none came. The instant the lock was off they pulled the drawer open together and rifled through the papers.

"Here," Troy said. He pulled out a folder labeled *project toolshed*. The rest of it was labeled taxes or deeds, making project toolshed stand out as the only potentially interesting item. She grabbed it and they tore back into the hallway just as a young servant man appeared at the stairs.

He screamed, then shouted, "They're here!" as he scrambled back down the stairs. Apparently, no one suspected Troy had walked in here unarmed. Or perhaps the man just feared coming up against a fire nymph.

"This way." Troy led her up another flight and Sadie began to panic that he was drawing them into a trap. Her lack of confidence only increased when he stopped suddenly and looked back and forth, like he was calculating something.

She stared at him anxiously, but he didn't budge in his concentration, even as the sounds of people running up the stairwell drew nearer. "Right," was all he said before choosing to go left. He led her into a large room and out onto a balcony, while the sound of something strange roared overhead.

Was that— Sadie stared at the sky above with her mouth open as a rather rickety looking helicopter swam into view. Despite its questionable appearance, she was still impressed. After all, she'd never seen any flying contraption in real life, and she couldn't help but pause to gape.

"Come on," Troy said, hopping up on the railing and holding out a hand. Their eyes met as they clasped hands firmly and he pulled her up behind him, and Sadie was grateful he wore gloves – they didn't need any further distractions, and they both seemed hyper aware of the other one's presence as it were.

Sadie clambered onto the roof, the file folder still clutched in her right hand. The see-through robe did little to protect her skin from the harsh tiles, but she rose quickly and walked on bare feet to the flat stretch of roof centered over the left wing of the house.

She watched, open-mouthed, as the helicopter landed in front of them. Luciana's head appeared and she was grinning from ear to ear. Troy ran over confidently and hopped in, but Sadie froze. It was so loud and the blades were spinning dangerously close to the ground. Troy ran back out and grabbed her hand. She crouched down, even though Troy, who was taller, stayed upright as he dragged her under the monstrous thing.

Once they were situated in the back, Luciana and a stranger peered back at them. The man gestured with his eyes to two headsets at their feet. Sadie secured them quickly and heaved a sigh of relief at the drastically muted sound, before reaching to secure her seatbelt.

"Welcome back, Sadie," Luciana's voice rang clearly in her ears. "I will be your ride this evening. Where would you like to go?" She winked at her in the mirror before pulling back on something and taking them into the air. The machine wobbled slightly and Sadie reached for Troy's knee. He placed his hand over hers and she immediately felt safer.

People appeared on the roof as they took off and one woman pointed a gun at them. Sadie screamed as Luciana swerved. If the bullets struck anything, she couldn't hear the sound as they bolted rapidly into the air so fast that her stomach churned with sudden nausea.

The weather shifted abruptly, the perfectly calm evening turning on them. Sadie's head whipped from left to right as she tried to peer out the doors to the ground below.

"Hold on," Luciana said. "It seems their storm nymph wants to make things interesting."

A strong wind hit them suddenly from the side and the helicopter wavered dramatically. Sadie shut her eyes and tried not to throw up. The feeling of Troy's hand in hers cut through the fear and nausea just enough to keep her grounded.

"Woooohoooo!" Luciana said with a laugh as she took them in a sharp upward climb to the right. They rose and rose and the wind slowly dropped off. When it seemed they were out of reach, the helicopter leveled out, and they set a comfortable straight path. Sadie's heart was beating out of her chest by the time she tentatively reopened her eyes.

"Now that was some trial by fire!" Luciana said. "Sadie, meet Edmundo. He runs rescue missions for people caught in hard-to-get-to places. He's been teaching me to fly this thing. What do you think?"

What? "You uhh... you're still learning then?" Sadie asked, trying not to betray too much of her lack of confidence.

"She has to get in practice somehow. Life is short," Edmundo said. "Don't worry though. I've got her." He put his hand over Luciana's and the two exchanged a decidedly flirtatious smile. Sadie was hardly comforted, but she relaxed the barest inch as the realization that she was actually out safe struck her. *Fuck you, Siphon.* All of the emotion she'd had to repress during her time as a spy came bubbling up. She hated that man *and* his entire fucking world.

Sadie shook out of her handhold with Troy to carefully peek inside the stolen folder. He released her reluctantly, and she avoided looking at him as she shifted to secure the folder from the breeze before opening it. Troy moved closer to peer over her shoulder.

There were several sketches of... something, and a lot of words she didn't know. But as she read a letter from some Dr. Skine, it became clear what they were looking at. This was the schematic of a bomb. And as the letter explained, the project was finished.

She looked up at Troy, expecting to share a look of horrified surprise, but he wasn't actually looking at the letter. His gaze was roaming over her. When he realized she'd caught him, he shook himself and focused in on the document in her lap. A minute later, his brow furrowed and his eyes began to flit back and forth rapidly over the rest of the page.

Finally, he looked up to participate in the silent exchange she'd been looking for earlier. As much as she wanted to get lost in the lust pouring off him, she was glad he'd caught up. Sharing the fear helped calm her frantic thoughts. It seemed that the Siphon plan was far worse than any of them could have imagined. The question now was, where exactly was that bomb? And when did he plan to use it?

Chapter 26

Interrupted

The tent was still as Amadi read the letter. He passed it to Hetia. "Look at the date," he told her after a minute. Her eyes dropped to the bottom of the page and flared for a second. Sadie hadn't noticed the date. She wanted to jump in and ask, but it didn't seem appropriate.

There was a commotion outside as someone was blocked from entering. "Sadie?" Jimmy called. The people allowed to stay had been few: Troy, Luciana, Patricia, Cobie, and a handful others Sadie didn't know. Jimmy had been elsewhere when she'd arrived.

Amadi gave her a nod and Sadie stepped out the door. "He can come in, Amadi's orders," she told the guard.

Jimmy appeared in front of her. They typically didn't touch in public, so she wasn't surprised when he came to a halt a foot away. She was surprised when he changed his mind and grabbed her face between both hands and kissed her. She was lucky she'd just fed off Troy, or neither of them would have had the conviction to break off the embrace. But after a moment of savoring being reunited, she put two hands on his chest and pushed.

"Are you okay?" he asked. Amadi had wrapped her in a blanket, which she'd dropped during the kiss, and Jimmy looked her up and down as he pulled back. "Whoa." The robe did nothing to cover her mostly nude body, and she delayed reaching to pick up the blanket.

Jimmy had never really looked her over in the heated way strangers sometimes objectified her, but he was looking now. His gaze lingered on the ropes under and around her breasts and neck. He reached out and pulled the robe free with one finger to get a better look at the rest of her.

"I still need someone to untie them," she said. "And it might take a while." Jimmy bit his lip at her flirtatious tone.

"What happened?" he asked as Troy stepped out of the tent next to them. His eyes flitted up and down her, locked on Jimmy's face, and then looked back at her. With the desire pouring off him, she was sure he would have gone hard just then if his body hadn't been so exhausted.

"Amadi wants you back in there," Troy said, his voice a wavering husky thing two octaves below his usual.

"Wait. Are you hurt?" Jimmy asked, gesturing to a bruise Troy had left on her hip. Sadie looked at the fire nymph and his face flushed slightly as he took in his handprint. Jimmy looked between them and she watched comprehension bloom under his worried expression.

"I'm fine," Sadie said, bending to grab the blanket. She led the way inside without looking at either of them, hoping to delay dealing with her complicated emotions a while longer. She heard the men follow her a moment later.

"But why is that significant?" Patricia was asking Amadi as they entered.

Amadi looked at Hetia, shot a brief glance at Luciana and then said, "Because that letter was sent the exact same week Eirik Pierce disappeared."

"Pierce?" Sadie said, stepping back into the tight circle. "Your father?" she directed at Hetia. Sharp, light grey eyes locked on hers.

"Sadie? Do you know something?" Amadi asked.

Sadie looked around, assessing the presence of each person before deciding to speak in front of them. She didn't know everyone, but Amadi had them in the room, and she had long since decided to trust him. She turned to the blond woman standing with one thumb hooked into a utility belt and her face expressionless. Hetia would have appeared casual if she hadn't been frozen in place.

"You were in a meeting with Siphon and your dad. Do you remember? You were probably ten or eleven."

Hetia didn't react at first except to look thoughtful. "Yes. It was... just before he died." She said this last part almost like a question.

"Hetia?" Amadi turned to her. "You and Eirik went to the Siphon estate?" For the first time since she'd met him, he sounded shaken. Sadie wasn't exactly comforted either that there was something significant that Amadi didn't know about.

"I – I'm not sure where we were. I'd... forgotten about it." Everyone held still as Hetia searched the air with her eyes as if calculating something. "I hadn't connected that man in my memory to Siphon until just now."

Luciana looked more somber than Sadie had ever seen her as she said, "It's understandable you wouldn't want to think about that time. Let your brain work on it overnight. More details will return."

Hetia gave Luciana a significant look and then nodded. Then she headed for the door, clearly done with this meeting. Sadie watched her cross the room and put a hand on the tent flap to open it. She froze. Patricia said something that Sadie didn't catch as she was too busy staring at Hetia's back.

"Arlington," Hetia said, turning back around. "Siphon asked Dad to go to Arlington."

Amadi moved forward and put a hand on her shoulder. "Do you remember why?" She shook her head, wearing a childlike expression as she looked up at the man who'd raised her. Sadie'd never seen her wear youthful innocence before, but in this moment she looked completely lost.

Hetia watched Amadi as he paced the tent once before seeming to make a decision. "We have had a surprising number of new recruits since word of the battle got out. There are many people that don't quite buy the Coalition-controlled version that went out to the media, or the rumor mill that the Maddoxes are fueling."

He looked at Cobie and the two people Sadie didn't know. "I've had word that the Coalition army is pausing to regroup. For how long isn't clear, but one of our spies caught a general declaring they were looking at a few weeks at least. We need to find out where this bomb is and when and how they're planning to employ it. Maybe it's connected to Eirik's disappearance. Maybe not. But right now, it's the only lead we have. Troy and Patricia, can I put you in charge of this?"

Troy nodded and Patricia said, "Of course. We'll do what we can."

"No," Hetia said in a quiet voice that nevertheless captured everyone's attention. "I've gone long enough not knowing what happened to my father. If we're investigating his death, I'm going to be there."

Amadi nodded, then sighed. "I thought you might say that. But Hetia, we'll need you in the coming fight. Maybe not right away, and definitely not in the next two weeks, but eventually. You could be the turning point between winning and losing."

She bowed her head. "I promise to come back before then. But the more of us helping, the better. Who knows how long it could take to uncover the details of a disappearance that happened fifteen years ago."

"And Jimmy and I spent several weeks in that city earlier this year. If you want to uncover secrets quickly, maybe we could help," Sadie said.

Amadi looked over the five of them. "Right, well there's no time to waste. You all should get some sleep. Tomorrow, you're headed back west."

They began shuffling toward the exit.

"Sadie, a word alone before you go," Amadi said.

She exchanged a parting look with Jimmy before falling back, while Amadi pushed up his glasses and waited until everyone had gone before speaking. "Did you learn anything else I should know?" he asked.

"Sorry. That one memory was the only half-useful thing I got and it was from Mia's perspective, so I didn't even hear any of the important details. She was kicked out of the room partway through for being a five-year old." Sadie bit her lip nervously.

"That's okay. You did good. In fact, you did remarkably well in such a short time. I'm glad to have you with us." Sadie felt a warm pride wash over her previous feeling of inadequacy. "Now let's talk about Hetia," Amadi said, and sighed.

"She has the remaining memory. Do you think I should tell her about what I can do?" Sadie asked.

"That's what we need to discuss. After what you just shared with the group, they're all going to have questions. You might not be able to keep it from her even if you wanted to. But if you do decide to tell her the truth, I wouldn't mention your other... skills."

Sadie raised an eyebrow in a question.

"Hetia, for all her hard exterior, has always been a sensitive soul. She wouldn't handle knowing you can see how she feels about you particularly well. Mae filled me in." He explained when Sadie opened her mouth at this last comment. "Maybe one day, but if you tell her that now it will only shut her down more. There's a chance Hetia will recall the details on her own over the coming weeks, but if she doesn't, I sincerely hope she decides to let you take a look around. But knowing her as I do, the idea of someone roaming around her head is probably her worst nightmare."

"I understand," Sadie said. "I'll tread carefully."

He paused to consider her before giving a decisive nod.

She didn't move to go as she realized she had some questions of her own. "Can I ask – the man you sent to me, did he get out safely?"

He gave her a confused look.

"The gardener's apprentice," she clarified.

"What's this?" he asked.

"You sent a man for me to feed off of the second day of my captivity. Uhh... didn't you?"

Amadi pushed his glasses up and swallowed noticeably. Then he dropped his voice even lower than they'd been talking. "Sadie, have you told anyone this?"

"Umm, no, I haven't actually."

"Then let's keep it that way, okay? Not even Jimmy."

She didn't like that. Her initial answer was a simple frown.

Amadi stepped closer and said in such a quiet voice that she mostly had to read his lips to follow. "I still have someone on the inside. Not someone who could get the kind of information you could, but someone very close to Derek Siphon. They have to play things safe in order to stay in that position, but they must have decided to take a risk and send you someone. They've survived this long because the only person who knows *anything* about them is me. And now you. Let's keep it that way."

Sadie nodded decisively. "I swear. Not even Jimmy."

"Good. Now get some rest. You have another important task ahead and you've been through a lot this week."

Sadie went to the door, but paused one last time. "Thank you," she said, and was glad it was dark enough that he probably couldn't see the sudden sheen of tears in her eyes. "For believing in me."

Amadi nodded in acknowledgement, and she went out into the night air to finish what she'd started with Jimmy.

Patricia was waiting outside. They smiled at each other. "Want to tell me a story?" her friend asked.

Sadie laughed. "I'd love to. Can you show me Jimmy's tent?"

Sadie told her everything that had happened as they walked first to where she'd be staying that night, and then in a loop around the entire encampment. Patricia made her skip over the sex parts, but Sadie didn't skimp on any of the other details, including telling her about her hidden senses and skills.

"Sorry I didn't tell you before," Sadie said. "Before I told Troy I had been keeping it all close to home, but after everything that's happened... I just – well, I want the people closest to me to know my secrets."

"It's alright. I... umm, understand." She gave Sadie a guilty look.

"Patricia? You want to tell me a story?"

She laughed and resumed walking, but cast Sadie a sly look over her shoulder. Then she sighed and dropped into a whisper. "I'm the reason Amadi trusted you. I'm the reason Amadi trusts anyone at all, actually. Hag's feed off life experience, as you know. But like succubi, every now and again we have additional skills."

Sadie bit her lip in excitement. "A few of us have a highly developed sense of when someone's story is false or not. When someone new comes in and tells their tale, if it stops feeding me at any point, I know that part's a lie. Simple as that. It can be a challenge when they tell half-truths, but I can usually tease out approximately which parts were real. *This* is my people's big secret."

"Damn. That's as big as mine," Sadie said. "It makes me worry over what hidden talents other feeders might have."

"Exactly. Which is why the best advice when you're infiltrating the Coalition is to control your emotions and to stick to truth as much as possible. Since you just never know."

"Hmm," Sadie said, grateful again to have made it out of there alive. As they fell into silence, another thought occurred to her. "Patricia, was your grandmother close to Hetia's father?"

Her friend frowned. "No. Why do you ask?"

"It's just, she seemed particularly struck by the topic of his death," Sadie said.

"Hmm, that." Patricia clucked her tongue as she stared intently at the path ahead. "Grandpa was killed twenty years ago now. He was a powerful politician. It looked like a car crash, but Luciana was a spy at the time and learned of the direct order from Siphon's mouth."

Sadie sucked in a breath. "I'm sorry. I didn't know."

Patricia shrugged. "That was for the best. The more you'd known, the harder it would have been for you to keep your emotions in check."

Sadie looked in the direction of the rest of the camp. "Luciana, she just seems so... upbeat all the time."

Patricia stopped walking, and they paused just on the edge of camp. In the distance, Hetia emerged from a tent, and Sadie watched her assured stride as she headed to intercept Amadi.

"She wasn't always," Patricia said with a shake of her head. "It took her years to shake off the daily pain of his death. But when she re-emerged into herself, she told me that she planned to suck all the life she could out of the years that are left." She squared her shoulders, and her gaze locked onto something in the distance. Sadie followed it to where Troy was working near the river. "She taught me that even if the world is crumbling around you, you have to take what's still right in front of you and hold on with all you have."

Sadie glanced from Troy back to Hetia in the distance. "This war might take everything," she whispered. "I don't think I realized that until now."

"That's why we have to live all we can," Patricia told her, "Because it's the only thing we have. And none of this is going to be easy."

Sadie put an arm across her back, hesitant to get too close with so much skin showing. "At least we won't be alone." Patricia smiled at her and Sadie watched the friendship line between them pulse thick and strong.

Sadie thought about her connection with Troy and her decision to trust him. Thought about Hetia, who would be coming with them. Hetia who had kissed her in the middle of a battle. Then she thought about the woman in front of her – Patricia, with her quiet strength and confident self-possession. As scary as all these new feelings were, Sadie was glad her circle had widened. It couldn't always be her and Jimmy. At least, that's no longer what she wanted. And Patricia was right, with the future so uncertain, she had to get what she could out of life.

They walked to Patricia's tent with their arms tentatively around each other, and paused to pseudo-kiss on the cheek.

"Sleep well." Patricia smiled knowingly at her. "I think Jimmy missed you."

"It's mutual," Sadie laughed, before breaking off toward his tent. She was anxious to be reunited for good this time, but as she meandered through the brisk evening air, her Jimmy laden thoughts were momentarily cut short at the sight of Troy.

He was heating up the shower water on the edge of a small stream, but froze when he spotted her. Dusting off his hands, he approached with a mix of hard to read emotions on his face. Though his internal sexual thoughts were bright as day.

They paused several feet apart and it seemed that for once neither of them could think of a thing to say. Eventually, Sadie shifted uncomfortably and Troy cleared his throat. "How are you feeling?" he asked.

She didn't know what to do with his gentle tone or the heavy desire and affection still pouring off him, so she swept a strand of hair behind her ear and pulled the blanket tight against the cold as she gave herself time to think. "Better," she said in the end. "Or I will be after some sleep."

Troy shifted his weight and ran a hand through his hair. Then he blew out a breath. "It was good working with you. We did well."

"Yeah. I guess we did."

They stood still through another pregnant silence. And then when she couldn't stand it any longer, she stepped around him, leaving an awkwardly large amount of space. "Good night then," she said, not looking back.

"Good night." His voice was muffled, like he had also begun walking away. She glanced back at him, but he wasn't looking at her, and when he did look, she quickly jerked her face back toward her own path.

Sadie wasn't sure where they went from here, but they'd have to work it out, because tomorrow they were starting a whole new adventure together. Though tonight, she had other things on her mind...

Jimmy wasn't in the tent, but she spotted him by a wooden fence slightly removed from the commotion of the camp. His back was to her as he gripped the top rung in his hands, which creaked under his weight, threatening to break.

"Hey stranger," she said, pulling up next to him. He hesitated a minute before looking at her, and when he did it was on a deep steadying breath. "What is it?" she asked, her smile disappearing.

He kicked at the lower rung of the fence and looked back out at the field in front of them. A cow mooed in the distance, and Sadie felt a twinge of homesickness.

"Arlington," he said and then fell silent again.

"Arlington?" she prompted when it didn't seem he was intending to speak again ever. She was anxious to get him into bed, so whatever he needed to say, he better hurry up.

"I'm not coming."

Wait, that wasn't possible. What had he just said?

"Uhh, what do you mean? You're not coming... to bed now?"

Jimmy frowned out at the field. "There's work I can do here. Good work. And you don't need one more person going with you.

Especially not a human, given what we know of the place. It doesn't make sense for me to go."

Sadie was stung. He couldn't be serious. "Of course it makes sense. You're coming to be near me. Don't you want—" She stopped as her voice threatened to crack.

"I would love to be near you," he said with quiet intensity, turning to face her. "But," he looked in the direction she'd come after her conversation with Troy, "I think I need some time. And space."

This couldn't be happening. She blinked back tears.

"Sadie." He looped his arms around her lower back and pulled her against him. "All I've known... for years, is wanting you. And that hasn't changed." Evidence of his arousal between them emphasized his point. "But I need some time to figure out who I am when you're not around. Maybe we both do. And... I need some time to deal with this Troy thing."

"Troy thing?" she asked.

He just looked at her.

"Jimmy, I fed off Troy when I was really hungry. But I do that all the time. Feed off other people. How is this different?"

He just raised an eyebrow at her. Shit, how did he know? He wasn't a succubus, he shouldn't be able to tell that. Sadie dropped her gaze. "It doesn't change anything between you and me," she said.

Jimmy stared back out at the field. "I know that. And I still need time."

She reached for him, a tear actually breaking free now. "But... we've only just started touching skin. I can't lose you now. Not now."

He took her hands in his, his gloves preventing contact. "Maybe this would be good for both of us. And now might be the best time, before we get too used to each other."

Sadie shook her head. "But I am used to you. I'm so used to you. It's too late." She began to sob in full.

Jimmy's eyes glistened as he looked at her and he grimaced. "I'm sorry. I don't want this to hurt you, but I've made up my mind. I need this. I think... *we* need this." He swiped a hand under his own eye to brush away a tear then cupped her cheek in his palm. "I love you,

Sadie. And I'll be right here when you get back." He kissed her before she could respond, and it served as an abrupt distraction.

By the time he'd got her back to the tent, neither of them had even the barest hint of tears in their eyes. He pushed her back on the sleeping pad and pulled open the blanket which had covered her. His gaze raked over her body, and it seemed like the conversation they'd just been having was some silly dream.

Jimmy was as hungry for her as ever and his lust pulsed as he soaked up every inch of her attire. She was going to do her best to make sure he forgot about their conversation, even if it took all night.

A few hours later, when he'd finally removed all the ropes and was desperately moving inside her with a primal ache that consumed them both, she couldn't remember the conversation herself. Sadie fell asleep sated, the most content she'd been in a long while.

And when she woke up, Jimmy was gone.

If you enjoyed this book, please consider leaving me a review or rating.
I truly appreciate it!

You have finished book 2 in The Carnal Fever Trilogy!
Check www.rileykade.com for the exact release date of book 3.

The Carnal Fever Trilogy:
Flames of Rapture
Heat of Unrest
Fires of Deception (out summer 2023)

Acknowledgments

Thank you to all my beta readers for their feedback and for talking about my characters as if they're real. You helped bring them to life. Thank you to my editor, Julie Mianecki, my interior designer Joe Donley, and my cover designer Ebook Launch for putting up with all my requests.

About the Author

Riley Kade is a romance erotica writer from the pacific northwest. She loves writing high-tension story arcs with big payoffs.

To stay up-to-date on new releases, you can sign-up for my newsletter on my website at https://www.rileykade.com.

9 781957 572031